Praise for David Mark

'Dark, compelling crime writing of the highest order'
DAILY MAIL
'Brilliant' *THE SUN*
'Exceptional... Mark is writing at the top of his game.'
PUBLISHERS WEEKLY
'A wonderfully descriptive writer' *PETER JAMES*
'A class act. Utterly original and spine chillingly good, when it comes to crime fiction, David Mark is in the premier league.' *ABIR MUKHERJEE, AUTHOR OF A RISING MAN*
'One of the most imaginative crime writers in the business, David Mark knows how to tell a good story – usually one that will invoke feelings of extreme horror and awe... in a good way, of course!' *S J I HOLLIDAY, AUTHOR OF THE LINGERING*
'Aector McAvoy, Mark's gentle giant, is one of the most fascinating, layered characters in British crime fiction. Mark is an outstanding writer.' *M W CRAVEN*
'Masterful' *MICHAEL RIDPATH*
'A true original' *MICK HERRON*
'To call Mark's novels police procedurals is like calling the Mona Lisa a pretty painting.' *KIRKUS REVIEWS*
'Mark writes bad beautifully' *PETER MAY*

INTO THE WOODS

Also by DAVID MARK

Novels
The Burying Ground
A Rush of Blood
Borrowed Time
Suspicious Minds
Into the Woods
The Guest House

The DS McAvoy series
Dark Winter
Original Skin
Sorrow Bound
Cruel Mercy
A Bad Death
Dead Pretty
Fire of Lies
Scorched Earth
Cold Bones

As D M Mark
The Zealot's Bones

INTO THE WOODS

David Mark

This edition first published in the United Kingdom in 2021 by Aries,
an imprint of Head of Zeus Ltd

A CIP catalogue record for this book is available from the
British Library.

ISBN (E) 9781800244016
ISBN (PB) 9781800246362

Cover design © Lisa Brewster

Aries
c/o Head of Zeus
First Floor East
5–8 Hardwick Street
London EC1R 4RG

www.headofzeus.com

Printed and bound by CPI Group (UK) Ltd, Croydon, CR0 4YY

For Snowdrop, with love

'The greatest blessings granted to mankind come by way of madness, which is a divine gift.'

Socrates

'The greatest peril of life lies in the fact that human food consists entirely of souls. All the creatures that we have to kill and eat, all those that we have to strike down and destroy to make clothes for ourselves, have souls, souls that do not perish with the body and which must therefore be pacified lest they revenge themselves on us for taking away their bodies.'

Knud Rasmussen, polar explorer and anthropologist

Prologue

Now,
And Then...

The girl is beginning to return. She takes possession of her own unconscious skin as if wriggling into a wetsuit. Graceless, she slithers her way into fleshy cul-de-sacs and dead ends. She comes to life as if somebody were blowing air into a deflated rubber doll.

She can't work out where her arms and legs should go.

Can't decipher up from down.

Can't remember how to breathe.

Gradually, she realises she cannot see. Her senses are all jumbled; smells and sights and sounds all swirled around like wet paint. She fancies she can touch colour; can taste crimson and iron. Can reach out with her hands and grope at great liquid handfuls of darkness.

She considers herself. She feels somehow waxy. Oddly soft. A pig-fat candle. Drowned flesh.

At length, she becomes aware of the high, ringing sensation in the centre of her skull. She thinks of piano wire, pulled tight and then plucked with a coin.

My name, she thinks. *I don't know my name...*

The fear is coming, now. Fear, and pain. Adrenaline is flooding her. Sensations and feelings start to log-jam at the knot of muscle and bone and nerve endings at the top of her neck.

Suddenly she is gagging on scent. Scorched feathers and yesterday's rain. Sandalwood and oil. Mushrooms past their use-by date. Meat: all sweaty leather and mildew.

She realises she can taste a little. Herbs and tobacco. Her tongue is swollen, too big for her mouth. Her lips tingle. There had been a drink. A cold, brown soup slopped from an earthen bowl. It had plants in. Some wormy tuber had touched her lip as she lapped at the brew like a cat with a saucer.

Memory again. Music. A guitar on a strap. Bare feet and the shimmering puddles within the underpass. The honey-drink. She can taste its sweetness. Can remember the touch of the green-gold bottle upon her lip – the reckless way they had passed it between them, brim unwiped, giddy on their new friend.

She tries to move. Blood rushes into her fingers, her toes. It cuts through the numbness. It's as if hundreds of pins are pushing out through her flesh. She squirms again. Her face is constricted. It feels like she's being squeezed. There's pressure behind her eyes and across her sinuses, as if she were hanging forward.

She's on her belly, on the table, looking down, staring at...

...and now she realises she can see a little. Darkness. Shapes. Soft edges and hard edges and something just out of sight.

The floor is moving. Snakes and eels wriggle beneath the thin carpet of leaves and paper and dirt. She blinks again, hard: eyelids pressed together like lips refusing the spoon. A fast, feathery panic flutters at her chest as she forces herself to see through the hallucinations and to focus on what is really there.

A memory, sudden and vicious. The girls. Her *friends*.

Following the stranger. Smoking his cigarettes. Drinking his honeyed wine. Tripping after him like ducklings after their mother, heads swimming with the sweet golden wine...

There had been a fire. Branches blackening around a small, red-gold flame. They had danced, and smoked, and drank. And then he had begun to tell them what he believed. He had begun to talk about his great undertaking. About the journeys. His *gift*. And he had made them drink. They'd gagged on it, scared and shivering and each wanting the other to do something, to say something...

She croaks, pitifully, and from somewhere nearby she hears a small, snickering laugh.

She smells sweat. Smells the high, keening song of earthy skin buffed with moss and wild garlic.

She gasps as she feels the first of the small, cold objects being placed upon her back. She tries to buck backwards but cannot seem to get her body to obey her commands. She feels insubstantial, floating like a kite above herself, the thread gossamer thin.

She pictures them again. Her friends. Her best and only friends...

There is an electrical charge within her – a copper wire inside her bones. For a moment she is a mosaic; a whole made up of a billion parts. Inside her skull, an orange glow, like watching a bright sun through closed eyes.

Again, the sound of drums. Wood and leather, rhythmic and swift: split wood beating a thunderous pulse on a perfect circle of taut skin.

She opens her eyes. They bulge like fish straining at the trawl. Through the haze she sees the earth below her begin to shift. Opens her mouth and feels her tongue flop forward as the leaves and the stones and the broken twigs rise up as if something is tunnelling upwards out of the earth. She tries to rise. There is a sudden weight upon her back; a bare, sweaty knee in the well of her spine, a warm flat hand pushing her head, stuffing her deeper into the face-hole.

A face appears from the darkness beneath her: a full moon emerging from black cloud.

She blinks: tears and ash. Tries to make sense of the thing that leers up at her from the ground.

Teeth. Eyes like gobstoppers. Bristles and hair and crusted spit.

A mask?

A *face*.

It's all leather and pig flesh – a mess of tusks and furrowed snout: the whole stained a dark tobacco-brown. She thinks of bog bodies.

Beneath, the ground bulges, rises; stones tumbling down; the stench of turned earth and bad meat rushing up to fill her nose, her mouth…

She stares into the eyes of the thing beneath the table; the thing that has lain in wait, submerged in the warm, wet earth. She glimpses dark, wrinkled skin.

She opens her mouth and sees the grotesque, porcine face extend its tusks in mimicry.

She sees the face beneath – the one that peers out through the open mouth of the boar.

Sees eyes she recognises, in a face she has smiled into a thousand times.

It lunges up from the earth.

And darkness falls.

Rowan Blake @Ro_Blakewriter

Just took a call from a Neo-Nazi with zero sense of irony. Threatened to burn my hands off if I didn't apologise for last week's *Guardian* column. Here's my response, mate. Just try it, you prick.

6:11PM August 23
19 Retweets 42 Likes

Antony Lukaku @h8crimez 8m
Replying to @Ro_Blakewriter
You're going to burn.
6:19 PM August 23
2 Retweets 19 Likes

PART ONE

PART ONE

I

The Eskdale Valley, Lake District, Northern England
Monday, November 19, this year
9.47am

The morning mist gives this landscape a blurry quality, as if the watcher's eye were still muzzy with sleep. It transforms the panorama into something oddly fabric in texture: the fells gathered into ruches and pleats; all mismatched swatches of tweed and hessian – felted twists and wisps of downy green wool.

A little cottage stands at the foot of the slumbering fell, half lost in the damp, grey air. It has a red chimney and a new roof of green slate. The two sash windows are big inquisitive eyes above the astonished mouth of the black lacquered door. It has been built of the same grey stone as the low wall that encircles it.

A sign hangs above the doorframe: white letters on black wood.

Bilberry Byre

A thinnish, darkish man stands in the doorway, squinting up at the grey clouds. He is barefoot, his mud-grimed feet turning slowly white from contact with the cold grey stone of the front step. He wears dirty jeans, the knees stained. He is wrapped, toga-like, in a tartan blanket, its folds lying across his shoulders and gathered around his waist. His skin is a gallery: a turmoil of intricate words and pictures.

Rowan Blake, fortyish, is glaring at the world as if he would like to punch it in the throat. He flicks his head back and forth: a deranged horse swatting at a wasp. He lowers himself into a crouch. Squats. Moves cautiously forward, braced... then swings: his head a wrecking ball. Something red and brown flutters up elegantly from the overhanging branches, and Rowan leans on the wall for support. He's sure he just heard his brain strike his skull: a damp splat, as if a squid has been hurled at a wall.

Rowan sags, beaten and sore.

'Give it a rest,' he growls, feebly. He squints in the general direction of the bird that has been driving him to distraction with its song. He can't see the little bastard.

Probably laughing at you, Rowan, says the voice in his head. *Gonna take shit from a tit? You gonna stand for that, son?*

Temper breaks like a flung glass. 'You're shit! You're a shit fucking singer. Your parents are embarrassed; your kids won't admit they know you! You're a shit bird in a shit nest. And that's a shit fucking tree!'

He stops, out of breath. Listens as the echo disappears into the damp swaddling clothes of mist and mountain and autumn air. He permits himself a small, half-mad laugh.

'Come to this, has it?' he mutters to himself. 'You're a joke, mate. An embarrassment. If they could see you now…'

Rowan forces himself to stop. Unchecked, he could well berate himself for ever.

He closes his eyes. Slumps back against the brickwork. Feels gloom settle upon him like ash. The unfairness of it all! Three great steps up the career ladder and each has taken him closer to the bottom. From journalist to writer. *Tick!* From writer to TV presenter. *Tick!* And from TV presenter back to square bloody one. *Dick!* A reporter without a story; a journalist without a journal. Self-employed bordering on full-time unemployed.

He feels his disappointment, his resentment, like a physical pain; some herniated lump of gristle right behind his heart. He'd served his time, hadn't he? Twenty years in newspapers, man and boy. He'd been right to take the money from the posh publishers down by the Thames. A two-book deal: two true-crime books, the first to be delivered inside twelve months. That wasn't a problem, considering he'd already written it. He got most of his money in one go. The agreed fee was supposed to be paid out in different stages – the signature of contracts, the acceptance of the manuscript, the hardback publication and finally the paperback. Rowan was struggling with some old debts and having outright fistfights with some new ones. He agreed to a slightly lower fee, if he could have the bulk of the cash up front. He'd quit his staff job at *The Mirror* before the transferred cash hit his account.

This is it, lad, he'd told himself, full of pride. *You're going to be a writer. You've made it!*

The book was a critical success and a commercial failure.

His series of interviews with serial killer Gary King were found to be illuminating and repulsive in equal measure. Critics said he had an uncanny skill for letting people believe they were speaking to a confidant. Rowan gave his all to the marketing campaign, writing endless blogs about his *poor-but-honest* childhood and his sense of journalistic responsibility to the truth. Writers whom he'd admired gave admiring quotes for the front cover and three serial killers wrote to him asking if he would like to poke around inside their heads.

Trouble was, not enough people bought it. That's what it came down to, in the end. There were posters and promos and appearances at every bookshop and library he was willing to attend. It just didn't do very well. King wasn't a proper household name and his victims were all middle-aged white men, which meant little public sympathy. If he'd favoured young blonde girls or vulnerable women, King would have made Rowan a fortune. Rowan had come to the conclusion that there is almost nothing more expendable than a bland, white male. If he ever fancied becoming a serial killer himself, he would definitely make them his targets. After teenage runaways and long-term addicts, there is little in society as replaceable as a man.

The publishers expect something more commercially appealing for book two. The brief has been maddeningly broad. Perhaps something from a victim's perspective, they'd said. A confession, perhaps. Or an unsolved mystery, like those ones on Netflix. Rowan recalls one tall, blonde, frightfully Oxbridge twenty-something looking at him over her chai latte and asking, quite seriously, if he knew of any unsolved cases that he might be able to solve. Preferably one with a personal angle...

Rowan raises his hands as if to push back a loop of hair, looking afresh at the things on the ends of his wrists – the things that now pass for hands. His palms and fingers are entirely mummified in bandages and polythene. They hide the grisly mass of peeling skin and yellow pus beneath. Last time he was permitted to look, some of the skin grafts were starting to look a little healthier. In other places he was still just blood and bone. He feels as though he has been wrung out like a damp cloth. Something inside him feels fractured; broken. He looks as if he has been drained; juiced – as if the right gust of wind could carry him away.

Maybe those bastard producers were right after all, he thinks, looking at the mess of cloth and plastic and skin. He sinks in on himself. *You couldn't appear on camera anyway now. Not like that.*

He snarls at the memory – at the unfairness of the cards that Fate had dealt him not so long ago. As he'd dug around for a new story, Rowan had been thrown another seemingly golden opportunity when a production company in Manchester approached him to present the pilot episode of a new true crime series on a digital channel. Rowan had given the role his all, convinced this was going to be a permanent gig and a truly life-altering moment. Three months after they finished shooting, Rowan was replaced by a former soap actress. She was going to present, to film the links, to be credited as "star". Rowan was reduced to a "talking head", a named onlooker offering a journalist's perspective, filmed in front of a wall of old books.

Rowan had told them to shove it. None of his old

contacts took him back. Nobody wanted to give meagre freelance budgets to somebody who had left on a megabucks publishing deal. And his book publishers were starting to ask for updates. For some pages or an outline at least. If he failed to deliver a manuscript before December 31, he would be in breach of contract. He would have to give a great chunk of money back. And he didn't have the money anymore. He'd drunk it and smoked it and snorted it benevolently from bellies both fleshy and taut. He'd had a wonderful time. Now it was gone. He found himself having to do late-night subbing shifts at right-wing tabloids; missing from his girlfriend's London flat for such long periods that she presumed they'd broken up. In her distress, she'd turned to a handsome gym bunny called Donnie for emotional support.

Then he'd been hurt. Hurt so badly that the only place to go was home.

Home, he considers. It's an odd word this little green-brown corner of the Lake District. His upbringing saw to it he never put down roots. Home was caravan parks and halting sites; a seemingly endless succession of woodland enclosures where he and mum and Serendipity cosied up inside the old American school bus that rocked with each lash of the wind. He grew up itinerant, forever on the move; both benefactor and victim of a Bohemian mother and a series of impermanent dads. For a while, school was also a young offenders' institute. The foster homes, care homes, and finally free. *Home*, now, is wherever his sister is and this moody coastal valley is where she has chosen to put down roots.

He stretches, elongating his hands. Emits a simian screech as the wounds threaten to open like flowers.

'You stupid sod,' he mutters, seething. 'Stop forgetting!'

Rowan is under doctor's orders to keep his skin covered. The wounds upon his palms have twice become infected. For a time he seemed to be more blisters than flesh: mottled strips of epidermis hanging from his palm like popped bubblegum; pus and pain in every line and whorl. Two weeks ago he was admitted to A&E – the doctors concerned he was developing sepsis and pumping him so full of antibiotics that his blood could have healed the sick. He ran a fever that turned his skin a shade of green; steam rising from his forehead while shivering so violently that the nurses feared he would break his teeth. There was talk of an induced coma. His sister was called.

Rowan spent five whole days in hospital before boredom and the absence of a bar persuaded him he would be best served by discharging himself. He didn't get very far. The pain in his hands reached all the way up to his shoulders. He couldn't steer his car or change gear without weeping. They found him in the car park, trying to reverse out of a parking space using his elbows.

His sister had made the decision for him. He was coming to stay with her. There would be no arguments. She would give him space. She'd just had the byre done up and although it was pretty basic and the toilet was outdoors, it would be perfect for his convalescence. He could take it easy. He could write, or at the very least he could dictate into a recording device. He could walk on the fells or skim stones, however inexpertly, on the silver-grey surface of the mountain tarns. He could meet new people, drink real ales and decide what he wanted to do with the rest of his life. He could get to know his niece, Snowdrop. They would take care of him.

Rowan still feels as though they took advantage of a sick man.

He looks down as his feet nudge a silvery metal mug, resting against the doorstep. There's a wildflower wilting on the sealed lid. Rowan grins. Bends down and picks it up with his right hand; his bandaged fingers and thumb looking like a sock puppet fastening onto prey. He sips strong, black coffee, and gives a little salute to the air.

'Thanks, Snowdrop,' he mutters. He glances around, hoping his young niece may also have gone to the trouble of bringing him a bacon sandwich, three Marlboro Red and a strip of Ibuprofen. Wrinkles his nose, unimpressed with the youth of today.

He sits on the front step, a little cold, a little feverish, and still a bit drunk. The bird starts singing again. He glances back inside, through the door into the tiny space he is currently under instructions to think of as "home". He's proud of his sister for how hard she's worked to spin straw into gold. The byre was waist deep in cow dung when she bought it. The bloke who did the renovations spent the first three days shovelling his way down to floor level. Even then he had a hellish job with the drainage and foundations. There are old mine workings honeycombing the ground beneath this part of the valley. Serendipity had to beg two more budget increases from her wife before the byre could be declared fit for human habitation.

There's a different kind of crap to wade through now:

imitation Welsh dressers, cut little landscapes in wonky frames; rag rugs and wicker baskets piled with logs and pine cones. It's homely but too twee for Rowan's tastes. The absence of hot water or a shower doesn't help. He doesn't mind visiting the outhouse now and again but he's encouraged his hosts to think again before advertising a holiday cottage that expects its occupants to wash their nether regions in the downstairs sink. Rowan is no stranger to roughing it, but he fancies that the fell walkers who flock to this part of the Lake District may expect slightly more for their 600 quid each week.

Rowan's descent into the warm milk of self-pity is disturbed by a sudden sound at his garden gate. He looks up to see a bundle of effervescence and sunshine.

'Hiya,' comes a voice, bright as ice. 'Uncle Rowan! Did you get it? Was it still hot? Is it strong enough? Uncle Rowan! *Namaste!*'

Rowan pulls himself up and turns his back. Alters his position so he is leaning with his forehead against the doorframe, his back to the front gate. Hears plastic soles striking stone and the shush of disturbed grass as she runs up the path.

'What are you doing?' asks Snowdrop, a giggle in her voice.

'I'm getting paid to hold this building up,' says Rowan, without turning around. 'A tenner a day. The lunch breaks are a bit fraught with peril but a job's a job. I can't be picky.'

He enjoys her laughter. Turns back, pulling a face that suggests he has been pressing his features too hard into the brick. She laughs again. 'You're so weird,' she snorts. 'Mum said you would be weird but you're like, way out there.'

'Says you,' protests Rowan, pretending to be outraged. 'You're the one dressed like a pantomime cow.'

She grins, her face naturally charming. She's twelve years old. She has a pale, lightly freckled appearance, red lips and the same blue eyes as her mum, Rowan's older sister. Two spots of perfect red colour her cheeks. Her hair is a shimmering mass of black and hangs to her shoulders in a jumble of ringlets. Some of the twists in her hair are intentional – pretty curls made last night with twists of paper and elastic bands. The others are more naturally occurring tangles; a mess of knots and snarls, twisting over and under one another like ivy. There is mud on her bare knees and up the side of her wellingtons. Her bare hands look cold. There is a bruise on her left thumbnail and the last flakes of purply nail varnish on the seashell-coloured cuticles at the end of her long, pale fingers. She smells of the outdoors; of cake baked in a steam-filled kitchen; damp clothes and chunky, old-fashioned soap. She has the air of a Disney princess who has spent a month living rough: a Snow White not above barbecuing her woodland helpers.

'You should be wearing red,' says Rowan, looking her up and down.

'Sorry?'

'And you should be skipping.'

The girl frowns, unsure. She really wants to understand. 'I don't…'

'Red Riding Hood,' explains Rowan, shaking his head in mock disappointment. 'Honestly, you're supposed to be a writer. Now I know who picked the bloody awful name. Bilberry Bloody Byre…'

Rowan has already made his feelings clear about what

he refers to as "the saccharine vileness" of the cottage's new sobriquet. It was chosen by Serendipity, his sister. Given her own moniker, Rowan believes she should understand the importance of getting a name right. Their mother has a fifty per cent success rate. Rowan suits his name. *Serendipity*, forever anxious, forever screwing herself into the ground with responsibilities, with her lost paperwork and sob stories, has always struck her younger brother as more of a Carol or a Mavis. *Bilberry Byre* is her choice. It's a thoroughly incongruous affectation, deliberately chosen to suggest a certain cosiness – as if the remoteness of the location and severity of the weather could be somehow camouflaged by the cunning use of alliteration and pastoral imagery.

'I lit the fire myself today,' says Rowan, with a slight air of pride. 'My shirt caught fire, but it wasn't one of my good ones.'

'I can smell it.' Snowdrop sniffs. 'Did you smoke yourself out? I told you to clear the grating before you put the kindling on. Your eyes look a bit pink. Did you take the ash out? Mum gets cross if you don't. And do you need more firelighters? I brought some more anyway. They're under the croissants. That's okay isn't it? Are they poisonous? Will it make the croissants taste funny? Where does the word "croissant" come from, Uncle Rowan? There's a girl at school says her mum calls them crab-rolls. She says they look like them. They don't, do they? You won't die from eating them, will you? I've got a book on chemicals...'

Rowan smiles and puts his covered hands to his ears. 'Dippy, you're going to make my head explode.'

Snowdrop peers past him through the open door. It's

smoky inside the cottage; the grey air peppered with the greasy scents of bacon grease and spilled red wine. Her eyes shoot to the stain on the rag rug in front of the open fire. Red wine and burned cloth. A small, rather pitiful flame attempts to devour a large stack of A4 pages and a sheaf of newspapers. The fire gives off a pitiful amount of light and makes the cottage feel gloomy, turning the windows into mirrors. The walls seem closer today than when the sun shines. The creak of the gate sounds more threatening, like violin strings played with a saw.

Snowdrop wipes her feet on the step and slides into the room like sunlight. She crosses to the far wall and flicks on a standard lamp with a gaudy, seventies-style shade. Yellow light fills the poky room; picks out the wooden ceiling joists, the soft flower-patterned wallpaper, the random smattering of watercolour landscapes and Victorian school photographs in their mismatched frames. A pile of books has toppled over on the little table, knocking dirty glasses and crumb-covered plates onto the flagged floor.

'Nothing we can't sort out,' says Snowdrop, brimming with optimism. She looks at her uncle, slouched disconsolately in the doorway, and puts her head on one side as if talking to a younger child. 'You're doing so well. You've had no practice at this. Who could cope with having both hands out of action, eh? Especially when everything they're good at involves being pretty nifty with their fingers.'

Rowan chews his lip. 'That sounded vaguely encouraging,' he says, moodily. 'Have you heard somebody else say that?'

Snowdrop busies herself arranging papers, muttering something about an overhead conversation between her two mums. 'Typing, drinking, fighting – that's what Jo said.

Said something about it being like Usain Bolt losing use of his feet...'

'That's a clever line,' he says, begrudgingly.

'And no matter what they say, I know you're working hard here. Just because you won't tell anybody your idea for book two, it doesn't mean you haven't got one. I mean, your deadline's Christmas, isn't it, so you'd be pretty daft to not even have a title by this stage!'

He listens to her happy life. Manages a smile. 'Yeah,' he grumbles. 'That would be the work of a fucking idiot.'

The voice, thoroughly disappointed: *Yes, my son.*

2

Violet peers up at the bruised sky – the low clouds pressing down upon the valley like a boot heel. She tells herself the specks of purple and yellow are sunflowers and crocuses.

She looks across the stark, still surface of Wast Water. Makes out the shape of the school, emerging from the gloom like an iceberg. Pictures the big wooden door. Imagines her way inside it: to a place of high ceilings, bookcases, triple-tiered bunk beds and big comfy sofas.

Violet is beginning to regret slipping away from the rest of her party and taking herself off to this isolated spot. According to Daddy, Violet makes lots of bad decisions. Violet is a "difficult child". A "problem child". A "naughty girl". Violet is *"Trouble with a capital T"*. Nor, apparently, is she still pretty enough to charm her way out of trouble. *Apparently*, she has tried it on one too many times. *Apparently*, it's time to make big changes before she gets too far down a road from which she won't be able to come back.

Violet has recently turned ten. It's clear to her that her best days are well and truly behind her.

Violet hopes that Daddy won't be cross at her for going off on her own. She also hopes that he'll be furious. *Apparently*, she's a Contrary Mary. When she's in charge, she intends to take that stupid word out of the dictionary. *Apparently*, such grandiose claims are half her problem.

Daddy is a busy man. According to Mummy, he's *"well-to-do"*. He's from *"old money"*. He makes their lives easier and it's the least they can all bloody do to act grateful and give him a moment's peace, for God's sake...

This school is Mum's choice. If Daddy had his way she'd be attending one of the boaters-and-knickerbockers places down in the stockbroker belt. But Mum likes Silver Birch and, eventually, Mum tends to get her own way. Daddy's done a lot of sighing and snorting, letting out little breaths of contempt each time the head teacher has spoken about the school's holistic approach to "whole child" education. He'd seemed almost evangelical as he spoke of his pride in helping a whole generation of children how to become "citizens of the world" and to appreciate their "inner lives".

'Hippy claptrap,' muttered Daddy, as if he hadn't already read the brochure cover to cover.

'...*eventually everybody will be taught this way, and even the word "taught" is something I have issue with. This is of course our flagship school and two further academies are on the verge of opening in the next eighteen months. Obviously we live in a capitalist world and as such we have to make sure we balance the books but it's important you share our vision that all funds go straight back into education. We're trying to create a family here – that's why we keep the numbers small. For those pupils lucky enough to be boarding with us it's a real home-from-home mentality. I actually feel very jealous – this is going to be the start of a wonderful chapter in your children's lives...'*

Violet had stopped listening around the time Mr Tunstall had told them that maths was interchangeable on the curriculum with art, drama, homeopathy or modern philosophy. At her last school she was deemed an exceptional student – advanced in all aspects of schooling and extremely literate for somebody who turns eleven on their next birthday. Where she struggles is socially. She can be a boisterous girl. She loses her temper; gets easily upset. When she was small she used to pull her hair until it came out. Mum says she has too many feelings inside her – that she's "highly strung" and "neurotic" and "trying to find her path"; Daddy calls her a bloody nuisance.

Silver Birch is supposed to be a fresh start. They keep promising her things will be different here. They tell her she'll find peace. She doesn't believe them. They don't understand that she's two people. She's Violet Sheehan. She's clever and sweet and caring and artistic. She's also Violet's shadow. Those who have witnessed her temper say it is like watching a fight between hissing cats. She is all claws and spit and venom.

'Oh, sorry... I'll go... I didn't see you...'

Violet turns. The girl who emerges from the woods matches her intonation perfectly. She's a fragile little thing. Frizzy brown hair and glasses speckled with raindrops. She's probably the same age as Violet but looks younger.

Her clothes look considerably older: a big Salvation Army duffel coat is fastened up to the top above a knee-length skirt with shiny wellington boots. She holds herself close: elbows tucked in, like a roosting bird. She makes Violet think of premature kittens – the litter last spring – just bones and patchy fur, dead in a cardboard box. Daddy had let her keep one overnight, the better to help her say goodbye. She'd held it until it went stiff. Even then she'd continued to try and manipulate the limbs; to open its closed eyes and to push her finger into the squeezed-shut mouth, the pad of her finger searching for the tiny sharp points of teeth.

'I'm Violet,' she says, introducing herself in a loud, proud voice, the way Daddy has told her to. She puts out a hand for the frail girl to shake but quickly withdraws it, feeling silly. Her own hands are powerful – to take this girl's paw in hers would feel like closing a fist around a handful of crisps.

'Are you with the tour?' asks the girl, and Violet notices how wide her eyes are, like freshly cracked eggs on a dainty side plate. 'Are you coming here? You should, you really should. I started last term and it's not like other schools.'

'I've noticed.' Violet smiles, and the girl seems delighted by this small act of fellowship.

'I'm Catherine,' she says, though she doesn't seem entirely sure about the truth of the statement. 'My Daddy's the vicar in Seascale so I don't board. He's very happy with how I'm getting on here. What about you? Where are you coming from?'

'South.' Violet shrugs and pushes her hand through her mound of dark hair. 'They think the witch doctors here will make me stop going off like a bottle of pop.'

'Do you have control issues?' asks Catherine,

sympathetically. 'We've got a teacher here who's good for that. Well, not exactly a teacher but somebody who's good at helping people. He's a healer. Mr Sixpence he's called, but don't be put off. He's not a weirdo, or maybe he is, but not in a bad way. Anyway, he's good at making you feel better. Positive visualisation is part of it but there's meditation and something called mindfulness on offer three times a week. Have you heard of reiki? We do that too. It's weird but it kind of helps. You get all emotional and these tears come out that you've been holding in since you were a baby. Mam says they're the tears we weep for the sins of mankind, but she chuckles when she says it so she might just be pulling my leg.'

Violet feels grateful for Catherine's presence. She's not great at making friends. She can be too loud. Too boisterous. She loves too hard – that's what Mum says.

'Is this what you do at playtime then?' she asks, sitting down on a fat rock at the water's edge and gesturing for Catherine to join her. 'Is there a playground? I didn't see one. I like the ones where you hang upside down.'

'I'm not allowed to do that,' says Catherine, sitting down primly. She smells like an old lady and she seems to give off an air of constant cold. Her teeth chatter a little as she talks, though it doesn't seem to cause her any discomfort.

'Not allowed to do what?'

'Hang upside down,' explains Catherine. 'There was a little playground for a while but Mr Rideal wanted that turning into a nature garden so it's gone. Like he said, we've got the trees and the lake so why did we need it? But I get problems with my balance so I don't go upside down.

I don't swim either, though I did try with one of those bright red caps on. People said I looked like a match.'

Violet laughs, an obnoxious, donkey-like bray. It lands between them like a rock thrown into still water.

'Daddy says I need to stop letting things get on top of me,' explains Catherine. 'I'm not one of the special pupils but he wants me to think about seeing Mr Sixpence. Maybe have a healing.'

Violet picks up a handful of pebbles and starts tossing them into the water. 'A healing what?'

'It's a thing we do here,' says Catherine, and she wriggles on the rock as if she's uncomfortable. 'Like I say, Mr Sixpence isn't really a teacher. He sort of looks after the woods and the grounds. He used to be somebody quite high up but now he lives in a little... well, it's like a bus or a van or something, but all painted up and made cosy and filled with his weird stuff. He sometimes comes in to give talks to the class about places he's been and things he's done.'

Violet nods enthusiastically. 'The witch doctor! I said there was one. Daddy said I was being silly but I saw him in the background in a picture in the brochure. He looked like – I dunno – something from a film. Have you seen *Sword in the Stone*? He looked like Merlin!'

'That's funny,' says Catherine, her voice a little less fragile. 'Daddy says that some of the blokes in the pub in the village actually call him Merlin. Others say he's a – what's the word? – a Druid, that's it. He's a very quiet person but when he talks to you it's like you're the only person in the universe.'

Violet isn't sure how to respond. At her old school, anybody talking this way about an adult to whom they weren't related would have had their school bag emptied into the toilets and their heads stuffed down shortly afterwards. Violet would have been in the thick of it, high on pack mentality, shouting encouragement without dirtying her hands. She doesn't want to be that person anymore. Catherine seems nice.

'How does this healing thing work then?' asks Violet.

'I don't really get it but one of the people who stayed with us – they went to him and seemed a lot better afterwards.'

'Better than what?' asks Violet, intrigued.

'Than before. Sometimes we put pupils up at our house when the boarding hall is booked out or it's been hired by one of the Scout or Guide groups that come to learn about flora and fauna and homeopathy and stuff. It's just part of being a vicar's daughter – you get used to it. This one girl, Honey-Rose, she was really nice one moment and then this complete raving demon the next. That's Mam's words, not mine. She'd get a bad phone call from home and start hurting herself. Like, really hurting herself. I saw her coming out of the bathroom once and the backs of her legs looked like she'd been sitting in a wicker chair. But she hadn't – they were all scars. Daddy said I shouldn't mention it to her. He said people had been bad to her but she was getting better. Mr Sixpence was helping her put herself back together.'

Violet sits quietly, processing it all. She watches the surface of the lake. It looks like liquid mercury. A spot of rain lands on the stone by her hand. She glares up again, the reddish hue of the Wasdale Screes looming in the corner of her vision, plunging down from the long ridge between

Illgill and Whin Rigg. She wonders if Mum and Daddy are looking for her.

'It's a funny name,' muses Violet. 'Sixpence.'

'Like I said, he used to be somebody important. A psychiatrist, I think that's what Daddy said, though I always get that confused with psychopath. Daddy says he went to the same university as Mr Tunstall and Mr Rideal but he was a – what do you call it? – a dropout. Went travelling and saw the world. He got caught up in a war once – he spoke about it at assembly, though we could barely hear a word he was saying. He mumbles a lot, but when he's healing people his voice is clear as anything.'

'How does this healing thing work?' asks Violet.

'I think it's a bit like hypnotism,' muses Catherine. 'He'll probably give another talk about it soon. You can hear it, if you come to the school.'

Violet looks at the small, shy girl, and hopes that she gets to become her friend. Hopes, too, that she doesn't spoil it. Hopes she doesn't make her usual mistakes. Sometimes she loves so fiercely that it looks a lot like hate.

'If I come to this school, do you think I might stay at yours sometimes?' Violet asks, staring off. 'You can show me around. Take me to meet Mr Sixpence…'

Catherine laughs: a small, snuffling sound, like a shrew with a cough. 'That's out of bounds,' she says, in a tone that brooks no argument. 'Mr Rideal takes you up to see him if he thinks it will help your development. There aren't many rules at the school but we're encouraged to let people heal in their own way so we don't ask questions about how it works. Honey-Rose told me she doesn't remember much of it anyway. Just him talking in a deep voice and this constant drumming.'

'Sounds really weird,' says Violet. She picks up a bigger rock and throws it, forcefully, into the water.

'There are bodies down there,' says Catherine, quietly. 'Because it's so deep, they don't decay. They just go white, like statues. Like candles, I suppose. Daddy said.'

Violet looks at the lake. She feels an overwhelming urge to clap her hands and shout – to make noise, to scream, to beat on the rocks and beg the world to notice her, to see her, to understand...

'We could have an adventure,' says Violet, trying to look excited. She comes across as manic: clown-like. 'If you know where it is. We could sneak up, see what people are doing...'

'They'd see,' squeaks Catherine. 'He uses a slingshot to kill squirrels, that's what Perdita in Form Four said. And he can hear you coming. He has bottle tops on a wire. Daddy said.'

'*Daddy said, Daddy said,*' mimics Violet, shaking her head. 'It's just for fun. But if you're too scared?'

'I am,' agrees Catherine, without missing a beat. 'It's not nice up there. Daddy's been and he said that Mr Sixpence just wants to be left alone. There are old mine workings in the woods up there, near the house where the boarders stay. He cooks on a campfire; reads books, plays music. He grows his own vegetables and plants flowers. He writes a lot. The last thing I want to do is disturb him. He's always been very nice. When the children were staying with him it must have been very cramped.'

Violet flares her nostrils, disappointed her new best friend is so worryingly sensible. 'He had pupils stay there too? I don't know if I want that. I mean, he might be a weirdo.'

'He's not,' says Catherine, forcefully. 'He doesn't do that much anymore anyway. Some of the pupils who weren't suited for school, they'd go and learn forestry skills and how to take care of yourself and stuff. Daddy said it was too much for Mr Sixpence and so Mr Tunstall – the head – put a stop to it. Mr Rideal had all sorts of plans to start offering alternative therapies to the public but Mr Tunstall stood up to him.'

'And this Rideal? Is he the creepy one with the hair like Dracula?'

Catherine raises a hand to her face, shocked. 'You can't say that! He's the owner, yes. He's put lots of money into this!'

'I'm sure he has. Still looks like Dracula though.' She gives Catherine a little nudge in the ribs, and is pleased to receive a similar one a moment later in return.

She suddenly knows that she and Catherine are going to be best of friends.

3

The phone feels awkward in Rowan's injured hand: a bar of soap in a wet palm. He fiddles with the gaudy pictures on the cracked screen, flicking clumsily through the audio files. Such technical advancements have disenfranchised the traditional journalist. His skill set is almost obsolete. There was a time when he could scribble down perfect shorthand in the pocket of his overcoat, a stub of pencil beneath his thumbnail – his jottings running neatly along the parameters of a betting slip or blank taxi receipt. Now all he has to do is press "record" on his mobile.

Sulking, he sips his coffee. His niece will have to help him get dressed soon. Will have to wedge his toothbrush into his padded paw and raise the water glass to his mouth. She'll fasten the buttons on his shirt and lace his shoes.

'Did you get the thing?' asks Snowdrop, taking a cloth from a voluminous pocket and starting to scrub the condensation from the windows. The frames are flimsy, the glass thick, but they show the bleak, forbidding vista of the back way up Scafell Pike.

'The thing?' he asks, bewildered.

She turns to him, a little hurt. 'I did you a present.'

'The coffee? Yeah, thanks…'

Snowdrop tuts, hands on her hips, hair sticking out like a damp chimney brush. He feels like he's being admonished by a cartoon. 'Wait there,' she mutters, and runs briskly up the rickety stairs that lead up to the boxy, low-roofed bedroom. He hears the floorboards creak and a moment later she is back down, holding a large folder decorated with scraps of multi-coloured paper.

'I left it out for you to see when you woke up,' she says, holding it out. 'I decorated it with stuff from the art box and some wallpaper samples. Do you like it? It's got your name on.'

Rowan glances at the words on the front, written in black marker.

Portfolio
Rowan Blake
Journalist and Scribe

He realises he is smiling. He reaches out to take it then stops himself in case his ruined hands might stain the pages. He likes the word "scribe".

'I'll do it,' says Snowdrop, hurriedly. She opens the folder reverentially. Slipped within a transparent plastic sleeve is a picture of a well-dressed, dark-haired man in a neat white shirt, wool tie, dark braces and a flat cap. He's staring up from the page enigmatically, as if he knows something that he might be prepared to share – for a price.

'That's from your book,' says Snowdrop, unnecessarily. 'I took a picture of it from Jo's iPhone and we printed it out with proper glossy paper last night. It took ages. The rest of them are all genuine though. That's okay, isn't it? I mean, you didn't have plans for it all, did you? Jo said I should check but I wanted it to be a surprise.'

Rowan watches as she leafs through the pages. He glimpses headlines. Bylines. Black and white and black and white. Sees the word "Exclusive" begin to repeat itself page after page.

'You did all this?' he asks, quietly.

She shrugs, a little embarrassed. 'They were going to go mouldy.'

His old cuttings had arrived a few days ago, along with the rest of his possessions. They'd been stuffed into boxes and bin bags and piled into his ugly, battered car. His latest ex-partner, Roxanne, had paid somebody she knew from work to drive it up to the valley and abandon it on her drive. Rowan had encouraged his sister to set light to it – to let everything he used to be go up in a puff of smoke. Instead, she and Snowdrop had set about sorting through it.

'You're a very good writer – you can tell that,' says Snowdrop, looking at a feature he had written in 1998. It was an article on a young girl in desperate need of a bone marrow transplant. Her father, an IT expert, had set up a website encouraging people across the world to be tested for compatibility. Rowan was working for the *North-West Evening Mail* at the time. Eighteen years old and full of poetry and ambition and bile. He'd won an award for the interview – his descriptions of the girl's chipped pink nail varnish and trusting blue eyes striking a chord with readers, and the judges of the Regional Journalism Awards. He seems to recall that the girl got the transplant in the end. Pulled through. He wonders whether she's thriving now or floundering like everybody else. He checks the date. Wonders if there's any mileage in a follow-up.

Snowdrop turns the page. 'I hope you like it,' says Snowdrop, and moves towards him in the hope of something like a hug. He nods his head, over and over, his throat tightening. He tells himself to hug her. To pull her in for a big squeeze and a tickle. He can't seem to make himself. Just stands there feeling silly and awkward.

'I'd forgotten most of these stories,' he says, with a cough. He crosses to the sofa and sits down. Snowdrop places the book in his lap, open on a random page. He gives a snort of laughter as he looks at the article he wrote one hot April day in '99. A teacher from Millom was running as an independent candidate in a local by-election. If elected, he was going to stop the "blight" of wind farms and prevent the building of an access road that was going to lead to increased HGV traffic near the chalet-style houses of a group of pensioners. He'd vowed to stand up for decent people and common sense. Rowan presumes he lost.

'It's in date order,' says Snowdrop, hoping for a compliment. 'Your first murder's on page nine.'

Awkwardly, Rowan slides the glossy pages forward. Sees his name, third in the pecking order behind the crime reporter and one of the senior hacks. Rowan was still a trainee, but he'd earned the acknowledgement.

He flicks forward, memories coming back like birds returning to the nest. He glances at another article. It's been cut out neatly and glued down onto black card. Jason Peters, a senior member of the Wasdale Mountain Rescue Team, had been awarded an MBE for dedicated service.

Rowan had spent twenty-four hours in his company for what turned out to be a 600-word double-page spread in the *Cumberland News*. They'd been called out twice. Once had been a false alarm and the other had culminated not far from the summit of Scafell Pike, where three tourists were turning blue in trainers and T-shirts, shivering behind a wall and agreeing that, with the benefit of hindsight, they should have set off for the summit a little earlier, or a lot better prepared.

He glances over the text. Snowdrop was right. He'd been good with words when he started out. They flowed out of him – often to the distraction of his senior colleagues who always seemed to delight in putting great red lines through his prose. His eyes fall on a paragraph midway through the article. Rowan had asked about memorable incidents; difficult discoveries.

'All you want to do is get people safely off the mountain. That's what you sign up for – not awards or people slapping you on the back. Yes, I've seen horrible things but it would be disrespectful to talk about the injuries people have suffered or the bodies we've found after a period of time. I do remember the feeling of helplessness that washed over me when those teenage girls went missing about ten years back. One of them was the daughter of a good friend and all I wanted was to tell him she was safe, that we'd found her. I've never known conditions like that. It was like the valley was fighting us...'

Rowan sits back, one eye closed. He feels a memory unfold itself from the too-small box at the rear of his mind. *Girls.* Missing girls in the Wasdale Valley. He has a sudden clear picture of himself, no older than nineteen, tie unfastened to his midriff, purple streaks in his hair, asking one of the senior reporters whether they knew what the mountain rescue man was talking about when he referred to "the teenage girls who went missing". The deputy news editor had given him a lacklustre synopsis. Said there had been a "bit of a hoopla" at the time. Three teenage girls from the hippy place in the valley. Word was, they'd gone off with a stranger. Witness statements suggested they might be somewhere on the back route up Yewbarrow. Others said they'd seen them scrambling over the Screes at Wasdale. Mountain Rescue had battled a tempest as they scoured the black fells looking for them.

He concentrates, trying hard to remember how his old boss had resolved the tale. Looking back, he realises he hadn't even listened to the conclusion. Had probably cut her off, drunk on youthful hubris.

'Mum knows one of the ladies in that story,' says Snowdrop, peering over the back of the sofa at the article. 'When we were making the portfolio, I mean. She read your article and said somebody from her writing group was one of the girls who'd gone missing.'

Rowan glances her way. She has his attention. 'I don't suppose she desperately wants to share the story of what happened to her, does she? Go on, be kind to your uncle, tell me a good-natured lie. Tell me there's a story in this that'll fix all my problems.'

'What problems?' asks Snowdrop, smiling. 'I know you're only pulling my leg about not having a second book. Maybe I shouldn't be distracting you when you're so close to your erm, what do they call it, yeah, your deadline, but if you did fancy showing me how to be a proper reporter;

well, maybe you could show me what to do with a story like this. I mean, we could do a follow-up.'

Rowan sinks into the sofa. A follow-up to what? If he were still a local newspaper reporter there may be some purpose to writing an anniversary piece – some nostalgic "remember when" article for readers to coo over, uttering inanities about what they might have been up to so long ago. He supposes he could check the date and see if there's a significant anniversary coming up.

'Google Jason Peters for me,' he says, sighing. 'The Mountain Rescue chap.'

Grinning, Snowdrop does as she's asked, her fingers dancing over the screen of the laptop as she sits on the floor by the fire. She pulls a face. 'Dead,' she says, with a note of apology. 'Lots of people said nice things when he died, which is good, I guess.'

The glow of the screen casts light onto her face and Rowan smiles as he sees how intensely she is concentrating. She has her tongue pressed against her teeth. He does the same when he's thinking hard.

'The vicar who gave the service,' reads Snowdrop, raising her finger to the screen. 'Reverend Marlish. I know him a bit. He comes into school sometimes, or he did when I was there last.' She rolls her eyes at this, sick and tired of her on-and-off relationship with conventional education, which she sees as an unavoidable consequence of being raised a little off the grid. Rowan, who didn't go to school until he was nine and took his GCSEs in a young offenders' institute, has every sympathy.

'There's a quote here, in the article, where he talks about how Jason always put others before himself.' She reads it out loud, putting on a deep male voice. *'Like so many others, I was spared grief by Jason and the team. He was a true hero – a lifesaver. Every time I hug my daughter I say a prayer of thanks that he brought her home.'* Snowdrop looks up, expectantly. 'Could be the same friend that Jason spoke about in your article, couldn't it?'

Rowan chews his lip. The Mountain Rescue Team keeps immaculate records. Would it be such a chore to trawl through the incidents from thirty years back and see if there are any more details? He can feel something unfolding itself in his mind, righting itself like crumpled cloth. He remembers a court case, maybe eighteen months back. Somewhere in South London was it? A stabbing or a shooting, he can't recall which. They all blend together after a while; an ugly melange of victims and villains, of perpetrators and witnesses, killers and the bereaved, all swapping faces with the dead.

But he always manages to remember attractive women, and there was no doubt that the detective inspector with whom he shared two machine coffees and a cigarette ticked that box with gusto. She'd been there to see some drug dealer get life for killing one of his teenage couriers. She was loud, funny and dangerously indiscreet and they'd got on famously. She'd been unapologetically forward, sharing confidences and encouraging him to give various colleagues a roasting in print for the misdemeanours she was happy to elaborate upon. He'd done her a good turn, hadn't he? He seems to recall that she'd said "thanks" a lot when she texted him, though he has no way of checking. Those messages would have been prudently deleted lest they be glanced at by his eagle-eyed partner.

Even so, he can recall the contents – and the picture of her dainty feet propped up on the bath taps that she had sent along with the rather suggestive message "*thinking of you*". Sumaira, that was it, wasn't it? Flirty eyes and a big mouth. She'd told him the case had made her mind up, hadn't she? Said she couldn't stare into the sewer of London's underworld any longer. She was going to accept a job up North. They'd chatted for a while as he'd told her about his own connections to Cumbria: his start in journalism, his sister's love affair with the Lakes. He has no doubt that he could persuade her to see the merits of renewing their acquaintance. Wonders whether his hands are up to it and decides there is no gain without pain.

Snowdrop comes and sits down beside him. She's warm and smells of the outdoors; of baking. She points at the picture that accompanies the article. It shows a young Rowan, wearing Mountain Rescue red; a ridiculous half-moon hat buckled to his head. He's talking with a spry, wiry man with a dark moustache and unruly eyebrows, similarly attired.

'You're only about six years older than me there,' she says, in wonder. 'Do you think I could be a journalist even younger than that?'

Rowan looks down at his feet. He wrote an article on this subject a year ago – a virtual obituary for court reporting and regional journalism; a desperate cry of anguish about the state of the media industry and how free content providers and the internet had turned journalism from a profession into a hobby.

'Apparently, you can be anything you want to be,' he says, meeting her eye. 'So if anybody can, it's you.'

She seems satisfied with the answer. She shifts a little, ducking into his eye-line. They sit in silence, watching the firelighters kiss the paper and twists of card; the haphazardly chopped tinder; the great hunks of sap-scented wood. She tries to rest her head on his shoulder. He sucks on his lower lip, his curiosity unfolding like an origami rose. He can sense an opportunity. Can see the faintest light of possibility: a haze of phosphorescence in the darkness. He's spun baser materials than this into gold. Has polished far darker turds to a truly dazzling gleam.

'Go on then,' says Rowan, trying to make it sound like a hard-won favour. 'I can give you a masterclass in what to do next, if you like.'

Snowdrop grins, little fizzing sparks in her eyes. 'Can we really? Can you show me how to be a journalist and a writer and find stuff out…?'

'If you stop dancing about, yes,' he replies, smiling at her and meaning it.

She stops performing her unsettlingly vigorous jig and considers him as if he were a particularly intriguing fossil. 'Uncle Rowan, you wrote a book once, yes?'

Rowan laughs, drily. 'I've written lots – I've published one.'

'And it got good reviews but not enough sales, is that right?'

'Oh I'm glad you're so well informed…'

'But everybody said you were great at getting into people's heads. I mean, you wrote about a serial killer and you were able to make him sound somehow normal. Said you were like a locksmith when it came to getting people to open up. Lots of people said it was very unsettling.'

'And?'

'Well, Mum's friend sounds like somebody who wants to talk.'

'Talk about what?' he asks, losing patience.

'What happened when she was abducted,' says Snowdrop, pronouncing each syllable as if he's simple.

'Abducted? It doesn't say that,' says Rowan, glancing at the yellowing newsprint in its glossy coat.

'No, but Mum says there's more to it. She was a bit surprised when she saw the article, actually. Last night – when we were making this. I don't think she would have put it in the portfolio if she'd been on her own. I saw her trying to put it to one side but I told her – every article from when he was starting out needs to be in portfolio. I've googled it – that's what you're supposed to do.'

Rowan sits forward. His fingers are tingling a little, and he wonders if sensation is about to return with a kiss or a punch.

He closes his eyes. He gives the order like an embittered submarine commander urging his crew to launch the torpedoes. There's a weary resignation in his voice.

'Go on then,' he says. 'Get the laptop, and the phone. Two pens. A lined notepad. Set them up on the table where the phone signal's best.'

'Yes,' hisses Snowdrop, performing a mini fist-pump. 'What do we drink?'

'Whisky,' says Rowan, slithering down into the embrace of the sofa. He raises a hand. 'I would type but I've got flippers.'

'Do you want a straw?' she asks, over the banging of cupboards.

'I haven't sunk that far yet,' he says.

He hears the squeak of the chair across the flagged floor. 'So,' she says, after a tiny hesitation. 'What do I do?'

On the sofa, Rowan smiles. Raises a bandaged hand and manages to close it, gratefully, around the tumbler of amber fire and ice. It's a twelve-year-old, all seaweed and peat. 'They should call this Snowdrop,' he mutters, and manages a gulp without spilling a drop.

'Dial this number,' he says, and begins to recite from memory.

Snowdrop energetically does as she's told. She stops three digits from the end. 'That's Mum's number,' she says, suspiciously.

'Aye,' he confirms. 'I want to know what she knows...'

'She'll be cross,' protests Snowdrop. She slaps her forehead. 'Damnit – that's rule one! I shouldn't have revealed my source!'

'No,' says Rowan, ruefully. 'That's way down the list. Rule one is simple. Be prepared to be unpopular. Can you do that?'

At the tiny table, Snowdrop draws herself up. Nods, solemnly. 'Whatever it takes.'

Rowan hides his grin behind the glass.

4

Silver Birch Academy, Wasdale Valley
Saturday, July 11, 1987
4.01pm

The girls are lounging in the little horseshoe-shaped bay at the edge of Wast Water, their backs to the school. This is a favourite spot. The trees form a screen. They're not up to anything naughty, but they still enjoy the sensation of being able to do what they want without fear of being observed.

Violet is in one of her moods today. She's quiet. Sullen. She wants somebody to say something negative to her so she can tell them how little she cares. She has a habit of chewing her cheek until it bleeds. Catherine, who has learned to read the signs, is doing her best not to be annoying. She doesn't really know what will trigger an outburst, as the rules seem to change every day, so she sits quietly beside her, trying to exude the warm, golden light that she has been reliably informed she can employ as both sword, shield and blanket. She tries to centre herself. To listen to her heartbeat and to breathe in tandem with the vibrations of the universe. More than anything, she tries not to be annoying. Violet's temper scares her.

Violet is glaring into the depths of the lake. She fancies that she can taste it somehow: all iron and dirt and vinegar on her tongue. If she concentrates hard, she can see what's below the great silver mirror of the surface. She can see down through the cold, still bleakness and make sense of the perfect dark. She can see the dead people. Can see their cold, bloated skin: white, like the belly of a fish. Can see dead eyes, staring upwards, into nothing. Can feel what they feel, the loneliness and rage.

Mr Sixpence is the only person she has confided in about her visions. Mr Sixpence tells her she has a gift. He wants her to learn how to harness it. To channel it. He has warned her not to listen to those who tell her she is ill. It is a blessing, he says. A gift.

Violet feels the pull of the water. If she concentrated hard enough, she thinks she could swap places with one of the dead. She could swap consciousness with one of the bodies, bound in plastic and pitched into the inky black depths by any one of the succession of murderers who have chosen this place to conceal evidence of their deeds.

She moves closer to Catherine. Screws up her eyes until the feeling passes. Turns to her friend and punches her in the arm.

'Don't!' hisses Catherine, wrapping her left hand around her skinny bicep. She looks hurt. 'I've asked you to stop doing that.'

'You're building up your tolerance,' says Violet, trying to sound matter-of-fact. In truth, she doesn't know why she keeps giving her best friend dead-arms. She doesn't know why Daddy used to do it to her. He seemed to enjoy it more than Violet does when she inflicts them on Catherine or the other girls at the boarding house. She supposes she just likes the feel of it. Likes the way soft skin responds to her own hard knuckles.

'I've got bruises,' says Catherine, sticking out her lip.

'Do it to me, then.' Violet shrugs. 'Hit me back.'

'I don't want to hit you. You're my friend.'

Violet rolls her eyes, all scorn. '*You're my friend, you're my friend.* God, Catherine, you're pathetic. A pathetic little girl.'

'I'm older than you, Violet.'

'*I'm older than you, Violet...*'

'Stop copying me!'

'*Stop copying me...*'

They catch one another's eye and start to laugh. They've been best friends for a year now. They sit together as often as they are allowed. Violet spends more time at the vicarage with Catherine and her parents than she does in the boarding house. She's going to spend the summer with them too. There had been talk of going home, but Mum has been suffering with her nerves of late and Daddy has too much on to be dealing with "a houseful" so she is going to stay with the Marlish family instead. She likes it there. They're a little bit feeble sometimes and she finds the prayers before dinner a little embarrassing, but she likes them both well enough. They always want to know her opinions on things. They want her to be happy. They ask questions about what she wants to be when she grows up, and about how her parents met, and whether or not she feels as though she's living a better "inner life" than she had been before Silver Birch accepted her.

Violet always finds it hard to answer. She doesn't think much about the future. Her parents never told her how they met. And yes, her inner life seems a little more peaceful than it had been when she was starting endless fights at her old school, but that's more to do with the fact that none of the wimps at Silver Birch are willing to say or do anything to piss her off. Sometimes the place seems so peaceful she wants to burn it down.

'Do you want to say goodbye to him?' asks Catherine, pushing her bushy hair out of her face.

'Who?'

'Whom, you mean…'

'Piss off. Do you mean Sixpence? I doubt he'll be there.'

'We can try.'

Violet looks at her friend. She's got a sheen of perspiration on her forehead. It's always there. She's the clammiest person Violet has ever met. Cold hands, but always a little veneer of sweat on her brow and her top lip. Her mum always insists she dress for winter, even when the sun is bright. They are allowed to wear their own clothes at Silver Birch, but Catherine always looks as though she's dressed for Sunday school, with her sensible shoes, knee-socks and long, neatly ironed skirts. Violet, by contrast, is pushing the dress policy as far as she can. Mr Tunstall and Mr Rideal both champion the notion of dressing independently and creatively, but Violet's ever-diminishing hemlines are becoming a cause for concern.

'You might not see him for the whole summer,' says Catherine, quietly.

Violet gives her a hard look, searching for a hidden meaning. Catherine knows that Violet is fond of the peculiar man who lives in the woods and who sometimes comes to give talks to the school. He's quiet. There's a gentleness about him. Violet said he reminded her of something from a Disney movie. She could imagine baby birds nesting in his beard and hedgehogs dozing contentedly in the pockets of his big camouflage coat.

His battered old campervan is parked up a little way from the water's edge, tucked in a small clearing in the woods behind the school. To command the pupils to steer clear would be to go against the ethos of the school but the teachers have encouraged the girls to respect his privacy. Most do. Violet cannot allow herself to obey even this most gentle of suggestions. She regularly stomps her way through the woods to chat with Mr Sixpence. There is something about him that both soothes and energises her. She always feels better after time in his company, even if they have talked about nothing but the weather or the volume of moss on the trees. She feels cleverer for time spent with him.

'I don't fancy him or anything,' says Violet, harshly. She puts her face in Catherine's. 'He's an old man. He's a weirdo. A weirdo like you.'

Catherine looks down at her feet. 'You don't have to be like that,' she says. 'Why would I think you fancy him?'

''Cause I said he was interesting.'

'So? That just means he's interesting.'

'Fine, then. Fine, if it matters that much to you. Let's go see him. Say goodbye.'

Violet turns and trudges off towards the trees. Catherine waits a moment, hands on her hips, gathering herself. She doesn't like to cry in front of Violet. It makes Violet feel guilty, and when she feels guilty, she's twice as mean.

Then Catherine follows her friend into the woods. She would rather die than be left behind.

5

Rowan is standing by the front door again, huffing out soft plumes of grey air. The ragged breaths gather about his face like unwrapped bandages before drifting away to muddle with the great white smears of mist and fog that colour the dips; the rises, at the foot of the fell. He has a sudden image of a battlefield: of pain and mud and jagged coils of wire; of trenches and bomb craters filled with toxic mustard gas – smoke trapped inside a glass.

He walks halfway down the garden and peers into the nothingness between the straggle of trees. He can see it being lovely here in the summer. If he had the inclination, he could put down some jaunty flagstones at the edge of the little stream. Could give himself a place to sit, his toes in the gurgling water, rubbing his soles over moss-slimed rocks. He can almost picture himself here, leaning back on his palms, gazing up at a sky of gold and blue.

A low growl erupts at the back of his throat. He curses, pissed off with himself. Each time he ends a relationship he promises himself the same thing – that he won't let fantasies undo him; that he won't spurn reality in pursuit of some idealised daydream. He keeps telling himself to focus on the here. On the now. He can't help thinking that being an early reader did him no favours. He grew up a Romantic, retreating into the pleasures of fiction even as the facts of his reality became harder and harder.

'Uncle Rowan! She's done! She wants to talk to you!'

Rowan walks back towards the house. Snowdrop is in the doorway, holding out her phone. She's wincing. Serendipity is a magnificent interrogator. She doesn't do shouting or swearing, but she has a way of sounding disappointed that could cause the most hardened of political prisoners to denounce their ideology.

'You okay, sis?' he asks, as brightly as he can.

There is a pause. Wherever she is, it's windy. He can hear the rushing of wind past the mouthpiece. 'I'm not having a go, Rowan...'

'No.'

'But I'm not sure I'm happy about my daughter becoming a Fleet Street hound.'

Rowan laughs. 'Sorry, is this 1978...?'

'I encouraged her to do creative writing. Maybe some poetry. I don't know if journalism is a career I could encourage...'

'Nor me,' says Rowan, dropping his voice. 'Look, we're just helping the day pass by. I'm healing. She's my helper. It's a game, really. I want to show her how the job actually works – or how it used to.'

He glances at Snowdrop, holding his glass of whisky and staring at the different patterns held in the ice. Rowan has lost whole days to such a pursuit. She gives him a thumbs-up, tells him he's doing well.

'Look, it's nothing anyway...' begins Serendipity.

'I told her as much. That's why we're workshopping this

particular story. It's educational. I'm just showing her how to check some facts.'

'I suppose...'

'So, she said there had been a kidnapping...'

'No. No I never said that. I mean, maybe I said "abduction" but it's not that I know anything. Not really.'

He hears her start to attune herself to the right frequency. Prepares himself for answers to questions he hasn't even asked.

'Look, Violet has been having some problems, that's all...'

'Sorry, Violet...?'

'Oh, well it was Sheehan then but it's Rayner now.'

'Ha! Yeah, that's it, that's what we had. So, you said she'd been having a hard time...'

'I don't know the ins and outs of it,' she says, louder now, as the wind whips up around her. He can imagine gulls and spray.

'But the abduction, after what she went through, she was always going to have difficulties...'

'No, that wasn't it,' protests Serendipity. 'She was great for ages. She was fine with not remembering. She was happier not to know, I think. She's such a riot of a girl when she's doing well. I don't know, things just started coming back to her. I didn't read the story in detail.'

Rowan stays silent, not wanting to break the spell. 'Read?' he asks, at last.

'Yes, that's why I know she's been having a hard time. She did this piece of writing for her group. About how hard it was to live without knowing what had been done to you. With fragmented memories. It was quite powerful, apparently.'

'And this said what had happened to her?'

Suspicion creeps into her voice. 'What do you actually know, Rowan?'

He grimaces. Game up. 'Enough to make a start...' he mumbles.

She growls down the phone, frustrated. 'Look, there's no drama here. I just mentioned to Snow that one of the articles she'd put aside for your scrapbook...'

'Portfolio,' he corrects her, amid demonstrations of appreciation from Snowdrop.

'Yes, portfolio. I said that one of the girls who the mountain rescue man was talking about might have been Violet, who I only know a little bit. She wrote a piece saying she'd never known what had happened to her when she was a kid but how she thought she was ready to confront it. Jo told me about it. It was on the wall at the library, in a display. I thought I might be able to help.'

'Go on,' prompts Rowan.

'And I told Jo to tell her about some alternative practitioners who might be able to help if she wanted to work through bad memories...'

Rowan smiles, pleased with his sister. She's always desperate to help and there's never a price to be paid. She wouldn't think twice about contacting a virtual stranger and offering to help them find their light.

'So Jo did that, and said I knew some people, and gave her the number of the house phone and she got in touch. We aren't friends or anything, but she's a nice lady...'

Rowan crosses to the table and leans over his niece's head. Painfully, he jabs the tip of his bandaged right hand at the keyboard, thumping in a name. 'Google that,' he whispers to Snowdrop. 'Then Facebook, Twitter, Instagram, anything new and funky I haven't heard of. Use "Sheehan" too.'

She looks up at him in dazed bafflement. He's talking to her like she's a senior reporter on an editorial team. He waves an apology. Gives his attention back to his sister.

'You're saying she was remembering?' He sounds dubious. 'You're saying she doesn't know what happened to her way back when? That she's no memory of whatever it was? That's hard to swallow, sis. Weren't there another two girls? Couldn't she just ask them?'

'I don't know the ins and outs,' says Serendipity, and now she has to shout over the gale.

'Bloody hell, could you shout up?'

'I mean, everybody's friends with everybody here...'

'You'd never do the wrong thing, sis. Whatever you do, it's always the right thing.'

As she waits, he wonders what she might be up to. He presumes she's out doing good deeds. Whenever he asks how she's spent the day it has invariably been on some lost cause – saving old sycamore trees from the council chainsaw or demanding better play facilities for the park in some dying fell-side village. She spends a lot of time at meetings, munching cheap biscuits in her fingerless gloves and trying to inject some compassionate liberalism into agenda items. He's amazed she hasn't yet thrown herself into the sea.

'It's not going to appear anywhere, is it, Rowan? You're not going to actually write anything?'

'Sis, it's just a little game. I'll make sure she does the

spelling and punctuation all the way through. And you said she had to be my hands for a bit. This is what my hands do.'

'I suppose it's not like the confessional,' she mutters, talking to herself.

'I don't want to set her off on the wrong foot, Dippy,' he says, using his childhood nickname for his beloved big sister. She gives in.

'Look, Rowan, you know how it is round here. People can buy into a lie or a story that crosses generations. People can look at new-born babies with an Afro and swear they look the very image of their blond-haired, blue-eyed dads. I don't think Violet told me anything that wasn't already public knowledge but it's not my story to tell...'

'Told you when?' he asks, casually.

'Months back. Spring, I think. I gave her the number for my friend, she's very good...'

'And who is she?' he asks, patiently.

'Shamanic priestess. That's where she was going to go for soul retrieval.'

Rowan smothers a laugh. He doesn't look down on any religious or spiritual practice but can't help laugh at the matter-of-fact way she can use "shamanic priestess" in a sentence, as if introducing a butcher or postman. He doesn't need to ask her about shamanic traditions, or soul retrieval. Both played parts of his childhood.

'Do you think you could come back to the house?' asks Rowan, moving agitatedly. He wants to pace. He likes pacing. The damn room's too small to do it properly. And *cobbles!* Who could pace properly on cobbles!

'I'm doing something, Rowan,' she says, patiently. 'That's why you've got Snowdrop, remember. I'm working.'

'Oh come on, I'm sure whatever albatross chick you're bathing will forgive you. Come on, this might be important...'

'What do you think I do, Rowan?' she asks, chilly. 'Albatross chick?'

Snowdrop is trying to get his attention. She's found Violet Rayner (nee Sheehan) on Facebook. Rowan glances at the profile name. She's signed in as him. He glances at the centre of the screen. It shows that they have two FB friends in common. One is his sister; one is a man whose name always gives Rowan a delightful trill of anticipation.

'She knows Pickle?' he asks. He leans back over Snowdrop's shoulder and jabs again at the keyboard. Pickle has commented on several of Violet's posts and she has done the same for him. In March, he'd left a comment below a mournful black and white picture she had posted – the words **"That's It – I'm Done!"** in big angry letters in the very centre. Thirty-two people responded with crying emojis. Pickle had left a comment urging her to come see him "for a decompression session". She'd sent back a thumbs-up and a smiley face. Sometimes, the poet in Rowan truly despairs.

'Oh she must be interesting then, Dippy. I mean Pickle's like a massive great magnet for the dangerous and the deranged. He's only up past the falls. I'll wander over, get some air...'

'No,' snaps Serendipity, too quickly. 'No, you aren't taking her to Pickle's.' She raises her voice again, fighting the wind. 'Rowan, do you hear me? He's not a good environment... he's not all there... he smokes every moment of the...'

'Sorry sis,' he says, walking towards the dead zone at the far end of the room. The signal begins to drop out. He smiles at her frustrated, tinny voice, growing fainter with each step.

"...*that thing... with the buffalo... no... always come back stoned... Ro... do you...?*"

'Lost her,' he says, sadly holding up the phone. He grins, suddenly transformed. He adopts an exaggerated swagger as he walks back to his niece. She creases her eyes and nose into a smile that seems to take in her whole self. He suddenly has a memory, sharp as cut glass. He sees her as the little girl she was: a toddler, a tot, not much more. Big multi-coloured dungarees and rainbow jumpers; a bow in her hair and pudgy pink bare feet. A mind like a rocket. Bright eyes. Always so eager to learn. And kind, too. Happy to listen and burble as he told her where it had gone wrong and why this girl or that girl had left him. He wishes he'd sent just one of the letters he'd promised to write her. Wishes he'd turned one of the silly bedtime stories he made up for her into a manuscript she could hold in her hand. Always too busy. He feels an overwhelming urge to somehow become considerably less shit.

'You did brilliantly,' he says and finds himself giving her a bump with his shoulder. It feels kind of good. She preens; a stroked cat. He moves, quickly. 'Pickle,' he says. 'Real name Gareth Church. Gentleman-farmer-cum-impeccable-weed-dealer. A giant of a man. A colossus. Philosopher and recognised global number one when it comes to remembering trivia and quotes from the film *Withnail and I*. He sort of killed somebody once but he feels bad about it...'

'Killed somebody?'

He grins. He doesn't know many people locally but of

those he's had the fortune to acquaint, Pickle is the only one he'd like to think of as a friend. He's been putting off going to see him, constantly pushing back arrangements for get-togethers, dinners, a "good smoke and some Lucozade out in the shed". He hadn't wanted to show Pickle just how low he'd fallen since the last time they'd got drunk together. He fancies he can brave it now. He wants to show his niece that as a journalist, you are guaranteed to meet some weird and wonderful people. Such a demonstration would fall into Pickle's skill set perfectly.

6

Rowan feels his mood lift with every step he takes away from the cottage. There's a mizzling rain slapping at his face and the low cloud makes it seem that he's looking at the world through a cigarette paper, but he's never subscribed to the notion that beauty only belongs to warm days.

'River sounds full,' he says, making conversation. He jerks his head back down towards the Irt – clucking and surging, hidden by the swirl of mist. Beside him, Snowdrop is glaring at his phone, occasionally losing her footing on the slippery surface as she gives the screen her full attention.

'Sorry?' she asks, looking up. Her eyes widen; two perfect drops of spreading blue ink. 'You're not out of breath,' she notices, approvingly. 'Mum's always out of breath by now.'

Rowan shrugs. He's never been much of a one for the gym and he treats his body the way a foot treats a shoe, but he's spent most of his working life ambling relatively large distances, eating up miles of pavement as he meandered from court to council to pub to office to home.

'There's one of the rules of journalism for you,' he says, brightly. 'Always buy comfortable shoes. A good reporter shouldn't be afraid of putting in the miles. A lot of news happens in cities, and nine times out of ten the reporter on foot can get to a scene before the reporter in the pool car. And then of course, you're not encumbered by having to stay sober...'

'I'll write that down when I have a moment,' mutters Snowdrop. She's got one eye closed, focusing all of her energy on the web page. 'I've heard of your friend Pickle before,' she adds, warningly. 'Jo says he's bringing house prices down. I didn't know he had a real name. Were you joking when you said he was a murderer?'

'That's the word the court chose,' says Rowan, ruefully. He decides she's old enough to learn how shitty the world really is. 'There's this old law called "joint enterprise". Dates back centuries to when people used to fight duels. Well, it's still in effect and sometimes prosecutors like to stick a murder charge on every member of the gang who was there when one of them stabbed a rival to death; or if a load of people go to somebody's house intent on violence and the intended victim is killed – the whole lot are culpable. I've written about it a lot.'

'What do you think about it?' asks Snowdrop.

Rowan laughs, taken aback. 'Me? What do I know? I just write about it, Snowdrop, and Pickle's case was one I'd heard of even before I got to know him. He and some university mates got drunk and thought it would be jolly funny to grab one of the lads from a nearby dorm and whisk him away like he was being kidnapped. He woke up as they were trying to get him out of his bed. He lashed out with this bloody great bayonet he kept under his pillow. It got one of his mates. Instinct kicks in and Pickle grabs the knife. Pulls it out of his mate's stomach, sober as a judge now. Ended the night with one dead, one dying and nobody being able to say who'd done what. Pickle stood with his friends, refusing to deviate from the story they all agreed on. At the last moment the other two changed their plea to guilty and pinned it all on Pickle. A very grateful Crown Prosecution Service gave them reduced sentences. Pickle was done for manslaughter in the end. Served eleven years. He was supposed to be a barrister or a doctor by now. Instead he does little bits of this and lots of the other, living in the last of his dad's farm buildings. He's a bit of a character. Sort of lost himself after prison and it took a lot of chemicals to bring him back. You'll love him.'

Snowdrop glares at her phone. 'Signal's about to go...'

Rowan trudges on, the slope starting to get steeper. He likes it here, boots kicking up mud and grit on the edge of the quiet, tyre-rutted path that leads through the tangle of woodland and up towards the falls. He can hear the distant growl of the tumbling water.

'Bit quiet of late,' says Snowdrop, over the sound of their feet crunching over damp stone. 'Only a few posts since the summer. Usual silly Facebook stuff like Mum puts on. What does your thumb-shape say about you? And celebrations of "friendship anniversaries". She's got over 600 "friends". She used to be quite busy on it but seems to have lost interest. She's got photos and videos and lists of favourite books and films and stuff...'

'What does she like?' asks Rowan, intrigued. 'Books, I mean.'

'Oh all sorts,' says Snowdrop. 'Weird mix. Everything

from *Harry Potter* through to crime fiction, a biography of some comedian I don't know, and a load of enlightenment stuff, the stuff Mum pretends to read. *Warrior Goddess*; *Grow a New Body*; *Inside the Divine Pattern*, or something...'

'I'll read it properly when we're back,' says Rowan. 'Is there a picture? Recent?'

Snowdrop fiddles with the phone and holds it up for inspection, displaying a screen-grabbed image of Violet Rayner (nee Sheehan). She's grinning for the camera; a big mess of dark hair piled up on top of her head and wooden earrings dangling down below the level of her slightly rounded chin. She's a few years older than him but he thinks she looks younger. She's got healthy skin and the whites of her eyes are bright as a new moon. Her dark eyebrows have been accentuated with pencil and brush but she wears no other make-up. There's something about her that suggests a fizzing kind of energy; a gleam in her eye that says she's enjoyed the kind of evenings out that don't finish until breakfast.

'Single,' says Snowdrop, as if reading his mind. 'I've got family, friends, workplace, past events. She's barely got anything set to "private" but I've sent her a friend request from your account.'

Rowan shoots her a look. 'My own account?' he asks, feeling the pressure of the climb in his calves. 'That's not always the best move...'

'You have other accounts?'

Rowan smiles, glancing ahead as the track slips back into the cold wet strip of forest. The light is muted as if the sun has been swallowed whole. He focuses on his steps and throws a look at Snowdrop. If his wounds didn't hurt so damn much he would be tempted to offer her a hand, though he couldn't say for sure whether it would be her benefit or his.

'I've got three accounts,' says Rowan, quickening his pace. 'I'm me, I'm a grandmother called Caron, and I'm a twenty-six-year-old mother of one from Canning Town.' He puts on a London accent. 'I work in childcare, don't I, but I hope to become a professional make-up artist. I'm quite acid-tongued when I want to be. I've got one of those *Live, Laugh, Love* pictures on my bedroom wall and I'm a fiend for my Prosecco.'

Snowdrop laughs, grinning up at him. 'Do you really? Do you really use different names? Pretend to be other people? Is that not a bit, well, wrong...'

'Wrong?'

'Well, it's lying. Pretending. I mean, people might tell you stuff and then be upset they'd been fooled...'

'I didn't invent social media, Snowdrop,' says Rowan, tartly. 'It came along on its own and hit my industry so hard that it's never got back up again. Don't forget, when I started in this game mobile phones were still a novelty and the internet looked like a fad. I found my first stories by getting to know people, by earning people's trust, by putting in the hard yards to prove myself. Christ, if I wanted to speak to somebody I didn't know, I'd have to sit with an open phone book in my lap, trying to find the right Mrs Smith of Workington. I wrote on a computer that didn't have a back-space delete function! I had to write letters to people to make arrangements for interviews. And faxes! You won't even know what that is, I bet. If the whole world has changed its mind about privacy, who am I to argue. People stick their whole lives out there to be vetted and filtered and judged. That's like leaving your diary open on the bed, isn't it? We're information gatherers, Snowdrop. That's what the job is.'

Snowdrop says nothing for a while, mulling over some moral conundrum. 'It's for the greater good though, isn't it?' she asks. 'Breaking stories, uncovering corruption, bringing down wrong-uns...'

'Sometimes,' mumbles Rowan, petulant. 'Sometimes we do good, yeah. But do you know why journalists want to go after the big story? It's to show off. It's for that wonderful word "exclusive". It's to say "*I knew this before you*".'

'That's quite a bleak outlook,' says Snowdrop, a touch disconsolately. 'But I know you mean them and not you.'

Rowan is saved from replying. His phone buzzes in his pocket and he manages to retrieve it without swearing too much. A call has gone straight to his voicemail service: another curse of the intermittent reception in this part of the world. He listens to the message from Harriet Kay, who runs the press office for Cumbria Constabulary. Her accent is local, her attitude too.

'*Rowan, this is Harriet from the police press office. I'm not sure you'll remember but we chatted a few years back when you were up here covering the murders on the coast? I'm just ringing because I got a message from the cold case review team. Apparently you're keen to speak with DI Sumaira Barnett about an old investigation. We're keen to do things through the proper channels so if you could make all such requests through me, that would be a big help. I'm here for a little while if you want to call back...'*

Rowan hangs up, a little disappointed that Sumaira had shunted him back to the press office without even returning his call. He quickly comes to the conclusion that she hadn't got his message and that some jobsworth colleague had taken it upon himself to keep her from getting back in touch. He prefers that version of the truth and decides to stick with it.

'Oh goodness, that's rank!'

Snowdrop isn't wrong in her exclamation. Rowan wrinkles his nose, the smell of red diesel and soggy hay climbing into his nostrils. He looks up, noticing a little watery light bleeds back onto the path. They're nearing the last stretch of trees. He detects movement high up in the corner of his vision. Squints at what might be a hovering bird, static just above the treeline.

Pickle's place emerges from the mist; the hazy suggestion of white stone and black roof delineating into the outline of a squat, sturdy dwelling made up of huge whitewashed boulders. A great sail of black tarpaulin is flapping against one of the holes in the slate roof: a raven's wing slapping fatly against the exposed timber.

'Is this where they film zombie movies?' asks Snowdrop, coming to a stop. 'Is it abandoned?'

Rowan grins at the run-down, seemingly deserted property. Gradually, more objects emerge from the gloom. There are two outbuildings a little further down the track and a battered grain silo blocks the view of the rising fell beyond. Vehicles in various states of disrepair litter what passes for the driveway. There are doors and windscreens missing in places and each has its bonnet up; great blooms of rust consuming the paintwork. He can make out an ice cream van, tyres gone, propped up on bricks and a green-slimed statue of a Roman deity. He walks towards the house, noticing a horse-box peeking out from behind a parked RV. The back of the box is open and Rowan can see that the storage space within has been given over to crates upon crates of cardboard boxes. He squints, and realises that the tinny high-pitched noise that has been pecking at his ears is coming from the dozens of tiny finches that are poking their beaks through the air holes of their cardboard prisons.

'He's grand,' says Rowan, quickly, as Snowdrop spots the birds. He jerks his head in the direction of the house. No two curtains are the same and each of the window panes seems to be plastered with sticky tape, holding together cracks in the glass. The front door is wedged open with a breeze block, offering a tantalising view of a mazy floral carpet and the edge of what looks, to Rowan's untrained eye, like a Wurlitzer organ.

'Pickle! Is that you, you sexy beast?'

Rowan turns at the sound of the great cheerful voice, spilling out from the nearest outbuilding. A grin breaks out on his face.

'Why's he calling you Pickle?' asks Snowdrop. 'He's called Pickle, isn't he?'

'He calls people "Pickle",' explains Rowan, hastily. 'We don't really know why. Every person he meets, he just calls them "Pickle" and that's kind of become his nickname as a consequence. It's weird.' He stops, feeling the explanation to be a little inadequate. 'Just go with it. He's a good lad.'

'Mum doesn't say so. Does he call her Pickle?'

'I should say so,' affirms Rowan. 'Probably does with your other mum too, though in her case I can see why. Probably to do with the vinegar.'

The man who emerges from the little brick outbuilding is, in every observable way, a catastrophe of a human being. Pickle is a lumbering mess of a man: with limbs that look as though they belong to a recently racked orangutan. He's six foot seven and would probably be taller still if he ever walked upright. Instead, his gait suggests he is trying to use his forehead to keep the rain off his wellingtons. As he lollops down the track, Rowan and Snowdrop take in the full horror of his clothes. Today he's wearing a police-issue, high-visibility coat and a bobble hat that sports ear flaps made from the pockets of old jeans. His face is dirt and oil and bacon grease and there's a rolled-up cigarette hanging from the bottom corner of his mouth. Like a half-pulled tooth.

'I've seen him before,' whispers Snowdrop. 'He ran the canoes on the lake at Ennerdale...'

'Aye, he lost that job,' says Rowan, discreetly. 'I think he still refers to that time as the "sinking of the Armada". He bought the canoes off a mate of his – more hole than wood. Patched them with some timber from his log pile. Got hold of some old Scout life vests that were discontinued around 1953. It was his finest hour. Didn't work, but you had to admire the gumption.'

'Did you write about that?' asks Snowdrop, nervously.

'No,' he says, shocked at the very suggestion. 'No, Pickle's the sort of mate that you don't want to throw away on a page-five lead. If you ever do throw him under the bus, you'd better hope you're bringing down a Cabinet member or a TV presenter.'

Pickle reaches out to take Rowan in a bear hug but then spots the bandages protruding from his sleeves. He stops a few steps away and Rowan catches the familiar smell: that wet-dog tang of clothes dried in damp rooms. He smells of smoke and wet grass. Rowan coughs, eyes watering, as he gets a sudden whiff of pungent cannabis. It seems to emanate from Pickle's skin and clothes and hair like steam from a compost heap.

'Heard you were around,' says Pickle, in a breezy Cumbrian accent. He gestures at the hands. 'You been to Glasgow, have you? They'll eat owt up there.'

'Deep-fried,' explains Rowan, grinning. 'Pickle here is a master in the cultural stereotype.'

'Indeed.' Pickle laughs, whipping off his hat and performing an elaborate bow. 'Stick around and we'll take the piss out of just about everybody. It's equal opportunities. None of it's offensive because I'm hardest on the English.'

'You're not English.' Rowan smiles. 'You're not even officially classified as human. You're a breed apart.'

'He's not human?' asks Snowdrop, moving closer to her uncle. She seems to be struggling with her manners. She'd like to shake his hand and introduce herself as she has been taught, but she's also remembering the instruction that she avoid strangers. Pickle may be her uncle's friend, but she doubts she's seen anybody stranger.

'Skin grafts,' says Rowan, and a little of the light fades from his eyes. He shrugs, holding up his hands. 'They're healing. My niece here is my hands until then.'

'Poor girl,' says Pickle, giving Snowdrop his attention. His pupils are pinpricks – the nucleus of an unfertilised cell. 'The stories those hands could tell, eh? What's he like to work for? Grateful? Diligent? Reasonable? I have my doubts. Once this lad's got the whiff of something in his nostrils he's like a greyhound out of the traps. You're Serendipity's daughter, aren't you? You've got a look of her. Batty, but likeably so.'

Snowdrop gives him a once-over, eventually deciding that being identified as "batty" by a man so extraordinary in appearance, is probably a compliment of sorts.

'I'm rolling, if you're tempted,' says Pickle, pointing back towards the barn. 'Got a fire in the brazier. Knocked a chimney into the roof with a sledgehammer when I was a bit stoned. Heather's got a video of the moment when I realised I probably shouldn't have stood on the roof to swing it. You should have seen me – went through in a cloud of dust and bricks and asbestos. Woke up with my face all bricks and bird nests. We pissed ourselves later...'

Rowan glances at his niece. If she understands what he is being offered she's not showing any signs. He wonders whether it would make him a terrible person if he were to go and smoke weed in a draughty barn with a convicted murderer and his twelve-year-old niece. He has a suspicion that the right thing to do would be to say no. Instead he hears himself telling Pickle to lead the way.

'Were you passing or did you want me in particular?' asks Pickle as their boots slurp noisily through the muddy path. 'You know the door's always open...'

'Aye, quite literally.'

Pickle looks down at his friend, his gaze softening. He

looks upon Rowan as if he's an injured bird. 'You okay? You look proper green around the gills. You've gone skinny again – the skinny you go when you're misbehaving. I'd have come to see you but I heard about the hands.'

Rowan swallows. 'What did you hear?'

'Just that you were staying at your sister's place to convalesce. I like that word, don't you? Convalesce, convalesce, conversation, conservation, let's rise up destroy the nation!' He starts to repeat the impromptu lyric to himself, jerking his beck forward and back to some imagined rhythm.

Rowan and Snowdrop follow him into the gloom of the barn. There are colossal holes in the roof and evidence of fallen slates and brick and timber mounded up in one far corner. A trio of plastic school chairs has been drawn up around a large metal brazier full of timber and coal. The grill from a commercial oven has been removed and placed across the mouth of the brazier and fat sausages are blackening, greasily, in the heat from the scorching flames.

At the rear of the barn sit a battered Land Rover and a quad bike, each covered in enough mud to disguise the colour of the paint. The rest of the space is somewhere between a modern art museum and a junkyard. Arabic rugs are turning to mulch on the soaking ground, pressed into the earth by the mound upon mound of stacked oddities. Towers of mismatched wooden chairs sway precariously in the shifting light. Cracked Tiffany lamps are bundled up in a haphazard pile of multi-coloured glass. He spots stage lights; a sign warning about the nearness of sharks;

a mannequin sawed in half at the thighs. There's a glass cabinet filled entirely with first-edition Troll toys – their big eyes and stoned smiles making them the perfect witnesses to Pickle's daily leisure pursuits.

'I saw you on the drone,' says Pickle, plonking himself down in the chair and gesturing for his guests to join him. From under his seat he removes a small assemblage of metal and plastic and paint. It has two propellers on top and a state-of-the-art camera underneath.

'New toy?' asks Rowan, sitting down.

'New venture,' he confirms, putting the drone down reverentially and removing a baccy tin from his pocket. He glances at Snowdrop. 'You fancy taking a walk to see the horses in the top field?'

Snowdrop sits down beside her uncle. 'We're working,' she says, firmly. 'You go ahead and smoke; I'll try not to breathe it in.'

'She's a good one,' says Pickle, approvingly. 'Maybe we'll get your mum up here for a smoke someday, eh?'

Snowdrop glances at her uncle. He gives a tiny shake of the head. Both are aware that for Serendipity, one smoke would be too many.

'It's about your friend,' says Snowdrop, pulling a notebook from her pocket and looking at Pickle accusingly. 'A friend from Facebook. We want to talk to her. I'm trying to be a reporter and we're trying to find out what happened to three missing girls thirty years ago, okay?'

Pickle glances at Rowan. 'Half-term, is it?'

Rowan shrugs. 'People play Doctors and Nurses. Why not Reporters?'

'Okay, boss. Ask away. You'll mean Violet, yeah?'

'Yes,' says Snowdrop, jutting her chin out and looking deeply suspicious. 'What's the nature of your relationship?'

'Wow,' says Pickle, eyes wide, playing along. 'You must be "bad cop".'

'Sorry, mate,' says Rowan, sitting forward. 'Youthful exuberance. You know the young ones, they've no time for the niceties.' He shakes his head at Snowdrop. 'There's a dance to this, Snow. We're English. We chat. We small-talk and gossip and slag off the politicians and eventually we get round to asking each other the thing we met up to talk about. It's not dynamic, but it's authentic.'

Snowdrop looks confused. Shakes her head at the pair of them. Pointedly, she takes the phone, opens the microphone function, and presses record. 'I'm waiting,' she says, eyebrows angled in sharp peaks.

Pickle reaches down and picks up a miniature snooker table. On the green baize is a bag of weed almost large enough to pass for a head of broccoli. Pickle looks at them both, picks up a Rizla, and sticks it to his forehead.

'White flag,' he says, by way of explanation. He starts to skin up a joint, fingers moving on muscle memory. Grins, and two gold teeth wink in the firelight. 'I surrender.'

'She good company?' asks Rowan, casually. 'Violet, I mean. When she came for a smoke?'

Pickle nods his head. 'Aye, great lass. Used to be more of a giggler but she's a chilled-out kind of stoner now. Likes to just lie back and float on the breeze for a while. Had to change the rota so she didn't bring down the room, y'know.'

Rowan laughs, delighting in Pickle's very existence. He runs the barn like a drop-in centre for those seeking temporary disassociation from the misery of their reality. Over the course of any twenty-four-hour period, he provides narcotics, succour and a listening ear for half the social stoners in West Cumbria. On any given day, bankers, teachers, farmers and any number of neglected spouses might find themselves sitting on a plastic chair in Pickle's barn, sharing tales of self-pitying woe or *giggle-till-you-piss* tales, eating Haribo and dipping Pringles in Nutella, wafting smoke and staring into the glowing embers of their own personal stairways to heaven. He's a valuable public service. The locals call such sessions "a decompression". There's a kind of community spirit to it. Marriages have been saved, rampages avoided and partnerships repaired thanks entirely to a couple of communal hours sharing the pipe of peace in Pickle's guru-like presence.

'She's a talker too,' he continues, lighting the joint and inhaling until his eyes cross. 'You know those stories we tell when we're drifting on the wave? The way that after a little while you're not telling anybody else but just straight-talking to yourself. Dreaming aloud, I suppose. Yeah, she was one of those. Good company, like you say.'

'Teacher, isn't she?' asks Rowan, casually.

'Did a bit of that, aye.' Pickle nods. 'Of course she'd say she was an interior designer first, teacher second.'

Rowan's starting to get the picture. 'She a seasoned smoker or a newbie?'

'She's the "old lag".' Pickle smiles, inspecting the end of a rotting fingernail and deciding that whatever organism is burrowed in beneath the cuticle has earned the right to stay there unmolested. 'The type who pops in for a stretch and pops out again. You know the sort. Every few years they'll enjoy six months of hitting it hard while whatever problem they're having goes away, then off it and back to reality. It's like medicine, really. She told me about the first time she smoked, I remember that.'

'Yeah? Go on.'

Pickle sits forward as if imparting a confidence. 'That's a good conversation starter, actually. Gets people talking. Hers was a belter. She said the first time she smoked she was still at school and some busker gave her a blowback from this massive great *hard-on* of a joint.'

'Is that rude?' enquires Snowdrop, pencil pausing on the pad.

'No,' says Rowan, shaking his head. 'It's when you bloke the smoke from your joint into somebody else's mouth, like a kiss. It's very sensual.'

'What's sensual?' asks Snowdrop, frowning.

'We're drifting away from the point, I think,' says Rowan, swiftly. 'At school? That might have been around the time…'

'Aye, I suppose.' He nods, seemingly in agreement with a voice in his head. 'She said it was pretty damned sensual, actually. "*Gave us all a go*", she said. Some pretty boy who thought he was so fucking cool because who used pages from the Bible for his joints.'

'He did what, mate?' asks Rowan, sitting a little straighter in his seat.

Pickle sniffs, momentarily transformed into a Victorian grand duchess passing judgement on a country cousin's lack of sophistication. 'Bit bourgeoisie for my taste. Very tacky. That was one of her darker smokes, for definite. She was here chatting with Helicopter Heather and Dan the Man with the Van.'

'Is that his full name?' asks Snowdrop.

'It is to me,' says Pickle, slapping his legs. Clouds of dust and assorted organic samples rise into the air. He gives Rowan the closest thing he ever gets to an accusatory look. 'There's something to this, I can tell. You know something you aren't saying. Don't do her any harm, Rowan. She's had her problems. Been through a lot.'

Rowan looks momentarily hurt. 'Pickle, it's a game. We can chat about something else if you like.'

Pickle shivers as a gust of wind thunders in off the mountain, stirring the fire and sending up a swirl of ash and flame: a collage in ripped silk and dirty snow. He stares at the spot where she had sat. 'Sorry, mate,' he mutters. 'Going through some stuff myself and it's a right downer thinking of Violet. She was pretty bleak once the tide took her.'

'Bleak?'

Pickle puts on an accent, imitating her. 'All this "*We didn't know, we didn't know.*" It was hard to watch, like. I tried to get her back to earth but she was all tears when she came back to herself. I felt awful, to be honest.' He leans in. 'You don't like to provide a bad high, do you? Not to people in pain. And she wasn't herself for a bit. Didn't talk much. I suppose we all have locked doors in our head and sometimes they fly open.'

'All your doors are open, Pickle.' Rowan smiles.

Pickle looks at the glowing tip of the joint and jerks his head as if trying to dislodge something from his ear. Whatever memory he's searching for, it comes back with a bang. 'Violet went missing for a few days when she was at school. The posh school up past Gosforth – the hippy place that cost an arm and a leg. It closed donkey's years ago but it was still around when she and her mates were all running about in knee-socks and blazers and pleated skirts. The other girl who went…' He conducts the air with his burning spliff. 'Yeah, the other girl, her mate – the vicar's daughter. Was it Marlish? And I think I remember something about the third one being a redhead though I never knew her.'

Rowan glances at Snowdrop and is pleased to see her pencil moving, even as the microphone takes down every word. He looks back to Pickle. 'I can hear the floodgates opening, mate,' he says, friendly. 'What else you got inside that fascinating head?'

Pickle laughs, open-mouthed – his molars packed with enough undigested pastry to feed a family. 'New scoop, is there? New book on the way? I did read your last one. It was compelling. They like that word – the book people. Everything has to be compelling.' He stops himself, lost in some labyrinth of mental cul-de-sacs.

'Violet, mate,' prompts Rowan, gently. He feels like he's talking to a suicide bomber in roller skates. The wrong nudge could see things end very badly.

Pickle gives him his attention: pupils swelling and diminishing in rapid bursts, as if controlled with a handpump. 'All right, here's what I know. Way I heard it, three went into the woods, and only two came back. But that's just between you and me, of course.' He glances at the phone. 'And for the benefit of the tape, I have smoked a great deal of marijuana…'

'Sorry, Pickle? Three went in, two came back…'

He glances behind him, peering at a row of potato crates that groans beneath the weight of clutter. Old papers, mulched magazines, empty pop bottles and crunched-up cans of energy drink. He turns back, satisfied that whatever had distracted him has slunk back into the earth. 'You do know what went on, don't you? It was big at the time.'

Snowdrop and Rowan fix their gazes on the fire.

'Remind us...' Rowan smiles.

7

Silver Birch Academy, Wasdale Valley
Saturday, July 11, 1987
4.44pm

'Look,' says Violet, wiggling her fingers in Catherine's
face. 'I've got claws. Purple claws!'

Catherine does as she is told. Her friend has removed ten
foxglove heads and placed them on her fingertips. It now
looks as if each tanned and slender digit is wearing a purple
witch's hat.

Violet swipes at the air, growling like a tiger. Catherine can
sense that in a moment her friend will test the effectiveness
of the makeshift claws by slashing at her face. Catherine
tries to distract her before the idea occurs.

'I thought we were seeing Mr Sixpence . . .'

'He's got friends,' says Violet, wrinkling her nose
at having to use such a saccharine word. 'Sat up there
like garden gnomes around the fire, waiting for him. I
scarpered before they saw but Rideal and Tunstall are
up there. Some tall bloke too.' She looks at her fingers,
then her eyes slide across Catherine's face and to the cold,

clammy hollow of her throat. 'I don't know if I feel like a cat or a witch...'

'I think they're poisonous,' says Catherine, quickly. She realises that she is sounding like a killjoy and back-pedals at once. 'But that's probably just a lie they make up to stop us having fun.'

Violet looks at the flowers on her fingertips. She makes a face. 'Actually, I think I've read that somewhere. Digitalis, I think. Shit. Have you got any wet wipes?'

Catherine shakes her head. 'Sorry, I didn't think...'

Violet rips the flowers from her fingers and glares at her friend. 'You didn't think? Says it all, doesn't it?' She reaches out and wipes her fingers on Catherine's coat, glaring at her, daring her to say something. Catherine looks at the ground.

Violet loses interest almost at once. She glares around her at the dense, dark wood. The treetops block out most of the light and the forest floor is a tangle of fallen branches and twisted roots. They came here with their registration class a few months ago – Mr Tunstall telling them all about the history of the wood. She tries to remember what he'd said. She remembers the names of the trees. Sweet chestnut. Larch. He'd said that most of the wood was planted around the time the school was built. Said it had red squirrels and that the sparrow hawks were vicious. He'd seen one tearing apart a blackcap in mid-flight. He'd talked about rhododendrons. Earned a snort of laughter from Violet when he said the numbers of great tits were on the rise.

They'd seen Mr Sixpence that day. They'd sat outside his campervan in two semi-circles, bums on the damp forest floor or becoming numb on one of the rocks or tree stumps. He'd shown them how to breathe. How to feel the universe flowing in and out of them. How to reach out with their minds and feel the cosmos. Then he'd made them find a favourite tree and hug it. She can see them now, only half laughing, wrapping their arms around gnarly, knotted trunks and pressing their faces to the bark. Violet had offered no words of scorn. She held the twisted rowan long after the other children had let go.

'Shall we be spies?' asks Catherine, and is surprised at herself for the boldness of the suggestion.

'Spies?'

'We could go listen. See how close we can get without disturbing them. You said you saw that lad in the Sinbad trousers last time you went up there by yourself. Bet we could get proper close.'

Violet closes an eye, scowling at her. 'You want to be spies? You?'

'We probably won't be back much over summer. It's just for fun.'

Violet appears to weigh things up. She glares down at the pulped purple flowers on the forest floor then gives a shrug. 'All right, but I'm going first. You follow my tracks. And if you step on a stick and snap it, you get three undefended punches, right?'

Catherine smiles, pitifully grateful. Violet rubs the remaining juice from the foxgloves off Catherine's front and smears her hand on the seat of her tight denim shorts. 'Sorry,' she says, though it's too quiet for Catherine to hear.

They move quietly through the forest, Violet several steps ahead, picking out a path that feels markedly different from the one they took when they visited with school. It feels as if Violet is leading them into the pages of some dark fairy tale. The further they go from the lake, the denser and darker the wood becomes. The mountains to the east shut out the sunlight so the ground never seems to dry out properly. Each step feels wetter than the last.

Two beeches have grown at odd angles, their trunks leaning inward and branches weaving around one another to form an archway. Violet is leaning against one of the trunks, smiling, proudly.

'Never made a sound,' she says, softly, and Catherine gives a tight, nervous grin in reply. She's starting to wish she'd taken the punches.

'Can we go back a different way? My feet are soaked. I don't like being spies…'

'Ssshh,' whispers Violet, and takes her friend's cold hand. It's an affectionate gesture, and reminds Catherine just how sweet Violet can be when she isn't trying too hard to be mean. She is about to speak when a sound from up ahead makes her freeze where she stands. She feels like an intruder. Her head fills with a thousand different terrifying scenarios. She's heard that some farmers and landowners shoot people found on their land. Without thinking, she squats down in the earth, dragging Violet down with her. Violet stifles a giggle. 'What are you doing?' she hisses.

Catherine pulls a face, exasperated. 'Sssssh,' she says, frantic. 'That's Dad!'

Violet raises her head from the forest floor. There are leaves stuck in her hair. Up ahead, in the clearing where Sixpence has parked his old campervan, she can hear raised voices. She squints: a hopeless attempt to make her hearing more acute. Catherine pulls her back down.

'Let's go back to the water,' she whispers. 'I don't like hearing when I shouldn't...'

'I thought we were spies.' Violet smiles, raising her head again.

'Violet, please...'

Violet cocks her head, listening hard. There are four voices, all male. Slowly, like a face forming in fire, the sounds become people, and the noise becomes words. She hears Mr Tunstall. Mr Rideal. Rev Marlish. Another man, too. His voice is softer, harder to hear, but it contains a solidity that makes it seem like an iron bar surrounded by the willowy branches of the other speakers.

'*...he did everything he could, you know that! He's a healer, not a magician...*'

'*Nothing was ever done that went against your wishes. He tried. The boy fooled him. Fooled all of us.*'

'*What you're asking is impossible. It goes against our every principle. I appreciate that you're upset but how can we possibly countenance that? This is a place for learning. For healing...*'

'*Let him tell me himself. Let him look me in the eye and explain why he took a sick boy and made him sicker. Taught him things that twisted him inside out. His mother's scared of him. His own fucking mother...*'

'*He comes and goes. Sometimes we don't even know where he's gone. That's why we stopped accepting the private sessions. The reiki. The healing. He only did those things as favours to old friends. We've pushed him too hard. He has problems...*'

'*Yeah, he fucking does. Me. He has a problem that he's going to put right. You're all going to put it right. You'll do*' *what I tell you to do or by God I will rain down vengeance on all of you. If you were to see the mess he made of her. My own boy. He came here to be put right and you sent me back a fucking monster...'*

Violet's smile fades as the language grows coarser. The tone grows more aggressive, the sounds of rising violence echo through the wood.

She looks to Catherine, who has her face buried in her forearm. She wants to snuggle into her. Her friend has no understanding of moments such as these, when words are no longer enough and only the thud of skin on skin, bone on bone, is enough to release the rage within. She doesn't know why the men are arguing. Doesn't know what service they are refusing to provide. They are protecting Mr Sixpence – that much is clear. But from what? What could the kind, gentle man have done to bring down such an enemy upon himself?

From behind, she senses movement, as if a shadow has folded her in its embrace. She snaps her head towards the tangle of woodland back towards the lake. Mr Sixpence sits on his haunches, his body streaked green and brown; great swirling handprints all over his gristly, knotted body. There is dirt in his hair; thick mud holding it back from his camouflaged face like lacquer. He has a finger to his lips; the nail painted a green that makes her think of old bottles.

He looks more like a tree than a man, thinks Violet. And his face, with his broken nose and tangled beard sinking into hollow cheeks – he looks to Violet like a carving on a church door; a satyr; some ancient representation of the Green Man. He blends in with the forest so perfectly that Violet could have lain upon his bare leg and been unaware she was not resting on a tree root until she registered the warmth of his skin.

He is looking at her. Looking at her with perfect green eyes.

He shakes his head: the movement no more than the quivering of a tree branch. Mouths one emphatic word.

'*Go.*'

She closes her hand around Catherine's and together they slither back through the archway and squirm back through the forest. Neither speaks. Neither says anything until the angry voices fade away, and they can see the top of Whin Rigg rising above the trees.

8

Snowdrop gives her uncle a damp nudge with her forehead – a dog trying to wake a corpse.

'Well?' she asks, raindrops spraying from her lips. 'Have I got a nose for this stuff or what?'

Rowan shrinks into his coat, deep creases of concentration lining his forehead. He scowls out at the rain, blowing in from all sides, bouncing off the forest floor like coins thrown at a trampoline. Above, the sky is the colour of stagnant water. The wind hurtles in from the coast like an angry tide: tearing along the ground, reaching up to grasp bedraggled trees that creak and groan in anguish. Rowan and Snowdrop have found a kind of shelter in the boggy entranceway of this half-roofed sheep pen. They're only a mile or so from home and probably can't get much wetter but the rain has battered them into submission. They shiver in the doorway, faces pale, hair slick, and the fronts of their jackets three shades darker than they should be. They have their heads together.

Rowan, still mildly stoned, is considering his options. There's a story here, though he's no idea what it is or what to do with it. The so-called "women's-interest" magazines still pay decent money for first-person exclusives and he's considering testing the waters. He's ghost-written a few himself in the past: lurid stories with headlines like *"My Boyfriend Ate My Leg"* or *"Grandad's Cross-Dressing Shame"*. There's usually a decent yarn somewhere within the text. Sometimes they'll take something with a bit of the supernatural to it. Messages from dead grandparents warning of impending transportation disasters is usually a good one.

If he does get a chance to speak to Violet Sheehan, he's pretty sure he can persuade her to talk about how her repressed memories of childhood trauma led her to seek out a shamanic ceremony. A couple of pictures, some *show-don't-tell* anecdotes about what happened during their captivity and it could be the best part of 500 quid. He makes a note to check which of the gossip magazines has folded in the past six months and which of the commissioning editors at the remaining titles has any legitimate reason to think him a prick. He's left with a paltry collection, but he seems to recall there was a nice woman at *Wo-Man!* magazine who had said she could always make use of proper old-school journalists.

He should probably buy Snowdrop an ice cream when they pay up. She's done well. Stopped herself from butting in too often and even nudged the subject back into line when Pickle wandered off. He wishes he were providing her with a less particular set of skills.

'I'm pinging,' says Rowan, the words sounding a slight echo in his skull. 'He nods at the pocket of his sodden trench coat, where Snowdrop had slipped the phone when the deluge began. She rummages, quickly while Rowan stands in absolute silence, uncomfortable.

'Violet's accepted your Friend request,' reads Snowdrop, as raindrops begin to jewel the screen. 'That's good. And she's sent a "wave" emoji, so that's a good sign.' She smears her finger across the screen, skimming Violet's profile. 'Not much more to see as a friend than on a drive-by,' mumbles Snowdrop, sounding briefly like a New York private eye. 'Few more pictures, few more "shares" of political stuff, animal welfare, a bit of a rant about the ignorant driver who cut her up on the Mungrisdale turn-off...'

Rowan watches the rain. Watches the trees bend in the gale: branches stirring the damp air.

'Pictures aplenty,' continues Snowdrop. She runs her finger down the screen. 'Lovely sandy beach... palm trees... lovely sandy beach... blue waters... oh good, a tree with coconuts...' She looks up, grimacing. 'This is not an interesting person anymore... sandy beach, oh good, a market, and ah yes, finally, a picture of her.' She turns the phone.

Rowan looks into the cheerful face of Violet Rayner. She's squinting against the sun, hand raised to push back a tangle of fringe. Her eyebrows are raised so the whites of her eyes seem too large. She looks paler than in the other image he had seen and she has lost a little weight. She looks tired. Behind her is a triangle of featureless green field. The picture is captioned **Let's Finally F**king Do This Thing!** and features what Rowan considers to be a truly certifiable number of emojis. She has garnered twenty-nine thumbs-ups and a lot of smiley faces. The number of enquiries about whatever this "thing" might be is dispiritingly small.

'April,' reads Rowan, and somewhat self-consciously uses the tip of his nose to navigate down the screen. 'Plenty of selfies before she went away – none since.' He shrugs. 'I don't know, might be nothing.'

'We could knock on her door,' says Snowdrop, brightly.

'She's away,' Rowan reminds her. He sags, suddenly tired, as if one of the strings holding him up has snapped in two.

'It's ringing,' says Snowdrop. 'Somebody called Aubrey. Hang on…'

'Don't,' hisses Rowan, waving frantically. 'Hang up, hang up…'

'Oh, sorry, I answered,' says Snowdrop, her smile fading as she glances at the darkening features of her uncle. Desperate to make amends she lunges forward, pressing the phone to his ear. He squawks in protest and suddenly he can hear his editor saying his name. Although her lips move perfectly around immaculate Sloane Square vowels, he forms a distinct impression of a small canine yapping at a postman.

'Aubrey,' he says, making it sound as if this is a real treat. In truth he has been ducking calls from both his agent and his book editor for months. He's tried to stay optimistic – to cling to the belief that something will turn up. He's never seen a newspaper with **"Nothing Going On"** as a front-page splash. There's always a story to be found somewhere. He just hasn't unearthed it yet. His policy to date has been to keep his new book's subject matter a closely guarded secret. At present, and with six weeks to go, he'd dearly love to be let in on it.

'Oh, Rowan, thank goodness,' she says, and this time he flashes on a mental picture of some fragile heiress in a black and white movie, clutching her pearls with long, elegant fingers. 'I've been going slightly gaga wondering if I might have said something at our last meeting that had caused some upset. I've been trying so hard to get hold of you; I've had poor Morwenna ringing every fifteen minutes. I hate to come down heavy-handed but I'm getting so much pressure from the sales team. Marketing too. They need something to put in next year's brochure at least.'

Rowan feels his skin prickling beneath the bandages.

'Rowan?' she asks, insistent. 'It's for the brochure, you must understand...'

'Oh so you do plan to put something in the brochure, do you?' he hears himself ask, petulant and stoned. 'That's good, that's good. Certainly a step up from the last one where you forgot about the paperback...'

'Rowan, we've had several conversations...' says Aubrey, with a sigh so heartfelt it seems to come from her toes. 'Every possible effort was made to ensure the King book hit big...'

Rowan can sense the word "bollocks" making its way brashly towards the conversation. He's about to give it the stage when he's diverted by a sudden trilling of the phone, which feels wet as an open oyster against his face. He realises there's very little point in arguing. If he ever had any moral high ground he has long since conceded it. She's right to be chasing her for a book she's bought. He's the twat for not delivering. He knows this, believes it – he just can't seem to stop himself from swinging every time he feels himself under attack. He glances at the phone, vision obscured by his soggy collar and the rain on the glass. It's only a message telling him he has unopened mail, but in the fraction of a second that he looks into Violet Rayner's tired eyes, he hears himself start to talk – fast and urgent, as if he hasn't got long.

'Aubrey, I'm so sorry, it's just I'm in this thing now. Properly in it. The things I've seen, Aubrey – I thought I was a hard man but I tell you, my heart's in bits...'

'Rowan,' she whispers, as if calming a feverish child: 'Just stop. Just take a breath and a moment. Are you okay? It sounds dreadful where you are...'

'I can't tell you where I am,' hisses Rowan, urgently. He looks at Snowdrop and rolls his eyes, his lips tight around an exaggerated smile. 'Look, I know this is unprofessional; it's just I need to protect the few people I care about and I've had to stay properly off-grid.' He glances again at Snowdrop, who is mouthing the words "off-grid" at him, questioningly. 'Every communication with the outside alerts them. You don't know what these people can do!'

'When can we speak?' she asks, her own voice falling to a whisper as if the people who she imagines to be threatening Rowan are leaning in to hear. 'I just need a few words, just an outline...'

'Three missing girls,' says Rowan, rain flicking from his lip to speckle the image on the screen. 'Terrible things happened to them. Two came back – what happened to the third? And why does nobody want the truth to get out? More importantly, why hasn't anybody asked these questions before?'

'Oh that's good,' says Aubrey. 'Will you call me? Or email a precis – just an idea...'

After hanging up, Rowan isn't sure whether he said goodbye. He decides it probably doesn't matter. His heart begins to thump as he realises what he's just done.

This morning, he had to find a story good enough to fill a bestselling true crime book – preferably with a personal angle. Now, it has to include a missing teenager and a conspiracy of silence. He'd suddenly very much like to go back to bed.

'Looks like it might be clearing,' says Snowdrop, gesturing across the muddy ground to where the folds of rain are becoming less ferocious. She gives him a nudge. 'Are you going to message her right now? What are you going to say?'

'It's "write",' grumbles Rowan. 'What am I going to write?'

'I don't know, that's what I'm asking,' says Snowdrop, completely missing the grammar lesson. She grins, excitedly, and she looks as though she would have no problem with going and jumping up and down in a puddle. 'Are you going to do a book? A book on this? On my story?' She looks at him, accusingly. 'Will I get a mention? Maybe not as an author, but like, a contributor? An acknowledgement or something. That would be so cool…'

Rowan feels his spirits sink into the cold, wet ground. He looks away, thinking of a way to change the subject. He freezes, spirits lunging downwards like a weighted corpse. A gaunt, jointy-limbed woman with iron-grey hair stalks purposefully into his line of sight; materialising from the grey murk with the demeanour of a fairy-tale witch intent on finding out why she wasn't invited to the palace for the party. She's much the same colour as the sky: her expensive, pencil-shaded coat blending in with well-pressed pewter trousers tucked into battleship-coloured wellingtons.

'Snowdrop,' she snaps, looking past Rowan. 'You have had me worried sick.'

'Morning, Kitten,' starts Rowan, largely for his own pleasure. 'That's a wonderfully literary outfit, you temptress. Fifty Shades of...'

'Rowan,' she says, stopping him as if pulling down a blind. She stands on the track, glaring at them both. He realises she is holding a rolled-up golf umbrella behind her back. She shakes her head as she gives him a once-over. 'Drunk again,' she declares.

Rowan gives an understanding smile. 'That's okay, Jo, you can come back when you're sober. Anyway, how are you? You didn't ride that brolly, did you? That's a point, where did you park your broomstick?'

Jo lets a tiny smile disturb her thin lips. There is a part of her that seems to relish these little interactions with her wife's hapless younger brother. She has made a small fortune since establishing her network of workplace consultants, scooping up dissatisfied educators and turning them into well-paid experts in impossibly tedious aspects of recruitment, marketing, consumer law and global logistics. She's a named partner in the Belgravia-based firm but spends most of her life ensconced in her palatial office at the converted farmhouse half a mile further down the River Irt. Rowan has never understood how somebody so drearily straitlaced ever came into contact with his effervescent sister, let alone whisked her off her feet, married her and agreed to act as stepparent to her precocious child. Rowan is actually quite fond of her, although he doubts he will ever express it. He remembers how Serendipity used to be.

'Serendipity said you were doing something educational,'

she says, sniffing the air. Rowan doesn't worry. The smell of the weed is definitely well hidden amid the cow shit and wet grass. She purses her lips. 'I'm going to the bank. Whitehaven. Serendipity has suggested it might be useful if I were to pick up some books. Do you have any requirements?'

Rowan and Snowdrop share a smirk. Jo has a way of talking that speaks of school matrons or some stern governess. 'That's kind, Jo,' says Snowdrop. She's never called her second mum by any other name than her given, though Serendipity is always "Mum". Rowan wonders if that must be hard. Realises that of course it must. His thoughts are interrupted by Snowdrop grabbing his sleeve. 'We could go with her,' she says. 'You can show me how to do research. Will they have those old machines from the old films…?'

'Stop saying "old",' mutters Rowan, feeling ninety. 'Look, most research is stuff we can do back at the byre online. Get a fire going, maybe have forty winks…'

Jo looks from one to the other, reading the situation as if it is written in large print. Rowan is a moment behind. *They're trying to keep me busy. They're trying to take me out of myself. They're trying…*

'That's decided then,' declares Jo, as if a judgement has been made. 'Snowdrop, you can come back and get a change of clothes before you go. Rowan, you could do with being wrung out as well, though I shan't be obliging. I won't ask where you've been as the answer will only upset me.'

'Tell me where you'd like us to have been,' says Rowan, nicely. 'Let's both be happy.'

'Snowdrop,' she says, ignoring him. 'When you're ready.' She puts out a hand, a sprinter waiting for a baton.

Snowdrop grins at her uncle and runs to Jo, taking the proffered hand with a practised familiarity. Rowan feels a pain in his chest: something like heartburn, or loss.

He stays where he is, brooding and feeling left out. The rain has changed direction, hurling great damp handfuls at him from what seems like a few inches in front of his face. Slowly – *because he's not even bothered, no way, whatever, no matter what anybody says, he's too fucking impervious to this kind of shit to be bothered, to feel left out* – he follows them, a little sulkily, down the path.

9

Silver Birch Academy, Wasdale Valley
Tuesday, February 2, 1988
10.28am

'Everybody warm and toasty? Remember, there's no such thing as bad weather – just the wrong clothes. That's it, that's it, come in, Philomena. You go and stand next to Calpurnia there – the heaters are on so you'll thaw out in no time. Everybody have a nice breakfast? How was meditation, Astrid? Excellent, good, good. Wow, what a fine-looking bunch. Violet, could you and Catherine shuffle up a little so that Delphine can sit down? Of course there's room...'

Violet rolls her eyes at Mr Tunstall. She moves half an inch to her left. Catherine follows her and gets an elbow to the ribs for her trouble.

'Stop crowding me!'

'I'm not crowding you, I'm moving up.'

'You smell like your dad. Like breakfast.'

'You had the same as me, Violet...'

'You had the same as me, Violet...'

There are a dozen pupils seated in haphazard semi-circles in the cosy, high-ceilinged space known to staff and pupils alike as the Map Room. When the school was still a private residence, this large, wood-timbered space was one of the main rooms for entertaining guests: peacock-patterned silks and Javanese furniture, splendid in the glowing warm light of the great black fireplace. Now it is a study space – beanbags and slouchy chairs, bookcases crammed with well-loved paperbacks and pristine textbooks, donated by any one of the New Age charities that have done their damnedest to be associated with a facility that offers a truly unique education, focusing as it does on hearts and souls as well as academic excellence. It's a pleasingly tatty room, with threadbare carpets concealed with big multi-coloured rugs, and the cracks in the walls are covered with old maps of the local area; contour lines grouped tightly together like the whorls in a thumbprint.

Tunstall starts to remove his huge outdoor coat and bobble hat, to reveal the crumpled suit and crooked tie beneath. He wears his hair long, almost covering his ears, and the plump moustache that sprouts from his top lip looks as though it is marking time until the day it turns into a butterfly. He looks at Violet. Tightens his smile into something more like grim resignation.

Violet and Mr Tunstall have had a lot of mediation sessions together recently. He is being very understanding. He's listening. He wants to help. He's making allowances for her unique set of personal challenges and extending her every courtesy even as she deliberately tries to sabotage the educations of children who do not find things as easy as she does. But she needs to meet him halfway. Needs to stop pouring scorn on what they are trying to achieve. Needs to stop picking on poor Catherine while pretending to be her best friend. Violet already hates him. The more time she spends in his company, the more she comes to realise that beneath his warm demeanour and hippy bullshit, he is really starting to hate her too.

'Some of you will already know Mr Sixpence,' says Tunstall, brightly. 'He's the glue that holds this school together. He's caretaker, groundsman, maintenance man and pot-washer-in-chief. He makes the best cup of pine-needle tea you'll ever drink and he's one of the most interesting men I've ever met. He's also my friend, and he knows lots of stories about what I used to get up to in my misspent youth, so you can imagine why I only let him talk to you all on special occasions.'

There's a dutiful titter from the assembled pupils. They're starting to remove their coats, apologising under their breaths as they catch one another with sharp elbows and cold hands; the snow on their boots melting, vapour rising to join the hazy grey cloud of condensation that is forming up near the ceiling rose.

'Mr Sixpence has spoken to us before,' says Amber, a thin blonde girl with gappy teeth. 'He told us about shamanism.'

There are nods from a handful of other pupils. Some, new to the school, have been looking forward to this. There is something intriguing about the quiet, strange little man who lives out in the woods and who sometimes helps the more challenging pupils deal with issues like temper and self-esteem.

'Is he going to tell us about the dead people?' asks Elora,

a robust twelve-year-old with dirty glasses and frizzy brown hair. 'I like it when he talks about the dead people. Mr Tunstall. Will he talk about the dead people, sir?'

Mr Tunstall turns to the door, where a ragged figure is leaning against the frame. Violet has seen him twice since the day in the forest and each time he seems to have lost more weight. There's not much to him now. He looks to Violet like a long-dead corpse that somehow never stopped growing hair or nails or teeth. He's not much over five feet tall and his skin hangs over his bones like towels folded over a rail. There are gaps in his top row of teeth but the lower set of canines are big and square and stained a nasty shade of toffee-brown. There is snow matting his straggly grey hair, held back from his lined, sunken face by a threadbare Russian military hat. He wears small, frameless glasses, perched midway down a broken nose. With his big unlaced combat boots and his woollen fingerless gloves, he looks as though he started partying during the Summer of Love and didn't stop until the Winter of Discontent. His eyes, green irises and tadpole-black pupils, sparkle with a quiet intelligence. He smiles at the girls, his tongue visible through the gaps in his teeth.

'Dead people, Elora? I might have one or two stories that appeal to your rather macabre fascination.'

Violet glances at Elora and sees her give a little fist-pump of celebration.

'Good to see you, Mr Sixpence.' Tunstall smiles, making way for the shambolic figure who takes his place in front of the fire.

'And you, Phil. Sorry, Mr Tunstall.' He surveys the room. There's naughtiness about him, a certain whiff of devilment that suggests he could at any time reach into one of the pockets of his voluminous Afghan coat and pull out a bottle of brown ale.

'I'll leave you to it, if that's okay,' says Tunstall, rubbing his hands together. 'Paperwork. Meetings. You know the drill.'

'No I don't,' he says. 'But I've heard about it. Sounds bloody awful.'

The girls laugh and exchange excited looks. This is going to be good.

'I'll be by this evening to discuss that other matter,' says Tunstall, pointedly. 'It's quite pressing, so I'd appreciate it if you could make sure you're around.'

Sixpence rubs his nose with the back of his glove. Gives a loud sniff. Finally he nods, and Tunstall, looking relieved, makes his way to the door. Sixpence watches him leave. Slowly, he turns back to the group.

'You look a lively bunch,' he says, his eyes stopping on each of the girls in turn. When his gaze falls on Catherine, she fancies that he gives her the tiniest, most fleeting of winks. He doesn't look at Violet at all.

The questions start at once.

'Sir, is it true you're a shaman – that you can talk to the dead?'

'My dad says you make a fortune helping rich people talk to their own souls, or something…'

'Sir, are there spirit animals? Really? Proper spirit animals?'

'Sir, my dad wants to buy a drum from you. He says you make them yourself. Is that right?'

Sixpence pats the air, smiling. He doesn't know who

asked which question, but seems happy enough to answer whatever comes at him.

'Am I a shaman?' he asks. He shrugs. 'No, I don't think so. I'm a shamanic practitioner.'

'What's the difference?'

'Quite a lot, if you charge for your services,' he says, smiling and staring at the map on the wall by the big mullioned windows. 'But whatever you want to call me is fine by me. I like to think of myself as a helper. Maybe a healer. If you need it in absolute basic terms, shamanism has been around for as long as human beings. There is archaeological evidence that suggests shamanism in one form or another dates back 20,000 years. And yes, we are guides, of a sort. We are messengers. Do you know the word "intermediaries"? Well, we're kind of a go-between, linking the natural world and the spirit world.'

'My dad says that's all hippy bollocks, sir.'

'Your dad's entitled to believe that,' says Sixpence, smiling at Violet. 'And I'm entitled to think he sounds like an arsehole.'

There are laughs at that. Violet joins in. When she feels it's okay to do so, Catherine follows suit.

'You're right, Elora – I do make my own drums,' says Sixpence, when the hubbub subsides. 'I have friends who bring me my materials. Different leathers, which I stretch tight over a frame. It's a part of the shaman's toolkit, along with many other ceremonial objects, like knife and staff and mask...'

'Cool!'

'And you heal people, yeah?'

'I try.' He smiles. 'I try to enter a certain kind of

state of mind; a higher consciousness, a place where I can journey between one world and another. In this state I can communicate with an individual's power animals...'

'Their what?'

'I am able to visit the realm of the spirits, to seek help and guidance and to heal those who need it. Shamanic practitioners cross the borders between reality and nonreality at will. We seek the portals that lead to the other side of the sky. The higher realm and the lower realm...'

'How long have you been doing this, sir?' asks Catherine, her mousy voice almost lost above the hubbub of excited vowels.

'Since I changed my ways,' says Sixpence, turning soft eyes upon her. 'I used to be a different person, Catherine. A different man, with a different name. I was in the Royal Navy, if you can believe such a thing. I wanted what other people seemed to want. Money. A girlfriend. A nice house and maybe a couple of kids somewhere down the road. I didn't get that kind of life. A different destiny chose me.'

'Sir?'

Sixpence looks down at his boots. He twitches his face, moving his glasses up his nose. A sadness settles upon him. 'I made bad decisions when I was a young man,' he says. 'I wasn't as kind as I should have been. I was angry a lot of the time. I think I was looking for something and I didn't know what it was. So one day I decided to seek it out. To turn my back on what everybody else believed to be the right way to live. I travelled. I saw the world. I learned how other people lived and I came to the conclusion that we have gone awry. We've lost our way. We've lost sight of what is important. It took a special person to show me the true way.'

'Some hippy like you, sir?' asks Violet, smirking.

'If that word helps you understand then yes, Violet,' he replies, quietly. 'But to me he was a teacher. A doctor. A philosopher and a guide. He showed me how to journey. I drank the herbs that he bade me drink and I opened my eyes to a different reality. He healed me. Retrieved the parts of my soul from the dark place where it was lost. And at length, he taught me how to open those doors within me.'

'Was this in the Sixties, sir?' asks Cassandra, with her cut-glass vowels.

'I don't know,' he says, quietly. 'I sometimes don't even know how old I am. None of it matters. I feel a connection with all things. A "oneness". I try to help people…'

'Daddy says you charge people to help them,' says Violet, obstinately.

He looks at her, his voice softening. 'I don't need many material things, Violet. I have my campervan, up there in the woods. I have enough to eat. I have books to read and records to listen to and I have friends who come to talk with me and listen to the birds. Sometimes, I have people stay with me so they can learn how to put right those parts of themselves that go wrong. This school – the school that is trying to open your eyes to see a different way of living – this school sometimes asks for donations. That's between the board and the patrons. But I would never deny my services to those in need.'

'What's it like, sir?' asks Catherine, quickly. 'The other place. You know my dad's a vicar, yeah? Well he says that heaven is a place of pure happiness; pure peace, pure love. Is it like that, sir?'

Sixpence turns his eyes upon her, pupils swelling to devour

the dark irises. 'Sometimes,' he says, softly. 'Sometimes the sensation is of absolute serenity – a peace, a place within a greater whole. Sometimes, if I journey in tandem with a particular soul, it is a darker, more menacing environment. Imagine being trapped for eternity in the worst nightmare you ever had. There are those whose minds are so troubled that such a realm exists within them. I have journeyed to such worlds to help retrieve their lost souls. I have glimpsed things that have terrified me.'

'Tell us, sir. Tell us what it's like…'

Sixpence looks at Violet. His gaze is so intense that the space between them seems to crackle with energy. Violet does not look away.

'I would not wish the knowledge on any of you,' he says, at last. He shakes his head. 'But there are those of you who will one day see.'

IO

The day is only a little past noon, but the cars and vans that swish down Whitehaven High Street all have their headlights on, pitching great circles of lurid yellow onto the grubby shopfronts and the condensation-streaked windows of this tired, rain-lashed road. The Lake District starts a few miles inland, and the difference in atmosphere and affluence is remarkable. Rowan knows from checking on his phone that he's worryingly close to the nuclear power station: a big silhouette of oblongs, orbs and squares. A mile the other way, the crumbling clifftop drifts into the village of Seascale; all rusty goalposts and untended playing fields; a wind-pummelled swathe of muddy beach and guest houses closed for the winter.

Rowan likes the grit of the place – the heartfelt lack of pretension. West Cumbria has a sense of itself that always seems to raise a coal-grimed middle finger in the face of gentrification. It's always seemed a place much more at ease with the opening of a new kebab shop than with any Italian-themed coffee house, as if doner meat and garlic mayo is intrinsically more in keeping with the spirit of this down-at-heel West Cumbrian harbour town than a skinny macchiato with extra foam.

But for all that he admires the spit-and-sawdust earthiness, his mood matches his clothes. He's still soaked to the skin; shivering hard enough to make his teeth rattle. He managed to change into a cleanish black T-shirt and steer his arms through the sleeves of a baggy cardigan but he couldn't face the rigmarole of stripping off his jeans, socks or boots. Damp material clings to his thighs, his calves, ankles, soles. His toes feel like chipolata sausages straight from the freezer.

He's taking comfort in the fact that he has left a perfect arse-print on the calfskin leather of Jo's vintage Nissan Figaro. She's told them she would be back in an hour, dropping them off in the car park of the DIY store and giving firm instructions not to cause mischief. Rowan had saluted, earnestly, then turned the hand gesture into one more in keeping with his feelings as she drove away in a burst of spray.

'I know I'm working, but will there be time to read?' asks Snowdrop, hopefully, beside him. She's changed into dry clothes; big baggy lumberjack shirt now spilling down to her shins, where rainbow leggings peep out above sequinned high-top trainers. She's wearing a genuine Lambretta parka and a floppy hat. She looks to Rowan as though she's raided the dressing-up box.

'You can do whatever you feel like doing,' says Rowan, scowling. He can smell a pub. Can smell hops and vinegar and the humid embrace of strangers in damp clothes. His head's spinning. The reality of his situation is starting to hit home, his thoughts grinding against one another like plates of pack ice. He has to give Aubrey something, if only to buy himself time. He's ducked them long enough. He's not ready to tell the truth to anybody so he's going to have to put his faith in a captivating lie.

Wincing into the cold wind, Rowan makes his way towards the big red oblong of the town library. There's a sale on in the off-licence. A two-for-one offer in Specsavers. Five sausage rolls for a pound in Greggs. He mooches down a side street, past a charity shop where a woman in her eighties is standing in the window trying to put a leather jacket on a mannequin. The windows are steamy with condensation and through the smears of damp glass, it looks to Rowan as if two corpses are preparing one another for a night out.

He pushes open the doors and steps into the warm, yellowy light of the library. It soothes him like a church. There are posters on the wall advertising author nights, book groups, tea mornings and computer literacy classes. A small woman with spectacles and extraordinarily frizzy hair is sitting on the floor with a toddler on her lap, reading from a colourful picture book. She's doing all the voices. Rowan pegs her as a first-rate parent.

'Can I go read?' asks Snowdrop, tugging his sleeve. 'I'll join you in a bit. I just want to see if my favourite book's there...'

Rowan waves a hand, trying to make the point that he couldn't care what she does, provided it doesn't cause him any headaches. She scampers off as if she's won a trolley dash through a sweetshop.

Alone, Rowan considers his options. He could dictate an email to his agent, explaining what he's working on and cautiously enquiring about a deadline extension. He could make a list of the few vague bits of intriguing information that he's learned about Violet Rayner and see whether it looks as thin written down. He could slip away, hit the pub and do some serious research on what kind of glass his problems look better when viewed through the bottom of. He gives a little growl to himself, aware that Snowdrop has high expectations.

Sulkily, he moves into the warm and towards the desk. A harassed-looking woman with greying black hair is attempting to repair a damaged paperback. She has strips of sticky tape hanging from the arms of her spectacles: a time-saving efficiency that Rowan admires. She's maybe sixty, and very neat; cardigan and polo neck: a gold locket and polished, unpainted nails. She looks up as he approaches. Looks down again, and then jerks her head up as if a hand has taken a fistful of hair and yanked it.

Rowan gives a good smile. 'Local history,' he says, by way of greeting. 'Newspaper cuttings. I'm not quite sure what I'm after.' He stops. Composes himself. 'Sorry, that was all a tad garbled. I'm just visiting, so is there a temporary password to use the computers?' He holds up his mangled hands, feebly. 'And somebody who could occasionally feed me crisps?'

The woman behind the counter is giving him a peculiar look. 'You're a writer,' she says, a little Geordie in her accent. 'Serendipity's brother.'

Rowan rolls his eyes. 'I'm thinking of wearing a sandwich board with that written on it. You know Dippy?'

'Oh yes, she's a marvel. Helped with the fundraising for the youth project and always brings us a treat when she pops in. She and her partner sometimes come to our book group.'

'It's wife, actually,' says Rowan, quietly, as if correcting a faux pas.

She recoils, mortified. 'Oh, yes, yes. Goodness, I do try and stay up to date...'

Rowan grins, letting her know she's off the hook. She breathes out, relieved. 'She said you were a bit of a devil.'

He smiles, delighted. 'I'm presuming she described me as a walking disaster area, yes? Hence the instant recognition?'

'Oh no,' says the librarian. 'No, it's from the photo in your book.' She casts a critical eye over him and registers her disappointment. He feels like a first-edition hardback that's been dropped in the bath. 'It's still a relatively good likeness,' she says, and he appreciates the lies.

'You've read it?' asks Rowan. 'What are the chances of that – meeting my one reader...?'

'Well, I've flicked through it,' she replies, apologetically. 'I ordered it in recently, you see. It wasn't one we stock but we can order almost anything. We had it when it first came out – just the one copy, but that wasn't returned and we didn't restock.'

Rowan isn't quite sure what to say. 'Well, if they didn't return it they must have enjoyed it. That, or they threw it off a cliff in disgust...'

'Perhaps.' The librarian smiles. 'It's funny how things come and go in waves. Whatever the reason you're definitely experiencing a new surge in popularity up here. I've ordered two new copies in the past week. There's a waiting list.'

Rowan gives a little bark of laughter. 'That's Snowdrop, I'm sure. Or Serendipity. Any decent feedback?'

The librarian nods. 'If you're still here next month you

can ask Eve what she thinks. That's Ms Cater. She has a copy. The other just whizzed out the door before lunch.'

'Cater,' he repeats. Something stirs. 'Detective?'

'She was.' The librarian nods.

'Maybe I should say hello. Do you have an address?'

'I'm afraid I can't give that out,' she says apologetically. 'Ask your sister – they're acquainted. Of course, round here, so's everybody.'

Rowan wonders if it matters. He's new in town, after all. Word gets around. Surely it would be natural to look for more information.

'You should come and talk to our creative writing class,' says the librarian, eyes opening wide as if she's just had an extraordinary idea. 'We're meeting Thursday night for a chat on setting and place but I know they'll drop that in a flash for a chat from you. The evenings when we have a speaker are always very well attended.'

Rowan makes a face. 'I doubt I'd be able to get enough books sent up from the distributor to make it worthwhile,' he complains. 'And I'm trying to only do paying gigs. I doubt you're about to offer me a few hundred quid to do it, are you?'

The librarian shakes her head. 'Sadly not. There are some lovely baked goods though – we all chip in for the buffet. There's always a bottle open and we're enthusiastic. We've published two anthologies, short stories and poems. We had one gentleman, a crime writer from Preston; he was drunk before he even arrived. He was very indiscreet about his day job. Solicitor for the Crown Prosecution Service! He was quite the scamp. We had a wonderful evening. I've asked Jo to sound you out about it but when I didn't hear back

I presumed you weren't up to it.' She glances at his hands. 'Sore?'

'Only when I breathe,' mutters Rowan. He's conflicted. He doesn't feel qualified to give anybody advice, but he knows it makes him feel good when people are interested in what he has to say. Most importantly, he might get to meet some new people. Every new acquaintance is a potential lead for whatever story might suddenly take the bait. And he's willing to admit to himself that Violet Rayner is starting to intrigue him. He remembers what Dippy had told him – she'd written a story. She was starting to remember. Perhaps if he went along he might be able to charm a copy of whatever it was she'd written. And it would help him seem less like some nasty outsider and more like a known quantity.

'You do know I'm not really a creative writer, yes? It's factual.'

'I thought some parts were rather beautiful,' says the librarian, smiling. 'I'm Julie, by the way. I'd shake your hand but I'm frightened what I might take away with me.'

'Can I bring Snowdrop?' asks Rowan, giving a polite nod in response to the sudden camaraderie. 'She's likely the only person who can stop me swearing or offending anybody.'

'Of course, of course,' says Julie, pleased. 'One of our members brings her little girl when her husband can't have her. She sits with her toys and we pass her from knee to knee. It's all very friendly. Of course, Catherine always feels like she's being a burden and she apologises about fifty times a night, but that's her way. Wonderful poet, you'll like her.'

Rowan chews his lip. Sometimes, he knows, a story will keep jumping up and down until it attracts the attention it craves. He's starting to wonder some hidden truth is clamouring to be exposed. 'Catherine? Rev Marlish's daughter?' he asks.

'Oh, you know the family?' asks Julie, surprised. 'Excellent. And you can see what Ms Cater thinks of the book, too...'

Somewhere, at the very rear of his consciousness, Rowan begins to compose the opening lines of his email to his agent.

Sorry for the radio silence, but I think I may be onto something...

'Here you go,' says Julie, handing him her phone. 'That's the piece she wrote for us. Violet, I mean. It might be useful. Very powerful.'

Rowan looks at the screen. Raises his bandages to hide the smile.

Creative Writing Assignment
Recollections
By Violet Sheehan

I have a decent memory. I'm good with faces, better with names. If we've arranged to meet next Tuesday at 6pm and I don't turn up by quarter past, call the police or question whether I actually like you, because I promise, I won't have forgotten. I know the star signs of all of my friends. I never get home to find I've run out of bread or milk. I send in the meter reading as soon as the electricity people ask for it and I can tell you where I was and what I was doing at pretty much any time in my life going back to three years old.

But there's a gap. You all know the gap I'm talking about. Or at least, it feels like you all do. There's a black hole, snipped out of my brain like a photograph pulled from an album. It feels like somebody has reached into my brain and sheared a piece away.

If you don't know what I'm talking about, then sorry for wasting your time. I can be a little paranoid sometimes. Maybe that's why I'm single. I've had my share of company over the years but I'm not very good at letting people get too close. I always wonder what they're really after. I can't imagine that there's anything about me they're eager to get close to. I suppose I look okay and I can't argue with the teachers and the shrinks and the bosses who have all told me I'm too clever for my own good, but I'm not really very nice. I was a horrible cow at school and I still don't know why. I never really knew how to act. It always felt as though I'd missed a class when everybody else had reality explained to them. People seemed better at living than me. They still do, I think.

Sorry, I'm waffling on. I was trying to explain. Some of you will know that when I was a teenager, I went missing for a few days. I met somebody who played the guitar and sang in a lovely voice, and he got me and my friends stoned and drunk and we spent a couple of nights partying in the woods while people went a bit nuts trying to find us. You might even be sitting there now, wishing you could ask me about it. What would I tell you if you did?

For a long time I would tell you the same thing I told everybody else. I don't remember. Whatever happened, it's gone. I don't think it's some sort of suppressed memory – a way of protecting myself from trauma. I think it's because I was so unbelievably out of it that I couldn't make memories at all. So whatever happened, it's not a memory to be retrieved, because it was never made in the first place. That's what Catherine says when I dare to bring it up. She's the same as me. It's just a gap in her head, and maybe that's for the best.

Is it, though? That's what I've been asking for a while now. Maybe coming to this group has helped. I like writing. I used to be good at it when I was young. I liked poetry when I was a teenager. I liked a lot of things that were a bit of an acquired taste. Catherine despairs of me, but after thirty years of friendship I doubt she's about to ditch me now. I don't tell her often enough what she means to me. I hope to goodness she doesn't cry like a toddler if this is the piece that's picked out for a reading.

I think I've been a bit harsher than usual with Catherine recently. I'm sorry for that, I think. She doesn't seem troubled by it the way I am. She accepts it all. It was her act of rebellion, a little interlude of partying and acting up and giving the vicar a reason to go out of his mind.

I don't think I can leave it at that. You see, bits have been coming back. You know that feeling when you see something random and it reminds you of a dream you had when you were a child? It's like that. Suddenly, I'm asking questions of myself. I have a memory of a dark, wet, sparkling place. I can taste the taste you get after you've had a filling – like iron filings and chemicals. More than anything else, I can see the girl I haven't let myself think about in three decades. Freya. Red hair. White lines on her arms. Older than us. She was there, I know she was. She never said goodbye. Left, like she'd left all the other schools.

I've started looking for her, Catherine. I know I said I wouldn't, but I have. I've started looking into myself as well. There are pictures there. Not memories, but echoes. Something that comes to me when I sleep. Do you remember the old caretaker? The man in the woods who used to talk to us about oneness and vibrations and journeys between different planes of reality? I've been thinking of him a lot. You tell me I shouldn't hang around with my friends at the farm but they're good listeners, and they help me find the frequency I lost that day. I know it will come back to me.

Eve is worrying about me too. She's been worrying for thirty years. Do you remember that day I called her Mum by accident? Oh my God I'm still so embarrassed.

So, that's where I'm at. I'm the girl with the gap in her memory – a story with a missing page at its heart. Freya's the answer, I'm sure. Freya, and the hippy man with the weird name. I've asked the girls to try and remember. They don't owe me any favours, but maybe they will. And, Freya, if you somehow hear that I'm looking for you, please get in touch. I know you're the glue that would put me back together. I need to know if I'm remembering the truth, or what they've told me to. And I know you're the one with the answers.

11

Yem How Wood, Wasdale
Wednesday, October 19, 1988
8.03pm

The woods that close around Arthur Sixpence reach out for him with black talons. They grab at his feet as he stumbles; whip at his face like a flail. It feels as if the forest is trying to claim him.

He hears his breath coming in ragged bursts and tries, desperately, to hold on to his sanity. He glances around, trying to get a sense of where he is, but he cannot make sense of forward and back, up and down, inside and out. He feels like a fly in a tangled mass of spider silk. The forest around him is a terrifying black mass; all whistles and trills and shuddering branches. He hears sticks snapping beneath his feet with the gunshot crack of snapping femurs. Sees the darkness disassemble; to pixilate and disintegrate into a million falling leaves.

He is lost now. Lost in the darkness.

'I tried to help you,' he hisses. 'I tried to heal you!'

He reaches out his hand and feels the knobbly bark of a tree trunk. He realises his feet are wet, that water has soaked past the lip of his boots. He splashes backwards, onto soft ground. His right boot slips and his knee hits the wet ground, hard. His teeth bang together and he mashes the side of his tongue. He can taste blood. He spits on the forest floor, raising a gloved finger to his mouth. Even through the leather he can feel the wetness.

Just breathe, he tells himself. *He'll come back. Just breathe. You're fit – you're not done yet...*

His cheeks feel raw as the wind slices against the tears and he wipes his face dry with the back of a glove. He screws up his eyes, peering again into the gloom. There are vague shapes, but nothing more. He takes a tentative step and realises his boots are now on soft leaves, rather than the hardness of the path. He shuffles forward again and strikes something firm. He curses and stops again.

Don't go any further, he urges himself. *Stay and wait. Stay near the water, where they can see you. Stay where there's still the chance of light.*

He removes his gloves and plunges his hand into the pocket of his coat. His hands close on metal. He grips the Zippo lighter. Pulls it free and spins the wheel. There is a tiny spark but the flame is swallowed by the wind. He curses and cups the lighter with his hand, trying to shield it from the gusts that seem to be growing stronger, whisking the detritus of the night. The flame catches but disappears again when he takes his hand away.

He flips the wheel on the Zippo and there is an explosion

of light and power as his world is turned red, orange and vermillion.

It feels as though a cold, bony hand has reached inside his chest and squeezed his heart.

This is happening, he realises. *This is when it all comes to an end. This is when he comes for you...*

'Please!' he shouts, looking back, desperately, at the great lumpen mass of the mountains. The clouds are purple and silver; roiling and twisting like skulls in a sack. He lights the Zippo again, desperate not just for light but for some kind of warmth.

There is a shape to the darkness – an outline of flesh and bone. A creature. Pale skin and a vile, misshapen pig mask where their head should be. His guts twist and it is all he can do not to clutch at his heart like the feeble old man he tries so hard not to become.

His senses are suddenly alive as the tumblers of understanding start to fall into place.

'No,' he says, and his voice is snatched away by the wind. 'No, it wasn't like you think. I helped you. Healed you! Your father...'

The figure steps forward, and suddenly Sixpence understands. Suddenly, he knows how very wrong he has been, and how very bad the things he has done. He turns, trying to run. He does not take more than a step.

Legs and arms entangle.

Hot breath, chaos and confusion and a hand pushing against a face.

Tumbling now, rolling in the dirt, enmeshed in one another. Then a flash of face, like a sliver of moon, flits by close to his own: a glimmer of snarling white, and there is a fist in his gut and he is on his back again, pinned under meat and bone, gazing up. His hands scrabble in the mud and dirt. Rake through wet leaves as the pressure builds in his throat. His eyes feel like they might pop.

He reaches up, and even through the leather of his gloves he recoils at the tough feeling of the wrinkled porcine skin; the yellowed teeth and rucked, rancid snout.

He tries to form the word "please".

He opens his mouth just enough for a single syllable to escape, and then something cold and hard and utterly unyielding is pushing through the soft skin beneath his jaw, crunching upwards to skewer his tongue to the roof of his mouth and fill the hot wet cavern of his face with cloying, iron-scented blood.

He's still alive when his attacker starts to drag him towards the hole in the earth; the small, hidden space beneath the roots of the big, bone-white yew.

He will wish, in his final hours, that he had not fought so hard for life. That he had not spent so much of his life seeking the spirit world. Soon, it is true and endless death that he will crave above all else.

12

Bing
Bing
Bing

'Fucking bong,' mutters Rowan, silencing his phone and returning his attention to the laptop on his knee. There's cigarette ash on the keys; on the back of his bandaged left hand and smudged into the tartan blanket around his shoulders. He's been concentrating hard. He can sense a story lurking in the words on the screen.

A small, sly thought slinks around inside his head like a cat in a locked room. What if this is it? What if this is the story? What if Violet is about to hand him a second chance? There could be something to this, couldn't there? Three girls from an apparently posh school, wandering off to God knew where. And Pickle had said only two came back – that rumours persisted about the third girl ending up at the bottom of the lake. Written well, it could even carry a whiff of the occult, couldn't it? A small rural community closing ranks? He can almost see it. Can see the accompanying documentary and the mornings spent on breakfast TV along with one of his grateful interviewees, spewing superlatives about how he exposed the truth, and helped a troubled soul find peace.

'Don't get carried away, son, don't get carried away,' he mutters, raising his glass like a toddler with a beaker and taking a decent slurp of red. 'Pickle said Violet had been trying to track her down, which kind of kills off the idea that she and her schoolmate did her in.' He scowls into his glass, wondering. 'Suppressed memory,' he mumbles, and it's as much a proposition as a query. He closes an eye. 'Don't think it, don't you dare...'

He doesn't want to look directly at the thought as it slinks, catlike, around the skirting boards of his mind.

It would be a better story if she were missing.

It would be a better story if she were dead.

Outside, the rain hits the windows like handfuls of grit; the wind testing the old building for gaps in the masonry, the roof joists, the hearth. Soot and ash keep swirling out from the fireplace with each fresh gust of wind. He could very happily sit here and get drunk until bedtime, but he can't help but feel that he's somehow trodden on the tail of something big.

Rowan is currently neck-deep in the digital archive of the *Cumberland and Westmorland Gazette*: a database of words and images so old-fashioned that Rowan confidently expects to see actual footage from the thawing of the last ice age. He's typed any amount of keywords and dates into the tiny little search facility but it's still a mixed bag of offerings. He's found the original article printed on the Saturday after the girls went missing: early November, 1991. They aren't named in the article and the detective sergeant quoted as being concerned for their welfare is an Evelyn Cater of Whitehaven CID. There's no byline on the story.

The next piece is from three days later. It's accompanied by an image of a small, wiry man with thick black hair, small eyes and an impeccably smart suit. His name is given as Derrick Millward. The still vastness of Wast Water takes up the background: divers in dinghies emerging, golem-like, from the thick mud of the water's edge. Rowan scans the text and smiles, gratefully, as he recognises the name of the writer. Chris Gardner was working as a subeditor at the *North-West Evening Mail* when Rowan started out. He was a quiet, diligent chap who'd eschewed the lure of London in favour of a quiet life, a steady job and a nice house just outside Millom, which he planned to share with his wife and their then baby daughter.

Last time he saw him was at the funeral of an old editor they had in common. Chris's wife had died of breast cancer three years before, he'd been made redundant from the Mail, and the house had halved in value due to a subsidence problem and the rumour of Japanese knotweed in the back garden. Chris was bearing up under the strain of it all. He believed there were people who had it worse. Rowan wasn't sure who.

Rowan performs a quick Google search for Chris Gardner, alongside a few words that might narrow it down. *Millom. Journalist. Subeditor. Unlucky bastard.* He finds him listed as a page designer for a glossy lifestyle magazine based in Kendal. Rowan follows the link. The front page is given over to a pretty middle-aged woman staring wistfully at a tree, all yard boots and Barbour and expensively bleached hair. The accompanying banner promises an exclusive interview with a landowner determined to build a natural burial ground on land in the Wasdale Valley. Rowan rolls his eyes. Gives an unkind tut of disapproval and mutters darkly about provincialism. Calls the number and wonders if Chris is in the mood to help an old friend.

'Hello, Features desk...'

'Chris!' says Rowan, brightly. 'Rowan Blake, all grown up. My God, mate, it's been far too long. What was it? Pete's funeral, I suppose. How's it going? You good?'

There is a pause before Chris answers. Rowan pictures him. He's probably fifty now. Glasses, like in the old days, but with thicker lenses. Maybe his hair has continued its retreat across his scalp. He's no doubt his clothes will be presentable: he was always a neatly attired chap.

'Well, of all the voices I expected to hear, you're way down the list,' says Chris, quietly. 'Where you at now? Did I hear you were at some website? Or was it telly research? I read your book, by the way. You do let your pen run away with you but you can still sprinkle the glitter.'

'I'm back up here, actually,' says Rowan, getting comfy. 'My sister – I don't think you'll know her – she's got a place near Boot. Old farm. They've done up one of the old outbuildings as a holiday cottage. I'm trying it out. I'm sure she'd be grateful of any publicity when it's a holiday let, if you were able to pull any strings.'

'Sounds great,' says Chris, enthusiastically. 'Bet you're going cold turkey, aren't you? Sucking on exhaust pipes, trying to get a dose of smog.'

'As long as I keep smoking my heart won't stop,'

says Rowan, flicking the computer screen to bring up the text. 'I'm actually looking into something local. Bit of telly interest, definite book deal on the cards. A kind of follow-up to the Gary King book but with a bigger scope. An exploration of the cases that don't resonate with the collective consciousness. What happens to the families of the people whose deaths never trouble the tabloids.' He pokes out his lower lip as he considers what he's said. He might actually be telling the truth.

'That's got legs,' muses Chris. 'You know better than anybody that if it's outside London or the victim's not a pretty girl from a nice white family, too often it sinks without a trace.'

'It's a disgrace,' says Rowan, and means it. 'But to do it properly I need some case studies and thankfully I've got a belter right on my doorstep. I mentioned it in the book but only in passing. I've been going through the online archive and apart from a couple of paltry snippets and a picture, it's barely had any coverage.'

'You mean the coven,' says Chris, flatly.

'Sorry?'

'The three girls from the hippy school. Lovely old house on Wast Water. One of those places with about nine kids to each year. Closed in the mid-nineties, I think. It was one of those hippy-trippy places, holistic approaches to learning and mornings spent saluting the sun. It was part of a group that was supposed to revolutionise education but I guess that went the same way as most of the best ideas. Silver Birch, I think it was called.'

Rowan chooses to say nothing. Lets Chris fill the silence. He can hear him settling back – perhaps picking up a mug with "Shit Happens" written on it in big letters and slopping a gulp down his front.

'I was on the Gazette then,' says Chris. 'You know me, I was never much of a one for reporting. Give me a desk and a design job any day. But I served my time. We thought we'd got a big one when it came in. It was Damian who got the tip-off from one of his police contacts. Did you ever meet?'

'Damian Crow? Tall lad? Too grey for his age? Aye, he was chief reporter when I started. Didn't like me very much.'

'Retired now, but he was a good operator back in his day. He had good links with the coppers so they'll have gone straight to him. News desk asked me to be on standby in case it came to something. It didn't take us long to get names.'

'Remind me,' says Rowan, fingers poised.

'I know there was a Catherine Marlish. Daughter of the vicar, if I recall. Lovely couple, her mum and dad. Couldn't do enough to help. I think they'd have given me the whole family album if I'd asked.'

'Freya and Violet were the others weren't they...?'

Chris pauses, the silence stretching out like chewing gum. 'Freya was a redhead,' he says, locating the memory. 'I think the surname was "Grey". With an "e". That's about as much as we ever got. Related to one of the pastoral staff at the school, as far as memory serves, but we never got the chance to print much. Initial appeal and a request for information. I had a pad full of notes from Rev Marlish about his daughter but the cops requested we hold off on publishing for "operational reasons" and we weren't in a position to argue. You lose your contacts in this job, what are you? Anyways, it came to nought in the end. Wasdale Mountain Rescue found Violet and Catherine somewhere over Patterdale way.'

'But not Freya?' asks Rowan. 'So what, they just thought "two out of three ain't bad"? That's a bit hard to swallow, mate.'

Chris gives a snuffle of laughter, though it sounds fake to Rowan's ears. 'I'm probably remembering it wrong, Rowan. Maybe they found her somewhere nearby and it wasn't mentioned in the first press release that came out. We might have printed an amendment, or just left well alone. We're a local paper and the nationals never took any notice because it was all over so quickly. If something had gone amiss, if she'd never been found or there was a suspicion of foul play, somebody would have kicked up a fuss by now, surely.'

Rowan glares into his drink and tries to keep his temper. He knows from bitter experience how many people fall between the cracks – how many girls, boys, women and men fade from reality like the colours in a sun-bleached photograph. He knows how many killers have preyed upon society's disposable people. How many lives have been snatched because their murderer didn't expect anybody to notice?

'You still there, Rowan?' asks Chris, forced jollity entering his voice. 'Look, if you're really interested you should have a look on the Mountain Rescue's online archive – it's pretty good. I think it was Jason – he passed away a few years back – who brought them home. He was always good with us but apparently he wasn't allowed to talk about the incident, so draw your own conclusions there.'

Rowan chews his lip and considers the screen before him. 'Who's this guy in the photo I'm looking at? Dark hair, fiftyish…'

'Come on Rowan, it was thirty years back,' protests Chris. 'Hang on, let me see what you're looking at…'

Rowan listens to the sound of fingertips moving swiftly over keys. He looks at his own, useless digits and swallows down a surge of jealousy.

'Oh right, right,' says Chris, up to speed. 'That's Derrick Millward. Local lad, though we're probably talking pre-war. Spent his life catching the worst of the worst. You might have heard of him, to be honest. Bit of a legend in some circles – old-school copper. He had some connection to the case, as far as I can recall. I think he was introduced as a "liaison" – somebody to make sure the family were kept up to date. He'd retired from policing but I think he had some connection to a private detective firm. Blackpool, I think? Was it Blackpool? Honestly, Rowan, you should have emailed me and I could have found my old notebooks.'

'You always were horribly efficient.' Rowan smiles. He narrows his eyes. 'Three girls missing,' he muses. 'You've told me one didn't come back. I've heard that before. What's the story?'

'It probably sounds more exciting than it was,' says Chris, apologetically. 'The coppers never did tell us the ins and outs. We got a very short press briefing saying the vicar's daughter and her mate had been found – that they were receiving medical attention and the families appreciated being left alone. Even on a local paper it was never big news. I only remember the bits I do because I wrote a piece a few years back about the retirement of Eve Cater and the case was one she remembered as being a significant one in her career. I don't know if I've got a copy of the piece. I know she got hurt, that's about all I can remember.'

Rowan turns his head as the dust in the grate puffs up. It looks as if a giant foot has thudded into the ground outside.

'Is this Millward still with us?' asks Rowan, tightly. 'He might be better with a door-knock than a phone call.'

'No, popped his clogs a few years back,' says Chris, ruefully. 'Good age, though. We carried an obit. So did the *Cumberland News* and one of the nationals. He'd been around. Saying that, there was nobody around for him when he was going downhill towards the end. I think the care home would have ended up in court if anybody had kicked up a fuss.'

Rowan decides to say nothing. Just swishes the blood-red wine in the well of his glass and hopes to God he's onto something.

'His number two's still around,' says Chris, helpfully. 'And I suppose after all this time there's nothing to stop you speaking directly to the girls. They're still local. You'll find Catherine through her dad, I think. He's vicar at St Olaf's, among others. You'll find Derrick there too. Buried there because of his connections to the valley. It's the smallest church in England so spaces are a premium. We carry a story every year where they appeal to people not to scatter the ashes of their loved ones in the churchyard. When there's no breeze it starts to look like there's been a nuclear winter! I tell you what, that place has a history worth a book…'

'It's really good of you to help out, Chris,' says Rowan, grateful. 'We should have a beer. How's that gorgeous daughter of yours, eh?'

Chris's tone changes. 'Ah, that's a sad one, Rowan. Poor lass. But I'm so proud of her. She's fighting it so bravely…'

Rowan lays his head back. Listens as Chris outlines a life so full of grief that Rowan wants to reach inside him and take it all away. He stops listening. Types Derrick's name into Google. Sits back, glass in hand, and begins to read.

Twenty minutes later, he drops his head back against the cushion, and breathes out slowly. This is starting to feel like something. He doesn't believe he's stumbled onto a genuine atrocity, but he knows he has the skills to make it sound like one.

He reaches down and his sore skin touches the cool glass of the whisky bottle. Splashes a good measure into a mug and takes a swallow. He realises he is nodding to himself as if listening to music. He can feel a kind of nervous energy within him. He listens back to his conversation with Chris and stops it when he hears the mention of the school by the lake. The "hippy" place. It takes him moments to find a reference to the Silver Birch Academy online: a story in the *Independent* published in 1993. He rinses his mouth with the last of the whisky and dives straight in.

A Sad End for the School That Promised a Golden New Age of Education

By Nicky McKenna, education reporter

'If things had gone differently, all children would have been educated this way. It's a source of great regret to me that we weren't able to keep the dream alive.'

So says Phillip Tunstall, the pioneering head teacher whose holistic approach to education was the driving force behind the controversial Silver Birch Academy, which has closed its doors after almost twenty years providing "New Age" education.

The academy, based on the shores of Wast Water in a converted mansion house built by wealthy industrialist Steadfast Hookson, was the flagship school for the Whitecroft Trust, which has run several co-educational schools across the UK. The Trust has now been bought out by an investment partnership and Silver Birch is among the schools to be axed in a cost-cutting drive.

Mr Tunstall, who remains a trustee within the organisation he started along with Cumbrian landowner and businessman Alan Rideal, told the Gazette that he was proud of what the school had achieved.

He said: 'It's always best to be positive – that's what we've always taught. We did things our way, a holistic way, where the school's responsibility was to fit around the pupil rather than the other way around. Spiritual, moral, social and cultural development has always been at the very heart of our philosophy and I can say with absolute certainty that we have turned out some exceptional human beings over the years. The school's aims and philosophy regarding how pupils live their lives and learn supports them in developing mature and responsible attitudes to living in a community.

Of course it is a blow that the school will close its doors

but the Whitecroft approach will continue and I have not lost any of my enthusiasm. I still believe in what we started back in the seventies, when I had lots of big ideas and even bigger hair!'

Mr Tunstall, 51, has been at the helm since the school's opening in 1974. Backed by philanthropist Alan Rideal, it has never had more than forty pupils on roll at any time and has actively resisted the normal monitoring and evaluation processes, preferring to offer a "holistic" approach to education favoured by pioneering educators overseas.

While some pupils have attended from the local Lake District community, many have been boarding pupils whose families were attracted to the first-rate facilities with the emphasis on a "home from home", and "universalist" approach to development. The school's philosophy was that pupils learned more when free from coercion, so many lessons were optional. The timetable was flexible, allowing pupils to pick and choose the times they felt most inclined to learn, but were encouraged to participate in meditation, yoga and mindfulness sessions alongside curriculum-based activities.

'All in all, we've done a lot of what we set out to do, but I think I would be lying if I didn't say that it hurts to see the doors close. I have a memory of the three of us standing in front of this ruin of a house and knowing what we wanted to do and how to do it. I'd like to thank the many people who have helped me to fill my head with such wonderful memories.'

The school has not been without its controversies. The local education authority has been at constant loggerheads with the school over its refusal to allow inspectors to see pupil records, while in 1989 the *Times* ran an exclusive story on alleged irregularities with the Trust's finances, claiming that the families of some pupils were paying three times as much as others to attend the school, while so-called "scholarships and bursaries" seemed to be given out without any fixed criteria.

Copeland MP Jack Guinness said: 'I've always admired what they were trying to do at Silver Birch but we need to have a uniformity of education in this country – a standard start for each of us. For all of its talk of inclusivity this was an elitist school that went out of its way to keep the authorities from becoming too involved.'

Rowan clicks his tongue against the roof of his mouth. Looks for further references in the archive to Alan Rideal or Phillip Tunstall. Exhales, slowly, as he finds what he's looking for in a banner headline from November, 2004. The search for missing fell-walker Alan Rideal has been called off. Tributes are pouring in for the Cumbrian philanthropist who poured money into local good causes.

'...*experienced fell-walker... died doing what he loved... Mountain Rescue conducted an exhaustive search... Wast Water, Screes...*' Rowan mutters to himself as he scans the article, clicking his tongue, again and again, until he annoys himself. He feels jittery now. Feels things starting to come alive. Scans the remainder of the page and finds no reference to a next of kin. The only named associate in the article is Phillip Tunstall, who went back to get help when Mr Rideal began to experience chest pains during their ascent of Great Gable. Tunstall's address is given as Bleng Hall, Nether Wasdale.

Rowan allows himself a grin. He stands and paces a little, tripping on the cobbles only twice. He feels fizzy with it. Jittery. He can almost feel the first line of chapter one, slithering around in his thoughts like a live snake in a bag of dead worms.

He calls DI Sumaira Barnett. The young man who answers her phone at the Cumbria Constabulary Cold Case Review Unit tries for fifteen agonising minutes to redirect him to the press office. Rowan keeps hanging up and calling back, hoping Sumaira will pick up on a different extension. He doesn't raise his voice or make any kind of threat – just keeps ringing back and asking to speak to DI Barnett. Eventually, he hears some muzzy expletives somewhere in the office and a harassed-sounding South London voice demands to know what he wants.

'Sumaira,' he says, smiling. 'It just occurred to me I still owe you a machine cappuccino and a KitKat. Can I drop them round this afternoon or are you going to charge me interest? If so, I can stretch to a bottle of red and a decent steak.'

She responds with a low growl. 'I knew I recognised the name. Bollocks. Now isn't a good time. Last year, when I was ringing you and you weren't replying – that would have been a good time. What is it you're after?'

'Some company,' he says, with a smile in his voice. 'I'm adrift in Lakeland. Withering in my bloom…'

'You've got a sister here,' she says. When she speaks again it's clear she's remembered something else. 'Did I hear that you'd had a bit of an incident with an online troll?'

'I'll tell you at dinner,' says Rowan, looking at his hands.

'I'm up to my eyes,' she protests. 'What is it you're after

anyway? I mean, I'm flattered you've looked me up but I know you must want something more than company.'

Rowan makes himself comfortable. Presses "record". 'What do you know about three missing teenagers, and the Silver Birch academy?'

She pauses before answering. Rowan listens to her breathe.

'I can be free by 9pm,' she says, at last. 'And I warn you, I'm an expensive date.'

13

Hotel Vin de Mere, Lake Windermere
10.14pm

'I think it's some sort of tapenade,' says Sumaira, cautiously. She pokes the dish with a finger. 'Smells a bit like posh olives? Is it pesto? I'm not brave enough.'

The substance in question is being employed as a sort of gastronomic cement: a khaki-coloured glue that adheres the vibrant hunks of yellow tomato and silvery radish to the piece of slate in front of her. The waiter had told her it was called "pistounade" and formed part of the fifth course, of the nine-serving taster menu. She'd laughed: a fulsome, pleasing cackle that had caused at least two other diners to tut out loud.

'You reckon those fit in the dishwasher?' asks Rowan, nodding at her platter. He's trying to be funny but it feels horribly false. He's uncomfortable; slick with sweat inside his faded black shirt. He's managed to eat some of the ludicrous little servings without asking for help but he can tell that Sumaira is itching to cut his meat for him and feed him like a child. He's unable to feel like anything other than a total arsehole every time he looks at the unwieldy leather gloves that hide the bags and bandages on his hands.

'How did you get here?' asks Sumaira, dabbing at a small drip of spilled mimosa on the tablecloth and trying to turn her finger into a sponge. 'I didn't see a skateboard in the car park.'

'My sister,' says Rowan, with a sigh. 'She gave me a lift and says if I ring her before eleven she'll come and pick me up. Any time after that I have to call a cab, which I can ill afford, so I'll probably have to ring my mate Pickle for a lift.'

'Pickle?' asks Sumaira, eyes widening. 'You're mates?'

'He's everybody's mate. He's Clifford the Big Red Dog. He's one of the good ones.'

Sumaira pulls a face. 'His record would suggest otherwise.'

'So would mine,' says Rowan, surprising himself. He hadn't intended to bring up his past, or his lack of funds. He can't seem to get a hold of himself at the moment. Keeps saying and doing things that offer no obvious advantage.

'We've all got a past.' Sumaira shrugs, sucking in her cheek so that a dimple suddenly appears. 'I wouldn't be a copper if I hadn't had dealings with the law when I was young.'

'I presume you know a little about my misspent youth,' says Rowan, holding her gaze.

'Enough,' says Sumaira. 'I checked you out after we met. I never thanked you properly, by the way. You could have made us look very bad that day.'

Rowan waves her gratitude away. He can't even remember what the story was or how he had chosen to report on it but a cop's gratitude is always a thing worth banking.

'I read your book,' she says, and begins to play with a fine gold necklace that hangs in the well of her throat. 'You're a good writer. You didn't glorify him, you just understood him. I thought it was brave.'

Rowan manages a twitch of a smile. It belies his true feeling. He feels sick: his tongue too big for his mouth, his throat dry and sore. His thoughts keep drifting away from him. He tries to centre himself, the way the shrink had told him to. He imagines himself in the place he feels safe. Imagines the space beneath the seats of the old school bus, tucked up warm and cosy in that musty little space, snuggled up with Serendipity, music turned down low as a pulse; her cold fingertips on his temples, his eyelids, telling him it will be okay, that it was just a nightmare, that the bad people have gone away.

'...a while to settle in and obviously it's a very different kind of ethos but we've had some good results and I'm definitely feeling better for the fresh air...'

Rowan realises he has missed some conversation. He drapes his arms over the wooden back of the small, cosy booth. He points at the pretentious montage on the table between them. Sumaira's slate is balanced on four small jars of different coloured sand, which in turn sit upon a squat, rustic tabletop. The table has been polished to a high gleam and reflects the distant ceiling; all wrought iron and exposed brick. Old bird cages hang from hooks and fruit crates full of curiosities are nailed to the walls.

'It's nice to see you again,' says Rowan, and means it. 'I know "nice" is one of those utility words, but it fits here. This is nice.'

Sumaira looks at him over the top of her huge, square

spectacles. She's somewhere in her thirties: tall, with highlighted brown hair cut too short at the front. She wears a fluffy V-necked jumper and a long black skirt with plum-coloured court shoes. She was wearing a designer duffel coat when she arrived; rain sparkling on the cerise fur trim around the hood. Her cheeks had been flushed, her nose pink from the glacial air. She'd seemed unusually nervous for an experienced copper, as if this was a date she had been looking forward to for some time. She'd kissed his cheek and commiserated about his hands, informing him that the bastards would no doubt get what was coming to them on the inside. Rowan doesn't doubt it. Arrangements have already been made.

'Nice?' She smiles, and pushes her hair behind her ear. 'Yeah, you're right. I don't tell people that very often, so enjoy it.'

'I'll make a note.'

'It'll have to be a voice memo,' says Sumaira, nodding at his hands. Rowan looks away before his expression betrays him. His phone is on the table between them, serving as a decoy. On his thigh, his voice recorder is taking down every word.

'So,' he begins. 'I was wondering…'

'You never called me,' she says, abruptly. She glares at him, eyes wide, seeking explanation or apology. 'I thought we got on.'

'We did,' says Rowan. 'But I was seeing somebody.'

'So was I.' Sumaira laughs. 'I'm not anymore. Well, maybe a bit. There's a thing with my builder that might become something. Maybe not. What about you?'

'I continue to attract women who deserve better,' mutters

Rowan, performing mental arithmetic as he tries to decide if he can afford another double whisky. 'Roxanne was the girl I was seeing when you and I met. She's with somebody else now.'

'Love's a bastard,' says Sumaira, and seems to mean it. 'You must have been sweet on her – you never called me back.'

Rowan shrugs. 'Maybe I was. I've never worked it out. I mean, she was lovely to look at and she knew how to keep me from coming unglued, but if I'm honest, we weren't a neat fit. She wanted more for me. Or more for her, maybe.'

Sumaira pretends to play a tiny violin. 'Tried to fix you, did she?'

Rowan drains his glass and allows himself to consider his latest failed love affair. He sits back in his seat. 'It's nice to have somebody on your side, but she always made it seem like we were a work in progress. Or I was, at least. Like I was a house that needed fixing up but the budget had got out of hand. She kept me right, I guess. Made sure I met my deadlines and went to work and didn't drink so much that I couldn't remember the stories I'd wheedled out of people in the pub. At least she made it look as though somebody loved me.' He gestures at himself, bitterly. 'I didn't look like this.'

'You look like you,' says Sumaira, casting a critical eye. 'That's how you're meant to look, I think. And if I'm honest with you, she wasn't doing that great a job of keeping you right when I met you. There was a haze of drink coming off you and I don't think you had a pupil in either eyeball. If you were dating a mother figure then I reckon you had a case for neglect.'

Rowan finds himself laughing. 'I don't think I was doing that,' he protests. 'She was younger than me, anyway. And I didn't like all that housewife stuff she wanted to do. I paid for a cleaner so she wouldn't have to pick up after me.'

'You could always have picked up after yourself,' says Sumaira, with a grin. 'Sounds to me like you don't know what you want. You're a Romantic, maybe. See the shine on somebody for a few weeks or months and then you start seeing the rotten wood beneath. I know your type, I reckon. You gave away a lot about yourself in the book. You can tell that it hurts you when bad things happen to good people, but then you identify so strongly with the bad. I reckon you spend most days unsure of whether you're the best thing since the Rampant Rabbit, or you're the Antichrist.'

Rowan chews his lip, biting back a smile. 'You should be a copper,' he says, and realises how much he is enjoying her company.

'I think I know what you're looking into,' says Sumaira, reaching into her bag and pulling out a slim, buff folder: a magician's puzzle of conjoined rings staining the front. 'Truth be told, I've been waiting for somebody to ask me about this one but it seems there are even fewer investigative journalists out there than there are decent detectives, so maybe I should just be grateful somebody's taken an interest. I wouldn't have had it to hand but I'd already dug it out for a Freedom of Information request – not that it ever went anywhere.'

Rowan angles his leg, raising the Dictaphone. 'Somebody else is interested?'

There is a clatter as Sumaira's shoe drops from her toe and lands on the floor between them. She smiles. 'Worrying you've got a competitor?' she asks. 'Don't be. Private citizen, not rival writer, though apparently she's got ambitions in that area?'

'Yes?' asks Rowan, aiming for nonchalance. 'Are you able to tell me?'

Sumaira shakes her head. 'No, of course not. That would be an appalling breach of confidentiality. But it's a Ms V Sheehan. Requested the information through the correct channels in July of last year. A standard letter was sent back while we performed due diligence on the request. God they're a pain in the arse. Anyway, the two files were linked.'

'Violet,' says Rowan, quietly. He locks eyes with Sumaira. 'Explain it to me like I'm an idiot. Explain like you would to a six-year-old child off his tits on Calpol.'

Sumaira lets out another laugh. 'In July last year, an FOI request was made...' She stops, and adopts a schoolmarm tone. 'That's the Freedom of Information Act and the Environmental Information Regulations, under which you have a right to request any recorded information held by a public authority, such as a government department, local council or state school. Or us. While searching out the information on an incident in 1991, we found the files cross-referenced in both hard copy and on the database, with a case that had been put forward for Cold Case Review when I first moved north. As it happened, we took a look and realised there weren't the resources to take it forward but we intended to keep a watching brief.'

'I know this one,' says Rowan. 'A watching brief is where you do bugger all, yes?'

'Precisely,' says Sumaira, brightly. 'Now, the case this person was linked to – well, that had a connection to the

Silver Birch Academy. I know you know all about that place.'

'Go on,' prompts Rowan, quickly.

'Three teenagers were reported missing in late October 1991. They were all pupils at the Silver Birch Academy. Went to Keswick on a shopping trip and didn't get the bus they were expected on. The dad of one of the girls went looking when they didn't come home. So did the housemaster at the accommodation. They couldn't find them. Eventually, they called us. It didn't take long to rustle up some witnesses. As it transpired, they'd met a bad lad – some busker in the subway near the pitch-and-putt. For some nice privately educated girls he must have been irresistible, don't you think? Anyway, they went with him. Gone for some heavy-duty partying in the woods. We think they got pissed, fooled around, and took what sounds a lot like magic mushrooms. Best couple of days of their lives by the sounds of it, though that's not in the file. Mountain Rescue found them in the end. They were in a bit of a state but that's hardly surprising. From the file it's clear there was some concern about sexual assault because they were found wearing not very much in the way of clothing.' She glances at the file, double checking. 'Covered in body-paint too. Sounds like they had themselves a proper little festival.'

'You have to elaborate, Sumaira.'

'I like the way you say my name.' She smiles, and looks back at the file. 'There's no forensics held on file because it never went that far but there are some old photos somewhere. All I've got here is the image description. It says "runic symbols" on back of Victim 1 and "possible blood-spattering" to Victim 2, though by the time they got to the nearest cop shop that was all pretty much gone. Rain was coming down like a sea.'

'Runic?' muses Rowan. 'That could be anything.'

'Yes, it could.'

Rowan glances towards the lake. 'Three girls missing, two found. What does it say about that? What did the girls say when it all calmed down?'

Sumaira spreads her hands, apologetically. 'There are a couple of handwritten notes from the senior investigating officer. She stood down the Mountain Rescue Team after the two girls were discovered, so she must have been in possession of information that the other one was safe. Maybe she toddled off home before the others. It doesn't say. It's crap record-keeping but it's also from a time before computers ensured we can't chew our toenails at our desks without having to log it.'

Rowan winces. 'It sounds iffy, Sumaira. I've heard rumours that she was never found. That she's at the bottom of Wast Water.'

'We've already found the people at the bottom of Wast Water,' says Sumaira, checking her teeth in the reflection of her knife. 'It's a huge spot for divers. Did you know there's a garden of gnomes down there? Divers put them out for a laugh. There's no bugger else down there.'

'Did it lead to any convictions?' asks Rowan, hopefully. 'This busker – he must have been in line for more than a slapped backside.'

'No follow-up worth the name,' says Sumaira, sitting back. She looks around for the waiter, seeking food and drink and a chance to talk about something less depressing.

'It seems there was a bit of pressure to sweep it under the rug. It was probably a bit embarrassing for the parents – people thinking your kid's been abducted then finding out they've just been partying their brains out. The file's pretty thin. The statements given show they don't remember very much besides the busker they met in Keswick, and some weird rambling about a medicine man, or some such.'

'The Medicine Man?' asks Rowan, and immediately imagines pitching the name to a news editor. 'You're sure?'

Sumaira opens the file and flicks through the sheaf of papers. 'Shaman – that was it. Like I say, the statement's a bit of a mess. This is the bad old days, remember. Not exactly softly-softly, and as for the record-keeping... We can't even find the third girl's statement. The file's a disgrace. CID talk about Eve Cater like she's this legend, but she must have been having an off-day when it came to putting in the paperwork.'

Rowan sits quietly. Waits for more.

'The girls were pupils at Silver Birch Academy,' says Sumaira, looking around and indicating an increasing readiness for more food. 'Holistic, hippy-drippy school that closed years back. Well, a statement was taken at the time from a few of the pupils, staff, and the pastoral team. It was privately owned, you see, and I think the men it belonged to, well they were very keen to get things sorted swiftly. There's a letter in the file from solicitors representing owners Alan Rideal and Phillip Tunstall, written a few days after it all happened, saying very complimentary things about our sainted Eve.'

'Indeed?'

'Well, as it happens, both of those names were familiar to

me, as they'd both been named in a briefing document I'd been shown when I joined CCRU. Missing persons report, made October 1988. One Arthur Sixpence.'

'Fuck off,' snorts Rowan. 'That's not his name.'

'No.' Sumaira grins. 'Not originally. He was probably a Bob Smith to begin with but he changed it both colloquially and legally so many times we can't actually trace him back to his origins. He was Arthur Sixpence when he went missing, so that's what's on the file. Anyway, it wasn't much of a case. Sixpence was this eccentric old boy who did odd jobs and a bit of happy-clappy yoga and stuff at the school. He lived in the grounds, which can't be bad as it's a lovely spot there by the lake. He had a camper in the woods. Kept himself to himself, as the best ones always do. No sign of him for a few days, so the police get called in. There's a bit of a scare for everybody when blood is found by a sniffer dog not far from his cabin, but it seems the coppers at the time weren't too concerned because it never went much further up the ladder. Sounds like a friends in high places situation to me, and it's hard to go back and check because the guy who bankrolled the place died in a mountain climbing accident and the school's been sold off to a Youth Hostels Association.'

Rowan gives thanks to the world for sending him Sumaira. She has a cab driver's approach to discretion.

'And I'm taking it Arthur wasn't found?' asks Rowan.

'Grown man went missing, didn't come back.' Sumaira exhales. 'It happens a lot.'

Rowan sits forward, elbows on the table. 'And the owners were questioned on that, were they?'

'Not as suspects,' says Sumaira. She flicks through the

file, checking a fact. 'It was actually a local man who called us in. He was a friend of Arthur's. A Mr Gordon Shell, from Nether Wasdale. God, don't they have funny names up here?'

'He worked at the school and yet nobody had been to check on him?' Rowan frowns. 'That's a bit...'

Sumaira suddenly looks sulky. 'There's supposed to be pudding, yes?' She turns back to him. 'I'm doing all the talking here,' she says, narrowing her eyes. 'You came to me about Silver Birch. Come on, what do you know? Is it one of these owners – have you found out something terrible?'

Rowan tries to look enigmatic. 'I wish I could tell you but I'm not sure I know myself.' He nods at the folder. 'The lady who requested that. Violet. She was remembering things about what happened. Maybe that led to her asking questions she shouldn't have asked. I'd love to talk to her but apparently she's away finding herself somewhere exotic, which means this line of inquiry is looking a bit dead in the water.'

'Oh yes.' Sumaira smiles, her eyes widening in delight as Jez approaches with a platter containing six tiny plates and enough dessert to cover one of them. She gives Rowan a moment's more attention. 'You should speak to Eve. I'd love to know what she has to say – especially about those friends in high places I just alluded to. She still has a personal interest in the case, that's clear. She was on the phone as soon as we started the FOI request, suggesting oh-so-politely that we might want to leave that particular bit of paperwork near an open window on a windy day.'

She shakes her head. 'Formidable woman, that one, so good luck if you do go up there.'

'I'm glad you're thinking of my personal safety.'

Sumaira frowns. 'Speaking of which, you might want to check in on this lady if she's been gone a few months and you've only got a few Facebook messages to show she's okay. I can tell you some stories about that, believe me.'

'I know.' Rowan smiles. 'I've written some of them myself. And yes, of course it's occurred to me that somebody else might be answering on her behalf, but I'm just a journalist, not the police, so the chances of me pinging the mobile phone tower and pinpointing the location are rather slim. Of course, if you want to help me...'

'I don't see you as high priority,' says Sumaira, running her finger around the crystal bowl and then sucking it.

'In that case, I'll take your advice. Go and make a nuisance of myself. Check up on her.'

'As if you were ever going to do anything else!'

Rowan sits back in his chair and decides he will probably enjoy watching her eat all the desserts. He gestures for her to enjoy herself and she tucks in. He wishes more coppers were like DI Barnett. She reminds him of a time when people said whatever they wanted to and then lied about it later – a time before recording devices and screenshots and a video camera in every pocket. He begins to feel nostalgic.

'This is so good,' says Sumaira. 'Seriously, I'm reaching a plateau of pleasure. Do you want a taste?'

Rowan meets her smile head on. He suddenly realises

that he is going to let her pay for dinner, and possibly drive him home too. She seems a thoroughly modern woman and he's no doubt she'll appreciate the gesture.

'Tell me,' he says, getting comfortable. 'Come on. Push yourself. Tell me your secrets.' Then, with a glint: 'We've got all night.'

14

Yem How Wood, Wast Water
Sunday, October 30, 1988
8.06am

The morning mist clings to the ground, soft as cotton. It drapes a veil upon the face of the clustered mountains that glare down into the cold, black gloom of Wast Water. Only the weakest tawny light bleeds through from the cold, vein-blue firmament behind the clouds. It puddles into the shadows and scars of Great Gable; of Kirk Fell and Yewbarrow, of Scafell Pike and Lingmell: casting tiny iridescent flecks of yellow and lilac into thick pelts of green and grey and dirty gold.

Gordon Shell doesn't look up as he trudges along the broken path. The view is as familiar to him as his own face, and he has long since stopped thinking of that as something worthy of further study. He walks with both hands behind him, coupled at the wrist, as if wearing handcuffs. He stoops a little, but it's the effect of habit rather than old age. He's spent his life here, in this wet, quiet valley, secreted away between the mountains and the sea. It's a panorama of ridges and peaty holes, harsh slopes, lethal drops. He has learned to watch where he puts his feet. He's broken both ankles and one leg. Knows the shotgun crack of a femur broken clean in two. Once found a climber at the base of Napes Needle, his skin the colour of a duck egg and his waterproofs punctured with spears of bone.

Despite the easy familiarity of the path, there is something of a spring in the farmer's step. He's on his way to visit with his friend. He enjoys the old hippy's company more than he enjoys anybody else's. He's not really one for friends, though he knows enough people to clutter his mantelpiece with unreciprocated cards each birthday. He has no shortage of associates; men he's known all his life, hard-grafting Herdwick and Swaledale men, fighting to keep their farms in profit, battling the weather, trying to live within nature and despite it. But Arthur is the first person in a long time to have actually qualified as a proper mate, like he used to have when he was at school.

He finds himself thinking about the first time he met the ragged little man, trying to ease the battered campervan through the narrowest of spaces on the little road that led up through Yem How Wood. Shell had stopped to help, once he'd explained his reason for being there. He was going to be working at the posh school – a caretaker of sorts. He'd been offered a room indoors but preferred the more familiar space of his cramped, sagging motorhome. Shell had talked him through the trees, gauging angles and throwing out gruff commands until the creaking old vehicle had negotiated the most unlikely of routes into a little clearing surrounded by larch and rhododendron. Anybody finding it would presume it had been there before the wood was even planted.

They'd celebrated the moment with a couple of tins of strong German lager and shared a roll-up or three by the fire. That was the first time since the sixties that Shell had sampled marijuana. It greased the wheels of their friendship, though Shell had found himself a little maudlin on the walk back to his lonely, leaky farmstead on the fell. In the years since, they have come to enjoy one another's company. Shell finds Sixpence fascinating. He didn't used to be sure whether he believed all of the older man's stories but that has never stopped him enjoying them. The story about body-paint and Diana Dors in a Yurt near Stevenage has woken him in fits of laughter on more than one occasion.

But for all his skills as a raconteur, it's his spirit that fascinated Shell. There's something about him; some strange elemental peace. He can understand why the women in Gosforth, in Seascale, in Whitehaven and Workington, all fall over themselves to keep him warm and fed. There's a charm to him, but it's more than that. He gives out a warmth, a gentleness, a sense of peace. In a different time, Shell imagines that men would have followed him. Others, fuelled by fear, would have persecuted him. He still hasn't made up his mind whether he thinks of him as a wizard or Jesus.

Shell pushes through the trees, following the familiar path. He watches where he places his feet. His grandfather was a youngster when Steadfast Hookson sunk his exploratory mining shafts into the land here, honeycombing the earth in search of copper and tin. He found nothing of any use; just a network of tunnels and caves that looked set to cave in if any of the geologists or black-faced miners did so much as sneeze. He'd filled in the holes and let the woods grow back, but there had been plenty of times over the past hundred years when the earth had given way and the older trees had sunk into the earth as if being devoured. He'd warned Sixpence about it as he manoeuvred his campervan through the trees.

'Riddled with it,' he said, nodding at the tangle of trees obscuring the gently sloping ground. 'Kids used to come up here looking for the entrance to some of the old shafts. Cavers too. We had a load of posh boys from university stomping around trying to find holes to crawl into before your new boss bought the building. Never understood it myself. Hobby for a dog, isn't it? Going scurrying about in holes…'

Sixpence had listened, head cocked, letting information sink into him like rain into soft earth. Then he'd spoken, softly, earnestly, his face half obscured by the thick exhalation of smoke.

'There's a place in Siberia. They call it the White Shaman cave. It was the home of the Khakas people. Mongolian descent. Pagan, if such a word can be used. They practised animal sacrifice. Human sacrifice. There are stalactites taller than a man, surrounding an altar on which there are still bones. That's where the shamans of the past performed their rituals. Some people say that it has absorbed the energies of these ancient healers. That it has a dark power. I heard a story when I was in St Petersburg. A group of students decided to explore. Twenty young men and women went beneath the ground. Two returned. One was completely insane. She spent the rest of her life in a psychiatric ward.

The other was found nearby, her hair turned grey, holding a little stone figurine. She was dead within a month. Nobody's been back. I'm rather tempted, if I'm honest with you. I'd like to feel those energies. I don't believe they can be a force for darkness. All energy can be used for good. If you'd permit me, I'd be glad to journey with you. There are pieces of you missing – I can see that. There used to be pieces of me missing too. Then I found my path...'

If anybody had told Shell that he would have listened to the little man's story with anything other than scorn, he would have dismissed the notion. But there had been something about the way in which he spoke of his beliefs. Something that suggested a knowledge of things that normal people could only dream of. Shell had listened. He had never allowed Sixpence to perform any of his healing techniques upon him, but he had enjoyed hearing about those who did. About the rich men and women who paid the bosses at the posh school for a chance to spend time in the woods with the strange little man as he banged his drum and sang his songs and surfed on their energies like a bird riding a thermal.

He's seen him in his full costume, a gift from medicine men in Peru who had shown him how to brew the potions that helped them to cross over. The mask was a thing of beauty and horror; a ragged leather patchwork of different shades of brown, stitched and twisted into something resembling a wild boar – yellowing tusks forming a portcullis around an open, snarling mouth. 'Is it real pig-leather?' Shell had asked. Sixpence just smiled, and told him that some questions were best left unanswered.

Shell listens out for the tell-tale signs of life coming

from Sixpence's clearing. He has no doubt he'll be awake. He sleeps outside most nights and generally wakes with the sunrise. He invariably gives the inside of the campervan to his guests. He's had no shortage of people staying with him during the years he's been Shell's friend. Some are not dissimilar to Sixpence in appearance: ragged troubadours in tie-dye and Doc Martens, following old ley lines and footpaths on their personal pilgrimages to wherever the spirits have told them to go. But others have surprised Shell. Well-to-do ladies, barefoot in skimpy white dresses. Handsome, well-dressed men squatting by the fireside with tears in their eyes and a joint between their lips. Children too. Wild-eyed, half-feral creatures, squatting on the steps to the camper; meditating, cross-legged, giving their faces to the first rays of the sun or helping to stretch soft leather over a circular frame to make the drums that beat out the rhythms of a world Shell does not claim to understand.

He moves through the archway formed by the two fallen trees, and stops. Tunstall and Rideal, the two men from the posh school, are sitting by the remains of Sixpence's fire. There is no smoke. The wood has burned Bible-black. Tunstall has his head in his hands as if praying. Opposite him, Rideal rakes, nervously, through the crumbling remains of the fire. Shell realises he should speak. Should cough or whistle to announce his presence. Instead he stands still. There is something about the postures of the two men that make him feel his presence would be unwelcome. He cocks his head and listens as they speak in short, angry bursts.

'...moved on, Alan. That's what he does. That's what he is. He's stayed still longer than we ever expected. It doesn't mean anything.'

'You're telling yourself that because you want to believe it. But he would have said goodbye. And he likes it here. Likes what we do. He believes in this.'

'Times are changing. You know we're going to have to change with them. We're going to have a proper curriculum. Proper tests. A roll-call of pupils, paying agreed fees...'

'That wasn't what we set out to do.'

'But it's what we have to do now.'

'He wouldn't leave for that. And not without saying goodbye.'

'Oh God, man, he was never our friend. What do we really know about him anyway? I let you have him here because he looks the part and because his bullshit helps pay the bills but the education authority was never going to let this carry on indefinitely. A bloody shaman? Having pupils to stay? Residential soul-retrievals for damaged children? Look where that got us.'

'He did his best. That boy was damaged beyond repair. And Pearl blames him. You heard what he said.'

'That problem was put to bed. That's over. He's just gone. We don't need to make a fuss...'

'He's left everything. His books. His crystals. Even his maps. What if he fell into the lake? Or a mineshaft? You know how obsessive he could get – all that nonsense about the Siberian caves – out here at all hours looking for holes into the earth. We can't just act like he didn't exist...'

Shell has heard enough. He clears his throat: a noise like a rutting stag in the still morning air. Steps into the clearing. The two men swivel towards him, startled, guilty. Rideal even looks afraid.

'I was looking for Arthur,' he says, gruffly. He doesn't know if he wants them to know that he has heard.

'Ah, Mr Shell,' begins Rideal, stammering. 'We were actually looking for him ourselves. But you know these Travellers – they don't stay still for ever...'

Shell is about to reply when something glimpsed out of the corner of his eye gives him pause. A little way from the fire is a jagged rock, sparkling with a rusty metal ore. Its point is sharp, like a tooth. Its tip is crowned with a thick, viscose red. Shell moves towards it and the two men follow his gaze. Shell squats down. Two fat flies rise up, sated and red. Shell angles his head. He sees a long grey hair tangled around the rock like the severed rope of an abseiler.

He turns to the two men, his expression brooking no argument.

'Call the police,' he says. 'Now.'

15

Rowan finds himself giving quiet thanks for the absence of mirrors in Bilberry Byre. He's laid out on the cobbled floor of the living room, not quite naked but a long way from dressed – mildly indecent in leather gloves and solitary black sock. A snipped tie-wrap handcuff hangs from one wrist and he feels like there may be a bite mark on his eyebrow. He has the dazed, sore look of somebody who has been run over, and enjoyed it.

'Don't get up,' whispers Sumaira, putting her spectacles back on and blowing him a kiss from the doorway. She's immaculate. 'I didn't want to wake you. You looked very sweet like that. What do you call that painting by Da Vinci? With the arms and legs sticking out? You look like that. Well, that or a starfish, anyway.'

Rowan wiggles upright, self-conscious. The only light in the room comes from the smouldering coals in the grate but they are enough to illuminate a scene of disarray in the small, cramped living room. They've broken the sofa, knocked a series of Coniston slate pictures from the wall and the contents of the log basket and fire bucket are scattered across the cobbles, interspersed with splinters of broken crockery. He isn't sure whether the sharp, scratchy pain in his back is smashed glass or Sumaira's fingernails, embedded in his skin like a cat's claws left in a tree.

'I wasn't expecting any of this,' begins Rowan, unsure what tone to take. 'I don't want you thinking I'm trying to romance information out of you…'

Sumaira gives him a grin. 'Rowan, I'm a detective inspector. I'm not some giggly girl. I do what I choose to do and tonight, I chose to have a lovely time.'

'Lovely?' asks Rowan, reaching out for his shirt and finding that it only has one button left. 'Are we using the word "lovely"?'

'You're the writer – you can find something more suitable if you'd prefer. Anyway, I have to be off. My fella's been texting since midnight.'

Rowan raises his eyebrows. 'Fella?'

'Don't worry your pretty head.' Sumaira grins. 'And look, I don't know what you're writing or where you're taking it but do try and be the best version of yourself about all this.'

Rowan sits up. 'And that means what?'

'People do get hurt, Rowan,' says Sumaira, squatting down in front of him. She's reapplied make-up and sprayed perfume but she still gives off a trace of sweat and sex that comes dangerously close to reviving him. 'Not all secrets are desperate to be dragged into the light, that's all. And maybe, if you're going to tear anybody's life apart, you should ask that person whether they mind. This Violet, she's obviously working through some stuff. Perhaps that's private.'

Rowan swallows. Resists the urge to say anything clever.

'I think it might be better if this was a one-time deal,' says Sumaira, gently. 'I mean, you're fun and I like you but you seem a bit needy, if I'm honest. A bit vulnerable. But I'd love it if we could be friends. You get your rest, yeah? It's been a blast.'

Rowan doesn't give in to the laughter until the door has closed and he hears her footsteps fade away down the path. Then he drags himself upright, and winches himself into dark trousers, round-neck T-shirt and a baggy black cardigan. He pops two of his painkillers from the dimple packet and knocks them back with the last dregs of a whisky he can't actually remember pouring when they arrived back at the little cottage. He checks the clock on the mantel: 1.24am. He could sleep, he's no doubt about that, but it feels like wasted time.

Clumsily, he fills the kettle and sets about trying to make himself a cafetiere with the posh coffee. As the kettle boils, he listens back to the voice recordings. His thoughts start to speed up: an athlete finding their rhythm on a treadmill. He pours the coffee and moves to his favoured position, on sentry duty in the entryway, door half closed behind him.

It's a cold, squally night, but there's a decent-sized moon and the clouds, so constant during the day, have unlaced their feathery edges to allow a glimpse of the stars. He angles his head towards the fell. There is dead bracken on the lower slopes of Scafell. In this light it has the appearance of an old bloodstain: coppery splatters upon woollen sheets.

'Right, just get it over with,' mutters Rowan, sliding off the gloves, teeth bared, trying not to squeal as the new skin tugs against the old wounds. He blows on the exposed fingers, turning the livid pink skin this way and that in the cold air. He spares a moment's thought for the prick who did it. The internet troll who called himself @h8crimez is on remand in a wing of Hull Prison, awaiting trial. So far, nobody has hurt him, though all Rowan has to do is give the word. He knows a couple of the wardens and half a dozen of the inmates and it wouldn't take more than a phone call for @h8crimez to get a mug of boiling sugar-water poured slowly over every millimetre of his sensitive parts.

Rowan doesn't know why he's holding back. He'd hate to think it were some sense of empathy: some whiff of compassion for a wannabe who got in over his head and ended up with a terrible choice to make.

For half an hour, Rowan sits in the doorway and drinks his coffee, his fingers hurting less as he dictates a few emails to people he has been neglecting. He apologises wholeheartedly to Matti, his agent, and gives him a masterfully vague precis of what he's working on. He provides a snippet of interview transcript: thirty seconds of Sumaira bitching about poor record-keeping in the bad old days and being pressured by Eve Cater to lose the FOI request. He doesn't know if he'll include the snippet in the finished work, because he's no idea what the finished work will be, but he's no doubt that Matti will be suitably wooed.

Next he contacts the assistant producer on the TV show that dispensed with his services in favour of a soap star. He keeps it light and friendly: dresses it up as an opportunity for them to have first refusal on a "global exclusive" he's been working on since last they spoke. He copies the text and sends the same exclusive offer to half a dozen other producers and the news desk at ITV, Channel 4 and Sky. He can't bring himself to offer it to the BBC. They always ask too many questions.

When he's done, he begins working through his mental checklist. He knows he needs to speak to Eve Cater, that much is certain, and he'd like to know a lot more about Derrick Millward. More importantly, he wants the Silver Birch pupils on his side. With Violet on her travels, he has to hope that Catherine will be keen to talk. He'll get to that at the book group. He doesn't want to start looking for Freya until he knows a little more and he has yet to truly make up his mind what he hopes will be the outcome of his search. He can't help thinking it would make for a far better story if she were dead, and while he knows this makes him a good journalist, he accepts that it makes him a somewhat terrible human being.

In the meantime, Alan Tunstall has to be worth giving a gentle nudge. He'll be an old boy by now but he was present when his business partner went missing, when the caretaker vanished from the grounds and when three of his pupils disappeared for a weekend. That makes him more than interesting to Rowan – it makes him positively entrancing.

'Tell me all about you,' mutters Rowan, a pen between his teeth, as he settles on the sofa in front of his laptop. Somewhere, he can hear a robin singing. Further on, a herd of chunky Swaledales have drifted into a bare, soggy field. At least two of the sheep appear to have a smoker's cough and Rowan keeps jumping, abruptly, as he hears the wet hacking sound.

It doesn't take long for Rowan to get an address for Tunstall. He's eighty now, and still lives at Bleng Hall, Nether Wasdale. Rowan performs a search on two real estate sites and cross-checks with the Land Registry. He's lived in the property since 1986, when it was transferred into private ownership by the Whitecross Trust, along with a large parcel of private woodland to the rear of the property that once formed the Silver Birch Academy.

'Nice perks,' mutters Rowan, pleased with the discovery. He puts the address into the search engine and finds several images. Some are in black and white and linked to newspaper archives – others are more recent and the captions are full of architectural terms fawned over by readers of magazines delivered free to homes of distinction. He clicks his tongue against the roof of his mouth and selects an image at random. He's confronted with a photo of a large, white-painted manor house: Georgian in origin and style, green paint around the sills and frames and doors. He flicks through the accompanying images. High ceilings, solid oak floors; a ballroom with timbered ceiling and cruise-liner chandeliers.

He flicks through the remaining images with a scowl on his face. He'd quite liked the sound of Tunstall from his farewell speech to the papers. He'd sounded genuine in his belief in a new way to educate the masses. There's something about seeing the excessive luxury of his home that makes Rowan instantly disbelieve his motives. He likes his heroes to suffer.

'...built by Steadfast Hookson in 1823,' reads Rowan, shivering suddenly, as he realises for the first time that he's cold, and tired too. 'I know that name...'

Rowan nods as he swallows down the details of the article, which appeared in *Country Living Lakeland* in 2009. The text made no mention of the occupants but did say that the "long-term residents" had attempted to stay true to the original spirit of the house, which was built as a companion to the larger property at nearby Wast Water.

'Steadfast Hookson,' mutters Rowan, stifling a yawn. 'Built Silver Birch Lodge in 1851 having grown wealthy in his native West Yorkshire trading in ores and textiles. Bought in to mining concerns in Eskdale, Wasdale, Borrowdale... helped fund the Ravenglass Railway and pay for the upkeep of three local churches... Victorian philanthropist, died in 1890, leaving the last of his fortune to notable good causes.' Rowan stops, scowling. 'Sounds too good to be true.'

He flicks the cursor over to Facebook and checks whether Violet has left another clue as to her current whereabouts. Sure enough, there's an image on her timeline – a dainty mandala framing a silhouette of a blissed-out woman in a yoga pose. The accompanying caption states that she's having the "best time ever" in Rishikesh, Uttarakhand, in the foothills of the Himalayas. Rowan licks his lips, as he types a simple reply.

I've got friends there – message me and I'll hook you up.

He smiles as he closes the screen.

He reaches out and pulls himself up by the doorjamb, barely heeding the pain in his palm. His head feels suddenly overfull; as if names and dates and addresses are going to start spilling out his ears. He needs to rein himself in – not let things get too big. Three missing girls. That's the centre of it. Two came back. What the hell happened to the other? Maybe Violet's looking for her. Maybe she's found her and they're busy chatting about the old times, when they were all kidnapped by a serial killer. Maybe she's presently in mortal danger and his search for her will lead him back into the good graces of his publishers and his bank account back into the black.

As he climbs the rickety stairs to bed, he gives thanks for the absence of a mirror. He isn't sure he could look himself in the eye.

16

Violet stands at the water's edge. She feels empty. Weightless. Her whole being seems insubstantial, as if it is resolve alone that stops her from disintegrating into protons and particles to be disseminated by the breeze. She considers this. Thinks of spores and bees. Decides she would like to be a part of a swarm; a speck in a shared consciousness. Would like to become nothing more than energy; cosmic vapour wafting into and out of trees and stones and raindrops. A pleasing thought dances through her mind. Perhaps she could become a sensation. An impulse. She would like to become a moment of somebody else's consciousness; her entire essence distilled into a stranger's unbidden sense of joy. The picture makes her smile. She imagines herself as vapour, fleetingly inhaled. Mr Sixpence will be pleased that she was paying attention as he spoke, so softly, about the lower world; about what lay beyond the veil.

The thought saddens her. They say that he's moved on. They say that he's been hurt. Elora says he's gone down into the dark world beyond our own and now exists entirely as energy, but Elora has a tendency to talk in riddles and bollocks. Either way, she'll miss him. He always tolerated her without it seeming like an effort. And he was interesting. Saw things in her that nobody else saw.

'You're the one they call Ultra, yes?'

Violet turns away from the great mirrored bowl of the lake. Looks back towards the school. It's a view she knows well, and today, with the soft rain drifting in from the east, the old building looks almost ghostly as it peers out from the ragged fringe of trees. Violet's twelve now but looks older. She's tall and well-proportioned; her eyes bright, her smile ever so slightly disdainful in its half-hearted curl. She's womanish in her baggy, pyjama-like top and trousers, her hair pulled back into a ponytail that exposes an elegant neck.

'Ultra, yes? That can't be right, can it? Here, love, help me out...'

Violet looks away from the water and into the unreadable face of a woman who appears to be modelled after a fertility icon: an earth mother baked in clay. She's small and smooth-edged, a sketch composed entirely of ovals and curves and circles. She's dressed in a suede bolero jacket, unzipped, which exposes an inflatable mattress of belly fat beneath her cream, cable-knit jumper. Her glasses are the same slightly ovoid shape as the face on which they sit – poorly maintained brown hair piled atop her head like shaving foam upon a palm. There's something about her face that makes Violet think of goblins. Her eyes are sunken and her cheeks seem to stick out too far as she talks, making her glasses twitch up and down almost of their own volition.

'It's Violet,' she corrects her, stepping forward and putting out a hand to be shaken. The little woman seems to appreciate the gesture. Her hand in Violet's is plump and warm, the nails bitten down and ringless.

'And you get "Ultra" from ultra-violet, yes?' asks the woman, one cheek twitching with a strange, lopsided smile. 'Could be worse. I'm Eve. Evelyn, to be precise. I'm a detective sergeant, and I'm a bit lost. Do you think you might be able to spare me a moment or two?'

Behind her back, Violet makes fists. 'Me? Yes, yes, of course. Um... Where you going?'

'Right now, nowhere. Bit steep that walk, innit? Thought I'd join you here for bit of a skive.'

'A skive?'

'Bunking off. Truanting. Twagging, as they say in Yorkshire. I'm supposed to be taking statements but I've got two decent constables who can do the job for me, which means I get the chance to go stare at the view and hope that the clouds shift.'

Violet can't seem to make herself smile. She's agitated. Twitchy. She tries to concentrate on her breathing but the imp in her chest won't let her be still. She feels hyper: revved up, as if about to run a race or jump from a too-high branch. She's known since yesterday morning that there would be questions – people in uniforms with notepads and serious faces, wanting her to be as helpful as she can be.

'You know why we're here?' asks Eve, her hands in the pockets of her coat. She looks clammy, despite the cold of the day.

'Mr Sixpence?'

Eve nods, satisfied with the answer. Behind her, she can see two tall figures, blue as the hydrangeas in the conservatory up at the dorm. She can make out the distant figures of Mr Tunstall and Mr Rideal, busy nosing around the two police officers like sheep at feeding time. Violet can imagine the differing ways in which the school's two most senior figures are dealing with the disruption to the usual school day. Can picture Mr Tunstall, calm and orderly, insisting that there is nothing to be alarmed about, voice smooth as molasses. Rideal will be squirming. Rubbing those big pale hands together, steepling his pale, pointed fingers, slicking back his brilliantine black hair to better pronounce the sharp widow's peak. He looks like the oil paintings in the library. Looks just like the men in his family who came before – who owned this chunk of the valley and who called themselves "squire".

There are issues between the two of them – arguments about the direction the school is heading in; about whether to expand, to formalise the Silver Birch philosophy; to turn the neighbouring accommodation building into another wing of the school and to apply for permission to build new dormitories for an increased catchment.

'Heck of a name.' Eve smiles.

'Apparently it wasn't always his name,' confides Violet, quietly. 'I heard he used to be something important but he gave all that up to live in his bus and catch squirrels and talk about weird stuff. He knows a lot about crystals. He's interesting.'

Eve pauses, appearing to be trying to work something free from a back molar with her tongue. She pushes a small, stubby finger behind her spectacles and wipes the glass.

'You know Mr Sixpence well?' she asks, when she's finished.

'Nobody knows him that well,' says Violet, honestly. 'He gives assemblies sometimes and if one of the regular teachers is ill he'll come and monitor but we tend to see him more when we're in the grounds. He looks after things. He talks to you if he sees you or if you ask him something. Some people are a bit mean about him, but I'm not. Honest.'

'Mr Rideal hasn't been able to tell me very much about his actual duties,' says Eve. 'Did I understand correctly – he's like a sort of guidance counsellor here too? Is that right? I don't know the phrase.'

'He's just Mr Sixpence,' says Violet and she becomes aware of an unpleasant, prickling sensation in the air. 'I think he makes drums when he's not doing other stuff. I've seen him stretching skins out on this circular frame outside his bus. He kills rabbits with a slingshot. Do you know what a slingshot is? He's really good with it, apparently. I don't think he likes killing things though. He looks a bit sad, sometimes. Maybe not. Um…'

'Going to be a storm,' says Eve, looking up. She licks a finger and holds it up. 'You can feel it, I bet. Hair like that, I can imagine it standing up like you've rubbed it with a balloon. Always gets me in my fillings. Sizzles, like sausages in a pan. One of my first jobs as a copper was guarding the body of a poor roofer who'd been hit by lightning. There was still smoke coming out of his ears and the leather around his steel-toed boots had peeled back like skin.'

Violet wonders if this is normal behaviour for the small

policewoman; whether she is in the habit of sharing grisly anecdotes with twelve-year-old schoolgirls.

'When did you last see him?' asks Eve, without making any attempt to produce a notepad.

'Mr Sixpence? It was about a week before Hallowe'en. I know he wasn't here by then because he's normally the one who helps make the pumpkin lanterns and we all have to keep the seeds for him. It was Mr Tunstall who oversaw that this year. So the time I saw him before that will have been the last time, if that makes sense.'

'And where was that?'

'Just in the woods,' says Violet, weakly. 'There's a spot I like to go – it's quiet and there are rhododendron bushes where I've seen a red fox slinking about. I just sit on the log and read my book until I get cold and then it's time to head back to the dorm, or to Catherine's – wherever I'm going.'

'That's Catherine Marlish, yes?'

'The vicar's daughter – my best friend,' confirms Violet. 'I don't mind staying at the dorm – I mean, it's a gorgeous big house and everything, but I prefer it at Catherine's. I don't really have any other friends at the boarding house.'

'I'm sorry to hear that,' says Eve, and appears to mean it. She leans in, two old pals having a gossip. 'Truth be told, it must be hard to find a good pal in a place like this. All a bit stuck-up, don't you think? I don't know, they just seem to act like they've got all the answers and everybody else is not much more than a lump of nothing. You're the first normal teenager I've met!'

'I'm only twelve,' points out Violet, as she gives in to a smile. She likes Eve immensely now.

'Bloody hell, you'd get served in most bars.' Eve laughs.

'Hey, just quickly – what was Mr Sixpence up to when you saw him?'

Violet tries to keep her face neutral. This was what she had been afraid of when the message came through at breakfast. Somebody had reported Mr Sixpence missing. The police were coming to talk to staff and pupils. They had to be as honest as they could, but not worry. Everything was going to be okay. She doesn't think she wants to tell her about the time she saw him naked and painted green, hiding in the woods while the teachers and Rev Marlish and the man with the deep voice had argued outside his cabin. That doesn't sound great for anybody concerned. But she's happy to tell her about the other thing she saw – the unwashed, strange-looking man she had glimpsed once before.

'He was talking to somebody,' says Violet.

'Oh yes?' asks Eve, conversationally. 'Who?'

Violet looks away. 'It's "whom",' says Violet, and wonders why she feels compelled to correct her. She shakes her head, angry with herself. 'I'm sorry; I'm a bit all over the place today. It's a bit of a shock. It's sad. I'm trying to work out what I feel.'

'Don't get your pigtails tangled,' says Eve, smiling. 'And don't worry about the "right" feeling. Honestly, between you and me I reckon Mr Sixpence as you call him has got a bit sick of cutting down trees and skinning squirrels and listening to a load of rich-kid hippies whinge about getting nervous before gymkhanas. He's a Traveller so I reckon he's travelled on. But we have a duty to follow up on a report of a missing person, which is why I'm here, on this miserable bloody day, having this chat with you. The quicker you can help me out with something useful, the quicker I can sod off back to a nice warm office and a mug of tea. You understand, yeah?'

Violet presses her lips together in case the imp says something silly. She can feel the gathering storm. There's a chill in the air; a purplish blackness to the sky. The air tastes somehow roasted. She wants to open her mouth, to pop her ears, but she doesn't trust herself not to spoil this new friendship before it's begun.

'I didn't recognise him,' she mutters.

'Him?'

'He looked like the people you see on the news – the ones that Thatcher keeps moving on. The ones who caused all the fuss at Stonehenge. He looked like that.'

'They all look different, love,' says Eve, kindly.

'Straggly, then. Unwashed. I didn't really see him properly at first because he was wearing a camouflage coat but he had these sort of patchwork trousers on, like Sinbad wears in those old movies. I think he'd been talking to Mr Sixpence. They looked like they could have known each other.'

'Did he see you?'

Violet shakes her head.

'Did Mr Sixpence? Does he know you and your friends? Do you spend a lot of time up there?'

Violet keeps her face inscrutable – tries to distil what is memory from what is imagination. 'We all know where his bus is but we don't go up there,' she says, brushing over the question. 'There are mineshafts that you can fall down and never come out of again. He gave us an assembly about that. So did Mr Rideal when he told us about the history of the two houses – the school and the dorm. Mr MacBride – he's the head of pastoral – he always jokes that there are secret passageways and underground rooms in the old part of the house. He's only joking though, I'm sure.'

'Were they talking, or arguing?' asks Eve, cocking her head as if trying to clear a troublesome blockage.

'Mr Sixpence doesn't shout,' says Violet, shaking her head. 'I literally saw them for a moment. It was Mr Sixpence who was doing the talking and all he was saying was that he couldn't make it happen.' She nods, agreeing with a mental picture. 'Couldn't make it happen so it was going to have to be a no. I think that was it. The younger man, I can't tell you anything else about him. I barely saw him.'

Eve purses her lips, her philtrum touching the tip of her nose. She sighs. 'Do you see him with other people, up at that spot? Where the fox lies down in the rhododendron, you say? I should imagine a man like him would enjoy a place like that. Somewhere pretty.'

Violet shrugs and hopes it isn't taken as a rude gesture. 'He lives up there. It's all pretty. Do you think he'll come back – it's just, I was hoping Mr Rideal might take me to be healed.'

Eve shoots her a look that is entirely at odds with all that has gone before. 'To be healed?'

'It's a gift he has,' explains Violet, dropping her voice. 'He helps. He heals. It's like reiki but deeper.'

'And what's reiki?' asks Eve, her brow furrowing.

'You should ask Mr Rideal…'

Eve seems to be having a conversation with herself. She sniffs, foully, and looks ready to spit. She changes her mind in deference to the company.

'Is it true?' asks Violet, suddenly. 'That Mr Shell, the farmer who called you – is it true he saw blood?'

Eve licks her lips. There are wrinkles in her top lip and they seem more pronounced after she wets them with the pink tip of her tongue.

'I think you and I might be friends,' says Eve, at last. She wets her finger and holds it up, looking past Violet to where the gathering wind is whipping up shark fins of silvery water. She watches as the fine strands of hair begin to swirl and dance upon her crown.

'Friends?' asks Violet, and her teeth feel fizzy with static.

'Oh yes,' says Eve.

PART TWO

PART TWO

17

If he were writing about this tiny triangle of South-West Lake District, Rowan would use the phrase "sleepy" or "picture-postcard" – rummaging around in the crumbs at the bottom of his bag of journalistic clichés for the simplest way to get the right picture into a reader's head. In truth, this little straggle of cottages and barns is well past sleepy. It's asleep to the point of coma. If it had nostrils, Rowan would be tempted to use a mirror to check for breath.

'You're a genius, son,' he grumbles to himself, wincing each time his damp jeans touch his skin or he hears his sodden walking boots squelch. 'Great idea, this. Fucking belter, you twat...'

He's reached the outskirts of a tiny place that he thinks might be Santon, or might be Santon Bridge, or which nobody has yet discovered and which is still up for naming rights. On a sunny day there might be shafts of golden light hitting the trees and turning the dew-damp earth into so many miles of crushed emeralds. Instead, he feels like he's lurched into some gory dystopian TV show. He half expects to see some slavering zombie emerge from one of the forbidding little lanes that split off from the curving grey road like the legs of a giant millipede. Each leads to a barn or a cottage or half-forgotten farmhouse – and all sodden to the bone.

Rowan has been walking for twenty minutes. He's been pissed off for nineteen. Earlier, Jo had been gracious enough to drop him off for a lunchtime shandy at the nice foodie pub in Nether Wasdale. He and Pickle had eschewed solids in favour of sampling the unexpectedly good range of single malts. Rowan's debit card hadn't worked when they'd come to settle the bill. He'd protested, appalled and embarrassed, plucking random numbers from thin air and claiming that the account contained that precise sum when he checked just a few minutes ago. In the end, Pickle paid cash, peeling off three greasy twenty-quid notes from the unseemly roll in one of the pockets of his overcoat. He'd been happy to oblige, if only to ram his largesse down the throats of the snotty-nosed ramblers who'd looked at him with disgust when he'd shuffled in reeking of weed and wet dog. Pickle had been his reliable self, offering a listening ear and a few choice words of support. He agreed with Rowan – there could be a story in all this. What he couldn't say with any clarity was whether that story could be turned into a pitch for a bestselling true crime novel before the New Year.

Over a measure of Lagavulin, Rowan had filled Pickle in on developments – brushing over the more physical details of his encounter with Sumaira. Pickle had nodded along. He didn't know very much about Silver Birch, but he certainly remembered the old boy who lived in the woods and used his healing hands on anybody willing to park their cynicism and let him loose on their chakras.

Before they clinked glasses for a final time, Rowan had mentioned to Pickle that Violet had accepted his "friend" request, and that he was going to speak to her creative writing group the following evening. Pickle had asked that he pass on his regards and to tentatively enquire whether she would be willing to pick up some cargo from a friend of a friend if her pilgrimage happened to take her near Kandahar. Rowan, feeling warm and convivial, had prodded the screen of the mobile and painfully typed out a jaunty hello.

Pickle is missing you! Hope I've kept your seat warm.

She hadn't replied. He'd chosen not to push it. Didn't want to risk upsetting her before they'd even had a chance to meet. Over the past twenty-four hours he'd become such an expert in Violet Rayner's social media profile that it could replace the poems of Seamus Heaney as his chosen subject on *Mastermind*. He senses a yo-yo character – somebody able to project ecstatic highs and ink-black lows, with precious little in between. He knows the books she likes – romantic, literary, New Age; a trio of self-deprecating comedienne biographies. Knows her favourite movies – *Grosse Pointe Blank*, *The Notebook*, *Whale Rider*. Has looked upon her seemingly endless photographs.

It feels a little like a relationship: the "getting-to-know-you" stage compressed into a couple of hours. He assessed her through critical journalistic eyes. Pictured each of the images as they will look on the pages of his new book: a little caption, a credit and a few solemn words; something sincere about "being pictured in happier times". He knows how she looks dressed up in everything from a Christmas elf outfit to a glitzy dress on a works night out, by way of swimsuit and floppy-hat shots during a two-week break in Marrakech. She'd still been with her ex then – a surveyor from Carlisle by the name of Sam. Her relationship status had changed to *"it's complicated"* over a year ago.

Rowan's sifted through her family contacts, her work buddies; her old mates and new acquaintances. There have been no photos of her since March. Each time she's updated her profile it has been with a generic illustration or a random bit of Far Eastern philosophy. He's beginning to wonder whether she might not just be playing a prank on everybody – whether she's secreted away in a back room of her house, shoving down snacks and drinking beer from the can, revelling in the illusion of being a hippy on a global search for enlightenment.

As the rain doubles back on itself in an effort to slap him twice, Rowan is beginning to regret turning down Pickle's offer to run him back to the Byre. It hadn't looked as far as this on the small glowing rectangle of his phone. He's cold, and the pleasing conviviality of a long liquid lunch has been replaced by a cold that seems to bleed into his bones. He keeps shivering inside his borrowed coat – some stiff, waxed affair that Snowdrop had purloined from a cupboard up at the big house and left on his doorstep along with a basket of warm pain-aux-raisins, a coffee and a strip of Ibuprofen. She'd left a note too, incandescent over Serendipity's insistence she join her at work rather than spend the day with her uncle. She promised that she'd be over later to "go over the files".

Rowan ducks into the cover of a line of tall evergreens. Violet Rayner's house is a little further up the road. She lives in a decent-sized Edwardian farmhouse at the end of a small row of terraced cottages. He can see its chimneys protruding over the big hedges that mark the boundary to the property. There's no smoke. If he carries on past it he'll emerge on the road to Holmrook within twenty minutes – home within the hour.

'She's not there, you tit,' he mutters to himself, tasting rain on his lips. 'You should have stayed in the bloody dry.'

Rowan already knows what he's going to do next. Even as he stands still, considering his next move, there is a part of him that is acutely aware he will go and poke around Violet's house. Worse, he knows what he hopes to find. In twenty years as a journalist he has grown used to a life of moral duality. He's been present at hundreds of murder sites and inquiries, countless for hunts for the missing-feared-dead. He has always hoped for two things. That the missing be returned unharmed, or that something truly unspeakable has occurred. Both are newsworthy. Both are tremendous stories. Rowan has often found himself hoping after two linked murders that a third corpse will be found, turning a half-decent yarn into a sudden front-page headline. Serial killers sell papers. He has a built-in calculator of a corpse's journalistic worth. It's a grotesque skill to have, but he has it nonetheless.

He lets himself in through the low, wrought-iron gate, slipping in to the long front garden as it swings open and clangs against the stone wall that circles the pleasant-looking house. It's Victorian, looks to Rowan to be as sturdy and unmoving as Her Majesty herself. Six big sash windows surround a black-lacquered front door. Proper iron gutters criss-cross a dark series of lines across the house's big stone face. Peeping out at the rear of the property are two brick outbuildings with faded white front doors. Neither looks locked, or particularly sturdy.

Checking behind him, Rowan quickens his pace and steps from the path to the long, soggy grass, cursing as he crosses nimbly around the front of the property and scurries on towards the rear. He glances at the darkened downstairs window. Sees the vague outline of a standard lamp, a mirror, the back of a large TV. Through the rain, almost slipping, he runs to the first outbuilding and uses his boot to pull at the unlocked door. He looks inside – a big white tank in one dusty corner and a complicated series of pipes and fuse boxes at the other. Boiler room. He spots a small white box on the dusty wall to his right and looks at the gauge. The tank is showing as empty. Rowan, shivering, manages to fumble his phone from the pocket of the coat. Quickly, painfully, he takes a couple of shots.

He steps back into the rain and moves to the second building. Tries the door. It won't budge. He yanks with his boot, toes under the lower half of the door, which hangs a few inches off the puddle-streaked stone floor. He hears the clank of a lock. He puts his face to the gaps in the damp wood, peering into pitch blackness and flaking the white paint from the wood with his eyelashes.

He groans, lowering himself in begrudging steps down to the muddy floor. He pulls a face as he angles his head to look underneath – rain soaking his upturned face and trickling into his mouth. He manages to switch on the light of the phone and awkwardly shines it into the darkness. It takes him a moment to make sense of what he is seeing. The torch beam picks out a bare, grey room: the mortar gone from between the bricks, which seem to be held up by beams of rotten wood and great hanging veils of spider silk. The floor is broken up and dirty, a mulch of old papers and glistening black plastic piled in one corner. He changes the angle of the torch. There's a rocking chair set back in the furthest recess: spindle-limbed and ribboned with cobwebs. In front, a fire sunk into the ground – ashes turned to dust.

He lets the light linger there for a moment, straining his eyes. Slowly he turns the beam. The chair is angled to face a bare wall. It has been painted white, and Rowan has a sudden fanciful notion that perhaps this is where Violet comes to project movies. He tries to picture her in the chair, feet on the lip of the firepit, watching old films flickering on the bare brick. He can't imagine why she would. Can't think why she…

He swallows, drily, as the image on the bare brick comes into focus. He thinks of cave paintings: ancient finger-paintings of elongated figures; ridge-back game and huge deer with splayed-finger antlers. Some of them overlap one another, layer after layer of stick figures, running, kneeling, holding hands. Something that might be stars spin around the crown of one larger figure: bearded, pinprick eyes; a suggestion of tangled crown and beard. Beside it are three smaller figures, holding hands, like paper dolls.

Rowan changes his position, breathing hard. Shines his torch at the entirety of the wall and feels as though somebody has stepped upon his insides. His breath catches in his throat as he takes in a colossal swirl of overlaid handprints, of scratches and scuffs scored so deeply into the neatly painted wall that in places it seems as though the outline has been scratched into the brick by bleeding, frenzied hands. Rowan sees perfectly round eyes. A face made up from swatches of different skin. It's a patchwork pig mask; crinkled leather and a snarl of yellowed teeth and tusks.

Rowan hears his heart thumping hard; a drumbeat, soft but insistent. It grows, louder, deeper, as he stares again at the great face on the wall. For a moment, in the light of the torch, the shapes upon the wall seem to move. They flicker, like tongues of fire; stick-men and long-dead beasts strobing in an orgy of ecstatic worship around the leering central figure.

A curl of paper pinwheels across the darkness, fluttering up and down like a dying moth. It skitters up against the gap beneath the door and Rowan, struggling to pull his eyes away from the mural, reaches out for it, painfully, with aching forefinger and thumb. His fingers close around a scrap of flimsy paper, a smudge of neat black typeface on its singed surface. The words swim in his vision. '...*grace is sufficient for you, for my power is made perfect in weakness.*' It's a Bible passage. He recognises the line. Recognises the paper too. A Gideon; the paper almost see-through. The edge is tattered, as if it has been torn. Something is nagging at him, some unpleasant feeling; the memory burrowing deeper out of reach; a tick somewhere in his flesh.

He suddenly needs to meet Violet Rayner. Needs to know she's okay. For a moment, the story doesn't matter. He forgets all thoughts of headlines and front covers and stops composing opening lines and polished lies in his head. Thinks of her. Of them. Three girls who went into the woods. The two who came back. The one who never did.

'Excuse me… hello, excuse me…'

Startled, blinking dirty rain out of his eyes, Rowan jerks away from the door, dropping his phone onto the unforgiving stone. He has a sensation of slamming back into himself, as if he has been drifting slightly outside his own skin. He blinks rapidly, tears running onto his cheeks. What the fuck was that thing? On the wall? Glaring out at him like he was prey…

'Yes, hello? Are you with the gas board?'

Rowan squirms on the ground, reaching out for the handle of the door, trying to pull himself up as his boots squelch on the grimy surface. His feet go out from under him and he lies sprawled on the ground. There's no time to get up before the woman who walks towards him across the grass is upon him. He can see her waving, swatting at the air, all the while pulling an *"I-don't-mean-to-be-a-nuisance"* expression. He loves that about the English. Hyper vigilant, but hyper polite. Willing to do time before running the risk of causing an offence.

He adjusts himself so it looks like he's lying down for some good reason, resting his head on his palm like a gigolo on a waterbed.

'Are you okay? Did you hurt yourself?'

She's mid-thirties and trim, with hair dyed a pleasing shade, tied up with a Frida Kahlo bow. She's holding what is either a very large baby, or a small fat man, on her hip.

'I'm grand,' says Rowan, struggling to be nonchalant.

'What are you doing?' she asks, trying to make it sound

funny but clearly keen for an answer. He takes her in. Pretty, heart-shaped face. Brown eyes. A nice smile. She's wearing flip-flops and messy dungarees, paintbrushes sticking out of the pocket on her front. Her shoulders are bare, the raindrops adding a pleasing sheen to the tattoos of Flamenco dancers and delicate arum lilies. The thing on her hip looks like a Galapagos tortoise without its shell. It's floppy and damp and looking distinctly unimpressed. It grips the lady like a gargoyle clinging to a cathedral roof.

'I think she's forgotten,' he says, rolling onto his knees then gingerly climbing to his feet. He notices her glance at his hands. He raises them, guilty. 'When they say you shouldn't play with fireworks, they really are onto something. But yeah, I'm guessing Vi has forgotten about today.'

'You know Violet?' asks the lady, putting a hand, palm down, over the baby's head. 'Violet's away.'

'Still?' asks Rowan, looking shocked. 'Oh for pity's sake. Well, that's my best laid plans gang agley.'

She pulls a face. 'Is that from *Of Mice and Men*? I did that at school. The book, not the poem. But I liked the poem. Sorry, I'm gabbling. I'm Rosie. I live next door.' Her expression softens as she sees how sodden his clothes are. 'Look, we're getting soaked. I'm just next door. Do you want to pop in and I can grab you a towel or something? Awful day, isn't it? Of course, it's never exactly Barbados, but I do wish this mizzle would lift.' She jerks her head. 'Coming?'

Rowan watches her as she turns away. Momentarily alone again, his mouth feels dry.

The thing in the bare brick room: the shape on the wall. They've unsettled him. He feels somehow unclean, as if his skin were rimed with some greasy lotion: big oily smears of bacon fat streaking the vulnerable flesh beneath his drenched clothes.

He follows her down the path, and with each step further from the locked door and its unnerving contents, he feels the chill within him begin to thaw.

Turning away from a harsh gust of rain-filled wind, his eyes fall upon the small strip of untended flower bed beneath the downstairs windows. He turns his back on the wind, narrowing his eyes. Wordlessly, he pulls out the phone, a fresh new crack glistening on the display, and takes a couple of quick shots. He inspects the images. The footprint is clear: a perfect impression in the wet mud. Five oval hollows and the deeper print of the arch and heel of a bare foot. Somebody has stood here recently, gazing in.

Rowan stares through the glass into the dark room: an explorer gazing into the untold wonders and mysteries of an unopened tomb. It feels as though millipedes and scarab beetles are scuttling and wriggling upon his skin.

He turns away. Follows Rosie towards the light.

18

This cold, dank air carries a trace of smoke; the memory of flame. It is not enough to disguise the putrid reek beneath. This is the smell of a wasted year; the obnoxious stench of a thousand bales of hay turning black and decaying: putrefying back into the earth after a season of endless rain.

DS Evelyn Cater knows the smell. She grew up in a small Yorkshire market town. Daddy always told her she should marry a farmer, if she could find one willing to put up with a lass who couldn't resist asking questions and who looked like somebody had dressed a piglet in a pinafore dress. Always had a way with words, did Daddy. He said she'd never go hungry if she did. Said she should marry somebody who thought they were getting better value for money the fatter their livestock became.

She hadn't taken his advice. Never did. Became a copper back when women police constables were about as popular as an uninvited house guest with chronic diarrhoea. She's done well at it too. The lads rate her highly. She's put bad people behind bars. She can punch her weight and never backs down from a ruck. Some of the old boys even forget that she's female – neglecting to shout "ladies present" whenever some foul language spews forth from a beery lip, or a colleague raises an ample buttock off the bar stool and blasts a gust of methane into the smoky air.

She feels comfortable in most environments now. Even here. She certainly didn't have to marry a farmer to get to understand the ways of the countryside. She's been here a year now, a member of the briskly efficient CID team based at Whitehaven nick, and she's getting good at reading the skies for signs of impending trouble. There will be violence tonight, she has no doubt. She can read the mood in the valley as clearly as she can foretell a storm from the prickling in her fingertips. Temper hangs in the air like a cloud of gas and she has no doubt that it will ignite before the dawn.

It's been a hellish summer. The torrent didn't let up from June through to August, turning the sun-bleached fields of golden hay into mile after mile of ruined earth. A whole year's harvest has been destroyed and the rivers have swollen so high that there is talk of redrawing maps. A farmer in the Eden valley reported maggots eating into the living flesh of a whole herd of Swaledales; the meat beneath the wool as rancid as the ground on which they feed. In times gone by, the farmers in Borrowdale might have bunched their fists at the heavens, demanding mercy after the ceaseless onslaught. Earlier still, there might have been sacrifices. Ceremonies with bone-handle knives and virgins dressed in white. Eve knows there will be violence tonight. Farmers have burned their crops – bundles the green-topped bales of useless hay into stinking feathery oblongs – and they've thrown petrol and flame upon the whole fetid lot.

'Will it never dry out?' asks Eve, sitting on the shallow stone step at the back of Shell Farm: a squat, mucky white building that seems to be sinking into the khaki-and-coffee fell-side, half a mile up from the Wast Water. She doesn't understand how anybody can farm here – it's all sheer rocks and scree. 'I mean, can't they stick it in a barn and see what happens? Does it need to be burned?'

Gordon Shell leans against the mud-clogged wheel of the old tractor, both feet planted in a puddle rainbowed with spilled oil. He talks without removing the cigarette from his lips. 'It rots in on itsel',' he explains. 'Can go off like a fertiliser bomb. Fire's the only way.'

'Must be a kick in the teeth,' says Eve, sympathetically.

He nods, a tired irritability creasing his mucky, lined features. 'Worst summer I can remember. That's the worst of this life – those days when you work knowing you're killing yourself for nowt. Breaking your back stacking bales that are going to go up in smoke. It's not even like you can move on. There'll be ugly great rectangles in the fields until Christmas, patterns on the new grass, showing just how bad it's been. It'll take a year or more to grow back.' He spits the tip of his cigarette on the ground. '1988 can fuck off, as far as I'm concerned, if you'll pardon my French.'

Eve listens. Files the information away. Looks up at the smudge of grey clouds and can't help wondering whether she could ever have tolerated a life like this. She reckons she could probably still play the role of farmer's wife – she has the strong forearms and the round, red cheeks that she associates with the cartoon caricature version of the role. She just isn't sure about the making jam and the beating eggs and making packed lunches for some taciturn husband. Can't see herself rubbing blood and afterbirth off a new lamb with a fistful of damp straw. Can't imagine tweezing white hairs from the black face of a champion tup. She'd rather just get on with what she's good at. Get on with being a copper; a thief-taker.

Not that her single-mindedness hasn't cost her dear. Her last three lovers have all told her she's too much like hard work. She's felt sorrow at the end of each relationship but she has never felt regret. She's twenty-nine, a detective sergeant, a respected copper with a record that shows more commendations than black marks. She had to move to this little corner of England to take a step up the career ladder but she doesn't view it as a sacrifice. She's learning to love it here, in this dull brown blob in the top left-hand corner of the map. It's only forty miles from one side to the other but the variety is such that on any given day she could be called to locations as different in character as the sun and the moon. Cottages; castles; urban sink estates glaring out into the sea. She'd thought that all mountains looked the same. Now she feels able to recognise the different fells from description alone. She favours the wilder lands; the rugged mountaintops with their serrated edges and hidden hazards; sudden drops and concealed mineshafts; waterfalls that pound the rocks with a cold, endless fury. She's starting to fit in.

'You've given up on him, then,' says Shell, without rancour. He's a red-faced, knotty specimen; middle-aged but with the sun-slapped, wind-whipped look of abandoned patio furniture.

Eve pulls herself up from the step. Arches her back. 'We'll never close the file,' she says, quietly. 'He's a missing person until he's no longer missing. But as we told you at the time, he's a grown man. We don't even know we have the right name for him and there are more fingerprints in his bus than we could sort through in a lifetime.'

Gordon gives a whistle and two black and white dogs emerge from the gaping maw of the barn behind him. They nose around his feet and he pets them, absently, as he chews his tongue, searching for the right words.

'He wasn't happy,' he says, at last.

'I know; you said that in your statement…'

'But you're not going to look for him anymore,' he adds, accusingly. 'Even with the blood. With what I've told you.'

Eve looks away. She's already said all this to her detective superintendent. She's not at all convinced that Arthur Sixpence just upped and left one day, leaving his possessions behind and saying no goodbyes. What's more, the science officers and sniffer dogs have identified a substantial quantity of blood staining the roots of a yew tree near the spot where he parked his battered old campervan and did his best to live a quiet life. Eve's spoken to plenty of people who knew him. None have had a bad word to say. He was quiet. A little timid. Kind. A bit awkward – perhaps a little odd. But gentle. That's the word people keep using. He was a "gentle" soul. Helped where he could. Did what he could. Eve is starting to wish she'd gone to the trouble of meeting him. She's heard about his healing ceremonies; his attempts to heal troubled souls. She'd liked to have seen how the trick was done.

Mr Shell, with whom Sixpence enjoyed regular campfire drinking sessions, had been clear when he made the initial call to the police: something bad had happened to his friend. He hasn't changed his mind. Eve hasn't been looking forward to telling him that her superiors have decided to scale down the operation. Eve's turned up nothing to suggest that Mr Sixpence is worth any more of their valuable time. One of the pupils at Silver Birch gave the vaguest of descriptions about seeing him with a young man, dressed in ragged hippy clothes, but both Mr Tunstall and Mr Rideal said there was nothing unusual about that. Lots of people from the Travelling community made their way to Mr Sixpence's bus over the course of any given year. Nor had they even been able to give much in the way of background detail on the man who offered "guidance and alternative therapies" to pupils, when life began to hit them harder than they could stand.

He travelled a lot – that much they were clear on. South America, India, Indonesia, North Africa – even as far away as Papua New Guinea. This was according to the housemaster, who had once questioned him on the places he had seen and would like to see again. Eve isn't sure how much to believe. Sixpence seems to have been in the habit of telling people stories that verged on the fanciful. He claimed to have visited parts of the Soviet Union; to have made his way behind the Iron Curtain to learn from mountain men in the cold darkness of Siberia. It was at that point that Eve realised that if Mr Sixpence didn't want to be found, he wouldn't be.

'You know he had kids stay with him sometimes, don't you?' asks Shell. 'Kids with problems. Kids who saw things that weren't there, or heard voices, or couldn't help themselves pulling the wings off their pet canary. He'd try and help them. He was a good person. He tried.'

Eve sees genuine sadness in the farmer's eyes – more than she would expect.

'I think I'd like him,' says Eve, as kindly as she can. 'I like most people who want to help others.'

Gordon nods, stuffing his hands in the pocket of his overalls. 'I don't like that Rideal bloke,' he confides. 'I don't like very much about that whole bloody school. I don't mind a bit of the hippy-trippy bollocks and if they want their kids to do all that bending and stretching instead of learning to play football, that's their look-out. But I know they took advantage of Sixpence. Pushed him further than he wanted to be pushed. He didn't mind giving the talks to the kids and helping people who needed it but Rideal was starting to use him like he owned him. He'd even had fliers and brochures done up talking about their remarkable on-site healer who led meditation classes and had studied spirituality all round the world. Sixpence was too much of a gentleman to ever make a fuss but it was wearing him out. He wanted to be free – that was all he'd ever wanted. And like I told you before, they weren't happy about calling you in. It weren't until we saw the blood that they got off their backsides.'

'This mistake,' asks Eve, intrigued. 'Did he ever elaborate?'

Shell shakes his head, angry with himself for never having pushed harder. 'He spoke about one of the kids who'd stayed with him,' he says, screwing up his eyes in concentration.

'Somebody who needed to find the lost pieces of himself. That's what he said, and I know that sounds like nonsense but you've got to remember that's how he talked. It was like being pals with a wizard sometimes – it really was. He just said that he should never have taken him through.'

'Through where?' asks Eve.

Shell shrugs again, blowing out air through his dry lips. 'He wasn't the easiest bloke to understand. He said stuff that made no sense to me, but I don't think he understood half of what I was going on about neither. For all that, we were pals.'

'He might still turn up, Gordon,' says Eve, and it sounds a horribly weak platitude.

Shell shakes his head. 'No, love. He's gone. Passed through.'

Eve decides that silence is the best approach. She gives him a nod, and lightly squeezes his forearm as she moves past him, giving both soggy collies a rub behind the ear as she trudges through the yard, the grey mass of the valley opening out before her like the pages of an unfolded book. She's left a uniformed constable waiting a little way down the hill, warm and snug in the patrol car. As she makes her way towards it she's surprised to see that there is a large silver Mercedes parked nearby, wheels precariously close to the edge of the road and the tiered drop down to the lake's edge. A burly man with receding hair and one too many chins is leaning against the bonnet, chatting to the PC. He's wearing a dark coat over a black suit, the trouser legs stuffed into green wellington boots.

Over the smell of the smoke and the farm – the cloying miasma of rotting hay, the iron tang of the distant lake – Eve detects a scent she remembers. It's a blend of pipe smoke, talcum powder and extra-strong mints. She finds herself smiling, unexpectedly, as the man on the bonnet comes into focus.

'Well, well, well,' she begins, wincing into the rain.

'It's 'ello, 'ello, 'ello,' says the visitor, and as he grins he exposes short, stubby teeth. 'Did I teach you nothing?'

'Everything, sir.' Eve smiles. She wonders if they're on hugging terms or if she'd be better served by a handshake. She does neither. Just stands and smiles at him; a child happy to get a visit from a kindly grandad.

By the edge of the road, the PC looks from one to the other; an umpire at a tennis match.

'This is Derrick Millward,' explains Eve, waving a hand. 'My old boss.'

'DCI, as was,' says Millward, nodding to the PC. 'Private sector now, of course. Better pay, shorter hours, not as many people trying to saw your balls off with a hacksaw...'

'Don't tell me you're not nostalgic,' says Eve.

'Can't let myself, Eve,' he says, affecting an air of wistful nostalgia. 'My head's awash with memories already. You know I grew up here, don't you? Farming's loss was the navy's gain. Then coppering since '51. Bet that makes me seem ancient to you buggers, eh? Did you know, I caught one of the last murderers to get the death penalty?'

'Lucky you, sir,' says Eve, deciding she should have hugged him when she had the opportunity. She's missed him. 'Are you here to see some old haunts or were you just keen to see how I've coped since you retired?'

'I've been watching with interest, Eve,' he replies. 'Doing bloody wonderfully. Doing me proud.' He cocks his head and pulls a face. 'Not so much with Arthur Sixpence though, eh?'

Eve listens to the sound of the wind playing with the branches of the trees below. Listens to the *pink-pink-pink* of grimy water falling from the mudguards to the puddles in the road. 'Sir?'

'I think we might need a drink, love,' says Millward. 'I reckon we can help each other out.'

Eve will always regret the speed with which she agrees.

19

Rosie lives in a sturdy, stone-built cottage that looks, to Rowan's inexpert gaze, as though it may have stood here for the best part of 200 years. It's an inviting, homely sort of place and seems to carry an intrinsic whiff of home cooking and freshly picked herbs. Five big windows, painted sage green, spread out neatly around a big purple front door. The front lawn is slightly overlong but there are neatly labelled bamboo canes in the sodden flower beds, predicting the names of the flowers that will bloom here soon. He glances up as he passes from the cold of the day to the heat of the house and spies a bushel of dried juniper; the berries black, tucked into the eaves of the porch. It's a local superstition, a way to keep bad spirits away. Rowan wonders what she's afraid of – why she came out so quickly when she spotted a strange man so obviously poking around in her neighbour's garden.

He pushes open the front door and hears her call out that she's in the kitchen, drying off. He follows the sound of her voice, leaving footprints on her terracotta tiles, noticing the occasional imprint of her damp soles upon the dry stone. He steps into the warm, yellow-painted kitchen; the drapes dark green. Used pots are stacked around a deep Belfast sink and the round kitchen table is a platter for a colossal buffet of pens, paints, papers and modelling clay. Pots, pans and old-fashioned gypsy-style tea kettles hang from a wrought-iron range. The baby, now draped in a soft blue blanket, sits on the floor by an empty bowl for cat food, looking up at his mum with an expression somewhere between reverence and hunger.

'We got it for the view.' Rosie smiles, picking up an oven glove and gesturing at the window. 'Money well spent.'

Rowan drips onto the flagged floor. He looks past Rosie, who stands by the window, rubbing her hair into a great frizz of static. Beyond her, the fells are a blur: the merest suggestion of something there, beyond the cloud; brooding and immense.

'I'm not great with my hands but a towel would be appreciated,' says Rowan, apologetically.

'I'm using an oven glove,' responds Rosie, raising her eyebrows in a way that makes him warm to her at once. 'I'm going to presume that's not quite good enough.'

'I'm not proud.' Rowan smiles. 'It'll do...'

'Stay there,' she commands, and disappears through the door, leaving Rowan and the baby to eye one another distrustfully. She pops back a moment later. She's stripped off the vest and dungarees and pulled on a baggy T-shirt and a pair of flared cords. 'That was bloody daft of me,' she says, exasperated with herself. She hands him a fluffy burgundy towel; her scent is all coconut and poster paint. He notices that she has a tiny ring through the cartilage of one dainty ear; a *daith*, rumoured to be good for preventing migraines.

'What was daft of you?'

'I keep leaving him places,' she explains. 'My mind does have a tendency to wander. I'd like to blame the artistic temperament but I think it's more a case that I've gravitated towards art because I was too scatter-brained for everything else.'

Rowan uses his fingertips to rub the towel through his hair.

'Sorry if I loomed up on you,' she says, looking embarrassed. 'I'm not one of those nosy neighbours.' She grimaces, as if there's something unpleasant under her tongue. 'That's not true. That's a total lie. I am one of those nosy neighbours – I just don't mean to be. I swear, I maybe look out the window half a dozen times a day and they always seem to be times when there's something going on – not that very much goes on around here anyway.' She gestures at the table and Rowan sinks onto a chair, his damp trousers feeling vile against his legs.

'We go a bit mad here sometimes,' confides Rosie, busying herself filling a deep kettle and looking through chaotically stacked cupboards. 'Not that it's not brilliant, of course. I mean, who wouldn't want to raise a child here? It's idyllic. But my husband has to work away a lot so for big chunks there's really just us. I go to the playgroups and the mums-and-tots groups but it's always a bit of an effort. Some days I could scream, I really could.'

Rosie leans up to fetch something from a high shelf and in the sombre yellow light she takes on the likeness of a painting by Vermeer – an apple-cheeked serving girl with a radiance that speaks of glowing embers; a rose-lipped embrace. He feels a vibration in his pocket. It takes him a moment to realise it's his phone. Embarrassed, he apologises and fumbles for the phone. It's a message from Matti, his half Finnish, half Jamaican agent, for whom a love of literature has not blunted his use of superfluous exclamation marks.

Sounds great!!! Call me, asap. Mat.

Rowan isn't sure whether to feel enthused or to slink further into the swirling vortex of panic that is churning in his whisky and stomach acid. *This has to be something,* he tells himself. *Has to be!!!*

'That's Violet,' he says, rolling his eyes: an old friend falling victim to a repeated pattern of behaviour. 'Full of apology, as usual! What a donut. I'll have her guts for garters when she gets back from her travels.'

'Oh you've heard from her, have you?' exclaims Rosie, excitedly. 'I was panicking, if I'm honest. Is she on now? Is she active? Put her on FaceTime. I'd love to see her!'

Rowan makes a show of stabbing at the display. Makes a face. 'Isn't coming back. Hang on. Violet? Vi... no, she's gone. Bugger. I can send a message from you if you like...'

'Drat,' says Rosie, petulantly. 'Oh. Oh well, if she's on, just ask her if she's able to transfer the money for the oil, as it's been a few weeks and I don't mean to be a pain, but... and does she want to do it again this year? Split it, I mean?' She stops, worriedly wringing out Rowan's towel, water dripping on her paint-streaked hands. 'No,' she says, shaking her head. 'It's fine. Let her focus on her chakras or whatever.'

Rowan smiles. Affects the demeanour of one who's had

this happen plenty of times before. 'Left you hanging, has she? Think of it as flattery. She only makes trouble for her really close friends.' He grins, hoping it's true, and is grateful to see his smile mirrored in Rosie's.

'It's nice if she thinks of me like that,' says Rosie, a touch sadly. 'I haven't really made many good friends since we moved. It's hard, and with not being allowed on Facebook anymore, it's almost...'

'Not allowed?' asks Rowan, intrigued.

'Oh, my husband has banned me,' she says, and then makes an effort to make it sound less patriarchal. 'I mean, with my consent, of course. It's best – I get drawn in.'

Rowan nods, understandingly, adding Rosie's husband to his mental list of people in dire need of a punch in the face.

Rosie deflates a little, putting the baby down on the floor – who she introduces as Otto – and dreamily handing him a lethally sharp paintbrush and a water bill to scribble on. 'It has been a bit of a nuisance, her being away this long without any warning,' says Rosie, looking genuinely pained for having said such a cruel thing. 'I'm so pleased that she's got the new lease of life and everything but she's literally just toddled off without organising anything.' She pulls a face. 'Sorry, she's your friend...'

Rowan laughs. 'There are always casualties on the road to peace,' he says, philosophically.

'Even inner peace?' Rosie smiles. 'I think it's great she's out of her slump, I really do, but I was there for her through a lot of things and now I'm here signing for parcels and turning away clients and talking to bailiffs because she's in such a zen-like state she can't be arsed to renew a direct debit.'

Rowan licks his lips. 'Has it been that bad? How long has she been gone now?'

'March,' she says, immediately. 'I know that, because that was when we agreed to split the price of the central heating oil. She paid me in cash the first time but the last quarters have gone by and it's getting expensive, paying for two lots. My husband is getting very irate.'

Rowan winces. On the floor, Otto sucks the tip of the paintbrush, his tongue turning slowly blue.

'I can't wait to ask her about it,' says Rosie, happy again. She looks like she's fighting the urge to clap her hands together. 'She must have seen so many things. Felt so many things. Hopefully they've perked her back up.'

'I did notice she'd been down,' says Rowan, vaguely, playing along.

'Well, you'll have seen from Facebook, of course. Always the life and soul, always ready for Prosecco and Ladies Day at the Races. She was terrific when we moved in, before Otto came along. She was so friendly. Of course, she's seen plenty come and go. We're her eighth neighbours; she told me that on day one. But she'd made us this hamper with local products, local cheeses and crackers and jam and chutneys and stuff...'

'Kendal Mint Cake?' asks Rowan.

'Of course.' Rosie grins. She turns it inwards, smiling at a memory. 'She and my husband are never exactly going to become friends – I think that's fair to say.'

'Dispute over a boundary line, is it?'

'In one way, yeah,' says Rosie, lowering her voice. 'He thinks she's a bad influence. Doesn't let her in the house, though if he sees a way to save a few quid he'd make a pact with a hell-beast.'

'What's happening with her post?' asks Rowan, nonchalantly. 'I could sort it for you, if you like. Get it to her and let her sort her own stuff out for a change.'

Rosie blinks, trying to look cheerful again. 'Eve's got most of it,' she says. 'Do you know Eve? Older lady? Bit scary?'

Rowan nods. 'Eve Cater,' he says. 'They're still in touch?'

'Well, you go through a thing like that I'd imagine it bonds you,' says Rosie, passing a pot of glue and a teaspoon down to her son, who has now taken on a distinctly Braveheart appearance.

'She's spoken to you about it?' asks Rowan.

Rosie nods. 'As much as she could, anyway.'

'As she could?'

'Well, obviously she doesn't know what happened,' explains Rosie, and Rowan does his best impression of an idiot who's just caught up. 'That's the big problem, isn't it? I mean, people talk when they've had a few drinks and there was a brief period when she was over here most weeknights, helping me work through the alphabet of cocktails. And yeah, she mentioned it.'

'The abduction?' asks Rowan, playing the odds.

'Well she didn't just blurt it out,' says Rosie, bringing him a mug of strong, dark tea. 'There's no sugar, by the way. Sorry. And yeah, she was telling me about how long she's been here. I mean, it's nearly twenty-five years so she had loads of interesting stuff to tell us about, and of course I remarked about how well she'd done to have such a lovely place when she must have been no more than twenty, and she was smiling because I'd got the sums a bit wrong, but not by much. She said she came into some money – an inheritance. Bought her dream house and my goodness she's done a wonderful job on it over the years. Some of those curtains cost more than my car.' She squeezes her face into an amazed smile at the thought of it. 'Can't be bad, eh? I tell you, if I suddenly inherited some dosh I'd buy me and Otto a big campervan and just take off; I really would.'

Rowan, resisting an urge to ask the current value of her husband's life insurance policy, tries to keep his questions casual. He's warming up. Feeling better. He sips his tea and nods appreciatively.

'Tickety-Boo,' she says, proudly, as she tries to claw back her status as a progressive. 'It's Fairtrade.'

'I suppose that's what makes it extra strange,' says Rowan, chewing his lip. 'She loves the house, like you said. Leaving it to the elements and the bailiffs seems heartless.'

'I've said the same to my husband.' Rosie nods. She looks at Otto and his blue-streaked face. 'I've been getting very concerned, if I'm honest. She answers like, one text in every five, and even then it's hardly anything more than a few words. And with not being on Facebook I've only got what I heard third-hand for proof that she's even alive.'

'What makes you say that?' asks Rowan, trying to show he takes her seriously.

'Well like you say,' mutters Rosie, over the edge of

her mug. 'I mean, she's not short of money and owns the house outright so the only reason a bailiff would be round is if she'd forgotten to pay council tax or a car rental or something. And why would she do that? Even if she has found enlightenment it wouldn't take a second to sort that out, would it? And the gutters needed doing in September and I got our guy to do it because I know she has it done every year, but...' She stops herself. Looks at him intensely. 'Can I tell you something?'

'Please do.'

'Look, it wasn't my business – my husband's right – but I couldn't help poking around. I mean, over a few Proseccos she'd given me what she knew, and that wasn't much. Whatever he gave them, it's turned their memories to mush about what happened.'

'What he gave them?'

'The busker,' she says. 'I mean, that's all she remembers now, isn't it? A few snapshots of these ripped-up memories. Something about dreadlocks and bare feet and a half a memory about smoking Bible pages as cigarettes. It's all just gone. She said she'd been okay with that for a long time. And then of course she started wondering, and then really wondering, and she'd always been a bit of a hippy in her beliefs, hadn't she? All that stuff about not being able to move forward while carrying baggage. That's what this became. She wanted to know – for better or worse. And then it became about the other one.'

'Catherine?' asks Rowan, keeping up.

'No, Freya. The other one. After it all happened they didn't get to see her again. The police made it clear she was okay, and she'd gone to be with family. I guess as she's got older and wiser she's started questioning that. She wanted to find her. Find this Freya.'

'So you helped?' asks Rowan.

'It wasn't hard,' she protests. 'I just went on a couple of forums. Websites helping people recover lost connections. All that *"hello, I'm looking for the nanny who raised me in 1943"* stuff. I said I was looking to find Freya Grey, who'd been a pupil at her school and who I would love to make contact with. And of course I signed it as Violet. Why wouldn't I? So the next thing Violet – I mean "me" – gets a friend request from Freya – surname now Morgan.'

'Good work.' Rowan nods, approvingly.

'As far I was concerned that was it,' says Rosie. 'Good for Violet – none of my business what came next. But of course next thing I'm pregnant with Otto and my so-called friend from next door isn't coming round anymore because she's on this new journey, getting spiritual and talking about soul retrieval.' She looks at Rowan for confirmation that she's said it right. He nods. 'And when Otto comes along she barely even has time to say hello. All that banging, it's no wonder she and my husband hiss like cats.'

'From next door, you mean?'

'Drumming.' Rosie winces. 'Hours of it. I mean, it's soothing at first, but it was making our heads spin and with a new-born baby in the house he had to have a word. He must have caught her on a bad day, enlightenment or not, and she gave him both barrels about...'

'Yes?'

'About our lives, I suppose,' she says. 'The way he treats me, or the way he seems to at least. Violet told him

I was miserable. Really miserable. All part of her journey apparently – confronting that which needs to be confronted. He was furious. And he went on my Facebook profile and went back and back and back until he found something he didn't like and said that was it, I was off.'

Rowan breathes in deeply. 'Drumming?' he asks.

'The shamanic stuff. All of this yoga and reiki and crystal-healing. It wasn't doing her any favours on the looks front – she was looking really, well, haggard last time I saw her, which is why it's great she seems to be picking up, but if something has happened, and somebody is pretending she's okay when she's not, how hard would it be to drop a few random posts on a profile?'

'No pictures of her,' says Rowan, softly. 'Not since March.'

Rosie glances at Otto. 'I hope she hasn't done that stuff,' she whispers. 'Has she said? On Facebook, has she said if she tried it? I suppose she must have, if she's travelling.'

'The stuff?' asks Rowan.

'Whatever it's called. That medicine-man drug they do in South America. It takes you – what was the phrase – "through the veil".'

Rowan sips his tea. 'Ayahuasca,' he says, quietly.

'Yes, that's the stuff,' says Rosie, passing Otto a pair of scissors. 'When I took her Christmas card round, getting on for a year ago, well she was warm as toast with me. Is she always like that? Hot and cold? I mean, she'd had no time for me for ages and hadn't given Otto a look, and now she was cooing over him and asking about what we'd been up to. I don't know, maybe I'd imagined the coldness, and I guess if she was getting into all the New Age stuff she might have just had no time for anything else. I don't want to sound mean.'

'You couldn't.' Rowan smiles.

'But she said we should have one of our sessions next time my husband was away, a proper natter. She said she'd written something that had helped her with some stuff and she'd have some stuff to tell me. She called it a "chapter two", whatever that meant. She said she'd read about recovering repressed memories, about these soul retrievals and ceremonies where you drink this potion and journey through the veil into whatever it is that's out there. And she laughed as she said it.'

'Said what?'

'Said, "Don't worry, I won't be knocking back the ayahuasca," and I didn't know the word so she said it again. I googled it later. It's dangerous stuff.'

Rowan nods, remembering. Rosie puts her empty mug down on the table and picks up her son like a blanket. He appears to be missing a large triangle of hair from his crown. It's stuck to his top lip.

'Of course, she didn't come over,' continues Rosie. 'And the drumming was worse than ever. Next thing we get this curt message saying she'd gone away for a bit – it went to everybody so you'll have seen it – and now here we are with me paying for her oil in a house that nobody's in. If it wasn't for Eve I'd be knee-deep in post.'

Rowan ducks into her eye-line. 'I think you've been a very good friend,' he says, and means it. 'I also think you've done the right thing in telling me. I'm getting concerned myself.' He stands up, business-like. 'I'm going to go and see Eve and see if she's had any other contact with her.'

'But you just did,' protests Rosie. 'That message. She's okay, yeah?'

Rowan nods, unable to help himself. 'Of course, I just think, well... it's best to be belt-and-braces when it's somebody you care about, yeah?'

'Yes, of course,' says Rosie, glancing distractedly at the window. 'It's still throwing it down out there – you should really wait it out.'

Rowan remains in a crouch, half up, half down. 'It's best I go,' he says, and it's sincere. 'I'll go and see Eve, like you suggest. Do you have any post to take to her, just while I'm here?'

She nods, brightly. Returns with a small pile of white and brown envelopes along with some cellophane-wrapped periodicals. 'Can I dry your clothes?' she asks, on impulse. 'I can't imagine anything worse than damp clothes.'

'That must be nice.' Rowan smiles. 'I can.'

'I'm sorry, I know that must make me sound like some demented housewife,' she says, huffily. Her fringe flops down a little. 'I'm not trying to get in your pants.'

Rowan changes his angle so he can look at her properly. 'I can't even get them off,' says Rowan, smiling.

'Will you tell me what Eve says?' she asks, some of the light leaving her again. 'Or just, y'know, ask her for a picture of herself – Violet I mean. Just something to show she's okay.'

'Holding a newspaper with today's date, yes?' Rowan smiles.

'And you'll call back?' she asks, and there's less little girl in her voice.

Rowan looks around him. The bright walls, the posh

curtains, the little plump baby and the delightful artist who's just given away for free what might make him a lot of money. He feels the pang of conscience and decides the decent thing to do would be to leave her well alone.

'I'll call back,' he says. He hopes he's lying.

INTO THE WOODS

20

Nab Scar Cottage
Tuesday, November 15, 1988
2.14pm

Derrick Millward is staying in a neat, white-plastered
yeoman's cottage overlooking the silvery stillness of
Rydal Water. To the rear, the mass of Nab Scar provides a
barrier of sorts from the driving rain, though the storm has
still managed to spatter the dark, mullioned windows and
obscure a black date-stone above the porch: *1654*. From the
other side of the lake, Eve fancies that the house must look
like a child's drawing.

'Bloke who runs the place is a decent sort,' explained
Millward, as he led her from the rain-spattered parking
area into the warm comfort of the little B&B. 'No awkward
questions or slurs to your reputation if you were to trust
yourself to be alone with me...'

He'd said it with a twinkle but there was no disguising the
note of regret in his voice. They both know she's safe with
him. Both know she wouldn't give a damn what anybody
had to say, even if he was to chance his arm.

'It's cosy,' noted Eve, as she followed him along a corridor rough-plastered with the same off-white render she'd noticed outside. She gave the owners a mental tick for interior design skills, nodding approvingly at the clever placing of mirrors opposite the arches of the small cottage windows: doubling the light in an otherwise dark, oppressive space. The stairs had creaked like the beams of a longboat as they made their way up the dog-leg stair, passing potted plants polished to a waxy gleam.

'In here,' he'd said, unnecessarily, as he opened the dark wooden door and led her into a bedroom so murky that the walls and furnishings seemed to swallow the light. Eve had been pleased to see an Oriental, high-backed chair by the door to the bathroom, plonking herself down immediately and looking up at tobacco-coloured ceiling beams – the same dark staining as the floorboards, upon which a vintage green and pale pink Chinese wool rug has been vacuumed flat. The big four-poster bed faces the window – three arched panels of glass exuding a church-like air: a triptych of fell.

'I'd have thought you'd be at the Sharrow Bay,' says Eve, taking off her wet suede jacket and removing her glasses to wipe the drops away using the hem of her baggy blue jumper. 'Times hard, sir?'

Millward crosses to the windowsill and takes a bottle of brandy from behind the pleated curtain. He pours a measure into a glass from the bedside table and hands it to Eve, who takes it with a nod of thanks. He clinks the bottle against the glass and takes a swig from the lip. Eve takes a sip. It's good quality but it's not her favoured tipple. The lads all think she's a hardened drinker but she's always been happy with a Malibu and lemonade; maybe a packet of nuts or two. She's a long way past doing whatever it takes to fit in with the men – quitting smoking because she couldn't stand the taste of it and wearing clothes built for comfort rather than catching the boss's roving eye. She's comfortable in herself. Knows who she is. Most of that is thanks to Derrick, her mentor and champion. She's never seen him drink from the bottle before. She only drinks the brandy out of solidarity – a way of showing him she doesn't judge.

'I'm getting by,' says Millward, in response to the question Eve has almost forgotten she'd asked. 'I thought about staying somewhere a bit posher but what's the point? Depressing walking up those stairs to something that looks like the bridal suite when you know you're only going to be hugging your pillow.'

Eve stays quiet while he removes his jacket and pulls a cardigan from a suitcase on the floor. He takes a towel from the rail by the window and tosses it to Eve. He pushes back his hair and sits down on the bed, looking at her with a likeable smile on his pinkish, waxy face.

'You've done well, Eve,' he says, at last. 'Going to be a DI, I hear.'

'Fingers crossed, sir,' says Eve, wondering who he knows at the Nick. 'We've had some good results.'

'We?' asks Millward, settling back. 'You need to learn to take the credit. It was you, from what I hear.'

Eve rolls her eyes, deeming the flattery unnecessary. 'We're not having much luck with Arthur Sixpence,' she says. 'You have an interest, sir?'

'I think "Derrick" is all right now,' he says, raising the bottle to his lips. 'I'm retired.'

'And a bona fide private detective, so I hear,' says Eve. 'You always did like your detective stories. Who are you channelling, Marlowe or Spade?'

'I reckon I'm more Miss Marple,' says Millward, wrinkling his nose. 'I think you might have the wrong idea about what the job entails. I reckon I did too. It's mostly legal work. Donkey work, if you like. Finding people who owe money, property searches, investigations into errant heirlooms and more probate than anybody should have to look into. I've got two staff but I'm not good at letting people do things I should be doing myself. I'd have a secretary but I'd end up making her coffee, I'm sure.'

Eve grins, remembering her boss's reputation for being soft as cream with his underlings and hard as frozen butter with suspects.

'It's Blackpool that you're based, still?'

He nods. 'No shortage of clients and it pays to be somewhere that you have a few contacts and where people remember which favours are owed.'

'I'll bet,' agrees Eve.

'Last April a woman came to see me,' says Millward, looking to the ceiling as if about to impart something that will tax him. 'Siobhan Pearl. Wife of Deaghlan.'

'Irish?'

'What gave it away?' he asks, smiling.

'Sorry, I'll shut up.' Eve mimes locking her mouth shut while he takes another drink. She glances at his neck as he reclines against the headboard. He doesn't look well. His skin looks like butcher's paper, the veins in his neck as clear as A-roads on a map.

'They own fairground rides,' he says. 'Settled gypsies, if

you go back a generation. They've done well. A lot more money than the taxman knows about. They're not people to be trifled with, if you'll forgive such an old-fashioned phrase. Deaghlan and Siobhan live in a great gaudy castle of a place overlooking the beach at Lytham St Annes. I got to know them well during my time with Lancashire Police. Daddy's solid. Fair. I trust what he says.'

Eve waits for more.

'They have a son. Cormac.' His hands tighten on the neck of the bottle. 'Difficult boy. You might say he was troubled. Sometimes it happens, I suppose. You give a kid every advantage and it doesn't matter – they're just bad right the way through.'

'How so?'

'I reckon Siobhan knew it from the first. Said he was born with teeth and talons and I don't know if she was joking. Either way he was a big brute of a lad. Walked early, talked early, a real early developer. By the time he was a year old he was big enough to swing the cat around by its tail.'

'Boys will be boys...' begins Eve.

'He had visions,' says Millward, flatly. 'Heard voices. They'd find him sitting talking to nobody and then he'd have these seizures where his eyes rolled back in his head like a shark's. Mum and Daddy did all they could on the medical front. Doctors, specialists, but it was the things there didn't seem any cure for that caused the problems. He was vicious, that was the truth of it. Liked to hurt things. He was a charming little sod when he wanted something but if he didn't get his own way then all bets were off. When he was six he broke the back of the family dog. Jumped on the poor thing with both feet. They'd find him in the stables, setting traps for mice but he'd twist the hinge so that it only caught them, didn't kill them. Daddy found him with a magnifying glass roasting one in his palm, happy as you like.'

'Jesus...'

'Well, that were another bone of contention. Family were devout but he'd have none of it. Screamed like he was Damien in *The Omen* if they tried to get him into his Sunday best. And at school he was always getting sent home for playing too rough with the other children. Took a pair of scissors to a little girl in his class because he wanted to – and I'm quoting directly – "swap bones with her".'

'Sounds delightful,' says Eve, wishing she'd savoured her drink rather than downing it. She could already use another.

Millward purses his lips, as if what he is about to say will be an effort. 'When he was eight, he hurt somebody very badly. There was a knife. She'd be dead if Mum hadn't heard the squeals coming from the stables and even then he'd already had his fun. Left her striped like a bloody zebra.'

Eve feels the tick start up in her cheek. She's thinking ahead.

'They didn't call the police in?' she asks, knowing the answer.

'Kept it in the family, so to speak,' says Millward. 'Spoke to their priest. He said the boy was rotten all the way through, though I think his feelings had been hurt because Cormac had once told him to go get out of his sight before he gave him stigmata with a screwdriver. Mum and Daddy were at a loss. That's when they heard about your school.'

'Silver Birch?'

He nods. 'Reputation for helping people find themselves, isn't that right? Holistic teaching – more carrot than stick. I reckon they'd exhausted all other possibilities by then. The Daddy, Deaghlan, he's an upright sort of a bloke, though he's tough as iron when needs be. I honestly think he'd have put Cormac down like a bad dog if Siobhan hadn't persuaded him to put faith in the school.'

'When was this, sir?'

'It was '79,' says Millward, from memory. 'They met with Mr Tunstall, with Mr Rideal. Took the tour, heard the pitch. Cormac dragged himself round there like he was a hungry man at a buffet car. He'd have made mincemeat of those children – the school was right to turn him down.'

'He didn't pass the admission protocol?'

'The school said no to taking him as a pupil. But Mr Rideal did offer access to a healing treatment that he thought might be good for somebody with Cormac's specific characteristics.'

Eve sits forward. 'Sixpence?'

'The same. Deaghlan had to say plenty of Hail Marys and Our Fathers to make it right with his own faith, but Siobhan persuaded him to try. She said there was something wrong inside him and that anything which could heal him had to be worth a try.'

'And?'

'And the boy spent the next four years living part of the time at home with Mum and Daddy – and the rest of the time up here, sharing Sixpence's old bus with him.'

'Did it change him?'

Millward smiles, and there's no mirth in it. 'Hard to say. He was better, certainly. Always super polite at home.

Helpful, kind, good with the younger children. I don't know if Deaghlan believed he'd changed or had just learned to hide it better but he wasn't roasting mice in the barn anymore and that was a positive step.'

'How did you come to be involved, sir?'

Millward stretches, loud clicks coming from both elbows and wrists. He looks at Eve as if he wishes he didn't have to share any of this: that he regrets having to offload the burden of what he knows onto somebody he cares about.

'He came home for good aged fifteen. Deaghlan was vague about it, no matter how hard I pushed, but something happened to spoil the status quo. Sixpence had told him he wasn't welcome anymore.'

'Doesn't sound like the sweet man I keep hearing about.'

'I never got the story on what led to the falling-out, but home he came – all dreadlocks and hand tattoos and looking like something you'd find in a riverbed the day after Woodstock. Even so, as far as Deaghlan was concerned he was pretty much a grown man now and could be put to work. He started him off running one of the slot machine places on the seafront. Changed the name of the place to "Cormac's" and tried to keep him on the right track. Didn't take long to go wrong. Went wild on a young lass who worked with him – I've asked around and nobody knows what it was that flipped him, but he just grabbed her as she went past him. Those who saw it reckoned he was like a dog that just couldn't help itself. Dragged her into a storeroom and throttled her until one of her eyes went black. Took three members of staff to drag him off and they're all too bloody scared to talk about it. All I could get from one of the lads was that he kept talking about "healing" her – about swapping her bones. It was a bloody miracle she survived. Even bigger miracle that she took Deaghlan's money and kept quiet.'

Eve feels an overwhelming desire to lock up both father and son. 'Where is Cormac now?' she asks, tightly.

'True love conquers all, apparently,' says Millward. 'Fell for a pretty girl he met playing the penny slots on Blackpool prom. A "hippy girl" – that was how the family described her later. Boots and no bra, no make-up. The ones who got the stuffing knocked out of them on the drive to Stonehenge. Mona was part of that crowd. The hippies, the nomads, the alternatives. She turned Cormac's head. Told his parents he didn't want the life they led. Wanted her. Wanted to bed down beneath the stars and to find his own little patch of Paradise. He started quoting people his family had never heard of – Johannes Guttzeit, Isadora Duncan, Carl Jung, Gustav Gräser...'

'I'll check them out.'

Millward takes another pull of brandy. 'Cormac left the family home in the first week of July, 1985. He took with him a canvas rucksack, a change of clothes, a handful of paperbacks, a toiletry bag containing a toothbrush and some Euthymol toothpaste, a hair-comb, nail scissors, an empty exercise book, three blue pens, a bicycle repair kit and the battery from his father's imported Plymouth Turismo. According to an eyewitness, he was picked up in a dark green Military-style vehicle with canvas sides. We think it might be a catering vehicle. The eyewitness reported two females in the back already. He climbed into the back and the vehicle drove off, heading east.'

Eve realises she's uncomfortable in the chair. Stands up and crosses to the bed, reaching out to take the bottle from her old boss. 'And where is he now, sir?'

'That's what the Pearls are paying me to find out,' he says, pressing his teeth together. He looks at her with deep, inscrutable eyes. 'Are we still friends, Eve?'

'Of course, sir,' she says, automatically. 'You know me better than anyone.'

He smiles at that, a memory hovering in his line of sight. 'You were never cut out to be a WPC. People didn't know they should be scared of you until you'd kicked them in the shine and stamped on their balls. Too good a brain to go to waste on woodentop work. I'm damn proud of what you've achieved, I really am. You were the only person I wanted to see at my retirement do.'

'Sorry sir,' she says, genuinely remorseful. 'I couldn't. That was the weekend of the sergeant exams.'

'You chose right, the way I always knew you would,' he says, fatherly now. 'You know the right thing and the wrong thing and there aren't many coppers I can say that about. So I'm going to tell you something and imagine that I'm talking to my old pal Eve, and not soon-to-be Detective Inspector Evelyn Cater.'

'You think he's hurt Mr Sixpence,' says Eve, pre-empting him.

Millward looks past her, gazing into nothing. 'That and so much more. He's been busy.'

'Busy with what?'

'Healing through pain, I think you'd call it. He's bedded down in the Travelling community, and the last thing they ever want to do is talk to the police. But those who've been

willing to share a beer and a bong with a private investigator
– they've all heard the rumours.'

'Rumours, sir?'

'A predator. Moving from place to place, camp to camp,
following the stars and working his way around some
old route made up of ley lines and forgotten permissive
paths. He finds the people who are vulnerable; replaceable.
Charms them into believing he can help them. Drugs them,
takes them. Those who have come back are never the same.
Whatever he spikes them with, they see things nobody
should have to see. One poor girl I met near Salisbury, she's
not much more than an animal after what he did. Just sits
with her crayons and draws these terrible stick-men. They're
like cave paintings: all these frightened people fleeing this
thing with the face of a pig.'

'And you're saying this is Cormac?'

'I'm saying that I'm looking for Cormac Pearl, and that
the person who may or not be committing these crimes
matches his description. Used to, anyway. He's got braids in
his hair, according to one witness. Another said he wears
different-coloured contact lenses; somebody else spoke
about him being barefoot with green toes. All we know
is that somebody is snapping up vulnerable people like a
whale with plankton. Camp to camp, festival to festival,
always keeping moving. The only thing we know for certain
is that he likes people to come to him willingly. He turns
their heads. In several cases we've seen the same book on the
shelves of those who have gone missing. A French book,
translated into English. *Shamanism: Archaic Techniques of
Ecstasy*. It's a study of the history of this... well, it's not
exactly a religion – more a way of life.'

'Any tangible evidence, sir?' she asks, a note of caution in her voice. 'Any actual bodies?'

Millward looks at her like she's a puppy who's just learned a trick. 'There was a body found beneath the roots of a yew tree in March. Been identified as a travelling musician by the name of Bingo. We're looking for a proper ID.'

'Cause of death, sir?'

'The pathologist found a small puncture wound right through the breastplate, corresponding with a perforation in the heart. Not a knife. A screwdriver, possibly, but more likely something used by a leatherworker or a carpenter. Do you know the sort of pressure it takes to push a blade through the breastplate? He's strong.'

Eve nodded, picturing it. 'A fight with a rival, sir? I presume it was all very "free love"…'

'There's more,' says Millward, looking at her hard. He's reciting information from memory – reading from the reports he knows word for word. 'A young, well-built male, found ploughed into a farmer's field near Minehead. A small, round-faced girl, no more than seventeen years old, found in a shallow grave in woodland outside of Banwell. A male and female, their bodies dumped at the same time in a marshy area of wetland off the road to Glastonbury. They were buried face to face – the skin fused over time. They were cheek to cheek when they were found. Uncoupling them tore most of the flesh away but it was still clear they were young, and fit. All with the same holes in the heart. All bearing marks of having been associated with what we call a "counter-culture". The same people that we knocked lumps out of at Stonehenge.'

'Why haven't I read about these cases, sir?'

'You have,' he said. 'You've probably spotted a line in a national paper about a body found here or an appeal for a missing person there. But you've never read another word about it afterward, I guarantee it. Because these victims, these poor young people – they're the drop-outs. They're society's throwaway people.'

'And they're definitely murders? I mean, if the skin was fused then you're suggesting that he was carrying out these murders while still at school. While still staying with Sixpence...'

'No,' he said, flatly. 'Not definitely. Not conclusively. And you're right to question whether I'm a daft old man who's made a picture from a few random scraps of paper. They could be suicides. Could be accidents. Could be the victims of all different types of misfortune. But there are enough similarities for me to believe we're looking for one person.'

'How much of this can you prove, sir?' asked Eve, as a chill raises the hairs upon her arms and the base of her neck. She fights to suppress a shiver.

'Not enough to interest any of my former colleagues,' says Millward, with a flash of regret. 'Not enough to get any serving force to take a proper look at this. Not even enough to take it to the press in the hope people will learn to be on their guard. But I know enough to make catching him and stopping him the most important thing in my world. Enough to persuade an old protégé to let an old dog try a few new tricks.'

Eve realises she's taken a fistful of the bedsheets in her hand. She doesn't know if she believes him, but she can see that there is something in his eyes, in his manner, that means this is all very real to him. 'This family,' she says. 'The Pearls. If you found him, what would they do?'

Millward holds her gaze. She realises that the muscle in her cheek is twitching again. She can hear the rain against the glass and the constant shushing of traffic on the nearby road.

Millward seems to make up his mind. Leans forward and lowers his voice.

'I'd let them put him down,' he says, without blinking.

Eve gives a nod.

And a bargain is struck.

21

Rowan feels a little like a giant bumblebee. He's wearing dark jogging pants along with an Australia rugby jersey, and is reclining in one of the brown wing-back chairs that fan out around a circular, bright yellow table. He doesn't know if Serendipity planned it this way when she pulled the first two items of clothing she could find out of the laundry pile and insisted he sit in front of the Aga in the kitchen and warm himself up.

He raises his glass, toasting his sister. Saint Serendipity – always willing to blow-dry a drowned rat.

Serendipity has looked after him like she always has, fussing and clucking and doing everything but press her lips to his sore hands and kiss them better. He's been fed – an acceptable vegetarian lasagne with some ghastly avocado and pumpkin-seed flapjack for afters. Had his glass refilled enough times to make the world a softer, gentler place. His hands have been re-wrapped; the wounds healing well; his hands and fingers more able to move under the new wrappings. Now the drowned sailor who stood on her doorstep two hours ago has been replaced with a slightly healthier version of her younger brother. She keeps smiling at him, looking like she wants to pat his head.

It's nice here, in Serendipity's madly patterned kitchen, at the heart of the large stone farmhouse that Jo has spent a very keenly worked out budget on transforming into a home of distinction. Warm, with the Aga belting out heat. The walls are a mixture of burgundy and teal and the low roof and dark wood beams make him feel as though he's sitting in some marvellous Victorian tavern, tankard in hand and pipe cupped in a grimy palm. He's having to squint a little to keep up the charade. Jo is seated at the other end of the kitchen table, a hunched praying mantis.

It doesn't take long to spoil it for himself. Slowly, inexorably, the doubts wash in. The questions about what is real and what is projection. Does he really believe something has happened to Violet or is he just pretending to so he has something to tell his editor and agent? He's worked this way before – starting with a headline and trying to make the story fit the mould.

'Were you sleeping?' asks Snowdrop, appearing in the doorway. She's in huge pyjamas and slippers made to look like half-peeled bananas. She looks recently scrubbed, her hair dried and brushed so that it gleams like wet coal.

'Not at all,' says Rowan, shifting position and smiling. 'How are you doing, Scoop?'

'Scoop?' asks Snowdrop, muttering a "hello, Jo" to the silent, spindly figure who taps away at a typewriter and puts circles around an expenses sheet at the far end of the table.

'Somebody claim an extra mile on the round trip to Kent, did they?' asks Rowan, raising his voice and winking at Snowdrop.

Jo, a sleeping lioness, does not look up from her calculations. 'We have those odometers fitted for a reason,

Rowan. If you take a wrong turn, it shouldn't be the company that pays for your incompetence.'

'You're all heart,' says Rowan, and thinks he sees a little smile on his sister-in-law's tightly pursed mouth.

There's a screech as Snowdrop drags a chair towards him across the chequerboard paving, crunching up the end of a large rag rug. 'So,' she says, expectantly. 'Tell me what's next. Tell me what we've got. When do we start writing? Will we have a joint byline, or will I be like an "additional reporting" credit? What do you reckon?'

Rowan listens. The beat of the raindrops upon the glass; the pinging of hot metal in the fire; the rhythm of Jo's fingers moving across her screen. Deep down, far back in his skull, he hears the faintest whisper of something dark. Looks into his niece's trusting eyes and asks himself the question he has refused to look upon. Why haven't you called the police? The answer bubbles up like hot, sulphurous air; a speech bubble from his gut. He hasn't called the police, because right now, this is all his. He doesn't know yet whether there's even a story to write, but he does know he has enough little snippets of intrigue to start whetting publishers' appetites.

If something bad has happened to Violet Rayner, it makes for a better story. If the sins of the past have returned to haunt a woman kidnapped as a teen, it all gives the story weight. And if he's the one who raises the alarm, and hands the police a dossier full of cover-ups and crimes unsolved, it's going to look damn good on a book jacket. And if it turns out that Violet spent a weekend in Blackpool getting pissed back in 1991 and that she really is having a ball on a round-the-world adventure, he can at least do his damnedest to charm her into talking to him about how it has felt to live with such a big part of her past missing.

He could probably get a few hundred quid for that off one of the women's magazines, which could keep him in liquor money and phone service until the right story does land in his lap. He just needs to keep them all away for a while. If he can show them he's working, the publishers might grant a contract extension, giving him time to find a replacement story, twice as good. He just needs time. Time, and a few hundred thousand pounds.

'Speaking to Eve Cater is going to be key,' says Rowan, as Snowdrop sets about scribbling down a plan of attack in her multi-coloured jotter. She puts wiggly underlines beneath the date and uses a love heart for the dot over the lower case "i" in "investigation".

'The old police officer, yes?' asks Snowdrop. 'Do you think she'll be keen to talk?'

Rowan shrugs. 'She and Violet are close, or so it seems. If Eve's collecting her post for her, they must have a pretty good relationship, which means she might know plenty that will help, and might well be only too happy to tell us the truth about 1991.'

'What do we think that is?' asks Snowdrop, scribbling furiously.

'I'll let you know when it comes to me.' Rowan smiles. 'Either way, she's very high on the list. And we need to know more about Derrick Millward, about the school – who worked there, what they remember.'

Snowdrop stops writing. 'Uncle Rowan, erm, surely if Eve thought there was something to worry about she would have contacted the police. Doesn't that suggest Violet is exactly where she says she is and that there's nothing untoward going on? I know that would be a blow but maybe we're getting carried away.'

'Nothing's set in stone,' says Rowan, optimistically. 'I mean, yes, of course she could well be absolutely fine…'

'Pity,' mutters Jo, from the far end of the table. 'Maybe one of the other ones will be in a more marketable state of peril.'

Rowan regards her, wondering if he should defend himself. He catches Snowdrop's eye and she gives a little shake of the head. It doesn't matter. They're both writers, in this together.

'Catherine,' says Snowdrop, brightly. 'Catherine Marlish. What's the plan, Batman?'

'No social media profiles, no obvious way in,' muses Rowan. 'So it comes down to the creative writing class. I'm going to have to play it by ear.'

'I've heard that phrase – what does it mean?'

'Make it up as I go along,' says Rowan, draining his glass. 'In the best scenario, Catherine will be delighted to have the chance to tell her story. She's clearly got a desire to be heard – why else would she want to write? I need to show her that I can be trusted.'

Jo laughs, a hard, dry sound. 'But you can't!' she snaps. 'You demonstrably can't be trusted to use her story in a way that will help her. Listen to you!'

'That's not fair!' begins Snowdrop. 'This is Uncle Rowan's job. He's a writer who can't use his hands and he's still managed to grab the tail of a story. Look how much he knows already! Catherine *can* trust him – trust us! – to tell the truth.'

'Snowdrop, he doesn't care about Catherine,' says Jo, looking pained. 'He doesn't care about what may or may not have happened to Violet. He cares about his bloody deadline and the alarming lack of funds in his bank account.'

Rowan turns towards the fire. It feels as though the words in his head have found a mouthpiece in his sister-in-law.

'You shouldn't talk to him like that,' huffs Snowdrop, slumping in her chair. 'He's not well.'

Jo shakes her head, coldly. 'Where was he, eh? When things were going well? How often did you see him? What about those trips to TV studios or placements on newspapers or free entry to museums that owed him a favour? None of it happened. Too busy. Too busy living high and living well. No thought for you until he literally had nobody to wipe his backside and suddenly he's the uncle of the year? Bollocks.' She gathers up her stuff, her face contorted. 'I'm going to work in the study. Snowdrop, don't be long. And, Rowan, if you drink the last of the bottle you'll find some methylated spirit in the garage. There's cranberry juice in the fridge if you need a mixer.'

Snowdrop tries to put herself into Rowan's line of sight. He listens to the sound of Jo's footsteps echoing away into the corridor then manages to drag his attention away from the fire. 'Sorry,' he says, squeezing one eye shut. 'She's right about all that stuff. I've been rubbish.'

Snowdrop shakes her head. 'Depends how you look at it. You do a lot of the things you say you will and I know you only don't do the other stuff because you're busy. And anyway, you're here. We're being journalists. Writers. You're making up for lost time!'

Rowan manages a smile. Nods a curt little thank you. Turns away before she sees the moisture in his eyes.

'I think we need to know precisely what led Violet into going away for all this time,' says Snowdrop, trying to squeeze a felt-tip pen between her nose and top lip. 'And it was Mum who gave her the details on who to contact for the shamanic stuff.'

Rowan considers it. Thinks of drumbeats and the firepit and the painting on the bare brick wall. She's trying to remember, that much is clear. She's been trying to journey – to seek lost parts of herself. She spoke of ayahuasca.

'Do you think you could ask your mum?' he asks Snowdrop. 'I mean, I could probably spend an evening going through her Facebook friends and cross-referencing with shamanic groups but it would be easier if she just said who it was she put her in touch with. You could sort of just bring it up in conversation, see what she thinks.'

He looks into a huge grin. 'Didn't even need to come up with a cover story,' says Snowdrop, wide-eyed. 'She said to me before you turned up sopping wet – she'd messaged her friend and said that her brother and her darling girl were keen to know more about shamanism. That's okay isn't it? We don't need to mention Violet by name – just see what sort of path she was on. Anyway, she's a lady called Sharon. That's funny, don't you think? Sharon the Shaman? I did, anyway. Her surname's Durning. There's nothing funny about that. She lives in a place called Redcar and she's a shamanic practitioner, reiki practitioner, a crystal healer and something to do with Egypt as well. I googled her. She was an estate agent before she got the calling to become a, well, whatever it is she uses as a title for all that stuff. Anyway, she's happy to talk to us about what it is she does and how it works.'

Rowan feels like a proud dad watching their first-born score the winning goal in a cup final. He'd offer a fist-bump if it didn't hurt. 'You are a marvel,' he manages. He gestures at his phone, sitting on the tabletop like a neglected paperweight.

'You've got messages,' says Snowdrop, reaching across and scrolling for him. 'Your agent's still waiting for you to call back, your BT bill is available online, Roxanne wants to know if you remember where her passport is – that's a bit rich, don't you think? – oh, and you've been accepted into Facebook groups for Friends of St Olaf's Church and… what's this word?' she asks, spelling out "alumnus". 'Okay, alumnus. They've accepted your request so you can now view discussion groups and photos from the "glory days" of the Silver Birch Academy, 1974–1992. Is that where they were pupils? Right, right.'

Rowan chews his lip, mulling things over. He hasn't heard back from his message to Violet and his quest to find Freya Grey online has proven fruitless. There are plenty of red-haired women of a certain age who answer to the name. He's messaged them all, claiming to be a friend of a friend. He might be well served by posting a message in the Facebook group. A simple "does anybody have a number for Freya" might at least provoke some memories. But to do that he might risk alienating the people who may come in useful when he is fleshing out the book. Stories can rise or fall on such judgement calls.

'Oh, you've had a message from somebody called Rosie,'

says Snowdrop, narrowing her eyes. 'There's a picture attached. Apparently she's thinking of you…'

Rowan lunges forward, grabbing the phone. He looks up and sees Snowdrop grinning at him. 'I knew you liked her,' she says. 'You went all doe-eyed when you mentioned her.'

'Oh shush,' says Rowan, rearranging his position. He'd like a cigarette and another glass of something warming for the road.

'Cup of tea?' asks Snowdrop, reading his thoughts. She looks at him with such hopefulness in her eyes that he feels unable to disappoint her.

'Perfect,' he says. 'Just what the doctor ordered.'

22

Rowan

Hi, and Namaste. My name is Rowan and I believe you're good friends with my sister, Serendipity. She mentioned you might be able to help me out with some details and background for a project I'm working on. Would you be able to help?

Sharon

I do know Serendipity, and her lovely daughter. She mentioned you may need a bit of info so please, fire away. What is it you need?

Rowan

A precis. Shamanism explained. What you're into, how you do it, how people respond…

Sharon

There are some great books that could help you. There's one called <u>Shamanism: Archaic Techniques of Ecstasy</u> – that's what got me started.

Rowan

Great, thanks, I'll try and track it down. You've been doing this a while, have you?

Sharon

Started when I was in my teens. I can't imagine another way to live now.

Rowan

Who got you into it? I saw on your website you've been trained in all sorts of disciplines. How good are you? Can you get rid of my headaches from there?!

Sharon

Some people think so. There are shamanic practitioners who offer remote services. They find your frequency and promise to fix whatever ails you no matter where you are. I'm not saying they can't do it but I have enough doubt about my own ability to not offer it as a service. If that's what you're after there are people I can recommend.

Rowan

That's amazing, I didn't even know that was a thing. I keep wondering what it is that you actually see when you're in a trance. I grew up a little bit outside the mainstream so I'm open to new ideas. In a nutshell, what is it you do?

Sharon

I personally do power retrieval, soul retrieval, & shamanic extraction medicine.

Rowan

Soul retrieval sounds fascinating. How does it work?

Sharon

I use the drum, my main shamanic tool, and beat it to the 'eagle beat' (quite rapid, this is the same beat as the theta brainwaves when we're asleep). This induces an altered, higher state as it were, and once I connect to the client, set my intention to spirit in the Upper World (where lost soul parts are nurtured & looked after) that I wish to find and return lost soul parts for the healee. The feeling I liken it to is more like a lucid dream. I journey upwards, calling on my shamanic guides for assistance & protection. Each experience is different, but generally I am met by various, ancestors, guides, & occasionally totem animals that are connected to the client. They are taking care of the soul parts in readiness for them to be returned; they are never truly lost.

The ancestor/guide etc gives me an item, could be anything, and I ask them what soul part it represents, i.e. an arrow for their direction, a candle to bring their fire back, and so on. Then I give that ancestor something back in return as a thank you, energetically of course. I carry on doing this until I'm told by my guides that all parts have been returned. The feeling is very spacey but also quite euphoric. I bring the soul parts back to the physical world, and each part is blown into the heart chakra of the client, then again into the crown chakra; a rattle is then shaken around the crown chakra, sealing the soul parts back where they belong.

Rowan
This is fascinating.

Sharon
All different shamanic cultures have their own way of doing this; however, the basis always seems to be very similar.

Rowan
Maybe it's the cynic in me but it sounds as though it might be open to mischief. People could easily prey upon the sort of person attracted to that level of "power". You must have met people you wouldn't feel comfortable allowing to ferret about inside your higher consciousness?

Sharon
I used to have a client who felt like that. I can't mention names. I have known a couple of people, usually male, that have manipulated vulnerable people in various ways, to boost their own ego, bank balance, sense of power, or libido. But I guess that happens in all walks of life. Please just ask if you need me to elaborate on anything to do with the healing I've just described, as I've just given you a basic idea, I guess.

Rowan
It's fascinating. Would love to be able to go on one of these journeys with you sometime.

Sharon

Shamanic healing takes between 90 mins & 2 hours. That includes the consultation either side of it and dependent on the time it takes, it's between £45 & £60 x

Rowan

Just while I have you, from the perspective of the plot I'm working on, I've read that in ancient cultures some shaman used their gifts for less noble purposes. Could you maybe elaborate on that?

Sharon

That's not a weird question compared to what I've heard in the past 😄 It's all about intention of the shaman and if the recipient "believes" it can happen, as no doubt the shaman will make sure that the recipient knows he's going to do it, a bit like a gypsy curse, if you get me? I, personally, don't believe it can actually be done, and only soul "parts" can be lost (yet they can be returned) but a lot of bad luck can be stirred up. And yes, someone with a "dark heart" could really believe it's in their power. Hope this helps lol x

Rowan

Is there any atonement or morality based afterlife? A heaven or hell of sorts? Big one, eh?!

Sharon

I think that different cultures believe different things, but generally, the belief is that everything has come from light and will go back to it, whether good or evil. I guess there are different levels. But to be honest, no one really knows.

23

Silver Birch Academy, Wast Water
Monday, July 2, 1990

'They're just going to make you take it off again, Violet.'
    'They're just going to make you take it off again, Violet…'
Catherine sighs. She's grown used to having her own personal echo. Every time she says anything even vaguely conformist, Violet takes it upon herself to imitate her. She wouldn't mind if it wasn't such an excellent impression. She even manages to get the slightly apologetic note into her voice; the sense that it's an awful responsibility having to impart such bothersome information. Violet believes that Catherine has chosen to model herself on the wrong literary heroines. Whereas she feels a kinship for Cathy, for Jane Eyre, for Estella Havisham, Catherine has chosen to identify with Anne from the *Famous Five*.

'I'm just saying…'
'I'm just saying…'
Catherine slumps back against the cold, damp wall. It was painted bright yellow last summer but it seems to be

fading, as if the old brickwork is leaching the vibrant hue from its surface. She watches as Violet applies an extra coat of lipstick. It's a dark, plummy colour and it makes her look as if she's been eating chips with too much vinegar.

'Like it?' asks Violet, smacking her lips together. 'I nicked it from Boots. Walked right past the security guard. He was too busy looking at my tits to notice.'

Catherine decides not to follow the security guard's lead. She gives an encouraging smile, and forces herself not to ask any of the questions that are demanding attention in her mind. When did she go to Boots? How did she get there? When were they apart? She has learned how to handle her best friend, and knows that above all things, Violet hates to be caught out in a lie.

'Bet that Freya will be jealous as hell,' says Violet, looking at herself in the mirror. She seems to like what she sees. She looks more grown-up than Catherine. Boys notice her. Her hemline keeps travelling north and she manages to look as though she's seen it all, done it all, bought the T-shirt, which surprises Catherine, who knows for a fact that the most she has done with a boy was a rather sloppy kiss at the Young Farmers disco.

'Freya?' asks Catherine, glancing at her watch and hoping that Violet will finish up soon so they can make it to drama class before the lesson actually ends. 'Why would she be jealous?'

''Cos she thinks she's all that, doesn't she?' Violet shrugs. 'Like she's something special.'

'She seems okay,' says Catherine, who hasn't really given the new girl much thought since she arrived the previous month without so much as an introduction to the form group. She hasn't spoken to them much. Hasn't spoken to anybody really.

'Okay? She's all look-at-me, look-at-me. Trying to be all mysterious, with her weird little spell books and her nail varnish. God, it's pathetic.' She sucks her cheek. 'Cool shoes though.'

Violet can't make up her mind about the new girl. Catherine quite likes seeing her friend so conflicted. She looks at her the way dogs consider one another, weighing up whether this newcomer is a threat. She wears a certain expression whenever she considers the red-haired Irish girl. It's one Catherine knows so well. It's sullenness, an air of being spectacularly unimpressed. Elora had put it best when she said that, sometimes, Violet looked as though her mouth was full of somebody else's sick. Elora has a way with words.

'Her voice is nice,' says Catherine.

'Why don't you marry her then,' snaps Violet, baring her teeth. There's lipstick on her incisors.

'I was just saying.'

'*I was just saying.*'

'What were you just saying?'

Both girls turn towards the door as the soft Irish voice startles them. Freya is watching them. She looks like she may have been watching them for a long time. Catherine is struck, again, by how much older than them she looks. She could be sixteen at least, and though she wears no make-up and lets her tangled red hair fall over her face, she looks more like a woman than a child.

'I was saying I like your shoes,' says Violet, all smiles. 'How are you? Settling in?'

Freya glances at Catherine, giving her the tiniest wink. She knows she's caught them out but isn't going to make a thing of it. She gives them a smile. It's the first time they've seen her teeth. Catherine is surprised to see that they're not in great condition; stained with a peculiar patina that makes her think of the inside of a teapot.

'Bit weird isn't it?' confides Freya. 'I mean, I just go wherever but this feels a bit like we're in a cult or something. I did the morning yoga session my first day – all that downward-facing dog stuff with my arse right up in the air. There was only me and the teacher! You buggers could have told me it was optional.'

Catherine laughs. 'We've done plenty of that. I still like the meditation sessions but there aren't as many as there used to be. Mr Sixpence did all that stuff. And the reiki.'

'Yeah, I saw that in the brochure. Reiki? I thought it was something you did to your garden in autumn.'

Violet laughs, a little too loud. 'Do you need the mirror? I was doing my make-up...'

'Yeah, looks great. I don't really wear it. Sensitive skin. I hate my freckles though. Do you think you could do mine some time?'

Violet can't help but grin. 'Yeah? I mean, yeah, sure. Like, whatever.'

'Who's this Sixpence bloke I keep hearing about?' asks Freya, coming closer to the mirror. Up close she smells nice, like biscuits and old soap.

'Old hippy who lived in the woods.' Violet shrugs, making room. 'Sodded off one night. The police came and everything. It was cool.'

'Yeah? What happened to him?'

Catherine feels herself being excluded and decides not to let it happen again. 'Police have left the file open but they seem to think he's just gone off on one of his pilgrimages. He used to give assemblies about it. He was a shaman.'

'A what?'

'They talk to the dead,' explains Violet. 'Or they think they can. They travel between this world and the other world. I dunno if it's rubbish but he was nice.'

'Wish I'd met him,' says Freya, smoothing her eyebrows in the mirror. The cuffs of her jumper ride up. Catherine sees white lines across the blue veins of her wrists. She looks away before the new girl can see.

'He won't be back now,' says Violet. 'His van's still there because they can't get it back to the road but they've had a bonfire with his stuff.'

'They?'

'Tunstall. Rideal.'

'I met them. They seem nice.'

Violet snorts, scornfully. 'Tunstall's all right, but he's wetter than an otter's pocket. Rideal's just a posh wanker.'

'What do your parents think of this place?' asks Freya, chattily.

'I couldn't care less what they think,' snaps Violet, angrily. 'They pay the bills and leave me alone and don't make a fuss when I get in trouble. They're perfect parents, really,' she adds, nastily.

'Your dad seems nice,' says Freya, plaiting her fringe and then unplaiting it again. 'He's the vicar, yeah? I met him on my induction day. Friendly.'

'He does his best,' says Catherine, loyally. 'He didn't know you were joining, actually. He was surprised that there was a new girl. He's on the Board, you see. He was a bit miffed. Said so to Mummy.'

'Mummy,' snorts Violet.

'It was all a bit last minute.' Freya shrugs. 'My family work away. My guardian's out in Saudi Arabia making money but the school I was at before couldn't take me for the whole summer so they got me in here, last minute.'

'Your guardian?' asks Catherine.

'I've moved around a lot,' says Freya, pushing her hair up like a matinee idol. The action exposes a patch of torn scalp; a perfect patch of ridged flesh, completely hairless. Violet spots it too and Catherine has to reach out and squeeze her arm to stop her commenting.

'What about your mam? Your dad?'

'Are you two coppers or something?' asks Freya, looking from one to the other. Then she grins. 'Do you smoke? I've only got a few cigs left? Do you know anybody who might pop to the shop for us? I'll share if you do.'

Catherine doesn't get a chance to answer. Violet jumps in for both of them. 'Smoke? Yeah, I love a ciggie. Trying to kick them but you know how it is. I reckon you could get served. We go shopping in Keswick sometimes. It's boring unless you like fell-boots but I need some things and I'm good at getting stuff past the security guard in Boots. There's a bus on a Tuesday. Do you want to come?'

Freya turns from the mirror and looks from one to the other, weighing them up, surveying them like she's choosing a Christmas turkey. At length, she nods. 'I'm Freya, in case you didn't know. Like the goddess.'

'The goddess?' asks Catherine, and she feels a strange prickling anxiety all over her skin.

'I'll lend you some books.' Freya smiles. 'I'm into things that not everybody understands.'

'Like what?' asks Violet, brightly.

Freya rolls up her sleeve. On her forearm, picked out in fine white scars, is a stick figure. He carries a spear, and shield, and there are crude tusks protruding from the ruined mass of his face.

'Like this,' she says.

24

An unnamed road on the north bank of Wast Water
12.48pm

'Second... Snowdrop, second yeah... up and to the right, that's third... Now turn the radio up... Christ, that really is some view... Sorry, nearly lost control there, bloody silly wooden steering wheel. Who'd have thought that was a good idea...? Fuck, are you hot? I'm roasting... Here, can you light this when you get a free hand? Good lass, cheers... Aye, turn it up, turn it up...'

Rowan's fingertips slip from the steering wheel and the little car lurches to the right, the tyres on the driver's side briefly chewing gravel and air. Beneath them is a fifteen-foot drop down to sharp rocks and icy black waters. Swearing, Rowan grabs at the wheel, swinging them painfully back onto the winding grey road that hugs the curve of the lake.

'Don't mention that to your mum,' mutters Rowan. 'Or any of it, really. We went for a nice walk. I wanted some air. We bonded.'

'Do I have to fib? She might be okay with it.'

Rowan shoots his niece a look. 'I'm going to educate you,

little one. Pay attention, after you've lit that fag. Look, lies are horrible, terrible things. They're a virus. They're bad for the soul and can spread like cancer. When coppers and politicians use them, they should be roasted on a spit. It costs me a little bit of myself every time I have to resort to an untruth or exaggeration. But – and like the rear end of your mother's wife, this is a big but – they're also a kindness. You see, it's the people who respond poorly to the truth who force people like me, and you, to employ the compassionate balm of fiction. Fabrication. Duplicity. One day, we'll all be able to tell each other things with full and frank honesty. Until then, best stay shtum.'

'Shtum?'

'Aye. It's an onomatopoeic word. It's the sound of a truth suffocating behind superglued lips.'

'Sorry?'

'Don't be.'

Rowan looks out at the burnished pewter bowl of the valley, ringed in places by dense, spiky woodland. It's a brutally cold day, the wind and rain assaulting the car like fists and boots. It's his first time behind the wheel of the vintage Nissan Figaro that Serendipity and her wife like to use for picnics when they feel like treating themselves to a little luxury. It's recently been restored to the pale blue of the factory floor. It's Jo's pride and joy. She takes the family Kia to work each day just so that using the Figaro feels more like a special occasion. Snowdrop hadn't believed her uncle when he said that her two mums wouldn't object to him borrowing it. But he'd shown her the message on his phone; a carefree acquiescence and instruction to "be careful". Rowan had been quite proud of the speed with which he had typed the message with his bandaged hands, and the ease with which he had mimicked his sister's text-voice. Mud streaks are already making a mess of the white-wall tyres.

In the passenger seat, Snowdrop is doing her best to obey his multitude of requests, holding his mobile phone to his ear while changing gear, operating the radio and attempting to light a cigarette on the broken lighter by the gearstick.

Rowan glances down to the lake. A VW Transporter is parked in a small bay a few feet above a shingly cove at the water's edge. It is being investigated by half a dozen Herdwick sheep. In the water, two men stand bare-chested, their skin alabaster white; steam rising from their shoulders and from swimming caps that make them look like spent matches.

Rowan rolls the car to a halt in the parking area at the end of the road. The copse of trees that surrounds St Olaf's is a couple of hundred metres ahead. There are several vehicles in the car park; mostly working vehicles – flat-bed pick-ups and bottle-green Land Rovers. There's a blue BMW, a black Jeep and battered red works van; its mudguards clogged up with torn grass and thick mud. Beyond the car park, the road peters out at the front of the big hotel. It's a long, imposing building that looks up to the task of doing daily battle with the elements. Its front is the colour of old butter and thick black gloss serves as mascara around the dark windows.

Rowan scanned the website before they left, taking a mental note of the names of the owners and a little about the place's history, in case he needed a tool with which to start a conversation with a taciturn local. He now knows that this is where British climbing began. It has been a hotel for two centuries or more, providing much-needed lodgings for the merchants and tradesmen who laboured over Black Sail, Sty Head and Burnmoor passes to ply their trade in adjacent valleys. It has played host to the great men of British climbing: Victorian upper-class daredevils who pitted themselves against the towering crags and made daily wagers with the elements. Many of those early pioneers are buried in the consecrated ground of St Olaf's.

Rowan climbs out of the car, wincing as his fingers touch metal. It's a cold, desolate spot. A cold breeze seems to lift from the lake, casting patterns onto the still silver surface, lifting the dead leaves from the pockmarked car park. For a moment Rowan's mind seems to spin and eddy, as if some part of him were drifting into the dank gloom. He feels cold all the way through.

Sharp air chafes his cheeks. Beneath the smeared pink salve, Rowan can feel virgin skin turning duck-egg blue.

'Good God, you look like Shane MacGowan's stunt double!'

Rowan turns at the unexpected greeting. It takes him a moment to recognise the small, bald-headed man who stands in front of a budget hatchback. Last time he saw Damian Crow was twenty years back and then he had seemed a colossus of a man: lantern-jawed and straight-backed; the sort of Biblical icon that Charlton Heston did so well. Age has withered him. He's probably a little shorter than Rowan and there's a touch of a stoop to his posture. He wears glasses atop a prominent nose and looks cold inside his waterproof and fleece. His smile shows teeth that are all his own, though whether he cherishes them is open to debate. They're a colour that Rowan could best liken to salted caramel.

'Bloody hell,' says Rowan, returning the smile. 'Good job we're meeting at a graveyard – you look like you need the lie-down!'

Pleasantries exchanged, Rowan holds up his hands. 'Ouch,' says Crow, wincing in solidarity. 'Have you got the little bastard who did it yet?'

Rowan nods. 'Wasn't so little, to be honest. If he'd been little, it might not have happened.'

'That was the problem, was it?' asks Crow, closing the car door and crossing to where Rowan stands. 'Just too big for you?'

'That and the crowbar, yeah.'

'I always imagined opening a place called The Crow Bar,' says the old reporter, wistfully. Up close, Rowan's gratified to get the smell of lunchtime ale and last night's fags. There's something reassuring about somebody who sticks with their vices in the face of all the evidence.

'You were always better this side of the bar,' says Rowan, as Snowdrop comes and joins him. She smiles, politely. 'This is Snowdrop, my niece.'

'A pleasure, love,' says Crow, and the flat vowel sound betrays his Yorkshire roots. He's been a local reporter since 1981 but is still an outsider in the valley. He gives Rowan his attention. 'You didn't mention whether there might be a fee for my expertise.'

Rowan grins. 'There's the pleasure of my company,' he says, doubting it will be enough. 'And an acknowledgement when the book comes out. And a chance to remember a time when you were as young and good-looking as I am now.'

'You always were a gobshite.' Crow smiles, then mouths an apology at Snowdrop. 'You should have seen this one on his first day in the job. Purple hair, tattoos all over him, earring in each ear. We thought the gaffer had gone mad for hiring him and by Christ he was a pugnacious little sod. Do you know what that word means?'

Snowdrop nods. 'Fighty?'

'Not far off.' Crow smiles again. 'Told me on day one he was going to have my job inside a year.'

'I never did,' says Rowan, surprised at the accusation.

Crow looks at him with intelligent blue eyes and nods, fulsomely. 'You bloody did, son. Couldn't tell whether to laugh or smack you in the face. I decided neither would end well for me. You've done well for yourself.' He narrows his eyes. 'Could have done better, of course, but couldn't we all?'

Rowan nods in the direction of the church. They fall into step, crunching over the pitted, damp floor.

'So, no fee?' asks Crow, a little disconsolately.

'I'm a one-man band,' says Rowan, apologetically. 'And if this story doesn't work out, I'm going to find myself in more debt than Germany circa 1919.'

'Chris said it was a book – not a story…'

'I don't know what it is – I just know it's got legs.'

'It's my story,' butts in Snowdrop, as they approach the little track that leads to the copse of yew trees that hide St Olaf's. 'We're going to share the credit.'

'I'll bet.' Crow laughs, giving Rowan a knowing look.

'Chris told you what I'm looking into, yeah?' says Rowan, hurriedly.

'The girls in '91?' Crow nods. 'I looked out my old notes for you. You must know something I don't because it wouldn't even make a footnote in my memoirs.'

Rowan looks away, over the low stone wall to where a ram with the largest testicles Rowan has ever seen is trying to mount a ram with the second largest testicles Rowan has ever seen.

'Bloody hell,' mutters Crow beside him, as he subtly manoeuvres Snowdrop out of the way.

'Country folk with country ways,' mumbles Rowan, and they share a nice moment as they arrive at the lych-gate. Even in the dreary grey weather, the churchyard looks inviting.

'Smallest church in England,' says Crow, with a touch of pride. 'Highest mountain, deepest lake. I've never much liked this valley though – a bit too bleak for my tastes. Always makes me want to go and become a painter or a poet or something.'

'Let me know how you get on with the "something",' says Rowan, leading the way. He knows from a quick glance at a local history website that there has been a place of worship on the spot for 500 years, but the current scout-hut-style building has only been here since 1892. The roof timbers are said to come from Viking ships. Before the grounds were consecrated, people from the valley had to carry their dead across the old Corpse Road to St Catherine's at Boot. He's read grisly tales about processions of mourners becoming lost in the fog crossing the fells – of horses, coffins, wagons and mourners all swallowed up by the elements. He wonders how much is exaggeration and how much fact. Wonders when that started to matter.

'He's over yonder,' says Crow, gesturing towards the furthest corner of the graveyard. Around them, headstones rise from the damp ground like shark teeth. He glimpses a perfect rectangle of polished black – a memorial to a climber lost on Great Gable in 1919. Steps between family plots: weathered inscriptions alongside fresh memorials, bright bouquets beside little plastic flowers weathered down to a translucent white.

Rowan ducks beneath the boughs of the overhanging yew and looks upon the grave of Derrick Millward. His name, together with date of birth and death, are etched in white letters on a simple grey headstone. There is a space beneath, and in the centre, a line by Yeats.

STEP SOFTLY: A DREAM LIES BURIED HERE.

'It was a good turnout,' says Crow, stopping to look past the church to the mass of Great Gable beyond. 'There weren't many people knew he was a valley lad when he first moved back here and this is a place where they have a hell of a long memory.'

'Space looks to be at a premium,' says Rowan, glancing at the shark's mouth of gravestones crowded in the small space.

'He was the last one to be planted,' says Crow, his hands in his pockets – a cigarette suddenly clamped between his teeth. He rocks on his heels, the heel of one shoe grinding into some greenish gravel atop the nearest plot. 'He got preferential treatment because he's from the valley but even then there were some buggers kicked up a fuss.'

Rowan can't help but imagine what lies beneath his feet. He crouches by the grave, a tired sort of tightness across his back.

'Some people come and scatter their ashes here without asking permission,' explains Crow, as Snowdrop looks for the right expression for her face to relax into. 'They've had to put a stop to it because it was starting to look like there'd been a dirty snowfall round here, so your chances of buying a plot are zilch. You can still be buried if there's a family plot though even then it's a pain for the ground staff.'

'I didn't know he had children,' says Rowan, focusing on the space on the headstone that waits for the next inscription.

'That'll be for her,' says Crow, a smile in his voice. 'He must have had to properly twist the vicar's arm to get him to agree to that. An unmarried couple in a joint plot? It's a good job everybody in Wasdale's so open-minded.'

Rowan glances back at him. 'Go on...'

Crow grins, delighted to know something that the younger man doesn't. 'She told me at Millward's funeral. They're going to be buried together. She wouldn't marry him but she's happy enough to go in the ground with him. She said she agreed to it because it was what he wanted. They'd been thick as thieves for thirty years and neither have any kids so I guess it was a comfort to him. By the end he deserved all the comfort he could get. Not that he's been allowed to rest in peace.'

Rowan stands up, legs creaking. He turns and leans against the grave, willing to flatter Crow if it means filling in another piece of the puzzle. 'Go on, Damian, educate your junior reporter.'

He sheds the years like an exotic dancer casting off veils. He makes himself comfortable, one flabby buttock wedged atop the headstone of a hard-working Borrowdale farmer. Locates a cigarette and lights it from the tip of his last one and blows out a plume of absolute satisfaction.

'You'll know the name Rideal,' says Crow, and seems gratified to receive a nod in return. 'He's the money behind the hippy school.'

'Silver Birch,' chips in Snowdrop.

'Well done, love. Aye, that's the place. I was still in short pants when it opened but it was always one of the schools that people knew little bits about – always a rumour about some celebrity or pop star or an artist having a nipper boarding there. It had decent enough grades from what I recall but it wouldn't stand up to scrutiny now. You can have all the New Age philosophies that you want – Ofsted wants to know you're doing things properly. That wasn't the case back then. They couldn't even give you a straightforward price on tuition fees and boarding. None of that was particularly important as the people at the top. They ran it more in a spirit of philanthropy than as a business.'

'Rideal was happy to lose money?' asks Rowan.

Crow smiles. 'I don't know about "happy", but "willing", certainly. Never had to struggle, that one. The way I heard it, he met Tunstall when he was at university.'

'Tunstall was the head teacher?'

'Aye, that's him. Scholarship lad from Consett, over near Newcastle. Went to one of the posh universities in Edinburgh. Rideal was studying economics while Tunstall was studying philosophy. Unlikely bedfellows but it was obviously a firm friendship because when Tunstall wanted to start his pioneering new alternative education provision, his old pal Rideal bankrolled it.'

'To the tune of how much?' asks Rowan, looking down the lake in the direction of the stately home where Silver Birch had previously flourished.

'Hard to say.' Crow shrugs. 'Rideal already owned the old Hall and the building that's now Tunstall's pad – up there through the woods. Even so, it can't have been cheap.'

'What was in it for Rideal?'

'You cynic.' Crow smiles. 'It was a chance to do some good, of course. Though he was a slippery sod, there's no doubt about that. It took Marlish a lot of his creative writing skills to come up with something good to say about him at the memorial service.'

Rowan shoots Snowdrop a look. She doesn't see it in time to keep quiet. 'He's dead?'

'I should hope so, love,' says Crow, licking his palm and stubbing out his cigarette. 'Took ill on the mountain, out hiking with Tunstall. This must have been ten years after the sale had gone through. Tunstall came barrelling back down the Screes for the Mountain Rescue but they couldn't pinpoint him. The smart money says he's under the mountain. Under the Screes. There are mineshafts and crevices and smuggler holes all over this valley. I've no doubt that wife of his didn't wait the obligatory few years to have him declared dead. That's somebody who knows how to spend.'

Rowan realises he's rubbing his sore hands along the smooth edge of the headstone. 'The Mountain Rescue has had their money's worth out of that school,' he muses. 'I've heard an intriguing whisper about the two girls they found.'

'Three, wasn't it? There were three, I'm sure.'

'No, two were found out at Borrowdale. We're interested in what happened to them – and whether there is any truth to the rumours about the third girl. Some say she's in the lake.'

Crow closes an eye, staring a hole in Rowan. 'I think I'd know if that were true, lad.'

'There was something on Facebook,' protests Snowdrop, unimpressed with his attitude. 'And Pickle says Violet has remembered all sorts of horrible things.'

Crow looks scornfully from one to the other. 'Facebook? And if you mean Pickle the stoner, I wouldn't trust him to count his own legs.'

'Rude,' mutters Snowdrop, pouting and turning away.

Rowan suddenly feels utterly ridiculous. He needs this to be true. Needs to be onto something with meat at its centre.

'There's more,' he says, trying to sound positive. 'I've heard whispers about them being found not wearing a stitch – strange markings on their bodies...'

Crow shakes his head. 'Hey, if it helps it sell you say what you like, mate – I just don't know anything about that. You'd be best speaking to Eve Cater, though she can be a cantankerous sod. I heard some charity was going to establish an award in her name. She'll be loving that. Always was a proud one.'

Rowan pulls a face. 'I can't make sense of it, Damian,' he admits. 'I'm not saying she wasn't a good copper but of the two cases she was involved in that I've looked into, she came up blank both times.'

Crow cocks his head. 'You mean the old hippy? What was his name? Arthur Farthing, or something?'

'Arthur Sixpence,' he corrects him. 'Caretaker-cum-spiritual-adviser.'

'We got about fifteen centimetres out of that, nowt more,' says Crow dismissively.

'I don't understand,' butts in Snowdrop.

'It's the way you measure columns in newspapers,' says Rowan. 'It's not very much.' He gives Crow his attention. 'I'm surprised it wasn't worth more – even if you'd just got a couple of complaints from parents about police traipsing over the posh school where they sent their little darlings, it's worth more than that.'

Crow breathes out, long and slow. 'Editor of the day was a golfing pal of Rideal's,' he says. 'You know how the funny handshakes and the nods and the winks go around here, and around plenty other places too. I won't say I was leaned on but there was no appetite for more. It was a shame too – I'd got some decent quotes from the farmer who called the coppers in.'

Rowan flashes a smile. 'Willing to share?'

Crow shrugs. 'I doubt it makes much difference now. Gordon Shell – I think he's still alive but he'll be geriatric-and-a-half by now – he was quite pally with this Sixpence chap. Reading between the lines, I think Gordon might have enjoyed having the occasional smoke on the old peace pipe, and that isn't a euphemism, before you start. He told me he'd meet up with Sixpence a couple of times a week, just to have a few cans and chat about the world. He said Sixpence had been around, seen the world. Spoke about him like he was a guru, which I suppose isn't that far off the mark.'

'Explain,' says Rowan. Then adds: 'For Snowdrop.'

'Well, Gordon was pretty clear that there was a damn sight more to Sixpence than some old hippy in a school bus. He'd travelled. Knew old languages – languages people don't even speak anymore. Fascinated with all the old caves up that way too – the mineshafts they dug centuries back. Forever looking for new ways into the ground. The way Gordon told me, it was like he was a sort of faith healer. He'd help people if they asked. If you got migraines he could talk to you until they went away. If you were feeling under pressure he could help put you back together. I mean Gordon was very cautious about telling me this – it was the mid-eighties and your lot were hardly popular.'

'My lot?'

'Crusties. Hippies. New Age Travellers. The Peace Convoy.'

Rowan says nothing. The silence becomes uncomfortable.

'I have got something underlined in my notes – a quote we never carried,' says Crow, quickly. 'Reverend Marlish, he was there with Tunstall and Rideal and a few of the parents and pupils, putting on a united front. He said Sixpence was "a prophet". Seemed strange to me a religious man would use that word. It was Tunstall who corrected him – he said Sixpence was a shaman.'

Rowan stares at the grave of Derrick Millward, trying to fit the bits together.

'Sixpence had no kids?'

'I've got a quote from Detective Sergeant Eve Cater,' he says, rummaging in his pocket for his phone. He squints at the screen, clearly looking at photographs of notes dragged out of storage after having his curiosity piqued. 'She said he'd done a lot of good by a lot of people and he had a family of sorts, but that was too vague to use and as it happened, we never ran much more than you've seen. She was grateful for that, as far as I can recall. Slipped a few exclusives my way.'

Rowan suddenly feels an urge to hold Eve Cater upside down and shake her until the secrets fall out. 'My brain's hurting,' he admits, and looks around in search of liquid sustenance.

'That way.' Crow smiles. 'Hotel and bar and the birthplace of British rock-climbing, if you're interested. I'd sit there and have a good hard think.'

Rowan nods. "Thinking" certainly rhymes with his plan.

25

The Coffin Road, Boot
Tuesday, October 29, 1991
4.44pm

Winter is on its way. There's no snow on the fells but there's a saw-toothed sharpness to the air. The russets and golds, the honeys and caramels of a few days ago are yielding to the bleached bone and pure velvet blackness of the year's end.

Eve breathes deep as she climbs. Sucks in the grey-green aroma of sheep shit and grass. Her boots crunch over the pitted surface of the rock-strewn path: a noise like teeth crunching through ice. She can make out the village of Boot spread out below: little white houses scattered across the lower fells like seeds tossed by a giant hand. She's already two miles up the Corpse Road. The view is far from picture-postcard but there is a timelessness to it that makes her want to write something poetic.

She looks up as she hears footsteps on stone. Sees Derrick. Smiles at the sight of him, in his big overcoat and woolly hat, moving over ground that he seems to have sucked up through the soles of his shoes since he moved back to the valley. He's sold the agency in Blackpool. He exists for one case now. One investigation. One pursuit that has become an obsession. She's forced him to come along today – to make the walk up to Burnmoor Lodge – to sit at the edge of the tarn, feet bobbing in water cold enough to squeeze the breath from their lungs.

They go at their own speeds – that's the unspoken agreement between them. He's better on the fells than her and she'd rather walk alone than be responsible for slowing somebody down. Their relationship is built on many such unwritten contracts. He never tries the door to her bedroom but she never brings anybody home when there is a chance he might see. He has never known if he sees her as wife or daughter.

'Slow down, I'll get to you. Don't hurt yourself...' She stops, short, as she sees the look on his face. His eyes are wide – his face, still puffy despite drastic weight loss, ripples like a disturbed lake as he careers towards her. His breath is raspy, like there's a boot on his windpipe.

'The vicar,' he splutters, reaching for her and grabbing her, hard, by the forearms. He's in her face, spittle flecking out from his lips. 'Marlish. He's at the lodge, up top. Gordon Shell came over on the four-wheeler, shouting like it was closing time... Him and Rideal – that slippery fucker – they were up there walking. Shell all but grabbed the vicar by the middle and slung him on the quad...'

'Easy, Derrick, tell me again...'

Millward bends double, panting. 'His daughter's gone,' he gasps. 'Gone missing. Her and her friend, the girl you know from Silver Birch. They were due back from Keswick hours ago…'

'Okay,' says Eve, soothingly. She tries to calm him. 'Derrick, it's not even late – they'll be back before we know it. Violet's turning into a bit of a terror, so they say…'

'No,' he shouts, making fists. 'They went off with a man. A busker.'

Eve feels as though there are cold fingers creeping up her neck and teasing through her hair. 'No… there's no way…'

'Him.' Derrick nods, his chest heaving. 'He's here. He's took them. He's took them to show us he can…'

Eve takes his arm and steers him onto one of the big stones that mark this choppy, disjointed section of the Coffin Path.

'Derrick, he wouldn't come back here. He's known here…'

'We took Pearl's money, Eve,' hisses Millward, eyes bulging. 'We could have stopped this. Told the proper coppers what we were doing; what we knew…'

'I'm a detective chief inspector,' growls Eve, furious. 'I'm a proper copper. I'm *the* proper copper! And I've indulged you in this wild goose chase because I like being with you and because I think Cormac Pearl might have something to do with the disappearance of Mr Sixpence. But we know nothing. Not real. Not for sure. So if you go blundering in telling my colleagues we know about this – that we know who they should be looking for…'

'That doesn't matter,' says Derrick, shaking his head. 'You know what he'll do…'

'No we don't!' snaps Eve. 'We have nothing that can

help. Let me manage things properly, Derrick. Keep things in-house. Keep things small...'

'There's already a piece going out on the evening news,' gasps Derrick, trying to stand and losing his footing. 'Eve, I'd never do anything to cause you any problems. I wouldn't tell them you knew anything, but I need to go in to the station and speak to whoever's running this...'

'I'll run it,' says Eve, firmly. 'I'll tell the team what they need to know. I swear to you, this isn't him. There might not be a *him*.'

'I'll never tell them about the money,' says Derrick, looking deep into her eyes. 'I'd die before I betrayed you.'

'There was no money,' hisses Eve, in his face. 'You got that? I'm a good copper. I'm changing the way things work, Derrick. I'm making a difference.'

'We need to stop him. He knows this area. If he has Sixpence he can hide the girls...'

Eve feels as though there is a hot snake coiling and uncoiling in her stomach. She's worked so hard. Given so damn much. She doesn't deserve to lose it all.

'The school,' she says. 'You search the grounds then – I'll organise things my end and try to get you some space to manoeuvre. I'll keep them away until you tell me you need me.'

Eve begins to move down the mountain. There's a police radio in the car. In five minutes she could be with Rev Marlish, telling him the importance of keeping this investigation strictly low-key, promising to do whatever it takes to get their daughter back safe. Things might be okay. They might still all work out...

'Eve,' shouts Derrick, and the tone of voice makes her

stop and spin back, facing into a wind that carries the smells of sweat and rain and the old, newly stirred earth.

'What else?' she asks, and it feels as though there is a steel band inside her bones, thrumming with an electrical current.

'There's a third girl. Catherine. Violet. And a new girl – Freya. She's a redhead.'

Eve swallows, drily. Crime scene photos flash in her mind. The man they're hunting has a thing for redheads. He cut the hair off one when he was a boy. He left Blackpool with one.

'Go to the grounds,' she instructs. 'I'll be there as soon as I can. It will be okay, Derrick. For everybody…'

As she turns and starts to run down the path, Eve feels a wave of self-loathing wash over her. She shakes it away. She doesn't want to look at the thought that was chewing at her skull as she stood listening to Derrick. Doesn't want to admit that while he spoke of bribes and secrets, she had glanced down at the rocky floor and sought the perfect-sized stone with which to smash his head until it came apart: until all the things he could use against her spilled out onto the muddy grass.

26

The rain has started coming down harder here, on this quiet mountain road clinging to the lower lip of the Borrowdale Valley. It blackens the pitted grey surface; its fissured shell twinkling, like iron ore, beneath the yellowed moon.

Were it a brighter day, Glebe House would glisten in salmon pink: a million-million grains of sandstone reflecting back the sunlight. Here, long past sunset on a wet Thursday in November, the stately home looks as though it has been made out of mud bricks. In this light, with the storm blowing in across the fells, it is a cardboard cut-out: a black silhouette picking out pointy chimneys, steep-sided roofs; a bar graph topped with spikes. Beyond it, behind it, past the high stone wall that marks the end of the private land, there are only fells and straggled copses of woodland. They'd stopped at the aptly named "Surprise View", flicking the headlights to full beam to gaze upon the valley's famed "inverted clouds" – a meteorological phenomenon caused by cold temperatures and high pressure. They had briefly been above the clouds, looking down upon a carpet of soft, dirty fleece.

'*Like beaks on a coffin lid,*' says Rowan, broodingly, as

the raindrops peck furiously at the roof of the car. They've parked with their backs to the fells; looking up towards the grand property with its imposing doorway, great crinkled columns of granite: a crush of dazzling black and white. The lights of a silver Range Rover glare, too bright, through the rain-streaked glass. Rowan closes his eyes but an image remains oddly stamped on the darkness; an ultra-violet outline of a middle-aged man in a baseball cap, fumbling about with the windscreen wipers and headlamps while chatting into a mobile phone. An old, conked-out-looking Volvo clatters into a space beside them: a damp clanking of chassis and surging gutters.

Rowan's happy here, in the dark of the classic Nissan Figaro. It's peaceful. He'd heard some nearby church bells chime a few moments ago; a pleasingly old-fashioned sound, rolling out of some mist-wreathed bell tower with a low and sonorous authority, shushing the raindrops and the cars like impudent children. He's content. Maudlin, but acceptably so. He's beginning to regret sucking down a lungful of Pickle's finest before they'd bundled him into the car: a downcast figure trudging beneath a big umbrella wearing a newly pressed shirt, good jeans and a crumpled corduroy jacket. They'd even given him a shave. He looks piratical with his sharp goatee, his pupils big Kalamata olives. His heart's racing. He feels paranoid and nervous. He can feel pressure building in his head.

So many problems. So many deadlines. So much money! You've fallen so far, lad. How did you fuck it up, howdidyoufuckitup? How, lad...?

'You'll be great,' says Snowdrop, in the back seat. 'I'll cough three times if you start to get into trouble.'

Serendipity, driving, gives her daughter a look of pure love. Dippy's almost glowing tonight, so proud of her baby brother and her unstoppable newshound daughter. She'd cranked up her happy pop music so loud on the journey that the Figaro's long-suffering windows rattled in the frames.

'There's not even anything to worry about,' she says, brightly. 'Uncle Rowan's been talking to people since he was little. He's a great public speaker. That's why the politicians wanted him – he's got a way with words and manages to say what he means without coming across as too much of an arrogant sod. If it wasn't for all the skeletons in his closet he could be making big decisions by now.'

Rowan looks at her as if she's mad. 'Dippy, I sometimes wonder whether you're watching the same film as everybody else. I'm living in a cow barn, unemployed...'

'Self-employed,' they chorus.

'...and I'm about to talk about creativity to people who are already better than me.' He looks at her sadly, a Labrador full of apology for having eaten the Easter eggs. 'Can't you say I'm ill?'

Serendipity laughs as she shakes her head and opens the car door. At once, a swirl of wet air rushes inside the little car, bringing a squeal from Snowdrop. Rowan raises his hands and looks at the brown, calfskin driving gloves they had forced him into amid a symphony of curses, screeches and tears. Beneath, the wounds appear to be healing. There was less seepage this morning when they changed the bandages and he only took the recommended number of painkillers with his morning coffee, rather than doubling up.

Grumbling, Rowan steps from the vehicle and gives it a pat on the roof as if it were a gun dog that had brought back a golden eagle. Dippy's driving style is a tad gung-ho for Rowan's tastes. The half-hour journey from Holmrook has been a succession of near-death bends and vertical drops and the Figaro's narrow wheels spun over nothingness on more than one occasion. Rowan has a memory of locking eyes with a terrified Herdwick as they blared past in a riot of stones and spray. He's sure it had given him a sympathetic glance as it jumped over the low stone wall.

He hears Snowdrop running around from the rear of the car to join him; her feet made elegantly clunky by big rainbow-patterned Doc Martens. She's paired them with polka-dot tights and a pair of dungarees. Her brown charity-shop duffel coat gives off the slight aroma of moist canine but Rowan finds it quite a warm, comforting scent. He feels Serendipity press against him as they troop across the driveway towards the bright lights of the big front door. She smells good; all home baking and cherry tobacco. He leans towards her, rubbing her head with his own. The hessian of her chunky coat is tickly against his cheek. He's overcome with a sudden gratitude for her; her presence in his life, her enduring affection for him despite his countless failings and absences. He wants to say something kind but can't seem to find the words. He's always been better written down.

'You look nice, Dippy,' he manages. 'Thanks for coming.'

She looks pleased and makes a show of tossing the tassels of her woolly hat, offering a glance at the purple-grey dreadlocks that snake down into the hood of her denim jacket. Serendipity is always fun to look at. Tonight, she's wearing a pleated tartan skirt and mismatched knee-socks, her pink toddler knees turning white in the teeth of the rain. Her make-up, phone, purse and snacks are stuffed into a backpack that bears the legend **"So Geek – So Chic"**. She'll be forty-five on her next birthday.

Rowan looks up as two glowing white headlamps rake through the darkness, illuminating high walls and pointed black spikes. Rowan thinks of searchlights. He looks at the rain-slicked vehicles lining the grand driveway. Range Rovers cheek-by-jowl with tatty farm vehicles and utilitarian hatchbacks. The new arrival is a boxy people carrier. Rowan glimpses a dint in the bonnet on the offside. He catches sight of the passenger: a small, pale-faced woman with glasses and frizzy hair. The tall, angular-looking man at the wheel gives a little flick of a salute by way of greeting. Rowan is aghast to see he's also wearing driving gloves.

'That's Catherine,' says Serendipity, leaning over. 'You're in luck.'

Despite her initial reservations, Serendipity has embraced Snowdrop's foray into Rowan's world and is now keen to see where their little investigation might go. She doesn't seem to be able to conceive of it as an actual marketable story – something for the page or the screen. But she'd like to find out what happened to the three girls thirty years ago and whether it prompted Violet to seek out the services of her shamanic practitioner friend. She's on nodding terms with Catherine Marlish, and has managed to flesh out her knowledge of the vicar's daughter through a few conversations with the most indiscreet of the local gossips.

She seems eager to fill in the gaps for Rowan, despite his repeated assurance that he just wants to get this evening over with, and then sink onto the sofa with a warm whisky and a cold compress.

'That must be her man, driving,' says Serendipity. 'Terence. One "R", which tells you all you need to know.'

'Dippy, I'm trying to concentrate...'

'Works at the power station. Some kind of engineer. They've been together a couple of years. He's got a daughter from a first marriage but Catherine's never had kids. She's still tied to the apron strings by the sound of it – lives in Mum and Dad's pocket. She's got her own place – Terence lives there now too – but she's home at the vicarage in Seascale most of her time, so I'm told... Oh look out, here's trouble...'

The security light above the arch spurts into life as the front door opens, eclipsing the warm sepia lamplight that bleeds out through the stained glass. A broad-shouldered, thick-set woman stalks onto the porch like a ship's captain demanding a closer view of the approaching icebergs. She's all pleated skirt and comfortable, wide-fitting shoes. Her brown jacket is fastened over a soft plum-coloured jumper and, even from this distance, Rowan can tell that the jewel that sparkles on the surface of the locket around her neck, is very real. Two cats streak out from the open doorway behind her. Rowan would like to think of them as pets seeking a breath of fresh air, but the speed with which they move suggests they've been held captive for some terrible purpose.

'You must be the writer,' she says, over the sound of rain

hitting stone. 'I'm Marjorie Hawkins. Anybody who knows me will vouch for the fact I'm an easy-going individual, but it had been hinted during the last meeting that perhaps tonight I would be giving the address. Goodness knows I've waited long enough.' She waves a hand airily. 'This is my house, by the way. It's Glebe. A lot of people say Globe, which suggests either an epidemic of myopia, or that nobody has the common sense to concentrate anymore. I have a granddaughter who simply will not sit still! Can't concentrate – always has to have something going *bibbety-bip* in her hands. I've banned it from the house.' She frowns, a deep groove in her forehead, like a coin hole in a slot machine. 'Everybody seems late tonight so it's not really a problem. Still, one does think that perhaps Moses miscounted. Thou Shalt Be Punctual would have made such a difference.'

Despite the rain, Rowan, Dippy and Snowdrop stand still, shoulders hunched, each seemingly disinclined to walk up the steps to receive their less than enthusiastic greeting. Rowan detected Surrey in the accent. He has a feeling he isn't far from a kitchen with an authentic Italian barista machine and fancies that the residents of this lavish pad have their courgettes and hummus delivered in wicker baskets.

'Well, don't dither. They're waiting for you.' She glares at the newcomers with eyes that make Rowan think of the cheap nylon bears won at the fair. Her mouth is a glossy smear of red jam and the corners dip further down in tandem with each noticeable augmenting of her nostrils. Her gimlet gaze sweeps left and the nostrils flare like an exhausted horse. 'Oh, how delightful. I see Ms Marlish has deigned to bring another infant. How nice that will be for everybody'. She looks a hole in Snowdrop. 'I suppose you will have somebody to talk to at least. But don't touch the piano if you're eating sticky sweets – it's just been French polished.'

Rowan turns to look at where Catherine and a doughy, bowl-haired girl of seven or eight are removing a treasure trove of items from the rear of the people carrier. Catherine is gathering up water bottles and food wrappers. A fistful of discarded paper and a white carrier bag flutter out of the door and are whipped away on the wind, tangling in the branches of a dark, spiky tree. In the driving seat, the man Rowan assumes to be Terence is smoothing his hair in the little vanity mirror. As Rowan watches, Catherine straightens up, arms full of assorted detritus. The girl – a vague outline in a school uniform and an anorak – stands mutely beside her. Catherine moves to the driver's seat, perhaps intending to say goodbye. She has to dart backwards as Terence slams into reverse and screeches back across the gravel. He could easily have crushed both Catherine's toes, and the girl's. Rowan glares a hole in the side of his head as he drives past, giving the same cheery salute.

'Well,' mutters Rowan. 'What a fucking knob.' He puts his hand out for Snowdrop, who has the sense to take it softly. 'Go see if she needs a friend,' he says, leaning down to her ear. 'Not for the story – just because she might really need it.' He stands up again to find Serendipity smiling at him.

'You're not such a bad sort, Rowan.'

Mrs Hawkins leads them into a lavish, high-ceilinged entrance hall. Beneath deep, Arabic rugs, the floor is flagged with rough, local stone; a chequerboard of dark greys and boggy greens. The walls, a toned-down teal, form a gallery space for huge, gold-framed landscapes, interspersed with fine lithographs and a handful of blocky, inexpert oil paintings; portraits that appear to have been done using the back of a spoon as both paintbrush and mirror.

'Lovely place,' begins Rowan, but Mrs Hawkins cuts him off.

'You have no books to sell, is that right? Well I suppose that's something. One does sometimes feel that these authors turn up just to turn one's home into a market stall.'

Rowan gives her a sympathetic look. 'One does indeed.' Behind him, Serendipity lets out a tiny laugh. Mrs Hawkins chooses to ignore it.

'We have some fine writers,' says Mrs Hawkins. 'Very fine. If you've planned to give some kind of lecture I must warn you that it may be a case of preaching to the converted. We're all writers together here; this isn't a tutor and pupil scenario.' She draws herself up and Rowan smells dusky floral perfume and a whiff of dry vermouth. 'Before my marriage I was a teacher of English literature at a very fine school in Leatherhead...'

The door bangs open as Catherine, arms full of rubbish, pushes her way inside. Her face is pale as milk and her fronds of tangled black hair cling to her skin, her collar, and her steamed-up spectacles.

'I'm sorry, I'm sorry, oh Mrs Hawkins I tried to phone but there was such poor signal and Terence does like to listen to Radio Three when we're on the road so

I had to whisper when I left the message, so you might just have a recording of some garbled words and a lot of Mahler...'

Rowan finds himself smiling at her. She strikes him at once as a sort of pleasing disaster: a whirlwind of good intentions haplessly executed. He's met her, or those a lot like her, countless times before: scatter-brained and stressed to the point of aneurysm, terrified of causing offence or upsetting anybody. Her voice is soft and breathy and fast and Rowan gets the impression that if she were to receive one word of kindness or a squeeze of the shoulder, she would burst into tears and disintegrate. With her arms full, her elbows stick out like wings.

'I'm Catherine, well, Kitty – actually, that's a pet name, so not everybody knows me as that, so Catherine's fine...' Her eyes dart from one to the other, all nervous energy. Raindrops fall from her coat onto the burgundy wool of an expensive rug. 'We've met, I think,' she says to Serendipity. 'And this is your daughter, I presume. Snowdrop, yes? What a lovely name. And what a lovely young girl. She and Imogen here are going to be such friends, I'm sure.'

Beside her, Imogen is stuffing a plump hand into a large bag of Monster Munch, eating them methodically, joylessly: crumbs on the front of her school jumper. Snowdrop gives Rowan a look that says: "I tried, but look what I'm working with".

'I haven't missed it, have I?' gasps Catherine, looking worried. 'I heard there was a writer...'

Rowan can't help himself. He gives a little flicked salute,

Scout's honour, two fingers touched to his forehead. She clocks the driving gloves.

'I'm Rowan,' he says, warmly. 'Kitty, was it? And no, you haven't missed it. I'm it – or if you ask my sister here, I've always thought I am. You take a moment to get yourself situated.' He twinkles a little: one of his better smiles. 'I was only killing time until you arrived.'

Mrs Hawkins coughs, pointedly. 'We are assembled in the Orangery,' she says, haughtily, and Rowan is delighted to hear Snowdrop laugh out loud.

'Orangery!' she repeats. 'Ha! Is there an Applery? Do we get there by walking down a Lemony Snicket? Orangery – that's funny…'

Rowan screws up his face, suddenly very nervous. He doesn't know what to say to these people. Doesn't know who he is or what he's for or what sort of piss-poor excuse for a life he's going to be living by the New Year. He feels Serendipity move closer to him and squeeze his forearm. 'You'll be great,' she says. 'If nothing else, you've stolen this old cow's thunder for an evening. That's a win.'

'Do you mind if we sit with you?' asks Catherine, breathily. 'I always used to come with my friend but she's off on her travels and if I'm honest I sometimes feel a bit, well, on my own…'

Up close, Rowan studies her properly. Green eyes in an almond-shaped face, a nice smile and skin so soft and pale it looks like warm alabaster. She certainly doesn't act like somebody aware of her own attractiveness. She reminds Rowan of the uncool crowd at school – the sweet kids who would blush tomato-red if smiled at or spoken to by one of the sporty boys. He leans towards her, sharing a secret.

'You have to promise me that even if I'm dreadful, you'll talk to me afterwards,' says Rowan. 'Don't run screaming for the hills. And if you've been bored to sleep, you have to give me permission to wake you, okay? I don't need accusations of inappropriate touching.'

Catherine colours, hiding a smile behind her hand. 'I promise.'

27

Seascale Vicarage
Saturday, November 2, 1991
11.06pm

Violet dreams, her body stiff as death. From here, face down in the damp bracken, the girl she is watching could be mistaken for a marionette. She drifts through the darkened forest in boneless, liquid half-steps: a fleshy white poppet trailed on invisible strings. Her arms are raised, yet her hands dangle down at the wrists, so that from elbow to fingertip both limbs take on the likeness of murdered swans.

Occasionally, eyes shut, she pats at the air.

'Catherine,' she whispers, in the clutch of the dream. 'No, Catherine, don't…'

Her bare feet catch on tree roots; risen from the muddy ground like swollen veins. Sharp pebbles puncture her skin, the sting eclipsed a moment later by the sensuous suck and pull of warm mud and dew-moistened grass. She is only dimly aware of these sensations. Could not speak if she wanted to. Her throat is afire, her tongue swollen; the taste of rotten bark filling her mouth and nose.

'*You have been chosen,*' comes a voice: an icicle melting in the centre of her skull. '*You will be reborn...*'

She sees him. The man with the green toenails. He had given them something to drink. Something sweet and sticky. He had taken them somewhere at once foreign and familiar. She had seen things. Done things, had she not? She remembers a voice, right in the centre of her head. And something dark. Something animal. She remembers fear.

The senses fade. For a moment she is back within the dream. She sees her friend, dressed in a long white nightdress. The hem is torn and the delicate embroidery is obscured beneath splashes of mud. In places, the material clings to her skin. She's plump and pink. There are patterns on her flesh; serpentine sigils and jagged circles, daubed in sticky fingerprints on the ripe fruit of her skin. She has motherly hips, rounded ankles. There is nothing in her eyes.

Violet tries to remember. To see clearly. He had sung to them in a language they did not understand. And there had been a man, reduced to sticks and scraps of skin. She has a memory of coming to. Of being face down above a slithering, crawling mass of sticks and leaves and twisting serpents. She had turned her head and in the darkness seen the flame-red of Freya's hair, clashing with the pale whiteness of her freckled skin as the man daubed symbols upon her flesh. Had it been at the same moment? Was she both beside her and beneath? And Catherine. Where was Catherine?

'Freya,' she whispers. 'What happened...?'

She is in a place between memory and fantasy, reality and nightmare. She is asleep on the neat, laundered sheets of her bedroom at Catherine's house. And she is beneath the earth, rolling from the table with a hard thud, landing naked upon the hard damp floor. She is seeing firelight reflected in countless bottles. She is looking up at a half-made man dangling from the bottom rung of an old iron ladder. She is turning, terrified beyond understanding, as the thing with the pig face looms from the blackness like a nightmare made flesh.

There is blood on her hands now. Blood on her chest and on her face. And she can feel Catherine's hand slipping wetly into hers as they drag each other, deliriously, for the tiny chink of light high above.

And now it is fading. The memory is coming apart like damp paper. Somebody is shaking her. Stroking her. Whispering her name.

She opens her eyes into the large, round face of Rev Marlish. He is smoothing back her hair, whispering her name, saying the same thing over and over, like a spell.

'I'm so sorry. I'm so sorry. Please forgive me. Please…'

'Catherine,' croaks Violet, again.

'She's okay,' says Rev Marlish, cuffing the tears away from his eyes. 'You had us so worried. You got lost. Do you remember that? You got lost in the woods. Gave us quite a scare…'

'A man,' whispers Violet. 'There was a man. A musician. I can't remember. We were in Keswick.' She looks at herself, clean and scrubbed and dressed in soft pink pyjamas. 'How did I get here? Where's Catherine?' She closes an eye. 'Where's Freya?'

'Don't you worry about that now,' says Rev Marlish. 'Catherine's fine. Sore head but she's the same as you. I think you took something. Maybe you ate some mushrooms in the wild, eh? Saw some peculiar things. Freya's heading back to Ireland, I think. We'll sort all that out later.'

Violet tries to sit up. There is a man with dark hair in the corner of the room, watching the exchange. He's old. Skinny. Neatly dressed.

'Who's he?' asks Violet. She feels wrong. It's as if there's a hole in her brain and things are pouring away like paint down a drain.

'Don't worry yourself,' Rev Marlish says with a smile. 'We all make mistakes. You get some rest. Don't think about this anymore. It doesn't matter. All's well.'

Violet sinks back against the pillows. Suddenly she starts forward. She has a memory of the small, goblin-faced copper. Remembers her reaching out. Remembers lashing out. Can see her lying on the damp forest floor, bleeding into the earth.

Then the picture is gone.

She closes her eyes. Feels it all fade away.

Slips into sleep, and darkness, and nothing.

The last thing she sees is the face of a wild boar; yellow eyes and monstrous tusks, eyes that burn like cigarettes.

And then it is gone.

28

Later, after the laughs, and the questions and the pitiable attempts to sign books in spite of his seeping fingers, Rowan is able to make his way back to Serendipity and Snowdrop for what he expects to be a more candid assessment of how the gig has gone. They're waiting for him in the shadow of some exotic-looking tree. Fairy lights wind their way around the trunk.

'You were great!' says Snowdrop, grinning at him and stopping just short of going straight in for a hug.

Serendipity, behind her, gives a tight smile. Her eyes are damp; her face flushed.

He'd spoken for an hour. Where the writing journey began, his idyllic childhood and criminal adolescence; anecdotes from his time as a hack; indiscreet celebrity anecdotes; a story or two about ways he'd tricked his way into people's confidences: giving himself a bit of a roguish veneer. He'd enjoyed himself. Julie, the librarian, had been seated front and centre and he could tell by halfway through that she was feeling good about herself for having snagged him as their guest speaker. He hadn't been able to see his sister or niece but he'd been gratified to see Catherine grinning, sometimes even chuckling, as he did his best to speak like somebody who actually meant what he was saying.

'Oh I'm so pleased we came!' gushes Catherine, bustling up behind Serendipity. She still has a big armful of assorted rubbish. Rowan can't understand why she wouldn't just ask to use a bin. 'Oh we were in stitches, weren't we? I hoped it would be informative but it was actually properly funny! Imogen was laughing too.'

Rowan looks at Imogen. She's staring at the screen of an iPhone, hair flopping forward, one cheek grotesquely pushed out to accommodate what could well be anything from a fistful of Fruit Pastilles to a rack of lamb.

'I wasn't sure if I struck the right tone,' says Rowan, uncertainly. Behind her, Julie the librarian is asking for any members who had handwritten their short stories should hand them in now, and for others to email the usual address. He hears the phrase "disseminated among the editorial panel" and raises his eyebrows at Catherine. She is looking at her shoes, awkward, flicking glances at her partner's daughter and clearly fighting the urge to say "this is nothing to do with me".

'Shall we go and say our goodbyes to the lady, Mum?' asks Snowdrop, nudging her mum. Serendipity looks mildly surprised at the question but seems to read something in her daughter's eyes that strikes some kind of chord. Serendipity plays along, making a great show of shouting 'Marjorie' in her most upper-class voice.

Rowan gives Catherine his full attention. 'There's an unedited version, you know,' he smiles. 'Much more X-rated. You haven't got a story to hand in?'

'No.' She shakes her head at that, as though a voice has

told her not to be such a bad girl. 'Well, I have, but I think I'll chicken out again. I'm struggling with a bit of the old self-doubt. I used to write when I was very young and I suppose if I'm honest I thought I'd be a real writer by now and in truth it's just ramblings and bits of silly poetry…'

'Some of the best books are nothing but ramblings,' says Rowan. 'You'll be in good company. Personally, I admire anybody who just does it, you know? Who just sees it through to the end. The difference between a published writer and an unpublished one is that the published writers actually finish the book. Don't give yourself such a hard time.'

Catherine looks away, muttering something about Imogen needing to get into a hot bath. Rowan has an image of a chicken simmering in a slow cooker. 'You're nice,' says Catherine, and it is said so directly that he finds himself a little off-balance.

'Am I? Even for a journalist?'

Catherine's laugh has a schoolgirl sound, a high, nervous giggle. She claps her hands like a Southern dame. 'Honestly, I'm so pleased I came tonight.'

'So am I.'

She suddenly pulls a face, as if agonising with a truth. 'I don't normally like journalists,' she giggles. 'I don't like people poking into stuff. It's grubby.' Her face changes, and she takes a small bite out of the air: a dog leaping at a moth. She makes a small squealing noise, pig-like to Rowan's ear, and then erupts into more giggles. 'They're swine, they really are.'

'You've had a lot of dealings, have you?' asks Rowan, glancing up to see another of the enthusiastic writers promising to get in touch on Facebook. Behind her is a well-built blonde woman in a waist-length Harrington jacket and bike leathers, who he hadn't noticed during the talk. She looks back as she follows the older woman out the door. There's a toughness to her, as if she's been hit plenty without ever tiring of hitting back. She gives the older woman a squeeze on the shoulders, congratulating her for something.

'All swine?' he asks, looking back to Catherine.

'Not you, I'm sure.'

'Oh yes. Worst of the lot. Don't talk to me, I have the integrity of a particularly sneaky gutter rat. I mean the sort of rat that other rats are disappointed in – like they ask him how he could stoop so low. That's where I'm at.'

'You're very clever,' says Catherine, and a tiny alarm sounds, way back in some distant bell tower in his mind. Just for a second, she'd sounded like she was mocking him. He swills the thought around like mouthwash and spits it back out. He's thought the worst of people before and it has always cost him dear. He wants to get tonight over with. A drink and a joint by the open fire and a brief bit of basking in an okay day.

'Am I boring you?' asks Catherine, ducking into his line of sight. 'Oh God, I am, I know I am. Terence is always telling me that I'm such a bore. I'm sure you must talk to so many interesting people, must just be such a snooze-fest. You drifted off right in front of me...'

'That is unforgivable of me,' stuttered Rowan, genuine in his remorse. 'I was thinking of what you were saying, actually, and my brain just followed it because it was interesting...' He realises he is recovering splendidly. 'That happens to me sometimes – I'll follow a good idea like I'm a butterfly collector and it's a High Brown Fritillary...'

'A what?' Catherine laughs.

'Oh it's quite rare, I assure you. You're not a butterfly catcher, are you? I literally only have one point of reference for butterflies. No further technical names. I'd be denounced as a fraud by any lepidopterist...'

'You do make me laugh.' Catherine smiles. She glances at Imogen, distracted. 'I really do have to get Imogen home,' she says, squirming. 'Terence will want supper. It's Thursday, you see. He has his meetings on Thursdays.'

Beside her, Imogen looks up, eyes full of scorn. 'Yeah, whatever.'

'They were supposed to go to the pictures tonight,' whispers Catherine, mouthing each word. 'She was a bit disappointed. This was a poor second.'

Imogen nudges her stepmum's leg. Gives her a look of mild interest then slowly turns to look at Rowan. 'It was all right. He's not that funny, but I liked it when you talked about the dead people.'

Catherine cringes. 'I'm sorry...'

'She's a sweetie, she really is.' He drops his gaze, suddenly bashful. 'I'd like to talk to you again. How do I get in touch with you?'

'Oh I don't think Terence would...'

'I promise, no funny business. I've a book project on the go and I need some respite.'

'Really, there's no way...'

Feeling her fading from him, he makes an impulsive lunge. 'Did I hear your dad's a vicar? I'm sure somebody said that while I was doing the signing. It's just, well, a character I'm struggling to get to grips with, she has a similar backstory to you and I really think you could help me find her voice.'

She cocks her head as if somebody has tugged her hair. She looks frightened. 'I don't think Terence would like that.'

'It could be a secret,' he whispers, trying to be charming.

'No.' She shakes her head, mouth a tight line. 'No, I can't do secrets.'

Rowan backs off, hands raised. He can feel the opportunity fading from his grasp. 'It's okay, I won't push. I just need some company, that's all, and you seem like you might be good to talk to.'

'I'm really not sure…'

'Let's not get into that again.' He starts to reach into his pocket for his cards and realises that to do so would be to take the skin off his hands. 'I'm sorry,' he mutters. 'Could you reach into this pocket and grab it…' He nods at his pocket and replays how everything that he's just said and done must have seemed to somebody who doesn't know that their opposite number has badly injured hands.

Imogen is sniggering and Catherine doesn't seem to know what to make her face do. 'I don't think Terence would like…'

'He said!' snorts Imogen, and something high in saturated fats blasts out of her nostril. 'He asked you to put your hand in his pocket! Oh my God, Dad's gonna do one…'

'Please,' hisses Catherine. 'Please don't…'

Rowan runs his tongue along the back of his teeth. 'I only wanted to give you my card,' he says, deflating.

'I know,' she says, meeting his eyes. 'I read about your hands.'

'I thought you didn't know about me before tonight?' he

asks, and immediately wonders if he was wrong to catch her in the lie.

Unexpectedly, Catherine reaches into his pocket and retrieves the card. She twirls it in her fingers, her manner suddenly less mumsy and mouse-like. She grins at him, impish and considerably more attractive. 'Thanks for tonight. You've inspired me.'

'Sorry?' he asks, confused.

'I'm going to hand it in,' she says, proudly. 'My story. Violet's not here to object, is she? Had to go running off looking into things nobody wants to remember. I want people to hear the truth – or the way I remember it, at least.'

On the drive home, Snowdrop reaches into Rowan's pocket and stops the recording device. He feels her do it but doesn't comment or move. He's hugging himself, cold in the passenger seat, icy wind whistling through the blowers and condensation streaking the windows. Driving, Serendipity stares into nothingness, her thoughts seemingly lost in the churning black sky and the brooding mass of the fells.

She doesn't see Snowdrop slip the folded wedge of paper into her uncle's coat. Four pages, double-spaced, A4. Printed black on white and folded lengthwise. Snowdrop is still tucking it in when her mum spins around to ask her if she is okay, and telling her it would be straight to bed when they get home. Snowdrop smiles back madly, wide eyes and a too-wide grin. Immediately she directs her mum's attention back skywards, pointing to some invisible kestrel hovering above a tar-black tree. Quickly, Snowdrop tucks the gleaming white fold of paper inside the dark folds of the coat. Rowan squeezes her fingers through the fabric. She breathes out, relieved.

The last thing she wants is for her mum to spot the words *"by Catherine Marlish"* on the title page. She doesn't want to get caught before Rowan has a chance to read it. She doesn't want to have stolen it from the pile of papers for nothing.

29

Allerdale Private Hospital, Kendal
Sunday, November 3, 1991
10.04am

Eve wakes up like a switch has been flicked. A moment before there had been bright lights and screeches and the desperate, rushing noise of tyres on wet gravel. There had been words: prayers and pleas and desperate apologies. Now there is only the soft drone of a fan radiator and the *click-click-click* of the moth that flaps fatly at the glass behind the blinds.

She keeps her eyes closed until her senses return. Everything hurts. She feels like one colossal toothache; that cold, sharp agony of an infected root. She has to fight to keep her face still. She wants to grimace. To grimace and roar.

Slowly, she takes inventory. Her legs feel jelly-like; numb, as if she's sat on a hard surface for too long. There's a sickening headache at her temples and her mouth feels dry; a sun-baked slug of tongue sticking to the white crust on her lips.

The pain in her guts is like the worst stitch she has ever had. The skin feels tight, as though two folds of flab have been pulled taut and glued together.

She can smell disinfectant and potpourri. Can smell talcum powder and rum.

She becomes aware of the soft, prayer-like intonation droning at her bedside. Adjusts the frequency in her head until she can hear Derrick clearly. His voice is so full of sorrow it makes her heart clench.

'...did the right thing. It wouldn't have made a difference, I know that. And they're okay, that's the thing. So don't you be thinking of dying on me, yeah? There's so much life in you, Eve. I saw that from the first. You're the first person I've ever met that I could truly see the point in. I know that sounds awful but you don't know what my life was like growing up. So much of the kindness was kicked out of me. I still became a copper though, didn't I? Tried to make a difference. And I swear, I cared about the victims in every case I ever policed. But I did my duty because it was my duty, do you understand? I never thought the lives I might be saving or the deaths I might be getting justice for – I never thought they were lives that properly mattered.

'But you, Eve. You're somebody who the world needs. I know you understand how it's all supposed to work. How people tell whatever truths the world needs to hear and that underneath it's all just about trying to find the most credible lie to live with. I know that wherever you are right now, you're giving yourself hell thinking you're a bad person. But you're not, love. They're okay. The girls. Violet and Catherine. They don't remember much and

Rev Marlish did as you asked him and kept everything small. Violet's daddy's neither use nor ornament and the mum's a whipped dog. As far as anybody knows, you were involved in an altercation in the woods while searching for the missing teenagers. When I found you I got on the radio to Mountain Rescue and they found them in no time. It's all going to be okay. They don't remember anything. Violet kept gibbering about the pig-face man but she's so pumped full of the home brew he gave them it'll be like remembering a dream...'

Eve clears her throat, painfully. She opens her eyes like a Hollywood glamour puss waking from a swoon.

'Did you catch him?' she croaks. 'Cormac...'

'We never say that name,' comes a voice from the other side of the bed. She blinks, rapidly, taken by surprise. She barely notices the surroundings into which she wakes – propped up on comfortable pillows in a mahogany bed; plush patterned paper clinging redly to walls decorated in art deco mirrors and George Stubbs prints.

In the chair by her bed sits a big man. He's pushing fifty and looks it, but there's an air of solidity about him that suggests he would be a formidable physical opponent. Big, clean, hairy-knuckled hands grip the arms of a wicker-backed mahogany chair. He's wearing a vest and a cardigan, and there's a strip of blue cloth wrapped around his neck, all but obscuring the gold crucifix beneath. A round, swarthy face is topped by a head of dark curls. He has a face that looks as if it has been beaten into shape by a hammer and an anvil: flat features here and risen, lumpen bones there. He's looking at her dispassionately: watching her as if she's a cloud drifting across the sky.

'Mr Pearl...' croaks Eve, trying to sit up. She flashes angry eyes at Derrick. 'What's he doing here? If anybody sees...?'

'Nobody will see, Detective Chief Inspector,' says Mr Pearl, his accent a soft, velvety County Wexford. 'This is a private hospital. The best. Better than most five-star hotels, so they say, though I've not spent much time in any of those. Spent time in hospital, though. Spent plenty. Never liked it. Always felt as though I'd been trapped, you understand. Always my biggest fear, that. Waking up with my hands tied. Daddy used to use a manacle on me and my brother, can you believe that? All to be frowned on these days but you knew you were in for a whipping when you felt the steel go on. There was a hatch in the hayloft. Nasty, smelly place. He'd hang us from a beam, dangling there with our shirts off while he went to town with the lash. Gave me long arms but I don't know if that's much compensation.'

Eve swallows again. Derrick moves to get her some water from the elaborate bedside table. Pearl sits him back in his seat with one hard look.

'Mr Pearl, there was no choice. I was hurt. Bleeding to death. We had to get the girls to safety. We'd have called you in but there was no time...'

'You were bleeding to death,' says Pearl, flatly. 'That can't be nice.'

'No, it wasn't,' spits Eve, bristling.

'But you were paid to find my son,' he says, and turns his eyes on Derrick. 'You were given a lot of money for a simple job.' He swings the searchlight glare onto Eve. 'And you have done very well from the information I've provided you, and from the many cash gifts that have been deposited in your account.'

Eve shakes her head. 'No. I never took money.'

'No? Odd. I have a savings account that shows regular payments to an account in your name, Eve. Regular as clockwork.'

Eve looks to Derrick, shaking her head.

'I've paid for you to have the best care that money can buy,' he says, drily. 'That's because I want you well. I want you in tip-top fighting form so you can take me to my son.'

'Your son's a murderer,' growls Eve. 'He's gone. He's missed his chance with the girls here but he'll need his fix somewhere. He'll turn up, but I won't be helping you find him. I should never have started on this road. Neither should Derrick. If we ever find him, he won't be getting handed over to you. He'll go to prison like any other killer.'

'No,' says Pearl. 'He wouldn't like that. He's a child of nature – that is why I had such hopes for Mr Sixpence. He failed me. He helped my boy grow stronger. Darker. Gave him a taste for things he would never have discovered alone. He has gone too far now. He needs putting down.'

Eve shrinks into the pillow, wrinkling her lip. 'You wouldn't kill your own son.'

Pearl shifts in his seat, straightening his back, and a shaft of light falls across his face. The irises of his eyes are completely black: fat scarab beetles that swallow the light.

'If any man has a stubborn and rebellious son who will not obey his father or his mother, and when they chastise him, he will not even listen to them, then his father and

mother shall seize him, and bring him out to the elders
of his city at the gateway of his hometown. They shall
say to the elders of his city, "This son of ours is stubborn
and rebellious, he will not obey us, he is a glutton and a
drunkard." Then all the men of his city shall stone him to
death; so you shall remove the evil from your midst, and all
Israel will hear of it and fear.'

'You're not in fucking Israel,' spits Eve, her throat all
but closing up as she speaks. She shuffles upright, the
heavy woollen blankets slipping down. She realises she is
naked. Sees the huge bandage stuck to her skin, all gauze
and blood and pus.

'The girl,' says Derrick, quietly. 'There was a third girl.
Freya.'

Pearl lets a tiny smile disturb the millpond of his face. He
nods. 'Turns out she hasn't got much in the way of family.
Nobody making a fuss. She'll write to the school, or maybe
to that nice vicar – tell them she's doing fine. And the police
will leave well alone. Give it time and people will forget
there ever was a third girl.'

'No,' says Eve, shaking her head. 'That isn't how things
work. We can still find her. Can make a story work...'

'She's gone,' says Pearl. 'You did right. Everybody's happy.
The other two remember nothing. It's over. Rest easy.'

'Deaghlan, please...' begins Derrick.

'Don't,' says Eve, glaring holes in Pearl's forehead. 'I'm
a DCI. I'm Evelyn Fucking Cater. People have been hurt.
People killed. Cormac took those girls and it's only pure
good fortune that two of them got out alive. We can still
find the other one. Still find Freya. I'd rather die than let
somebody like you have a hold over me...'

'There is no Freya,' says Pearl, quietly.

'Derrick, hand me the radio. I'm calling all this in...'

Pearl jumps forward so quickly that it seems as though a bomb has pitched him forward. In an instant his nose is against hers, his eyes distorted and huge against her own, and he's grinning into her mouth, baring his teeth like a cornered rat.

'You'll do what I tell you to do, Eve. You'll show me where he's been playing his games. And when I've done what needs to be done, I'm going to go and lie down beside my wife and we're going to drink a fine Jameson's full of all her lovely pills. And we're going to fall asleep and go to Mother Mary our Blessed Virgin, and we are going to hold hands with Jesus for all eternity. And if Cormac's soul ever gets there, I will embrace it. And the only speck of darkness in that perfect place will be my memory of a debt unpaid. It will be my memory of you, taking my money and my information and promising to deliver my son to me, and failing in that task. So you will do what you've been paid for, Eve, or I will come back from Paradise just to stick my fingers in that hole in your gut, and pull you apart until you burst.'

Eve refuses to let the fear show. Holds his stare.

'Try,' she whispers. 'I'm a DCI. You wouldn't...'

She doesn't even see his fingers move. Just feels the sudden, burning penetration as he stabs his hand towards her wound and prods obscenely at the ruined flesh. She tries to bite back the scream. Clamps her teeth down on her top lip. Tastes blood, as she squirms on the bed, wriggling against his fingers like a skewered insect.

His voice, in her ear: 'Try me.'

*

Creative Writing Assignment
By Catherine Marlish

His feet are naked; toenails painted a shade of green that makes me think of old glass bottles and mint jelly.

I'm fourteen, and I've never seen nail polish on a man before. Never seen a man in baggy harlequin trousers or with braids in their scabby beard; wrists wrapped up in a gaudy maypole of beaded bracelets; lips singing around a cigarette. I certainly never imagined I would see such things today. Not so close to home. Not in the little subway beneath the footbridge on the edge of Keswick town centre. Not on a Tuesday.

'*He looks so cool…*'

'*Does he heck as like – he looks a proper tit. Looks as if he's been swimming during a fly-fishing contest!*'

'*He must be freezing.*'

'*Don't look. Come on, he hasn't seen us…*'

'*Go give his feet a rub, then. Stick them in your armpits.*'

'*You're gross.*'

'*You're gross.*'

The stranger stands with one foot half submerged in a puddle, the other planted on the grimy cement. The bulbs in the underpass are bathing him in a warm, sodium glow. His shadow, stretching away to the far end of the subway, has the likeness of a gnarled and knotted tree.

'*You fancy him.*'

'You fancy him.'

'Let's go say hello then.'

'Piss off!'

The singer's eyes are closed, head raised slightly, as if preparing to receive the sacrament. His fingers, grimy around the nails, inked across the knuckles, move lightly over the strings of the battered guitar, hanging from his neck on a length of cord – half as thick as the ratty dreadlocks that gather in the hood of his sodden purple coat.

We're sheltering beneath the little pagoda by the park. Freya is sitting cross-legged on the floor, a pile of books spread out around her as if for sale. I suppose we look out of place in this touristy part of Lakeland: a black smudge among the green and brown. There are guest houses and mountaineering shops a little further up the street; all crampons and Gore-Tex and fleece. The shops are mostly empty today. Many have shut early, including this blue-painted kiosk that offers a little protection from the swirling wind. In summer, it sells ice creams and Kendal Mint Cake, rents out old golf clubs and gaudy pink balls to families willing to endure a round of crazy golf. On this ugly February day, the shutters are down.

It was the same up at the boating lake. Nobody was renting out the rowing boats. The ducks and geese pecked miserably at the gravel near the water's edge. The quacks seemed decidedly half-hearted.

From where we're huddling, we have a perfect view of the busker, his guitar case open in front of him, two solitary coins catching the light.

'What the hell is he wearing?' asks Violet, scornfully. 'Oh my God, he looks like he needs to be sheep-dipped. Can you imagine kissing that? Bet he tastes like shoes.'

I laugh, the way I always do when Violet says something loud. I don't agree with her though. I actually rather like the look of him. And his voice. There's something hypnotic about it. Something that makes me think of honey.

'What's he expecting to make today anyway?' asks Violet, unthreading her hair from the inverted crucifix necklace that hangs, as if for extra blasphemy, in the shallow cleft of her expensive and somewhat unnecessary bra. 'There's nobody daft enough to be here. Keswick's so boring.'

'I think he's just singing because he likes it,' I say. 'Shall we give him some money? I've got my bus fare. I can just keep 10p for the phone and ring Dad for a lift…'

'I need to borrow that for some chips anyway,' says Violet, carelessly. 'I spent my allowance on the new boots.'

'Oh, right. Sorry,' I say, automatically. I make a mental note to start saying "allowance" instead of "pocket money". I still haven't forgiven myself for saying "playtime" instead of "break" in front of Freya.

I sit silently for a while, staring out through the misty rain. *Keswick* rain. That's what Mam and Dad call it: a kind of haze that hangs in the air and soaks to the bone. It blackens the tarmac, which twinkles like iron ore, in the light of the half-moon. It darkens the trunks of the trees: turning sycamore and elder into great columns of steaming charcoal.

'Crusties – that's what people like him are called,' says Freya, quietly. 'New Age Travellers. There's something called the Peace Convoy, people living this kind of gypsy life. They smoke pot and campaign to stop nuclear bombs and bring down Thatcher and stuff. I saw one of them on the news. He wore a cloak and said he was the true heir to Camelot, or something. I'm pleased they're on our side.'

'Our side?' I ask, wondering what she means.

'Outsiders.' Freya smiles. 'Alternatives. Goths. They're against the machine, just like us.'

I like this feeling. Like being part of the same swarm as Freya. I look at her out of the corner of my eye. So cool, so stylish: sitting there with her spell books and her dog-eared grimoires. Today she's reading a tatty paperback: a strange abstract painting on its cover. *Shamanism: Archaic Techniques of Ecstasy*. She's promised to loan it to me once she's done. I'll have to hide it from Dad. He doesn't object to the blasphemy but he wants me concentrating on schoolwork.

Things have changed at school these past couple of years. The inspectors have been in. We have uniforms now and the yoga and reiki are strictly timetabled. All that stuff started being phased out once Mr Sixpence moved on. We still get pupils who haven't done so well at other schools but we don't spend as much time putting them right.

Freya certainly doesn't seem to have any issues. Doesn't hear things or see things or spend her spare time holding the carp's gills closed, down at the ornamental pond. She's just nice. She could have had her pick of friends. Instead she chose dowdy old me, Catherine Marlish, and Violet, who everybody else is a little bit afraid of.

'They wear those in Peru,' I say, pointing at his tatty coat. I'm remembering a picture in the parish magazine. 'They're made of alpaca.'

'What's an alpaca?' snorts Violet.

'Like a llama. Apparently they're dead warm, and they dry quickly too. They make them at one of the missions Daddy raised money for...'

'I told you, stop saying "Daddy",' snaps Violet, embarrassed. 'It makes you sound like a baby. I've started calling my dad by his first name. He hates it. Then when I get in bother I call him "Dad" and he's like a toddler with a sweet. You should try it. Or call him Reverend! Did you hear that, Freya? Did you hear what I said?'

Freya, chuntering to herself, makes a show of rummaging in her rucksack to find her cigarettes. Makes a show of lighting up, her black fingernails artfully chipped, skin pale against the black of her fingerless gloves. I suppose to the untrained eye we are all dressed pretty similarly but it is Violet who looks as though a lot of money has been spent to appear this carefree. She wears a black pleated skirt, eye-wateringly short, with knee-high stripy tights and brand-new Doc Martens. Her ankle-length greatcoat is black with silver buttons and matches the woollen hat that holds back her sleek black hair. Mummy brought it back for her from a trip to Camden Market, a place so remote and exotic to me that it may as well have been purchased at a vintage boutique on the moon.

I feel shabby by contrast. My coat came from a pile of donated men's clothes, dumped in the doorway of the vicarage. It smells of old men: all talcum powder and slippers, Old Spice and fatty food.

'That language is mad,' says Freya, cocking her head towards the music. 'What is it? I can't make it out.'

'Probably gibberish.' Violet laughs, dripping with disdain. She doesn't seem to be enjoying her cigarette. She winces with each drag. I can't help notice that the smoke doesn't seem to be going into her lungs. It just hangs around in her mouth before she blows it back out.

'He's all right,' confirms Freya, casting a slightly more expert eye over the busker whose song echoes off the walls of the underpass. 'He's his own person. Nice voice.'

'I suppose,' says Violet, correcting herself. She's in awe of the new girl.

'He's stopping,' I mumble. 'Oh God, he's looking, he's looking!'

It seems to take an age for the final note to fade. It echoes off the walls of the underpass. The singer has almost crossed the short distance between us before the cadence disappears into the misty air.

I glance at Freya. She's altered her pose. Looks suddenly older. More like an adult than a child: eyes burning like cigarettes. Violet, at her side, allows a sulk to slip onto her perfect features.

Different-coloured eyes, I think, as his features become clear. *One brown, one green.*

All the little pieces of him drop into my mind like coins into a slot.

He's got a tattoo on his neck.
There's a silver cuff on his ear.
He's wearing clown trousers.
Chest hair. Proper chest hair...
He smells funny. Like the bottom of a pond. Like fox
blood. Like raw meat.

He stops in front of us. He seems to be listening to something nobody else can hear. Violet gives a little giggle.

'Namaste,' he says, at last.

'Eh?' asks Violet, the noise coming out like spit. 'Where's that from?'

'It's a greeting. A blessing. Loosely, it means *I bow to the God within you.*'

I already know what namaste means, and Violet should too. Mr Sixpence used to say it – the quiet, kind man who used to talk to us about the colours of the soul and the importance of feeling at one with the universe. Up close, the singer sort of reminds me of him, though he's probably forty years younger.

'You're smoking a Bible?' asks Violet.

I look at his right hand. A light grey-blue smoke is rising up from the thin cigarette he holds like a pen.

'That's a Gideon, isn't it?' asks Freya, quietly. She plays with her hair, red and fiery, and he looks at her the way I've always wanted to be looked at.

He raises his cigarette to his lips and I hear myself let out a tiny gasp as I realise that his tobacco is contained within a page of a hotel Bible. I see the word "mercy" being devoured by the glowing red flame.

'I liked your song,' says Freya, head cocked, plaiting

her hair with her fingers. 'What language was it?'

Lazily, he flicks a glance in her direction. 'I don't know,' he says. 'It just comes out of me. I think it might be Sanskrit.' His voice is hypnotic. Accentless. 'It's the voice of those who walk with me. Of my guide. They lend me their strength as I search for my own.'

'What are you doing here?' asks Violet. 'Not much money to be made on a damp Tuesday in Keswick...'

'I go where I'm needed,' he says, and his smile shows teeth edged in brown tobacco stains. 'Perhaps where I'm called.'

'What does that mean?' asks Freya.

He ignores her. Looks back at me. 'You have an interesting aura,' he says, eyes fixed on mine. 'Emerald green. You could be a healer. And the pink, it's almost luminous. Sensitivity, compassion – you understand more than you allow others to comprehend.'

There's a sudden gorgeous warmth inside me. I feel a pricking sensation across my shoulders; a suppressed shiver tickling the backs of my knees. It feels for an instant as if I can see the outline of things; the indigo-purple framework of the trees, the lights, the white-painted guest houses with their rain-pummelled hanging baskets. It feels as if I could reach out and smear the colours into a new shape; as if I am looking at a world still painted in unfixed oils.

'The spot behind your heart,' says the man. He leans forward and touches my chest. 'That is where our ancestors believed we kept our soul. If you concentrate, you can feel it. I can teach you how to feel it.'

I feel Violet's hand at my hip, a slight tug upon my

coat. Hear a rhythm, a beat like a train moving over railway sleepers. I become aware of a delicious golden heat spreading throughout my body. It is as if I'm elongating; stretching like a cat, becoming more. I feel sensuous. Feel delicious.

He steps back. Surveys each of us in turn. His gaze lingers on Freya and for a moment he seems about to speak to her. He stops himself: an almost imperceptible shake of the head. Raises his blasphemous roll-up and takes a drag. Proffers it to me. I find myself leaning in, nose and lip touching his dirty fingers. I inhale the profane offering. Freya, moving quickly, does the same.

'What are you doing?' asks Violet, looking shocked. She's staring at me like I'm a stranger. She looks like the girl I met by the water's edge, lost and thoughtful, back when we were little more than girls. I wonder if she's jealous and I like the thought.

'Chill,' I say, and it feels so silly in my mouth that I start giggling. 'We're not harming anybody.'

'You'll get germs,' snaps Violet. Her world seems to be shifting and I'm enjoying it. Enjoying the limelight; the attention.

'Forest green,' says the man, his eyes moving over Violet's body like searchlights. 'Sensitive to criticism. Jealous. Lacking in personal responsibility. A pretender. Unkind.'

'You can't say that to me,' says Violet, and her eyes start to fill. 'You don't know me; you don't know anything about me...'

'I do,' he says, and somehow his voice is a calm and

kindly thing, like a damp flannel upon fevered skin. 'I see things. I understand. I see what is within. I can help you.' He looks at each of them in turn. 'Don't you want to be whole again? Don't you want to put the pieces of yourself back where they belong?'

'Don't be mean to her,' says Freya, shaking her head. 'She's nice. She's been nice to me.'

Violet wipes a tear away, defiance and misery making her striking features suddenly seem very young. 'You're just a smelly man,' she says, petulantly. 'Just a man with no shoes. With no money. Her dad's a vicar. She's never even kissed anybody so I don't know why you're going all gaga over her. I bet you live in a caravan or something.'

At this, he smiles. Smiles so wide that his ears seem to move, like a cat's.

'Do you want to see?' he asks. 'All of you.' He turns gimlet eyes on Violet. 'I would dearly love to help you find your path, as I have found mine. I am a healer. A guide.'

'I knew a guide once,' I say, and my voice sounds dreamy. 'He talked like you.'

The singer stares at me, his mismatched eyes blending, Cyclops-like, into one shimmering orb. I feel like he's pulling me towards him with his mind.

'I would love to help you both,' he says, to Violet and me. He shoots a quick glance at Freya. She holds his gaze as something passes between them. Something I've taken a long time to understand.

In a swift movement, he turns away. Walks, sure-footed, across the damp grass.

I'm the first to follow.
Freya next.
In time, Violet will come too.
She would rather die than be left out.

PART THREE

30

Violet sits in the front pew, shivering. It's colder indoors than out. She wears her bone-white exhalations like a scarf: wraith-like shapes stark against the pure black of her coat and the inky curtains of loose-hanging hair.

It's peaceful here, in a melancholy way. It makes her think of damp Sundays at Catherine's house: Mum and Dad gently arguing; the sour fug of boiled greens and roasting lamb; one of the weekend boarders inflicting clandestine dead legs during the ad breaks in the Grand Prix; Rev Marlish fussing with his notes for the evening sermon.

She trembles, as if somebody is blowing on her neck. Raises her eyes from the cold flagstone floor. Glances up at prayer books and psalm numbers. There's a damp patch on the wall behind the altar. A page marker lolls from the splayed pages on a big, red-bound Bible: a tongue of silk dangling in the frigid air. Technicolour disciples gaze down from the stained glass, faces serene, halos golden. One is captured mid-blessing, his hand raised, three fingers extended. He looks like he's asking the others if they've stolen his glove puppet. The blessed onlookers seem bemused: fat angels and unfeasibly clean shepherds, shouting out a chorus of denials from the white clouds that adorn the masterful painting on the far wall. The image seems to shimmer in the pinpricks of heat that rise from the candles, and Jesus, sat atop the mural like a fairy on a cake, looks at once beatific and sinister in the rippling air.

She tries to pray. Feels like a dickhead and stops herself. Screws up her eyes and scratches at the cold, red skin on her knees. She feels dirty. Stained, as if there's a smudge of grease somewhere inside her that she can't reach, no matter how hard she scrubs at herself with the black, chemical-scented soap.

Violet lowers her head. Folds her lips in on themselves and tries again. How to start? What to say? *Dear God? Dear Lord? Our Father?* She wants to scream, and cry and take a hammer to something beautiful.

Hello God, she mutters, her lips barely moving. *It's me. Violet. You know my friend's dad. Um, I don't really know how to do this. I think you wouldn't like what I've been doing. What I've been seeing. Um, I've been trying to remember. To make sense of what I feel. I don't know what to say. Um, please bless the poor. And the weak. And the hungry. Um, please bless the people who deserve it and, well, help those who don't to become better people. If you want. I mean, just do what you're doing, really, I'm not offering advice...*

She stops, appalled at herself and feeling ridiculous. Tries again.

Is she okay, God? Freya, I mean. Nobody will talk to me about her, you see. They just want to forget. People always say that it's better to talk about things and not bottle them up but that's what they want me to do whenever I mention it. They want it to not have happened. But it did happen, God. You know it did. He tricked us. Made us believe he loved us. All that talk of how special we were, what we could become – all those lies about greater truths and higher selves.

Violet opens her eyes to find her vision clouded by tears. She realises she has been speaking aloud, the words gathering softly about her mouth. She feels like sucking them back in: inhaling the uttered secrets before they can be swallowed up by anybody else.

Is she alive, God? I don't know how badly he hurt her. He hurt me – I know that. It still hurts sometimes. But I'm here. Catherine too, and somehow it seems to have all done her some good. There's a light in her now that wasn't there before. She won't talk about it either. The police have made it plain – we talk and everybody finds out what happened. Everybody finds out what we did. They've got their own secrets to hide.

I know they think we've got more to tell them but I promise, I don't. All I remember is waking up on the floor, all muddy and bloody and numb. Catherine was shaking me, crying like she'd never stop. All her fingernails were gone. There was dirt all over her. And Freya was gone. He was gone. And nobody will tell me what really happened. They're scared of something. Sometimes I think they're scared of me...

She suddenly realises that she doesn't really believe

anybody is listening. She'd expected as much. She'd harboured hopes that here, in the quiet and the cool of the church, she might feel something divine. That she might be filled with God's love and to let her fears and sadnesses be washed away upon the divine flood of His love. Instead she just feels daft.

A fine, ghostly memory scuttles across her mind. She feels it as a physical thing; all gossamer and spider legs scampering across the inside of her skull.

Him.

The clearing in the woods. Cross-legged on a fallen branch, eyes closed, the sun throwing tiger stripes across his upturned, tranquil features. She and Violet and Freya, naked as the dawn, heavy-lidded and languid in their ecstasy, passing the pipe between them as they daubed pretty patterns upon one another's skin – the dry earth turning to paint as they splashed libations of aniseed-scented liquor into their palms.

She shakes her head. Raises her hand and rubs at her forehead, kneading at the tense areas above her eyebrows. The headaches have been getting worse. She feels sick more often than she doesn't. Sometimes she can't even raise her arms.

Amen, she mutters, and feels something inside her flare briefly, then die.

She feels a sudden breath of cold air upon her neck – a door creaking open and a gust of mountain air surging into the church as if fleeing whatever waits outside.

There is the soft click of a closing door.

Alone, in the dark, her sniffles and tears gradually become

the words he taught her. She reaches into the darkness with all that she is.

Slides onto the cold flagstones as if she is made of straw.

31

Seascale, West Cumbria
10.16am

Fine rain greases the cracked tarmac beneath Rowan's feet. Chilly air sprints in from the cliff edge in a swirl of salt and sand, gathering up the dead leaves and the chemical stink and hurling it back inland. Rowan has only moved seven or eight miles from the lonely greenery of the valley, but this is a different world.

'Keep going,' he repeats. 'You won't think there's a house there, but there is...'

He hopes the nice lady in the post office in the village hadn't been pulling his leg. Chris had managed to discover that retired Detective Chief Inspector Eve Cater lives in a clifftop bungalow just outside of Seascale. Serendipity had dropped him off in the village on her way to the appointment with the education authority – Snowdrop looking gloomy and horribly unlike herself. She'd been made to slick her hair down, to wear sensible shoes and to wipe the mismatched nail varnish from her fingers. Serendipity had squeezed herself into one of Jo's work outfits and scraped her hair back into an explosive ponytail. Both looked as though they were heading to a court case that could lead to the gallows.

He'd trudged around for a bit, acquainting himself with the likeably down-at-heel village on the very edge of West Cumbria. The woman who ran the little café hadn't been able to help but she'd sent him to see Sara, who ran the post office. Rowan had run in as if out of breath. Given a Bafta-worthy performance as an exasperated man trying to follow instructions – the satnav in his imaginary car refusing to co-operate. *How do I find Ms Cater's place?* he'd asked, exuding a studied haplessness that always seems to bring out the maternal instincts of women of a certain age. Sara had drawn him a map and given him a free KitKat to keep his strength up on the walk.

He reaches the end of the track and emerges into a wide stretch of grassy clifftop: old farm buildings and rusty machinery spaced out erratically around a small grubby-white cottage with a sun-bleached door. The house has its back to him; its face staring out towards the nearby cliff edge – a fisherman's wife awaiting a ship's return. It's a bleak, desolate place to call home but there is something about it that Rowan finds appealing. He can see himself here, writing bad poetry by lamplight, the single-glazed windows rattling in the crumbling frames, the ceaseless gale howling down the chimney to stir the ash in the grate. He's known a lot of coppers in his life and none have chosen to spend their retirement in such a location. It's the sort of place where Rowan can imagine a medieval prison: some hellish stone tower perched on a promontory, the howls of the prisoners lost amid the crashing waves and the screeching gulls.

A small red car is parked a little way ahead. Rowan notices mud streaks up its side and pressed into the tread of the tyres. More mud hangs from the wheel arches, where tufts of wildflowers and a ragged fistful of grass sticks out of the space between the plastic and the metal. He glances in the dirty windows as he makes his way to the back door. A tartan blanket covers the back seat. There's a cardboard takeaway cup in the holder and a blue binder on the passenger seat. It's spotless on the inside.

He looks towards the house. The windows are dark and he can only see his own image reflected back, rain-streaked and distorted. He glares through himself, into the dark. Wonders if he should just turn around and go home. *This is where it becomes real,* he tells himself. *This is where you find out whether you're following a story or making things up.*

She emerges from the gloom like an iceberg. At first she's just a single blue light, a dot of gaudy azure, static in the darkness. Then, like an image forming on photographic paper, she becomes Evelyn Cater. Rowan finds himself being scrutinised by a small, round, elderly woman: her grey curls framing a round face. Her features are sunken, unpretty: dark eyes and a Roman nose, fleshy around the neck, as if she is sinking into herself. She's smoking an electronic cigarette, the tip glowing bright with each drag. It casts an eerie light, a blue halo, like a police lamp, illuminating a plain round-necked sweatshirt atop a floral shirt with a twisted collar. She's staring straight at him, her face inscrutable.

Rowan suppresses a shiver. For an instant he feels like a child. Can imagine a coterie of giggling schoolchildren hidden somewhere nearby, watching as the bravest of their number knocks on the door at a witch's cottage. He tries to make himself look innocent. Manages a smile and a roll of the eyes and an elaborate pantomime of gestures, pointing at the door and signalling that he had tried to phone, that he could just have a moment of her time, that she should think of him as a welcome presence.

She looks at him for a long while, her face completely immobile. Behind her, he glimpses an oval mirror, hung on wire from a thick nail. Sees wallpaper patterned with feathery pink flowers – a crack running from ceiling to floor. There's a small sideboard, doilies covering its surface like fresh snow. Pictures in frames, black and white, faded colours: all too indistinct to make out.

Rowan finds her gaze unnerving. He imagines her in the interview room, stare burning holes in a suspect. He feels like a document full of spelling mistakes being given a once-over by an editor. Wishes she would smile. Or just blink.

A full thirty seconds goes by before Ms Cater gives the slightest of nods and recedes back into the gloom. Rowan stays still, uncertain, watching the gulls and the crows fight for thermals and scraps of food in the bathwater-grey sky. He looks around at the forgotten farm buildings. The rusty iron guts of a tractor stick up like dinosaur bones in the open doorway of a red-roofed barn. Beyond, he sees shelves packed with stained tins of paint; sees wires and bulbs and a snarl of cables hanging from a metal hook. Car batteries are stacked like bricks.

He turns at the sound of a key turning in a lock. She's standing in the doorway, one eye closed, the e-cig still wedged between her lips. She looks a bit like Popeye. She looks her age too. Beneath her jumper she's soft and plump: clementines in a hessian bag. The lines in her face are an Ordnance Survey map of a mountain range – tight contours marking impossible peaks. When she talks, it's clear the vaping is a recent compromise. Her throat rasps with the tell-tale roughness of a lifelong smoker.

'Before you start, I'll be having none of it,' says Ms Cater, raising a small, plump, ringless hand.

'I'm sorry?' asks Rowan, his rehearsed opening gambit fading on his tongue. 'None of what?'

'Whatever it is you're selling,' she snaps. 'If it's pegs, I'm up to my eyeballs. If it's insurance, I've got nowt valuable. I can't have double glazing because it's a listed building and I don't have a clue what PPI is, although it sounds like a dirty thing to me.'

Rowan finds himself grinning. He likes her at once. 'None of the above,' he says, standing on the path by the door. From behind her he can catch the smell of stale cigarettes and damp. Something else. A scent like burnt jam; acrid and sweet.

She disappears for a moment, the door swinging open invitingly. He wonders if she's extended an invitation. Before he can move she's back, thick bifocal glasses sitting uncomfortably on her nose. She glares at him before her mouth twists into a harsh grimace. 'I'm reading your book,' says Ms Cater, and she does not sound like a fan.

'It's a new service,' says Rowan, trying for charm. 'We're going door to door, visiting readers, filling in any gaps in the narrative and checking you're happy with your purchase...'

She doesn't smile. Lets him talk until he stops. 'I wondered if we might have a chat,' he says, weakly. She has a way of leaving silences, or making him feel awkward, that he has always associated with a certain type of police officer. He has no doubt that if she pulled him over for speeding he would confess to having three bodies in the boot.

'A chat?' she asks, removing the e-cig. 'Now why would you be wondering that?' Her lips smack as she talks, a sibilant shushing sound. She's toothless, and isn't wearing dentures.

Rowan gestures around him at the cold and the rain. 'Could we maybe talk inside?' he asks. He raises his gloved hands. 'I'm hiding a multitude of injuries here. I need to take my painkillers and a glass of water would be very much appreciated.'

She snorts, scornfully. 'Don't try that bollocks, lad,' she says, clearly disappointed in him. 'I've seen your sort in action enough times to be on my guard. Saw some prick from *The Mirror* rip his own trousers just so he could knock on the door of a grieving wife and ask for a needle and thread to help him cover his dignity. Stole a photo off the wall while he was alone in the doorway. It was in the paper the next day. I'd have ripped more than his trousers if it impacted on the case.'

Rowan tries to exude an air of apology – heartfelt regret at what some of his unscrupulous competitors were willing to do. Makes a mental note to stop wearing jeans and to invest in cheap polyester trousers with a rippable seam, just in case. He weighs up the likelihood of Ms Cater falling for any of his bullshit and decides to drop any pretence.

'If you're reading my book, you'll know a little about

me,' he says, closing one eye to mirror her expression.
'You'll know what I do.'

'Aye,' she confirms, a tiny smile twisting her lips. 'You're
good at talking to people, I'll give you that. You got more
out of Gary King than the copper who took him down, but
then, all the copper could offer was a shorter life sentence.
You were offering fame and fortune.'

'No fortune,' says Rowan. 'He didn't make any money.'

'But you did,' she says, and he sees her reaching for the
door.

'A little,' he admits. 'Not enough to compensate me for
the hours spent in the company of somebody who made my
flesh crawl.'

'Sounded like you got on, from what I read,' says
Ms Cater.

Rowan shrugs. 'That's the job, isn't it? You were a copper
more than thirty years. You're telling me you've never been
nice to a killer to get them onside?'

Ms Cater removes her glasses, as if she's seen enough.
'Serendipity's brother, aren't you? Thought so. You comfortable
in the Byre, are you? Christ, it comes to something when
that's where you choose to convalesce.'

'You know a lot,' says Rowan, as somewhere overhead
a gull screams as if on fire. 'Reading up on me, were you?'

Ms Cater nods, almost imperceptibly. She seems to be
having a conversation with herself. 'I'm only guessing,'
she says, 'but I reckon you're here to ask me about Violet.'

Rowan chews his lip, unsure how to proceed. The
recording device in his pocket is only picking up the sounds
of the gale and the faintest muffle of conversation. He wants
to get inside and get comfortable. He's good at getting older

ladies on-side. A few compliments, a few variations on the theme of *"you're never really seventy-five are you?"* and usually it's less than half an hour before they're giving him everything he wants over fruit scones and loose-leaf tea. Evelyn Cater doesn't seem like a standard OAP. She looks as though she's cracked a few kneecaps with a hammer and isn't above doing it again. He has a vision of some crook-backed East European peasant woman, carrying twice her bodyweight in hay: a cast-iron will and bloody-minded refusal to succumb to age.

'You have her post, apparently,' says Rowan. 'Rosie says you've been picking it up for the past few months.'

'Does she now?' replies Ms Cater.

'I'd hoped to have a chat with Violet myself,' says Rowan, keeping his eyes upon hers, even as he feels the urge to look away. 'Apparently she's been gone a good long while. Finding herself, is that right?'

She looks at him for a long moment. He feels as though he's being weighed on a scale.

'I'm writing a book,' he says. 'There are unanswered questions.'

'About Violet?' asks Ms Cater, suddenly scornful. 'Who's asking questions?'

'I am,' he says, and it sounds absurd to his own ears. 'About what happened in 1991. When they went missing.'

Ms Cater's face sets like concrete. She glares through him. 'Fuck all happened in 1991, son,' she growls. 'She and two of her mates got drunk and spent a weekend living large. Then they came home.'

'It really would be better to talk inside,' says Rowan, moving towards the door. He sees Ms Cater stiffen where she stands, and he suddenly realises that the left side of her body has remained concealed behind the wooden door since she opened it. He wonders what she's holding. He's been on enough rural properties to be painfully aware how easy it is to obtain a shotgun licence. Easier still for a decorated ex-cop.

'I think I'd like you to go,' says Ms Cater, flatly. 'It's not how it's done, you see. Not here. You don't just turn up and expect people to dance to your tune. I've got things to do.'

From behind her, he hears a second voice; brighter, younger. Somebody is shouting her name. Ms Cater gives a jerk with her chin. 'Violet's none of your business. There's no story here. You'd be as well to fuck off before you get properly hurt.'

Rowan gives a bark of laughter, holding up his hands. 'Carl Jung said there can be no coming to consciousness without pain.'

'Did he? Well he sounds like a prick as well.'

Rowan stands still, weighing his options. He wants her onside. He doesn't know whether he's played this wrong or whether she would have greeted him the same even if he'd turned up carrying flowers and cash. He feels his temper stirring, partly at the mean old bitch in the doorway but mostly at his own feckless self.

'Freya Grey,' he says, throwing the name out like a trump card. 'We're talking online. Violet and me are too. I'm seeing Catherine Marlish too. Lovely girl – gifted writer. If you want to get a message to Violet, just tell me. I'll pass it on.'

Her lip curls. She looks like she wants to spit. 'Leave it,' she says. 'No more.'

'It's amazing what you learn when you pull a thread,' he continues, twin points of red temper on his pale cheeks. 'All the stuff that unravels. You can weave the most extraordinary tapestry of lies but one loose thread and it all comes apart. I thought you might want to make sure you were on the right side.'

She flares her nostrils as if there's a bad smell. From behind her he can hear her name being called again. It's friendly, a sing-song call for "Eve".

'There's no threads to pull, lad. There's nowt to find out. Violet's having the time of her life. Freya doesn't need owt dragging up. Catherine's a soppy sod but she's doing okay. Don't spoil it. It's all the way it should be.'

Rowan wants her e-cig. Wants the warmth of a fireside. He doesn't know if he can take things forward without her help. He starts thinking about the other officers named in the case. Wonders whether he can find a next of kin for Derrick Millward. If he's buried in the Wasdale church then Catherine's father will be bound to know. Perhaps he could leave her to stew a little and come back when he knows more. Perhaps she's had a bad morning. Maybe she's not always got a face that could curdle breast milk.

'I'm sorry if I've come at a bad time,' says Rowan, softening his demeanour. 'I'm struggling for transport and your number isn't in the book. I wouldn't have bothered you if I didn't have some real concerns about Violet. I don't know if you're on Facebook but all these posts she's been sharing – none of them have pictures. And she made no preparations for going away. I'm told you're good friends, so that means you know how out of character this is…'

'No more,' says Ms Cater, holding up a hand like a traffic cop. 'I've asked nicely. Now I'm going to tell you to fuck off.'

Rowan gives a sad smile, beaten. Nods, and the rain runs down his face. For a moment, Ms Cater's demeanour seems to soften. Just as quickly it is gone. The door slams shut with an air of absolute finality and Rowan is left with just the damp air and the howling gale and the mournful cawing of the birds. He turns and trudges back the way he came, grinding his teeth together. He's got a long walk back into the village and an even further walk home. He hadn't really imagined things going wrong. He'd presumed that by now he would be sitting in a comfortable chair, sharing stories and bringing some much-needed distraction into an old lady's life.

He looks up at the roiling clouds as he stomps past the tatty outbuildings and back into the unfinished tunnel of spiky hedges and trees. He's offered a little protection from the wind and manages to get his phone out of his pocket without too much discomfort to his healing skin. He's recorded nine minutes of static and air. His heart sinks as he scrolls through his messages. Matti, his agent, has had a chat with his editor and they're really excited about what he's going to deliver. They really need to see some pages, and fast. Rowan growls as he dismisses the message and flicks past an unsolicited message from Snowdrop, telling him she can't wait to hear how his chat with Ms Cater has gone. He's considering throwing the phone at a low-flying gull when it pings in his hand. It's a message from Violet, finally responding to his cheeky missive, sent while smoking with Pickle. It's terse in tone, thoroughly dispiriting.

Away at moment. Peace and love.

Rowan looks back towards the cliff. Sometimes, it would be easier to just give in to the masochistic impulse. He can see himself lying smashed on the rocks below, his body undone, guts and bones a grisly sculpture across the sand. He keeps trudging on. There had been a pub in the village, hadn't there? He's sure he can persuade the landlord or landlady to open early. He can make good on any promise he makes about how much he intends to spend. He's got a thirst, suddenly. Can feel a nervous prickling in his skin, like the air before a storm.

There is a sound behind him like distant thunder. He glances back and sees the little red car trundling slowly towards him over the pitted track. There's a blonde lady at the wheel. He recognises her at once. She'd been at the writing group.

He makes a show of star-fishing himself against the hedge, sharp twigs pressing into his back. She slows down, the window sliding down. He gets a smell of bleach and lemon-scented wet wipes. Smells something a little like damp dog. She's leaning across, her face open and friendly. He bends down to the open window, managing a weary smile. He takes a quick mental picture for later analysis. His age, near enough. Blonde hair, quiffed on top and shaved almost down to the skin at the back and sides. She's wearing glasses, spotted with raindrops. Beneath a sensible fleece jacket he sees the bottom of a blue apron, rumpled around the thighs. At her neck is a glimpse of blue cord that disappears down into the folds of her clothes.

'She didn't bite then?' asks the driver, grinning. 'I wince

when I hear the way she talks to visitors, I really do. Don't take it personally. I've seen her reading your book and she was properly engrossed. Sat with it like she was doing a crossword, underlining bits.'

'You don't have to be extra nice just to compensate,' says Rowan, pretending to sulk. 'Truth be told, I probably got what I deserved.'

'Was there anything I could help with?' she asks, looking genuinely keen to help. 'I mean, I could sweeten her up for you if you tell me what you're after. My name's Vicki. Well, Vicki-Louise, actually.'

Rowan shrugs. 'Rowan, like the tree. I'm not sure what I'm after. Somebody mentioned a case she'd worked on and I thought she might be able to fill in some gaps. Didn't work out.'

'Ah.' Vicki nods, as if this was only to be expected. 'Not one for talking about the past, our Eve. She's a sweetie underneath but since she's been on her own – well, you can imagine. The last house before the power station, moving closer to the cliff edge every year... it's hardly going to keep your spirits up.'

'Is there nowhere more suitable?'

Vicki shakes her head. 'Not a chance. She'd shoot the first bugger who suggested it.'

Rowan pretends to suddenly recognise her. 'You were at the group, weren't you? The writing group – at the posh house with the woman who sounded like Penelope Keith? You stood out. Youngest by about thirty years, I'd say.'

She rolls her eyes, tutting. 'I reckon you were saying much the same to the vicar's daughter. My mam enjoyed herself. Said you were very cheeky, but said it in a nice way.'

'You didn't hear the talk?' asks Rowan, doing mental calculations.

'I just picked Mam up,' she says, apologetically. 'She loves it. I told her for years to write her stories down but she's doing it at last and she's loving it. I'm always telling my old lords and ladies to get their memories down before they fade. It must be awful to have been here and nobody remember.'

He jerks his head back up the road. 'I doubt you'll get Ms Cater along to something like that,' he grumbles. 'Writing is supposed to come from the heart, and I'm sensing a distinct absence of apparatus.'

The driver gives a polite smile. 'You'd be surprised,' she mumbles, and the car rocks slightly as the wind catches her words.

'Sorry,' protests Rowan, cupping a hand to his ear. He notices her looking at the glove and wincing in sympathy. She already knows what happened.

'Do you need a lift somewhere?' she asks, raising her voice. 'I've got a house to do down at Ravenglass but the lady isn't back until teatime so it's not a bother.'

'You have a cleaning firm?' asks Rowan, taking a guess.

'Not exactly a firm.' Vicki smiles. 'But yes, I clean. I've got three young kids and one big one at home so if I'm not earning money for cleaning I'm usually picking somebody's stuff up for free.' She gives him a little grin. 'What was it you wanted from Eve, anyway? She's not the sort who enjoys a chat, though she's always nice to me. I got tickets for a spa day at the Sharrow Bay last Christmas – I proper filled up when they fell out my card. My mate Violet said not to worry about it – that it was her way of putting up with being a cantankerous cow some days. She suffers, you see.'

'Suffers?'

'She's not very well, I'm sure you spotted that. She won't talk about it and she won't accept a lift to her appointments but she's been at the hospital a lot this past year. Still, she's doing good for her age.'

'Violet Rayner, is that?' asks Rowan, guilelessly. 'Small world. She's a friend of Catherine's, isn't she? My sister too, of course. Have you heard from her on her big adventure?'

'Just what I've seen online,' says Vicki, shivering as a gust of wind finds its way into the car. 'I hope she's back soon though, because Eve's house is going to start sinking under the weight of her bloody post. If it wasn't for the wood burner the recycling bin would have burst.'

'All right for some,' says Rowan, rolling his eyes. The car looks warm. Vicki does too.

'So?' she asks, invitingly. 'I can't leave you out in this.'

Rowan opens the door and ducks into the passenger seat, wiping the water from his face and muttering grateful thanks. Some tinny, cheesy pop music is bleeding out of the stereo. She switches it off, the sleeve of her fleece rising up to reveal a swirl of tree roots. Beneath the ink, he catches sight of thin white scars.

'I haven't eaten,' says Rowan. 'Would you get into trouble with any of your clients if I was to buy you a tea and a sticky bun?'

She grins, impish, and he sees smoker's teeth and the glint of the silver stud that pierces her tongue.

'I don't think I'd risk trouble for tea and a sticky bun,' she says, turning back to the road. The wipers carve a silhouette of Sydney Opera House onto the mud-streaked glass.

'How about a pint and a packet of dry-roasted?' asks Rowan, turning to face her. He's suddenly enjoying this game.

Vicki smiles. 'Sold.'

32

Santon Bridge, Wasdale. The home of Violet Sheehan
January 8, this year

The wall is cool against Violet's forehead: damp, like a vodka bottle straight from the freezer. It's a pleasant, sensual feeling. She rolls her head from side to side, as if grinding out a cigarette butt with her brow. Trundles her face from side to side, pressing first one cheek, then the other, against the clammy green surface.

Left.

Right.

She pulls back. Looks at the image her sweat has created. Sees a butterfly: two symmetrical wings patterned with circles, captured mid-flight. She leans in and draws eyes in the condensation with a bruised knuckle. Crafts a garish smile. Daubs imperfect teeth. Tusks. Smears the imprint into something vague and grotesque, a mess of meandering tracks and overspilling features, trickling into and over one another. Sees wrinkles gathering at eyes, running into nose, mouth, dripping, blooming, to puncture and trickle into nothingness.

She feels dizzy as she stares, watching her likeness bleed and dissolve.

Violet remembers this feeling. This sensation of staring into one's own eyes. She has done this many times. As a child, she used to like saying her own name, again and again, monotonously, never rising, never falling, over and over, eyes swimming in the edgeless pools of her own reflected vision, losing all sense of herself, just shapes and words, noises and textures, splitting, like single-celled creatures beneath a microscope, halving themselves, again, again, becoming more and less than themselves...

The ayahuasca tastes bitter on her tongue. Bitter, like burning sage. But behind it there is a sweetness. A memory of nectar. Of something honeyed and warm and wholesome. She flashes on a memory. Sees images that fight for the surface like drowning sailors.

'Catherine,' she gasps, and for a moment she can see her friend, dressed in white, blue marking on her skin. She sees a girl with red hair and white lines carved into her arm. She can see a man with green toenails, standing above her, head cocked, as a drum beats nearby like the heartbeat of the earth.

She has a moment of perfect clarity. She sees herself here. Now. In the little room at the back of her house on the quiet road between the valleys. She can hear the gentle, calming voice of the shamanic healer who strokes her back and guides her mind and tries to reach inside her to pull out the fractured pieces of her soul and the ripped pictures of her memory.

She needs to remember. It has been too many years. For

three decades she has left a part of her mind boarded up and shut down. For thirty years she has tried to pretend that she believes what they told her about those nights in the forest. For thirty years she has told herself that Eve Cater is her friend because she likes her, and not because she is staying close, looking for signs of her memory coming back – of one day recollecting perfectly what happened in that place beneath the ground, when she and Catherine woke to find themselves in a place of bones and broken glass; the body of Arthur Sixpence dangling from an iron ladder high above.

A scream rips upwards and out of her throat. The memory is perfect. Clear as day. She feels warm blood upon her skin. The shaman's blood. Sees herself clambering towards the light. She hadn't stopped for Freya. Had just clambered, drunkenly, up the jagged slope and clawed her way into the darkness of the forest. She had lost sight of Catherine. And then something startled her, and she had lashed out, unthinking, just as she had when the pig-faced thing tried to touch her. She had hurt Eve. Had spilled her blood. Had ripped off her clothes and dragged herself through the roots and branches and fallen trees and hadn't stopped running until she fell into the arms of the Mountain Rescue men. Catherine was with them, sobbing, terrified, eyes like skulls.

She had let them soothe her. Calm her. Had given in to sleep. And she had let go of the memories: disappearing like flakes of ash above a fire.

She knows that she will not rest easy again until she finds Freya.

Finds her, and asks her why so many people lied to

cover up the fact that she never came back. That she and Catherine had left her there to die. Left her with the body of two dead shaman, trapped at the bottom of an old mineshaft filled with bones.

33

The Harbourmaster in Whitehaven is the sort of pub where Rowan feels instinctively comfortable. It's not so much spit-and-sawdust as phlegm-and-fibreglass. The cosy pubs in the valley are infinitely nicer to look at and he's got nothing personal against landscapes or log fires or exposed wooden beams, but there's something delightfully honest about watering holes where the main aim of the clientele is to get cheaply pissed.

It's at its quietest now, just after lunch. Those who started drinking at breakfast time have gone home for a microwave meal and a doze. The evening crowd has yet to come in. The handful of men and women who mill around the bar drinking pints of Foster's and Carling are damp from the fine rain and Rowan keeps hearing snatches of their conversation. He has to suppress a smile as dialect words half-remembered from years before bubble up from the mouths of the pleasantly pissed.

Daft raji.

Proper charver.

Her gadgi; his bewer.

Aye, that's proper bari.

On the table, his phone vibrates, moving itself closer to a

sticky streak of spilled beer. The bottom of the pint glasses have left a careless Olympic symbol on the grainy varnish of the tabletop.

He squints at the screen. He's downed a couple of pints of the local real ale and it's done nothing to help his headache. He feels as though his eyeballs are expanding in the sockets. If he could use his hands he would be massaging his sinuses. He doesn't feel able to ask his companion to oblige in his stead. Although he and Vicki are enjoying getting drunk together, he isn't sure they've reached the stage in their relationship where he can safely ask her to knead his Eustachian tube.

'You Bobby Dazzler,' mutters Rowan, as the words come into focus. An hour ago he left a post on the Friends of Silver Birch Academy Facebook group. He's gone for a soft, deferential tone, in keeping with the general character of the fake social media persona he's selected for the role.

Thanks so much for letting me join – I won't bore you all with the details but I'm putting together a bit of a surprise do for one of our number (she's blocked from seeing this, ha ha!). I want as many of her old friends to be there as possible so watch this space for more info. Which of you good ladies were at the school in 1991? A list of all her classmates would be such a help. And if any of you see Violet on her travels, tell her she has to get back in time for the festivities. Lol!

He smiles to himself as he stares at the list of names, provided so helpfully by the site administrator. Sees Catherine's name in among others that, so far, mean nothing to him. An older pupil, her avatar showing an attractive brunette with a Botoxed forehead and inflatable lips, has promised to dig out some class photographs for him. He notices a couple of friend requests from members of the group. Accepts them both and opens an accompanying message. It's from a sweet-sounding lady called Natasha.

Hi there Rowan and welcome to the Group. I don't want to sound like a killjoy but there were a few shenanigans back in '91 that might make things a little awkward on the party front. I'm not sure if you know but Violet and two of her friends were in the paper at that time because they went off with this busker they'd met in Keswick. We had an assembly before they came back and Mr Rideal and Mr Tunstall said we all had to be very understanding and leave them be and not ask questions in case it upset them. The other girl – I think her name was Fleur or Freya or something – didn't come back to school but somebody told me she'd gone back to Ireland and she's never been in touch with any of us. She wasn't at the school very long. Anyway, thought you should know. Have a great time and do let me know when it's time for the big shindig. xx

Rowan clicks his tongue, aware that his leg is jiggling up and down.

It's a fascinating old building…

types Rowan, as quickly as he can.

I've been having a proper snoop around and it's such a shame that things didn't work out for the owners. Seems to me that one of them should have bought some lucky heather when it was offered. Am I right in thinking one of the owners was lost while fell-walking? And who's this Mr Sixpence I keep hearing about? Hope I'm not disturbing you. Violet does talk about her school days with a lot of affection, which is why I want so many of her classmates there. I don't want to put my foot in it though, so if I'm making a faux pas just shout at me! xx

He hits "send". Glances around, his fingers steepled at the tips. He suddenly wants to have some space in which to think. The jingle of the slot machine and the bursts of raucous laughter from the table by the window are starting to grate on his nerves. He looks up, irritated. Two middle-aged men are beerily pawing at a younger woman with slicked-back, batter-blonde hair. She's putting up with them because they're buying her drinks: bottles and glasses and crisp packets spread out on the table like casualties from a battle. As Rowan watches, one of the men raises his buttocks from the red velvet bar stool and emits a long, trumpeting fart. He laughs, delighted with himself, as his mate slaps him on the back and tries to belch an echo. The girl's dutiful smile stops well short of her eyes.

He looks back at the phone. The trio of dots indicate she's typing a response. He feels himself becoming restless, as though he's sitting at a stop line on a deserted road. He reads the reply quickly, thinking fast.

Mr Sixpence! Ha! Yeah, he was a proper character. We all used to make up stories about what he'd been like before he went a little bit peculiar. He was my first experience of a proper hippy, though he wouldn't have called himself that. He was like a guidance counsellor as much as an odd-job man. He knew loads of stuff and it was nice to have an occasional teacher who could go from telling you about the philosophies of Carl Jung to instructing you in reiki healing and teaching you how to catch squirrels.

I'm sure wherever he disappeared to he was gratefully received, though we missed him after he'd gone. It was sad seeing his old camp left to go to ruin like that – it was nice him being there in the woods, smoking by the fire, telling his stories about all the places he'd seen and the people he'd helped. He's probably long dead now but if you happen to find a relative or a next of kin, tell them Mr Sixpence was always our favourite.

Rowan rubs his cheek, little points of light burning in the darkened windows of his eyes.

Wow, at my school the most exciting teacher was the head of geography, and that was just because he had a wig that could defy the laws of gravity. We used to think he'd trained some horribly mutated platypus to cling to his shiny scalp! Anyway, I'll leave you to it. Before I go, do you think Violet would want Mr Tunstall to get an invitation? He's still around isn't he?

He looks up nervously, listening to the clatter of bottles

hitting the table; of bar stools screeching across the scarred
floor. He can hear the two drunken arseholes trying to work
out which actor played James Bond after Roger Moore.
The effort of thinking seems to be paining them. He keeps
hearing the leader say "Morgan. That Morgan bloke. Slick
fella." Rowan realises that his brain has got stuck on the
word "Piers" and replaced Brosnan with a truly horrifying
prospect. Either way, he is resisting the urge to tell them
that they're wrong about this, and a lot of other things too.

He wouldn't come! Lol, that's priceless! No, he won't
even come to reunions, though that's hardly unusual. I
think we've maybe seen two or three of the old staff since
it closed. He's a bit bitter, I think, though he's got himself
a very nice house out of it and he didn't do badly when
the Trust wound up, or so I heard. He's geriatric now
anyway. Last I saw him was at a memorial service at St
Olaf's. They have one every once in a while for those
lost on the mountain. He was there for Rideal, I suppose.
Didn't look well but he was civil enough.

Rowan plays it safe with his reply.

You don't sound like you were a fan of Rideal's...

She's back on in moments.

He didn't have much to do with the school. Good at
speeches and even better with the finances apparently
but not somebody you'd think of as a neat fit in a school
that pushed alternative, independent thinking. He was

much more of a suit, though I guess the world needs a few of those to function. And to be fair, when Sixpence went missing and there were fears for his safety, it was Rideal who gave the assembly and told us he had no doubts the old boy was having the time of his life somewhere. Same when there was the other incident in '91. He was good at stepping up when the outside world came sniffing.

Even so, we weren't exactly blubbing when we heard what had happened on the mountain in 2004. I mean, what was the silly sod even doing up there? He'd had bronchial problems going back years. That was what made him so creepy to us girls, I suppose – this snorting, horrible breathing noise, like a pig with its nose in the trough. Sorry, I don't suppose this is any use to you, is it? I do rattle on!

Rowan looks up, as he hears the girl mutter the correct answer to the Bond conundrum, slightly louder than the previous four times she has tried to get a word in.

'Bollocks, no it's not. The bloke from Flash Gordon? He never played Bond.'

'He did…'

'It's Timothy Dalton, you wanker,' grumbles Rowan, trying to concentrate on a reply. He realises he's said it loudly enough for heads to turn.

'That's better.' Vicki laughs, stumbling back from the ladies' toilets, trying to straighten her tabard and tuck herself in without spilling the last of her pint. The beer, she insists, is for sustenance and nourishment. It's the trio of double vodka tonics that are the indulgence. Rowan isn't sure she'll make it to Ravenglass or whether she will be in any fit state to wield a vacuum when she gets there.

'I'm sorry about that lot,' mutters Rowan, gesturing at the table and putting his phone away. He shoots a glance at the barman. He's probably younger than the woman. Perhaps twenty, no more. A tight T-shirt, grimy glasses and a body that's all joints and gristle. Rowan feels a swell of pity for the lad. The two boorish dickheads are twice his size. The nearest has a roll of fat at his neck like a pug. He's wearing a Fred Perry tracksuit top with shiny blue jeans and white trainers. He's around Rowan's age, and still sports a hairstyle made famous by the footballer Lee Sharpe around 1992: short hair gelled forward and snipped in a perfectly straight line at the fringe. His mate is wearing a checked shirt beneath a short bomber jacket – chunky gold chains around his neck.

'Which lot?' asks Vicki, looking around. 'Oh, you mean Daz Shipley?' She looks back to Rowan. 'Fancies himself a bit. I would say he's harmless, but he's not. That's Robin with him. He went to school with my first boyfriend. Ploughed his dad's Peugeot into Santon Bridge when he was fifteen. He escaped unhurt but thankfully his dad had the presence of mind to break his jaw. He's talked a bit funny since. If you do end up writing a book about this place, don't waste a page on those arseholes.'

Rowan is enjoying Vicki. He's learned more than he needs to. She's from Carlisle originally, which makes her positively cosmopolitan in these parts. She lives in a three-bedroomed terraced house near the seafront in Seascale with four children and a lodger: a reclusive Polish man who works in one of the posher Lakeland hotels. She's been married twice, she has an older sister called Beth, and she cleans for seven different private clients in the West Cumbria area. She worked as a care assistant at a retirement home for a few years but was placed on a zero-hours contract a while back that couldn't guarantee her the hours she needed.

For all that he is now well versed in her life, Rowan is beginning to wonder whether there is anything further to be gained from the exchange. He's bought all the drinks so far and he hasn't got the energy to sleep with her. He's considering making a show of draining the last of his pint. Wonders if it would be rude to leave her a tenner for a cab and to wish her well with whatever comes next in life. He'd quite like to smash Shipley's head through the fruit machine as he goes. Wonders if the pain to his hands will be worth the satisfaction of punching at least one of them in the face.

'It's a shame you never met her partner,' says Vicki, unexpectedly. She'd been gazing at a picture of a racehorse on the wall behind them and it takes Rowan a second to work out that she isn't referring to the animal.

'Eve, you mean? Ms Cater?'

Vicki turns back to the barman and signals for two more drinks. Ruefully, Rowan realises he's not going anywhere yet. He watches as Vicki retrieves her phone from the pocket of her tabard and sends a quick message. She spins the screen. 'They're my boys,' she mutters. 'Tyler's got my eyes, don't you think? My dimples are cuter though.'

Rowan nods, encouragingly. 'Who was her partner?' he asks, steering her back on course. 'And you mean romantic partner, yes? Not that they owned a business together.'

'Romantic in a way.' Vicki shrugs, as the drinks appear on the edge of the bar. She looks at the barman, expecting him to bring them over. He looks away, pretending not to see her. She stands up, noisily, and returns a moment later with a double vodka for herself and a pint of the local ale for Rowan. He'd swap it for a glass of even the cheapest whisky if given the chance.

'In a way?' Rowan smiles, taking a sip.

Vicki makes a show of narrowing one eye at him. 'Don't think you've got me fooled,' she says, mischievously. 'I'm not buying this "little-boy-lost" act of yours. I know what you're doing.'

Rowan takes a longer swallow, buying time. Decides to just take whatever's coming. 'And what am I doing?'

'You're writing about what happened,' she says, pulling her chair closer to the table. 'Violet and Catherine and the other girl.'

'Freya,' says Rowan, meeting her eyes. 'Freya Grey. Do you know the name?'

Vicki shakes her head. Sips her drink. 'I don't know the vicar's daughter very well but Violet's been a visitor at Eve's place for as long as I've been cleaning for her.'

'And how long's that?'

'Five or six years, I reckon,' she says, chewing her cheek. 'I looked after Derrick first and then Eve needed a bit of help with a few bits at home so I stayed in touch.'

Rowan licks his lips. He glances at the two men who sit at the table by the bar. Shipley has turned away from the girl and is staring at Rowan. His cheeks are flushed and he seems to be sucking spit through his teeth; a whale feasting on krill. 'Tell me about Derrick,' he says, giving Vicki his full attention. 'You looked after him?'

'When I was a care worker,' she says, rubbing her

finger around the top of her glass. 'Lovely place not far from Kendal. It wasn't cheap but you get what you pay for. Like I say, if they'd given me a proper contract I'd still be there.'

'I've heard he was a decent soul.' Rowan smiles, sensing that Vicki feels a warmth towards Derrick. 'Good copper, by all accounts.'

'He had plenty stories to tell,' says Vicki. 'He was frail, obviously, though that wasn't unusual. He got cross when he couldn't do things and he never got comfortable with being looked after, not really. He had dreadful arthritis and he suffered terribly with pain in his joints. He'd fallen in love with the Lakes when he moved back up here and I know it hurt him that he couldn't do much walking like he did when he was young. He always wanted the window open in his room. Loved it when the wind was properly blowing. He was somebody who liked the outside.'

'I've read the obituary,' says Rowan. 'No children.'

Vicki shakes her head. 'He was married once but that had long since broken down. No, I think his significant other was Eve, though you wouldn't have put them together. He was a charming so-and-so, very softly spoken, very thoughtful. He was clever too. He could barely hold a pen but I'd read him the clues from the crossword and he'd always know the answers. When he didn't he'd insist I look them up. He couldn't stand not knowing things. I'm just grateful there wasn't too much suffering. When he went downhill it was quick.'

'Physically or mentally?' asks Rowan.

'Both,' says Vicki, softly. 'It happens that way. He started having nightmares. It breaks your heart to see them like that, these old men who used to be, well… I suppose you'd use the word "formidable". He'd been a copper and a private detective and he'd done a lot for a lot of people. Eve told me when she'd come to visit. I think she wanted me to know just who it was I was looking after.'

'The article about his death was a bit vague,' says Rowan, glancing back at Shipley. The other man is looking at him too, whispering in Daz's ear. Rowan ignores them, focused on Vicki.

'Well, you can't blame the care home, not really,' says Vicki, draining her glass and staring at the tabletop. 'He might have been vulnerable but he wasn't a prisoner. He'd picked Levens House because he'd always loved the outdoors and he'd always felt pretty confident taking a walk in the grounds. That was one of his pleasures in life.' She smiles at a memory and Rowan is surprised to see tears glisten in her eyes.

'I can see him now. He was always so smart, right to the end. Even when he was losing his way, when he couldn't remember things properly, when his eyesight was going – even then he wanted a daily shave and wore a suit and tie. He'd never let me do his hair. That was one of his pleasures. He only had a few strands left on top by the end but he would slick it back with a metal nit comb and a blob of Brylcreem. You could tell he'd been handsome once. Like I say, him and Eve weren't a neat match but you could see what they meant to each other. She'd visit every day. Read to him. Sit out in the grounds, even when it was raining. I sometimes think she asked me to clean for her just to keep that connection after he was gone. She still likes me to talk about him when I can – anything I remember, any daft joke he might have told. She misses him. Maybe that's why she gave you short shrift.'

Rowan stays silent, flicking his eyes back towards the two half-drunk men. Daz jerks his head, his chin jutting out. 'Help you?' he shouts, and it's a challenge. 'I can take a picture for you if you like.'

Rowan sighs, ignoring him. Vicki begins to turn around but Rowan shakes his head. He wants to hear more. Doesn't want her to get distracted.

'You don't work there now,' says Rowan, making sure he looks her in the eye. 'You could tell me about the way he died and it wouldn't be a betrayal of confidence. And I'm very good at protecting my sources.'

'I'm sure you are.' Vicki smiles, pushing her hair out of her eyes. She looks tired suddenly, as if the drink and the conversation have exhausted her. She stretches, hugely, something cracking in her shoulders.

'There was a suggestion of suicide in the article I read,' says Rowan, cautiously. 'An open verdict, but I can read between the lines.'

Vicki presses her lips together, shaking her head. 'It was ugly. He didn't deserve that. I didn't know he had that kind of hate in him.'

'Hate? Who did he hate?'

'Himself,' says Vicki, sadly. 'You wouldn't do that if you didn't, would you? I mean, I've had couples take overdoses in the past so they could die together. One pair, they'd been together sixty-plus years. Dressed themselves in their best clothes and took a month's worth of their heart pills. Fell asleep holding one another's hands, staring out the window at the sea. Not a bad way to go. Better than Derrick.'

'I don't want to bring up bad memories,' says Rowan, aware he is lying. That's exactly what he wants to bring up.

'It wasn't me who found him, thank God. I think that would have done me in. Poor Radka – she's one of the Polish ladies... well, she got such a scare. It was a week before she stopped shaking. It wasn't unusual, him going for a walk after the evening meal. That was still a pleasure for him and it didn't matter a jot if it was raining or hailing or if it was waist-deep in snow. He'd take a shuffle around the grounds. You could always tell where he'd been from the pipe smoke. He'd leave a grey trail hanging in the air. I can still smell it after all these years. It's a nice smell. I fill up when I think of it.'

'What happened, Vicki?' he asks, tenderly.

She looks past him, staring deep into a memory. 'It was suffocation,' she says, closing her eyes. 'The thing on his face almost smothered him and he'd taken a handful of pills just to make sure. His notes were almost illegible but he was saying goodbye. I think the coroner would have said it was undoubtedly suicide but Derrick's mind had gone a bit and I still don't know if he really intended to end it. I hate to think of how much he must have kept to himself. If I'd known the nightmares were getting so bad I could have done something, but he was one of those old-school men. You'd find his bed wet through, his pyjamas soaked, but he wouldn't admit to fear. I think it got to him in the end.'

'The thing on his face,' repeats Rowan. 'Can you tell me?'

Vicki's cheerful mood has disappeared along with the last of the ale. Rowan pushes his half-full glass towards her but she ignores it. She winces as she talks.

'It was a mask,' she says, her lips sticking together as

the whispered words rush out. 'Radka thought she'd found a monster. She'd done her 10.30 check and his bed was empty. It was an awful night and she thought she should go and check he was okay. She had no doubt she'd find him out in the grounds at one of his usual spots, puffing on his pipe like a steam train. It took her half an hour to find him. There's a chapel in the grounds, you see. Levens House used to be a private residence. It's a lovely old building, with a little brick church set in a square of wood. We'd have the odd service there, on warm days, but it was always too draughty to use regularly. As far as I was aware it was locked when it wasn't in use but one of the maintenance staff must have forgotten to turn the key properly because Derrick got in without a struggle and his hands were little more than claws by the end. You should have seen how he struggled with his matches trying to light his pipe. He was determined, I'll give him that.'

'The mask,' nudges Rowan. 'What did Radka see.'

'It was like something you'd buy in a joke shop,' says Vicki, frowning at the ugliness of it. 'A pig mask. This horrible pink thing that he'd pulled right over his head. It was so realistic – the snout all wrinkled like it had been pushed in and slits for the eyeholes. He tied it tight around his neck. Used one of his ties. Just sat there in the cold and the dark and breathed the last of the air. Best clothes and a pig mask. Like I say, Radka hasn't been right since.'

'Jesus,' mutters Rowan. 'There must have been an inquiry. I mean, that's pretty damn suspicious...'

'All a bit above my pay grade,' says Vicki. 'We did have a staff meeting not long after where the owners told us the police weren't looking for anybody. As far as they were concerned it was either a suicide or an accident and neither was going to lead them to a righting of a wrong so it was left well alone. His funeral was pretty. Barely a dry eye in the house. I just hope he's at peace now.'

'Who told Eve?' asks Rowan.

Vicki shakes her head. 'I didn't have the pleasure. It was days after he died that I saw her and by then she had her hard face on. She was sorting through his things. I wanted to ask her what the goodbye note had said but it wasn't really my place. Next thing was when she asked me whether I could do a bit of cleaning for her, just a couple of days a week. I'd quit the care home by then. Too many bad memories.'

Rowan rubs his gloved hand across his chin, weighing up what sound like inconsistencies. He feels the stubble rasp against the soft leather. He glances up at the sound of a chair squeaking across the floor. Shipley and Robin are moving towards him, their body language speaking entirely in capital letters and exclamation marks.

'Where the hell would he get a pig mask?' asks Rowan, perplexed.

'I don't know,' says Vicki, and it's clear she's wondered the same herself countless times. 'It's just such a horrid thing to happen. I always thought he was proud of being a policeman but towards the end he'd go on about being filthy, being a beast, being a pig – muttering in his sleep with tears running down his face. He stopped using the communal areas, retreated inside himself...'

'Here we go,' mutters Rowan.

Vicki turns at the sound of a raised voice. Whips her head

back to Rowan in alarm. 'Don't get involved,' she hisses, quickly. 'They're just dickheads really.'

'I saw you looking,' spits Daz, standing unsteadily by the table. 'Want a bit, do you? She's cheap. Posh boy like you could afford her I'm sure.'

Rowan looks up, eyes on Daz. There's a tingling in his gut but he'll be damned if he's going to show fear.

'Posh boy?' asks Rowan, quietly. 'Are you out of your fucking mind?'

'You look posh to me,' says Robin, behind him.

'I should imagine everybody looks posh to you, mate.' Rowan smiles, giving him his attention. 'That's what comes with being a couple of steps down the evolutionary scale. Maybe if you were in a cage full of monkeys you could aspire to being middle class but even then I have my doubts.'

'What's he saying?' asks Robin, nudging Daz. 'Is he taking the piss? Daz, is he taking the piss?'

Daz leans forward, both hands on the tabletop, looming over Vicki. She growls a complaint but when she tries to wriggle free he puts a hand on her shoulder and holds her where she is.

'I know you,' growls Daz. 'Know your hippy sister too. Fucking lezza. You're the writer.'

'I'm *a* writer,' corrects Rowan. 'If there was only one, my sales would be better.'

'You're a cheeky shite,' spits Daz, his breath all lager and tobacco and pickled onion crisps. He sneers at Rowan's gloved hands. 'What's with the gloves? Not want to get your nancy-boy hands dirty?'

'Nancy boy?' asks Rowan, breaking into a smile. 'Can you hear yourself? How old are you?'

'Old enough, you cunt,' says Daz, pushing forward until they are almost nose to nose. Rowan can see pastry crumbs in his back teeth and there's white powder crusting one nostril.

'I've had a spot of bother,' says Rowan, brightly. 'I've got some nasty injuries under here. I'm recuperating, which is the main reason that I'm sitting here politely and you're not bleeding.'

Daz laughs, loud and bitter, turning to his aptly named sidekick. 'Do you hear this wanker, Rob? Do you fucking hear him?'

'Fuck it,' mutters Rowan, under his breath. 'Fuck it all.'

Daz turns back to face him and Rowan lunges out of his chair like a spring. His forehead slams into the bridge of Daz's nose and he hears the crunch of displaced cartilage and a spray of hot sticky wetness on his face. Daz crumples back like a collapsing building, knocking over glasses, tangling his feet in the chairs. Beside him, Robin's mouth opens in absolute shock and Rowan turns on him, blood on his forehead, hair hanging loose across his face, eyes wide around pinprick pupils.

'Do something,' begs Rowan, and picks up an empty glass, wielding it like a dagger. 'Fucking do something, I dare you.'

Robin backs away, hands raised. Behind him, the other customers are popping up like meerkats. The girl at the table has her hands to her mouth, her mascara sticking her spindly eyelashes together. He gives her a smile and an absurd thumbs-up. She doesn't move.

Rowan becomes aware of a thudding in his chest. There's a taste of sour fruit and iron on his tongue. His head is starting to throb. He's panting, half mad, as he gives his attention back to Vicki. The blood has drained from her face but she holds his gaze. There is no pain as he retrieves a card from his pocket and places it down on the tabletop for her. She takes it, her hands shaking. He stands and wipes his face with his gloved palm. He's suddenly greasy with sweat.

'You saw,' he mutters. He raises his voice for the benefit of the barman. 'I never started that.'

'You bloody finished it,' whispers Vicki.

Rowan stands, legs shaking. Manages to pick his way out from the booth, glass still in hand. Robin is leaning over his fallen mate, who is making a grotesque, porcine snuffling sound; blood forming a slick goatee on his chin. Rowan rolls his eyes, his mood changing, suddenly full of regret. 'Recovery position,' he mutters, heading for the door. He puts the empty glass on the bar. The barman nods his thanks, though Rowan isn't completely sure which service he is grateful for.

'I'm not like this,' mumbles Rowan, pushing open the door and feeling the cold air slap his hot face. He glances back at the other drinkers. 'I'm not like this,' he says, again.

Nobody speaks.

He barges out and onto the street, his chest tight, blood surging in his ears like pebbles rolled by the tide.

Bends double, and pukes two and a half pints into the gutter, all bile and acid and flat real ale. He staggers away. Reaches for his phone as if it is a holy relic. Manages to stop the recording at the third attempt. Names the file "Vicki". Controls his breathing and phones Serendipity.

'Please,' he says, and finds he cannot turn the word into a sentence. He just repeats it, tottering down towards the harbour in the swirling rain, his face full of pig masks and blood. Then again, for emphasis: 'Please.'

34

Rowan stares out at a blur of rocks and trees, disappearing greyly down to the water's edge. The taller trees have been decapitated by fog. Beside him, he sees Serendipity looking at his hands.

'They'll heal,' she says, quietly. 'Eventually, everything does. It hurts for a while but if it doesn't kill you, it persuades you to come back stronger. I know I said I wouldn't ask, but what are you going to do to the man who did it?'

He sucks his cheek. Closes an eye. Eventually he shakes his head. 'Whatever it is, it's best you don't know about it.'

'I don't like the thought of you hurting people, Rowan. You're not like that. Not really.'

'I don't know what I am. Neither do you.'

'I know that you care about people. That's why people talk to you. Why you write with compassion.'

Rowan sniffs, cold and sore. 'I can put on a good act.'

'It's real,' says Dippy, and Rowan is amazed to see tears in her eyes. 'I know you're a good person, I really do.'

Instinctively, Rowan puts out a hand. He wants to make her feel better but doesn't understand what's wrong. She seems cross at him in her usual way but there's something more. She chatted nonsense on the drive back to her house from the side road in Whitehaven where she had picked him up; shrill inanities about her day and Jo's plans for the garden and how Snowdrop was bugging her for a new laptop so she could start to write her masterpiece.

'Dippy, I'm sorry if I've done something daft and not noticed it. I don't always get the bigger picture – you know how I am. I'm trying, I promise. Don't be worrying about me...'

She sniffs, wiping her tears with the heel of her hand. 'I don't know what's wrong with me. I just want to be right about you. Snowdrop loves you so much and I want you to be worthy of that. Just tell me – do you think this Freya person that Violet was looking for, do you think something bad happened to her?'

Rowan opens his mouth, preparing to bluster – to spill some vagaries about being able to make a story out of it whatever happens. But his sister's expression stops him. 'I don't know,' he says, under his breath. 'I think this busker might have done bad things to them. It makes sense they never spoke of it and if there was a third girl it makes sense that she put plenty of miles between herself and where it happened. It even makes a kind of sense that Rev Marlish would use some influence to make sure the coppers underplayed anything that did happen – especially if his daughter had managed to bury the experience so deep that it took three decades and a shitload of ayahuasca for the memory to surface. But then I think about this Arthur Sixpence, vanishing from the site and his mate's belief that something bad happened. I think about a private detective assisting a former protégée with a case and her refusal to talk to me about it. The language she used – it's sorted.

Leave it alone. There's something there, I know it.' The more he talks, the more sure he becomes.

'Erlik,' comes a voice, from behind. Rowan turns. Catherine Marlish is standing in the kitchen, pale-faced, hair stuck to her cheeks. There's a bruise on her cheek and her bottom lip is scabbed with dried blood.

Rowan turns to his sister. 'Dippy?'

'Catherine's fallen out with her husband, Rowan,' sniffs Serendipity. 'She lost her nerve after the talk the other night. Rang Marjorie to ask for her story to be returned. It wasn't in the pile, as you know. Snowdrop took it. For you.'

Catherine steps through the door and into the cold grey air. Up close, her injuries are easier to read. The bruise on her cheek is a palm print; the cut on her lip around the place a thumb would strike if she were struck with a big open palm. Rowan feels sick.

'I got upset,' says Catherine, meekly. 'Started getting hysterical. He had to calm me down.'

'What a fucking hero,' hisses Rowan, through gritted teeth.

'He doesn't know his own strength,' stammers Catherine. 'And I was losing my mind. I should never have written that story, let alone handed it in. Violet said not to. But why does she get to have it all, eh? It's her out there looking for Freya. Her who's remembering all this stuff and putting horrible pictures in my head that I don't want to see again...'

'I read your story,' says Rowan, gently – moving towards her as if trying to shush a nervous pony. 'It's very good. You're an excellent writer.'

'You didn't tell me the truth,' sniffs Catherine, fresh tears gathering. 'You're writing about what happened. About me. About what he did…'

'And what's that?' asks Rowan, softly. He glances at Serendipity, looking for some sort of moral how-to guide. He doesn't want to push but he can't let it go. 'What happened in those days before you were found, Catherine?'

She reaches for the wall, her hand going white at the knuckles as she leans her weight on the damp brick. 'I don't know,' she says, falteringly. 'Truly. I remember meeting him and I know that he gave us something to drink…'

'Where?' asks Rowan, quietly. 'After you left the subway where did you go?'

'He had a van. Well, more like a really tiny camper. It was a mess. All painted up with swirls and shapes and the inside was disgusting. It smelled like when grass has been left to go mouldy.'

'And where was it parked?'

'Near the lake – where the theatre is now. Where you get the bread for the ducks.'

'And he told you his name?'

'Erlik,' she sniffs, looking down at her feet. 'It was like we got high on him. It was the most grown-up thing I'd ever done. And Freya was there so we knew it would be okay. She was older than us, or seemed it at least. She knew how to look after herself. So when she drank from the bottle we thought it would be okay. I swear, I don't remember anything properly after that – just shapes and sounds and that smell: all rusty and wet. It's all just a dream until I'm waking up in my own bed and Daddy's holding my hand and telling me it's over and never to think about it again. And that's what I tried to do.'

'And Freya?' asks Rowan.

'Mr Tunstall and Mr Rideal said the school had got a letter from her. She'd been upset about what happened. The school pretty much kicked her out.'

'And Erlik? He abducted you. Drugged you...'

Catherine shakes her head. 'I don't know if that's true. He chatted to us. We got in his van. He offered a drink and we accepted it.'

'You were underage,' says Serendipity, quietly.

'Yes, we were, and that's bad, sure. But I told Daddy when he asked me and I've told everybody else since – I don't remember anybody hurting me.' She looks at Rowan, embarrassed. 'I was still a virgin, I promise.'

Rowan sucks in a breath, unsure whether he wants to embrace this fragile, broken soul, or to shake her until she stands up for herself. 'You weren't wearing any clothes when you were found,' says Rowan. 'There was paint all over you. Symbols...'

Catherine shakes her head. 'No. No that's not true. Eve said. We got drunk, took things we shouldn't have, but it all worked out okay...'

'You sound like you've been hypnotised,' says Rowan, shaking his head.

'Ask Violet,' she says, childlike. 'Violet remembers more than me but if anything like that had happened she would have told me. She's friends with Eve. And Eve looked after us. Violet should never have started making me remember. She was happier not knowing too. All that stuff with drugs and chanting and drums and that horrible thing she painted on the wall. I thought she was trying to scare it all out of me.'

Rowan tries to hold her gaze. 'I've seen it. It's a wild boar, isn't it?'

Catherine shudders. 'She was trying to be like him. She'd sit and smoke Bible pages and chuck bacon fat in the firepit, trying to make her memory come back to life. I didn't want to do it but the memory of everything that came before – it just pinged into my head. I remembered him. The busker. Erlik. And when I said it out loud, that's when she started to remember too.'

'I know that name,' says Rowan, quietly. 'Erlik.'

'She wouldn't stop,' sniffs Catherine. 'Wanted me to be a part of it with her and kept telling me everything she was learning.'

'And that was?'

She takes a breath. 'In shamanic mythology he's a god of death. A monster. The face and teeth of a pig with a human frame. A deity of evil, darkness, lord of the lower world and judge of the dead.'

Rowan glances at Serendipity. 'I remember,' he says, softly. 'Mum's lessons.'

Serendipity chews her lip. A cold breeze lifts her hair. 'He's what other shaman are fearful of,' says Serendipity. 'He piggy-backs the journeys of others. He seeks out souls. Imprisons them forever in a place that's neither life nor death…'

Rowan feels a memory lift off like ash from the fire in his skull. Back before he went wrong. Went bad. Back when he was small. That night, parked up in the woods; the sound of bullet-hard apples bouncing off the roof of the school bus; an angora shawl around his shoulders and his feet near enough to the stove to pass for warm.

He'd been snuggled down with Serendipity and Mum, listening to one of the older men talk about the bad thing that had happened at a camp they knew. Telling them about the man with the mismatched eyes who had tried to buy mandrake and ayahuasca from a dealer they shared. The dealer had told him she didn't dabble with that stuff and told him not to ask again. He'd taken a nail to her. Driven a four-inch spike into the bone of her breastplate, slamming it home with his palm.

The man had escaped when the screams roused the families from the other shelters on the site where they had made camp. Slipped out of a smashed window, leaving a flap of skin hanging on shredded glass. His victim named him as Erlik. Told Mum to be careful. To look out for strangers and to believe her gut when it suggested a person shouldn't be trusted...

'It's Hungarian,' says Rowan, surprising himself. 'The god of death. A very powerful figure in shamanism.'

Serendipity looks sideways at him. 'You remember?'

He shrugs. 'I'm good at playing ignorant. People enjoy explaining things they're an expert in – educating the uneducated. I'm happy to play that role.'

'When in truth...'

He smiles, weakly. 'We grew up with this, Dippy. If it wasn't howling at the moon or making potions for the Wiccan gods we were dabbling in Pagan rituals and reading each other's tea leaves. Mum's mates always told me I had a touch of the old ways about me too. Had me convinced that the things I used to see were manifests – gifts from another form of consciousness. They said I could be a healer. Then when reality got its hands on me I discovered there was another way to view it. I was ill. I couldn't see auras, couldn't read souls. I needed medication and care.'

'And now? What do you believe?'

Rowan looks up at the sky. 'I don't know. People who believe too deeply in things tend to become zealots. Extremists.'

'Is she in trouble, do you think?' asks Catherine, quietly. 'I'm not allowed on Facebook but people say she's having a good time on her travels. She's okay, isn't she? And Freya – she's okay too? It shouldn't be like this. It was better before. Better before this all came back.'

Rowan closes his eyes and wishes he knew what kind of person he wanted to be. He smiles at Catherine, and feels grateful that he knows how to lie.

'Yes,' he says. 'I'm sure she's fine.'

She swallows the deceit like wine.

35

It's a little after 3pm and Rowan's back in the doorway of the Byre. The impenetrable cloud serves as a lid of sorts – a grimy, grey-black plug hammered atop the green of the valley.

In his ear, Sumaira is in full-blown detective inspector mode, sounding cross, disappointed, exasperated and far too busy to have to deal with her needy dining companion's problems right now.

'I bet you think you were being chivalrous,' grumbles Sumaira, with a sigh that could knock over a pot plant. 'Headbutting a wanker is only good for the soul temporarily, Rowan. After that, it's just another headache.'

'They were asking for it,' mumbles Rowan, rubbing his head with the back of his hand. 'I mean, that's not a confession, Detective Inspector. I'm not saying this happened...'

'I'm looking at the bloody footage as we speak!' she snaps. 'There were three uniforms stood around the screen watching it when I walked through CID! All laughing like bloody drains. It's pure good fortune that you chose to nut somebody that everybody else would gladly throw bricks at. The barman didn't even want to hand over the footage, but Shipley was making a fuss. At least, I think that's what he was doing – he was just making noises like a cow in distress.'

Rowan presses his lips together. 'I appreciate this call,' he says, sincerely. 'I would never have used your name. Not for this or anything else. If there are consequences, I'll face them.'

'Stop it with the noble knight crap,' barks Sumaira. 'You nutted him because he pissed you off and I can respect that a lot more than I can respect the idea you felt some girl, whose life you know nothing about, needed protecting. Do you know how insulting that is?'

'I don't know what I thought,' begins Rowan, then stops. He has to face the truth some time. The presence of the girl had simply given him a veil of decency with which to clothe an act of violence.

'I take it your meeting with Eve didn't go well,' grumbles Sumaira, though some of the temper seems to be leaching out of her voice. 'I've ducked three calls from her this afternoon but the messages were pretty bloody clear. Some pain-in-the-arse writer knocking on her door, stirring up trouble, making accusations. She's threatening to come in and make a formal statement, which at least means I'll get a chance to ask her to translate some of the notes left in the file. It's all frigging hieroglyphs and cuneiform to me.'

Rowan kicks at a stone, sending it skidding away across the slick grass. He looks up to follow its path and sees movement in the trees; a flash of dirty blonde against the dark tapestry of mist and trees and gathering dark.

'How are the hands anyway?' asks Sumaira, who seems to have decided the lecture is over. 'And the rest of you, for that matter? I hope you don't think I was rude slipping away the other night but it's all a bit complicated at my end.'

'You should see a doctor about that,' says Rowan, automatically, craning his neck to see who is making their way to the gate.

'You sound very glum,' says Sumaira. 'Is it not going well? What exactly is the story you're writing, Rowan? I'm intrigued.'

Rowan scowls. 'It's all connected,' he says, wincing at his own vagueness. 'A school with a hippy caretaker who goes missing and is never seen again. Three teenage pupils who meet a busker who smokes Bible pages as roll-ups. The school closing down and the head teacher getting to keep this great bloody house a few hundred yards away from the main building. A copper hanged in a pig mask; Violet starting to remember, to question, to try and get back into the headspace she used to inhabit when she was young. And then there's the ayahuasca. That's potent, powerful stuff and it takes a master to make it. Maybe the sort of master who spent time in South America on a spiritual journey. I don't know, but there are too many things to add up to nothing, don't you think? I mean seriously, what do you think? I'm really asking.'

Sumaira pauses before replying. 'I think you're in the right job,' she says, a smile in her voice. 'If you were a copper, you'd never get a conviction. You'd need evidence and forensics and witness statements. But you're a writer. A journalist. Which means that even if none of it's true, you can still make it sound as though it might be.'

Rowan licks his dry lips. Hears the squeak as Vicki

pushes open the gate and walks up the damp path, carrying what looks like a case for a musical instrument in her left hand. She's wrapped up against the drizzle in a fluffy green parka.

'If somebody did mistreat those girls in 1991, that person should pay for it,' says Rowan, quietly.

'That's your prime motivation, is it?' asks Sumaira, not unkindly. 'That justice is done? You're telling me that if it came to it, you'd put justice ahead of your own interests?'

Rowan doesn't reply. He manages a tight smile for Vicki, who stands a little in front of him, pale-faced, shivering, like a house cat locked out on a grisly day.

'I'm not trying to be a cow,' says Sumaira. 'But look, you said the other night that you were a little concerned for Violet. Have you considered the fact that maybe there's nothing untoward here at all? That maybe she got drunk and stoned with this busker, had a blast of a weekend, and has chosen not to remember anything more? And yeah, if she's gotten into this shamanic stuff and gone all New Age, then that's hardly a surprise, is it? She went to Silver Birch – she had a grounding in alternative lifestyles and medicine. And yes, maybe she did track down Freya. So what? The fact that her Facebook statuses don't show a picture means nothing at all. Maybe she's slimming and wants to come back to undiluted applause. There could be so many reasons, Rowan.'

'The busker,' says Rowan, softly. 'You can't tell me you don't want to know who he was. I mean, he and this Arthur Sixpence could easily have moved in the same circles. How do we know that he didn't send this busker to finish something he started, eh? Or what if the busker snatched the girls, drugged them and brought them to him for some horrible purpose?'

He hears another sigh from Sumaira. 'The busker, as you call him, remains unaccounted for. There's a statement in the Cold Case Review documents giving a piss-poor description. Twenties, hippy-looking, with baggy trousers, dreadlocks and a floppy hat, which could be just about anybody from the alternative scene at that time. His toenails were painted green, though that doesn't help a great deal. The description matches an unknown person of interest in so many cases it could make your head spin, but then, so does anybody white with a shaved head and a gold tooth, and we're not accusing anybody of that description of being a secret serial killer.'

'I never said that,' mutters Rowan. 'I don't know what I think...'

'I think you know this is bullshit but you're not going to admit it because it could get you out of a hole,' says Sumaira. 'I think since you got hurt you haven't known who you are or what you're for and a story like this, however much bullshit it stinks of, however much pain it might cause – I think you're willing to dismantle anybody who stops you showing the world you're still this barely house-trained pit bull.'

'Can I stop you there?' asks Rowan, politely.

'Of course...'

Rowan hangs up. Gives Vicki his best smile, and steps back into the clutter and gloom of the Byre. She follows him; a smell of fallen leaves and wet clothes; furniture polish and cheap soap.

'I should have called,' mumbles Vicki, as Rowan prods

at the half-dead fire and grabs her a hand towel from the kitchen. She ruffles her hair, gratefully, exposing a face that looks a lot less vibrant than when they parted.

'I'm so sorry about what happened,' he begins, and places his hands upon her forearms, moving her closer to the fire. She manages a tight smile, looking past him towards the muzzy hump of the slumbering fell. 'I'm not a thug, I want you to know that. I went too far – I thought he was out of line but not as out of line as me.'

Vicki waves a hand, swatting ineffectually at an invisible fly. 'I've seen enough fights in the pub to be able to eat popcorn and offer encouragement,' she says, a sudden sparkle in her eyes that looks, to Rowan, like the beginning of tears. 'No, look, it's not that; it's about what I told you earlier, about Derrick…' She seems flustered, angry with herself. She pulls a balled-up handkerchief from her sleeve and dabs at her eyes. Rowan gets the impression she's more accustomed to giving both nostrils a thorough excavation and clear-out, and admires her restraint.

'Please, sit down,' he says, gesturing at the sofa. 'Look, is this a social call? I'm honoured if it is, though as you can imagine I've got so much to do…'

'Thanks.'

'Can I get you something?' he asks, playing the gracious host.

'I thought I should show you something,' says Vicki, taking a deep breath that seems to settle her a little. She gestures for Rowan to pass the small case and she takes it from him with a nod of thanks.

'Trumpet recital?' he asks.

'Hardly,' says Vicki, weakly. She undoes the silver clasps

on either side of the handle and opens the battered old container. There's a smell of pipe smoke and camphor and the distinctive mildewy scent of damp paper dried in an airless room. She opens the lid and looks at Rowan with big eyes: serious now.

'You're going to write about this whatever I do, I can tell,' says Vicki, sincerely. 'I checked you out properly after you left the pub. You're the real thing, aren't you? I read some of the quotes people gave you about your book. They said you were tenacious. And I saw what you did when you thought Shipley was mistreating that young girl. I know you're going to keep at this so I've told myself that if I help you, I'm doing a good thing. That's right, isn't it?'

Rowan nods and puts his hand upon her forearm, his leather gloves ludicrous: his splayed hand resting on her bare, pale skin like a chimp's foot. 'I don't think you're the sort of person to do anything for the wrong reasons, Vicki,' he says, and lowers himself onto the arm of the sofa. 'You strike me as one of the decent people.'

She shakes her head. Drops her eyes. 'This is Derrick's,' she says, nodding at the open lid of the box. Rowan wants to peer inside – to see whether this whole act is worth his while.

'You two were close,' he says, warmly. 'If you have it then it's because Derrick would have wanted you to. What is it you're hanging on to, Vicki?'

Vicki waits an extra couple of beats more than is comfortable, looking into his eyes as if trying to style her hair in the reflection on his irises.

'The letter he wrote when he did what he did,' she says, at last. 'The one he left for Eve Cater. The one she gave to the coroner before the inquest. It wasn't all that he left behind.'

'No?'

'The one he left for Eve was in an envelope on the windowsill in his room at the care home, sealed up tight and with her name written on it in his shaky handwriting. That was none of my business, was it? I would never have touched that. But this – in the wardrobe beneath his good walking boots – the ones he couldn't wear anymore – this was for me. He said so. The letter said so.'

Rowan's mind is racing ahead. He understands. Vicki never told anybody that her favourite patient had left something for her. Not Eve, not the police, not the coroner. She'd taken it because it was for her, and now she was going to share it with a journalist.

'What was in the letter, Vicki?' asks Rowan. 'It was an emotional time. I'm sure any sensible person could forgive you for not wanting all and sundry poring over a private message...'

'That's it,' spurts Vicki, relieved. 'Exactly. He'd written it for me, hadn't he? Eve had her letter and that was up to her, but he'd always been so fastidious and such a nice old boy and it made sense to me that I should still try and do my best by him. So after I read it, and found the box, I sort of thought it best to let sleeping dogs lie. I mean, it was clear it was suicide. Nobody suggested anything else. And he wouldn't have thanked me for suddenly telling the world he had all these reams of gobbledygook stashed away – page after page of ticks and swirls and gibberish.'

'Can I see?' asks Rowan, sitting forward.

She nods, energised now. Reaches into the case and pulls

out a handful of faded, folded pages. On top, in barely legible script, is a short note.

'Dear V,' reads Vicki, sniffing. '*You've always been a good friend to me and you have kept me going through some horrible times. I want you to know how sorry I am it has come to this. I think one day people will start to say bad things about me, and the people I've helped, but I want you to know that I did everything with the best of intentions. In the morning, they'll find me dead. I don't know whether I'll swing or bleed or drop from something high but I know I'll be dead. That's okay, love. I'm ready for what comes next. Judgement. The veil. Whatever they'd have had us believe. I've had enough, if I'm honest, and if I can do this last thing well then maybe Eve will have a chance to get through until it doesn't matter anymore. I can't bring myself to put her in harm's way, not even now. There's a few years left in the old girl and I want her to have them in peace.*

'*There's a box in the cupboard beneath my old boots. There are some papers in there. It's going to sound odd, love, but I want them in the casket with me. Don't be frightened. I'm not off my rocker. It's important to me. I want them deep. They're in a plastic wallet and you can just slip them into the silk. I've arranged it all in advance – chose the casket at the same time I took the plot at St Olaf's. There's space for it. Just visit me at the Chapel of Rest and slip it in. Don't let Eve see. I want her to die a grand old dame before that happens. It won't matter to her after that, and when they sink her into the ground on top of me, I reckon our secrets will come up by the shovelful. I don't know how old you'll be by then, but I know you're a good person and I want to make sure you know I always appreciated you*

– and this kindness. If you feel obliged to show Eve, or if you think the authorities should be told, I will understand. I simply ask that you do not. I'm putting my faith in you, alongside...' She stops reading, her throat dry.

'Alongside?'

She clears her throat. 'Alongside this 12,000 quid,' she finishes.

Rowan sits back. 'Ah,' he says. 'I'm with you.'

'What could I do?' asks Vicki, colour rising in her cheeks. 'I mean, that was a new start for me. A better life. But to take it I had to do what I was asked, didn't I? If I wanted the money, I had to keep the letter away from Eve. And he knew I would do it; he knew.'

Rowan looks around for something to drink. 'You looked where he said?'

Vicki nods. 'It was like he said it would be. An envelope full of papers.'

'You opened it?'

'He'd sealed it shut but I had to!' she wails. 'How could I not look? I had to know what I was sticking in the coffin with him that was so important.'

Rowan raises his chin a fraction. He's not going to speak again.

'They were police reports! Witness statements, maps, aerial shots, names. Things he shouldn't have, should he? He shouldn't have had them. And he wanted me to pretty much see that they were buried. That would be like destroying evidence or something, wouldn't it? I could have got into real trouble.'

Rowan chews his lip. Nods.

'I'm a bad person,' says Vicki. 'I took his money but I

didn't do the thing he asked. I never told Eve about the letter but I didn't put the folder in the coffin. I was too scared to go through with it and there was always somebody else there saying their goodbyes. I nearly plucked up the courage at one moment but then that cranky arsehole who ran the hippy school barged right through me, sobbing like a baby... and so I've just kept it. I haven't had the guts to throw it away and Derrick had been so clear he wanted it found, but not until long after Eve was dead and gone. I mean it was very ghoulish, wasn't it? I thought it was just like him – very Edgar Allan Poe. He said they used to call him Corvus, after the raven, because he had this slicked black hair when he was young. I could see him getting a kick out of this, in a weird way. But what was he doing it for? I mean, I've read the pages and it's dry really – and there's nothing earth-shattering in there. The missing girls you were asking about – statements, background stuff, social services and childcare reports. Like I say, stuff he shouldn't have.'

Rowan looks at the sheaf of pages, trying not to lick his lips. 'Can I see?' he asks.

Vicki cocks her head slightly. Sniffs. There's a fraction of a smile playing at her mouth. 'I did wonder, given that this may be quite important to your book, whether there might be a fee payable,' she says, in a way Rowan immediately dislikes. 'I mean, I'm probably going to end up looking very bad and that might need some element of compensation, don't you think? I mean, I haven't solicited this. I'd have kept the files under the potting shed like before, but then you start asking questions and suddenly it kind of makes sense. Maybe this is what he would have wanted. Eve's not long for this world, I reckon. You should see the pills in her bedside table, and don't get me started on the homeopathic shite she brews up, stinking out the kitchen like she's steaming her smalls.'

Rowan stands, crosses to the fireplace and makes a show of gazing out the window at the gathering dark.

'So you'd leave the burden of guilt to me, would you?'

'I'd imagine you're used to it.'

Rowan closes one eye. 'How much? Just to look?'

'I need ten,' she says, almost apologetically. 'Look, it's like you were saying after you nutted Shipley, this isn't who I am. I don't do this. Derrick made me an offer and I took it and I couldn't do what he wanted, but now I can honour his wishes, and make enough money to buy Tyler the quad bike he's after and pay off a couple of bailiffs. What would you do if you were me?'

Rowan gives a small bow. He can't dispute the logic and he actually admires her pragmatic approach. He can feel himself almost salivating at the thought of poring over the pages held out on her lap. He turns back to the window, looking through the haunted revenant of his own reflection and seeing a thin beam of torchlight flicking through the near darkness.

'You can have a percentage...' he begins.

'Nope, I can't wait for all that – I need it now.' Her voice has risen a notch. He realises that she all but threw herself at him when he visited Eve's house and had gone along to his talk – obviously looking for a payday and a scapegoat from the off.

'I don't have any money, Vicki,' he says. 'Look at where I live. Look at the state of me. I owe the publishers money, not the other way around. I'm standing on the thinnest of thin ice and I'm taking a hot steaming piss on my shoes. I will see you right, I promise, but I can't give you what I haven't got, and without sounding too melodramatic, I've just come to the conclusion that there really is a story here, an important one, and that means some of my other suspicions might be true, such as what might have happened to Violet Rayner, so it's really important you show me what's in there.'

'Are you serious? Are you playing the morality card?' She claps her hands, hooting with derision. 'Fuck, you'll do anything. I need ten, Rowan. Maybe another writer might like to pay it.'

'You said the contents were "dry",' ventures Rowan.

'Yeah, they're dry if that's what you'd call a list of victims dating back to 1978...'

'And you have that there, do you?' asks Rowan, his whole manner changing. For a moment he's back in the young offenders' institute, back to the wall, baring his fangs as the bigger boys took their turn. His voice drops low. 'Right there, in your dainty hand. What's to stop me taking it?'

Vicki sits up straight, eyebrows raised. She seems scornful rather than shocked. 'Are you threatening me? Over this? You're going to get rough with me over something so pitiful?'

He sags, disgusted with himself. 'I'm sorry,' he says. 'Truly. I'm at the end of my rope, here. There's a lot riding on this for me. Professionally. Personally. I feel like it's my last chance, I suppose, and you're standing there brandishing a Holy Grail of stolen documents in front of me. But I can't give you what I don't have. My car's a piece of shit but you can have that. I've got some books and albums and a guitar I could sell, or give you, if you like

The Levellers and Otis Redding. And Serendipity might lend me something. But Christ, if I was you I would go and give them to somebody else. Maybe just go and hand them straight in at the nick. I know a lady. A good cop. Strategically scatter-brained and very fair. Give them to her and rest easy that you've done the right thing. Tell her you put the money in the church poor box or something. I'll pick up some journalistic work when it all comes out – whatever it is. And the police will do things properly – not blunder around in the dark...'

The door swings open and Snowdrop bursts into the room, her cheeks pink, the torch held in a hand that protrudes from the sleeve of a bright yellow raincoat. Her mouth opens in a perfect O as she spots Vicki.

'Hiya, Snowdrop,' says Rowan, affecting a textbook cow-eyed melancholy. 'This is my friend. Hey look, you know the book I was writing, well, look, this is hard to admit, but I think I'm going to have to pull the plug...'

'Oh for fuck's sake,' mutters Vicki. 'Any more and I'll be drowning in my tears. You don't half lay it on thick.' She brings her hands down on her knees. 'I want ten,' she says, again. 'But I'll take the car and the books as a down payment and the rest as soon as you bloody can. For that, you get this much.' She peels off a centimetre of paper and card and places it on the sofa. Then she peels off a single page from the remaining pile. Glances at it and gives a nod. 'You'll need that, I reckon.'

The page shows a list of names and dates, written in a neater hand than the scribbled text of Derrick's letter. There are eighteen names on the list. At the top, are five words, deeply underlined.

The Missing and the Dead

'I'll see myself out,' says Vicki, as Rowan sinks into the chair and invites his niece to sit beside him. 'I'm pleased that this weird shit is bringing you closer together. Or something.'

As she pushes out the still-open door, she mumbles something about "fucking weird family".

In the chair, by the light of the fire, drinking the red wine from the picnic hamper, Rowan and Snowdrop start to read.

Neither notices the fire go out. By then, the chill within them has spread far beyond the reach of the flame.

36

Sun-Wheel Holistic Therapy Retreat, Monadhliath
Mountains, Inverness
January 23, 2020
8.11am

The woman reaches down to pick up a stone. She wants to hold something solid: to fill her pockets with weight so she does not drift away. She starts to bend down and notices that her feet are bare. She thinks of her feet as ugly things. *Trotters*, her last man called them. Her little toe crosses over the next one on both of her feet. There is hard, calloused skin upon her soles. *Like sleeping with a cheese grater.* That's what he said, whenever she drifted from her side of the bed onto his side.

Such teasing always served as a gateway. The insults would drift up and over her as if she were lowering herself into water. Chubby ankles, toddler legs, pudgy knees, dimpled arse. He'd reach over and grab her belly. Squeeze great handfuls of her. She'd be crying by the time he reached her nipples. *Rubber-fingers*, he called them. Pulled out his phone and shoved pictures under her nose; sows suckling their young: swollen purple teats, bruised and sticky with greenish milk. Her tears would stoke his temper. He'd call her weak. Tell her she disgusted him. That by forty-six she should know her strengths and how to cope with a little banter about her appearance.

Peevishly, fatly, he would turn his mass away from her, shaking his head into the pillow, muttering about how he was trying to have fun, to make her laugh, that she could take the piss out of him if she wanted and he wouldn't fucking cry about it. It would fall to her to apologise: clinging to his sweaty shoulder like moss.

She does not hold him entirely responsible for the things she had to do to him, but he was certainly complicit in his own painful demise.

She had explained it to him, at the end. She needed to be cherished – to be venerated as a goddess the way a stranger had worshipped her for one perfect, exhilarating summer thirty years before. He had adored her feet. Had caressed every part of her. Had reached inside her and stroked her soul. He had seen what she truly was – what she was capable of. He had made her feel alive. Had made all of them feel alive. Her. Catherine. Violet. Under his guidance they learned to embrace their higher selves. They became one.

The memories flow like lava, burning away the flimsy defences she has constructed these past years. She has pieced her soul back together countless times. A litany of counsellors, psychologists and pill-happy shrinks have wriggled their way into her skull and poked around. Some have done so out of kindness; others through grim fascination, probing at her agonies and colouring in her darkest recollections as if her mind were a butterfly pinned out beneath a microscope. Doctors have bickered over her exact condition. She is encyclopaedic on their suggested diagnoses. Post-traumatic stress disorder; dissociative personality disorder; paranoid schizophrenia; bipolar with psychosis.

She has indulged them in their ham-fisted attempts to heal her with talking therapies and dialectical behavioural therapies. She has even taken the pills. But none has removed the sensation that the man who loved her, and whom she loved in return, is walking around inside her mind, keeping her company until she crosses over to where they can be reunited.

Freya has grown powerful, these past years. Agony has made her strong. She has been forced to do things she once considered unthinkable, in order to feel close to the one soul that truly brought her to life.

She feels him moving inside her; fingers kneading, nipping, squeezing at her fleshy places. Hears his voice.

Come to me. Come to where I wait, sleepless, tormented, yearning...

The doctors claim that his voice is a chimera; an audible hallucination brought on by guilt and past trauma. Sometimes, they convince Freya that he is not real. Then the voice becomes angry. The pain in her gut and her brain becomes unbearable. And she does as she is bid. She journeys. She jockeys upon the soul of the strangers who surrender to her will.

'Please,' she whispers, still bent over. 'I've done so much. Taken so much. Let it end. Please, let it end...'

She gasps, as something twists at her belly. It feels as if

fingers have taken a handful of her innards and pulled them like the roots of a tree.

'Please,' she begs again. 'Cormac. Don't make me…'

The pain comes again. She raises her hands to her head, rubbing at her temples as if trying to stop her skull from bursting open. She needs it all to stop. Has done things for which she knows there can be no redemption. She has killed, and killed again, just to hold hands with a murderer in the place where life and death collide.

'This time,' she hears him say. 'This time you will be strong enough to lift the veil. You will reassemble me. Breathe life into my dead bones.'

She screws up her eyes. Sweat drips from her forehead. She spits, bloodily, onto the floor, flecking her bare feet with frothy red droplets.

'Yes.' She nods. 'Yes, I swear.'

She knows what she must do. He will be stronger there. Stronger, near his bones. She can already feel his excitement, eddying and swelling inside her. She can almost taste him. He's always there, floating just out of reach. It used to be that he came to her in her dreams. She would see him in his entirety, his haunting eyes, that half-smile, the gentle lullaby of his syrupy voice. Now she carries him with her at all times.

Freya looks back down at her feet. Long ago, she was told that it was possible for a true creature of light to reach into the essence of another and to switch them off – to squeeze the heart in the fist of the mind. To push another through the veil as if it were an open window.

Freya looks up. The mountains are changing colour. The clouds seem wrong. The sky is fizzing with a lurid golden static; a fizzing wire of ultra-violet vibration seems to thrum above every leaf and branch, every pebble and blade of grass. She feels an energy within her; something at once familiar and new.

She turns to look at the big stone farmhouse where she has been a resident these past eight years. They are nice to her here. She teaches sometimes. Gives classes to the new practitioners. Tells them about the places she has been. The journeys to Peru, to Siberia, to South America, ever searching, ever learning. All she asks in return is a place to pitch her tent, and that they do not ask too many questions. She doubts they would like the answers.

She begins to walk, barefoot, towards the house. As she approaches the stone steps that lead up to the big front door, she is stuck with a hammer blow of memory. Sees Violet, moving through the tangled copse of trees, scratches on her skin, clothes ripped, muddy handprints upon her forearms, sticks in her tangled hair. Sees Catherine, bleeding from the mouth and nose: flies already landing in the crusted crimson pool, her eyelids flickering, looking up through the pleached trees, the arched branches, soundlessly pleading for help. Remembers her own strangled yell, cut off at its apex. She has a sense memory: her muscles perfectly recalling the way the bark of the yew tree felt against her skin and the rich, metallic flavour on her lover's hands as he stuffed his blood-smeared fingers into her mouth, pushing her lips open, pressing his lips and tongue into her hot, wet mouth.

As she trudges back into the cool of the main hall, she hears it. Hears the whispers. Hears the low, throaty voice. It resonates inside her; a tuning fork plunged into her skull.

'I give you all she was.'

'*She is my gift to you.*'

'*One day you will understand.*'

She glimpses. Remembers the surge of white-hot ecstasy as he moved his healing hands above her. Felt herself cross over. Felt death and rebirth and the sudden, certain knowledge that here, in this moment of execution and resurrection, she glimpsed Paradise. She will offer the same to Violet. Will take her to that place beneath the earth. Will be a passenger upon her soul as she journeys between worlds, again and again, over and over, until Cormac's bones start to sprout flesh.

Thinks: *I am coming home.*

37

It's cold inside Bilberry Byre. Even if he hadn't drunk half a bottle of Bushmills and gift-wrapped himself inside a quilt, Rowan doubts he would be able to press his damaged fingers against the keyboard. He's shaking a little. There's a sensation of intrusion in his mouth. He can feel fingers in his throat, pressing down on his tongue. If there were any food in him he would be struggling to keep it down. The whisky has already turned to acid inside him. He can taste bile and misery. He's no stranger to the taste but he can't explain it to himself. He knows his strengths and weaknesses and only doles out portions of self-loathing when it is deserved. He isn't sure what he's done wrong. He followed a story, and now he's in it. He just doesn't know what to do with it.

'Focus,' he mumbles to himself. 'This is the good bit. This is what you do...'

He can hear himself slurring, his voice thick with drink. Snowdrop went home a little after 8pm. It hadn't been the fun and games she'd been hoping for. He'd been short with her: distracted and preoccupied. He kept barking out orders, telling her to get her fingers off the keys of the laptop if she couldn't do things properly. Kept telling her to make a call to this number or that number while she was still busy with the previous task. He kept sighing at her, grumbling, telling her she'd never get her foot in the door at a newspaper if she couldn't handle the pressure.

It wasn't until after she'd made her apologies and told him she was going to go home that it occurred to him what a wanker he was being. This was supposed to be a bonding exercise for an enthusiastic pre-teen and her hapless uncle. He'd turned it into a hunt for a serial killer and unearthed decades-old corruption and a missing woman.

He's slumped in the armchair in front of the dead fire, laptop on his knee, phone on the arm of the chair. The only light comes from the little anglepoise lamp on the table beside him. It throws his shadow onto the wall. He spent ten minutes playing with the silhouettes, making birds and spiders and wolves with his fingers before the effort of stretching his tender new skin became painful. He's saving his energies for more important things. Needs to roll cigarettes and unscrew the cap of the various medicines that will see him through until the morning. Sometimes he needs the dark, and a glass, and the peace to lash himself without leaving a scar.

He's come to a conclusion almost subconsciously. These past days he has changed his mind without noticing it. At first, he'd seen a scenario with enough big grey areas to drop a narrative into. He'd seen an opportunity to take an insignificant missing persons case from thirty years back and pump it up into something compelling. Somewhere along the way he has begun to believe the bullshit. He believes that Violet, Freya and Catherine were abducted by persons unknown and subjected to something terrible. He has seen no evidence that Freya ever came back. Violet began to remember things – terrible things – and sought out alternative therapies to try and recover her memories. She hasn't been seen in months. He believes that Eve Cater is complicit in a cover-up. He has suspicions about the disappearance of a hippy caretaker-cum-guru by the name of Arthur Sixpence, the "suicide" of retired cop Derrick Millward, and the disappearance on a mountainside of Alan Rideal.

If he were a police officer, he does not think he would be able to make a case stick. But he's not a police officer. He's a journalist and writer and he holds himself to a far lower level of accountability.

'Explain it to yourself,' he mumbles. 'Pitch it.'

He starts to think in headlines and opening paragraphs; sees his byline on the front page of both red-tops and broadsheets and imagines his glossy hardback on promotional tables in every bookshop from Waterstones to Waitrose. Each time he considers it there's a tightening in his chest; a prickling sensation all over his skin. There's sweat at his temples, and inside the gloves his hands feel slick with grease.

'Make a decision, you twat,' he mutters, and his breath is tight in his chest. 'Are you going to do the right thing, or the thing you already know you're going to do...'

Some of the names on the cover sheet given to him by Vicki mean nothing to him. He can find no record online or in any newspaper archives. But three correspond to names on the UK's missing persons database: a charitable website groaning under the weight of pictures and names, dates and disappearances. Rowan had felt hot tears prick at his eyes as he'd stared into page after page of smiling faces: children, teens, women, men, all colours and creeds, ethnicities, religions. Page after page of staring into the features of those who vanished without trace, and for whom somebody, somewhere, still holds out hope.

Among the names on Derrick's list was one Cormac Pearl. He went missing in June 1985, disappearing from the family home near Blackpool, aged nineteen. The mugshot shows a good-looking, dark-eyed lad; young for his age, with longish curly hair and slender, strangely feminine features. He's smiling for the camera: an incongruous thumbs-up obscuring a portion of his lower face. He's bare-chested, but the image is black and white so it's impossible to say if it was an intimate snap, or simply a candid moment on a sunny day.

Beside it is a graphic projection of what Cormac might look like now. Digital software has been employed to age his fine features. Hairless, a little jowly, the fifty-something version of Cormac Pearl looks thoroughly unremarkable and any hopes Rowan held that he might recognise him were quickly dismissed as fanciful. Despite that, he is getting better acquainted with the young man's disappearance, cross-referencing the name against the National Crime Agency's missing persons archive: a grisly database full of digitally reconstructed faces of corpses as yet unidentified. He knows that Cormac was the only son of Deaghlan and Siobhan Pearl, but can find little other information online about the family.

He's managed to track down an In Memoriam announcement in the *Blackpool Gazette*, dated 1992. Siobhan died at a private nursing facility after a short illness. She was forty-four. The family asked that donations be made to a charity set up in memory of their son. The accompanying memento mori was in Gaelic but translated as: "*No matter how long the day, the evening comes*". He glances at the screen again and begins to think about the Irish families he has had dealings with – great sprawling clans of half-cousins and step-nephews spread out across the globe, united by the faintest bonds of blood.

He widens the internet search and changes the language settings. Quickly finds mention of Siobhan Pearl and her untimely death: the accompanying classified notice incomprehensible to his English eyes. He runs it through a translation service and the jumble of consonants turn into names he can search for. Sisters, brothers, nieces. He sits forward, all other thoughts forgotten. Types a half dozen keywords into a generic search engine and finds himself grinning as he spots what he's looking for. He often hopes to be proven wrong in his cynicism about the nature of people but it hasn't happened yet. People need to share. They need to have their stories told.

The internet has been a true leveller: an equalising platform granting the illusion of an audience to those who may otherwise have had to stand at bus stops shouting their stories into the air. The family history website administered by one Tegan Pearl, based in Boston, USA, is an abominable collusion of lurid yellows and pinks and seems designed entirely to give the user a migraine. Rowan has to squint to navigate his way through the mess of anecdotes, family trees and links to other, paid-for sites, with links to the family surname. He searches under the name "Cormac". It comes up with two hits. One is under the heading: "*A Prayer for Cormac*".

Hey Pearls of the World, I know you probably all say a prayer for the whole clan but can I ask you to say a special Hail Mary for poor Cormac, who's been gone thirty years now. For those of you who don't know, Cormac is the only son of Uncle Deaghlan and Auntie Siobhan, from the Wexford branch of the family. Cormac went missing in June 1985 and despite Uncle Deaghlan's best efforts, he's never been found. The pain of it all put Siobhan in hospital, where she picked up a virus and died. She was too young.

I have such lovely memories of her (we're third cousins, on Dervla's side) and I'll always remember how welcome she made us when we visited them in England when I was still not much more than a girl. I don't have many memories of Cormac but I remember a nice young man who let me play with his sister's toys and didn't mind me riding on his back like he was a horse! I still get a Christmas card from Uncle Deaghlan and I know it would mean a lot if you all included him in your prayers. I think we all know that Cormac isn't coming home but some kind of closure would help everybody, I think. Much love. Thank you. God bless.

Rowan clicks his tongue against the roof of his mouth. Reads the comments below the posting. Sits forward, jockey-like, as he sees the comment left in January, this year, by somebody named *eviec41*.

What a blast from the past! Seeing all these names has really got me feeling nostalgic. Deaghlan always managed to scare the life out of people but he always struck me as a good man who bad things just kept happening to. I'd love to send him a letter or a card if you could give me an address please? We lost touch after Siobhan passed away. Does anybody else remember the wake? By God that was a proper funeral – it took me a month to sober up!

Below, a user named *gadflypearl* has included a black and white photograph, taken in 1992, at a country hotel in County Wexford. It's a group shot: a great tide of black suits and black dresses, mourning veils and pale, downturned faces. Sitting at a round table, resembling the pint of porter she holds in a small plump hand, is Eve Cater. She's talking to a tall, broad-shouldered man. He wears a swatch of material around his neck, the knot peeking out from his open-collared shirt. There's a chill to the way he holds himself; something in his pose that speaks of a grief held in so tightly that to move would be to risk fragmenting.

Between them, sits a girl in her late teens: unpretty, awkward, hunched over herself like a vulture defending a kill. The image is monochrome, but her face is pale and the hue of her slicked-back hair speaks of a fiery red.

Freya.

38

The Wasdale Valley
February 15, 2020
8.30pm

'I am cleansing this sacred space. Here, we are untroubled by time. There *is* no time. Here, we are each governed by the same heartbeat: our pulse is the creaking of the fire and the beating of my drum. This is a place of freedom, untainted by negative energies. This is a gateway for the spirits, a barrier between two worlds: a veil between the here and the hereafter…'

Violet is perhaps three feet above the ground, close enough to make out the carpet of mulched leaves, of gravelly dirt and scattered straw that forms the floor of this small, round construction. Feathers and bottles hang on lengths of twine from the fan of thin wooden poles that spread out from the central column. Had there been a fire in the entranceway? A black cooking pot? She fancies she saw a pile of books, pages creased at each corner, tossed carelessly into a tangled clump of grass and roots. She cannot be sure what she saw and what she remembers. It has been this way for a long time.

This past year has been excruciating – her mind a labyrinth of locked rooms, bursting open to allow glimpses of tusk and snout and tooth. This place, this here, this now, it has been some thirty years in the making. This is what she must undergo if she is to come to understand herself. To heal, she must suffer. In cruelty, she will find truth.

She concentrates, hard, trying not to let the strange droning incantations seize the edges of his consciousness. An upturned milk crate had been placed beside the table. She had glimpsed crystals: green, purple, lapis lazuli. She hadn't paid attention. Had been too busy watching the shadows of the trees move across the forest floor; too busy catching droplets of fine rain upon his dirt-grimed face.

She experiences a moment of absolute clarity. A memory so bright and fresh that it seems newly painted. Sees herself, sitting up in bed, hair wild, eyes red, grinning at her laptop screen like a crazy person as the message pinged through from the one person who could provide answers.

Freya.

Freya – who promised to help her. To heal her. To tip the ayahuasca down her throat the same way the boy had done three decades before. Who promised to hold her hand as the visions came.

Violet feels herself grow light-headed. Her limbs are too heavy for her body; her thoughts a soft swirl.

She hears movement. Senses a shape draw near as the light in the room flickers and fades.

Freya...

She realises she has thought the name instead of spoken it. She cannot seem to make her mouth obey her commands.

She has so much to ask. She came here for answers: to embrace what happened in the darkness thirty years ago.

Freya has been so kind these past weeks. Has taught her so much.

The thoughts evaporate as she moves closer; her scent briefly penetrating the mixed aromas of the small, hot space. She smells her sweat. Smells the high, keening song of earthy skin rubbed with moss and wild garlic. Pictures her; the woman she has become. Shaved head: rounded, sun-darkened skin; painted symbols upon hands, feet, bare arms. She has the look of a fertility totem.

She tries not to wriggle as she feels the small, cold objects being placed upon her back. There is a smoothness to the stone at the small of her back. The others are more jagged, their make-up crystalline, and there is something oddly sensual in the way they prickle her skin. There is an unexpected warmth to their surface, as if they are generating heat.

She feels her eyes close again. Takes a deep breath. Smells dead flowers and disturbed stones. The forest floor seems to be moving, as if snakes and eels are wriggling beneath the thin carpet of green. She can taste the bitter, brackish liquid on her tongue. There's a sickness in her gut, swelling like a living thing.

Memory hits her like a wave.

She sees herself underground; the *pink-pink-pink* of water tumbling down a jagged crevasse, hidden beneath the roots of the tree where Mr Sixpence used to help those who came to him when nobody else could. She can see him now: the tall, grey-haired man, the braid in his beard, the blue ink on the backs of his hands. Can see herself and Catherine

Marlish draped around one another, skins not their own, adrift in delirium, giggling and puking and crying as the man with the green toes banged his drum.

An image pushes itself up from the pile of dead leaves in her memory. A picture long since submerged – hidden from herself in the place where bad dreams go. She sees Freya, as she was then. Sees the new girl who'd been so kind. Sees her stroking the hair of the singer from the subway. Sees the thing dangling from the bottom rung of the old iron ladder high above. Here, at last, she sees what she should have noticed all those years ago. She sees the look that passed between two kindred spirits. Sees the truth about the man with mismatched eyes, and the red-haired girl who helped him find troubled souls upon which to prey.

Through the haze of hallucinations, Violet becomes aware of the clamminess of her skin. It's too hot inside the yurt. It's a dank, dark heat. She feels as though there is a crust forming upon herself; a rind of salt and dirt. It is as if the canvas walls of the little round dwelling are made of flesh. She pictures deerskins. Sees the carcasses of flayed animals heaped into a gory red mound of festering flesh. Sees the woman who stands above him: imagines her crimson-handed, squatting above the forest floor, a bone needle in her hands pulling lengths of sinew through the tattered buckskin pelts of slaughtered doe.

The smoke is catching in her throat. It feels as if there is something in her mouth; some fruit-slimed peach stone blocking her oesophagus. Freya's voice has changed; slow, breathy, a wood flute playing a funeral reel. It makes her limbs feel heavy, her skin turning to rubber. She hears the rustle as she moves around the space. She smells something sweet and floral. Feels a sudden tickling heat at her feet; a warmth just the right side of painful. There is an electrical charge within her – a copper wire inside her bones. She becomes aware of the connection between them. She smells a rich, green tang of sage. For a moment she is a mosaic; a pixilated image; a whole made up of a billion parts. Inside her skull, an orange glow, like watching a bright sun through closed eyes.

Her mind fills with images the way another's eyes might brim with tears. Her feet jiggle up and down as though she is running. She feels as though there are ants beneath her skin.

A hole, black and wide as a whale's mouth, opens inside her skull and she pours through it as if being sucked into a pit of tar.

39

Evelyn wakes in the kitchen, face down on crossed arms. There's an empty bottle of Famous Grouse on the table and two Mars bar wrappers scrumpled up on her paperwork. A mugshot of Rowan Blake's face is staring up at her from the inside flap of the red book. She fell asleep while reading. Dreamed of tall, angular figures moving towards her through fire-blackened trees; the shadows and the objects that cast them indistinguishable; bindings about her elbows and ankles; soft earth in her throat.

Groggily, she reaches out for the last dregs of her water glass. Tips it into her mouth and swallows, drily. She's pleased the whisky bottle was almost empty when she unscrewed the lid. She'd have kept on drinking were there more to drink.

Her gaze returns to the kitchen window. The day is already darkening and she can see more of her own reflected kitchen than she can the steel grey sky and squabbling gulls in the space where the cliff disappears into nothingness. She pulls herself up and stumbles to the light switch, turning it off in the hope that the darkened room will give her a better view of what lies beyond the glass. Instead she sees only herself; small and round and old; her face pudgy and slack, creased and rumpled with the pattern of her watchstrap temporarily embossed on the wrinkled skin of her cheek.

A belch bubbles up: chocolate and spirit and bile. She grimaces. Wonders when the crossover happened – when she went from being able to knock back six pints and a revolver of chasers and get up the next day ready for a bacon sandwich and a ruck. Hospital, she reckons, giving it some thought. The stabbing. The operation – when they cut parts of her away.

She leaves the darkened kitchen and makes her way to the living room, flopping down into a floral Ercol chair. She's started making old-person noises too. Started groaning when she lifts herself out of low seating and responding with elongated vowels to pieces of news. She's already promised herself that if she starts to eat her dinner with a spoon or piss herself any more noticeably, she'll chuck herself off the cliff without a backwards glance.

The door into the hallway is half open, half closed, and as she looks at it her mind plays a cruel trick. For a moment she sees him, with his dark hair and his big teeth and his neat tie, smiling at her in that way of his, telling her she was doing a grand job, wondering if he might be able to spare a moment of her valuable time.

She feels a tightening of her throat. Closes her eyes and lets herself fall into it: to tumble over the lip of the precipice and into the person she used to be. Two years of chasing

shadows. Of coming up with lie after lie, disappearing from
her real life in increments. Two years of watching Derrick
grow more intense, more obsessive, in his pursuit of a man
that she was beginning to suspect did not exist. It was Eve
who put the miles in, criss-crossing the country, tracking
down camps and communes, wrapped up in a world of
psychedelia, of communion with nature; of the blissful
struggle of life outside the lines. Her notebooks groan under
the weight of names: one-word monikers of people who
may have come to harm, or who may have simply moved
on to another camp; another life. Young women with names
like Happiness; like Delilah and Morning. Young men:
Water, Kaftanman, Squirrel Red. In a scattered community
of itinerants determined not to play by society's rules, she
has found it impossible to determine what qualified as a
missing person. And everywhere she has asked about
Arthur Sixpence, about Cormac Pearl, she has drawn the
same response.

'Sure, we've heard the rumours – but we look after our
own. We welcome people in but we wouldn't allow anybody
who gave us a bad vibe. We're about peace. About nature.
About love...'

The break came in 1990. A contact has nudged them
towards a halting site further north than she had ever
imagined herself needing to travel. Mr Pearl had bankrolled
the journey. He provided the car, paid for the hotels, and gave
Derrick an envelope thick with cash in case he needed to
be persuasive. She can see herself now, pulling up at the bank
of Loch Linnhe, high up in the tip of Scotland: the car so
full of Derrick's smoke that it had been like driving in fog. It
took the best part of nine hours to reach Raspberry Lay-by.

They'd had to have the car pulled out of mud twice before they were able to make sense of their scribbled directions and weave their way to the secluded spot where a ragged community of families had made a home.

Suspicious, bright-white eyes peered out from mud-crusted faces. Children played in the dirt, bare-legged and snot-faced. A man with an arm missing at the elbow and a straggly ginger beard emerged from a canvas tent; his belly hanging over a pair of camouflage trousers and a tangled collection of necklaces stuck in his chest hair like moths in a spider's web. He was carrying a canvas backpack.

'You're police, yeah?' he asked, his accent pure Glasgow. 'Thought you'd come eventually. She left this.' He held out the sack as if it were a bomb. 'I've heard you've been asking. If you want my opinion she's probably dead, but she might just have found a place to get him out of her head.'

Eve and Derrick exchanged glances. The Glaswegian set the bag down on the floor. Derrick crouched down. Retrieved a gold pen from his pocket and opened the top flap. Written on the canvas in felt pen, framed in a childish love heart: *Cormac and Freya 4 Eva.*

'Where did you get this?' asked Derrick, his voice catching.

'She left it. Only stayed a night. She was running, I'll tell you that. I've asked around and there's nobody further north than us so she's not fallen in with anybody friendly. She said she didn't want to live that life anymore. He'd gone too far. He was going home – that's what she said. He was going home.'

'Is there somewhere we can talk in private?' asked Derrick, glancing around. People were emerging from tents and battered vehicles to gawp at the two newcomers as if they were some aquatic life form that had grown legs and climbed a mountain.

'Not much to tell you,' said the man, not unkindly. 'She asked if she could join us for a night. Ate with us. Sang with us. She didn't tell us anything other than her name and we're not the sort to ask questions. It only rang a bell with me because I've an old pal who spoke to one of your officers at a folk festival near Cambridge back in May. That'd be you, I reckon,' he said, smiling at Eve. 'He said you were pretty. He was right.'

'But you do believe in him, yes?' asked Derrick, his tick more pronounced than ever, his chin jerking as if pulled by a string. 'You do believe he's real…'

She arches her back, feeling the old wound pull on her stomach. She feels as though she is coming to the end of things. She wonders if this is how Derrick felt in those final days – as if he'd been spread too thinly over too much bread. Whether he'd let go of life in tiny steps or whether death had come in one great colossal punch.

She looks around for the letter – the one she's pored over more times than she can count. She reads it daily, always looking for a new, more palatable truth. Each time she finds herself coming to the same conclusion. Derrick didn't write this, and if he didn't write it, then perhaps his suicide was a lie too.

She reads it again, eyes tired, even though she could recite it from memory.

Dear Eve,
I know you're going to be cross with me for a

little while. You're going to grumble and bang things down and probably drink too much and eat the wrong things, and you're going to say I was a coward who took the easy way out. You'll be right about all of it. All I ask is that you forgive me. I'm doing this for the right reasons. I'm letting go. I'm tired, Eve. Tired of carrying all this horrible darkness inside me. I'm tired of the bad dreams. I'm tired of being scared.

I have to do this so your last years aren't for nothing. I have to do this so you're free to grow old the way you want to. I know you don't believe in an afterlife or any of the hippy nonsense we spent so long looking into, but it means so much to me that we're going to share the same patch of ground. It meant more to me than any wedding, though I reckon you were more likely to say yes to this than to any other question I popped. I want you to know, I understand. I won't ever judge you, Eve. You had your reasons; I had mine. I'll be waiting for you, forever grateful to be your friend.

With love,
D. Millward

Eve thinks that she could have left it at that. She could have persuaded herself that it really was a goodbye letter from an old, fragile man who simply couldn't stomach any more suffering. Then she heard about the way he was found. About the mask, and the way he would wake, shrieking, in the cold dark space of his bedroom. Somebody sent him that mask – she knows that. It was on his bed, in a padded envelope. Somebody had left it there for him. Had he really staggered out to the old chapel, slipped a noose around his neck and pulled the ugly pig mask onto his face. Had he really dropped from a pew and strangled, slowly, in the dark? She would rather believe that than the alternative. Would rather believe he did it to himself than that the sins of the past were coming back to haunt her.

She looks again at the picture on the inside flap of the book. Rowan Blake. She'd seen it in his eyes when he knocked at the door – seen the hunger, the desperation, the need for this to become something he could use. She knows he won't stop. It will all come out, in time. Everything that she achieved will be wiped away in one great black headline. The crimes she covered up and the people she left to die; the money she took and the killer she allowed to walk free. She made a terrible error – a decision made in temper, in the funeral shrouds of a cold hospital bed.

There is a creak from the floorboard beneath the doorway into the kitchen. She has a memory of that little bedroom at the guest house on Rydal Water – Derrick on the big four-poster, herself sat in the high-backed chair, talking about the disappearance of a healer and speculating about the connection to Cormac Pearl – the boy who heard things; saw things; who stayed with him for years having almost killed a member of his family.

She turns, slowly.

Sees her.

Sees the one who fooled them all.

The one they saw as a victim, but who was always more huntress than prey.

Eve doesn't try to bargain for her life. Doesn't apologise or ask that her good deeds be weighed against the bad. Doesn't tell her that for nearly thirty years she has lived with some vile, carcinogenic lie bleeding its poison into her old bones.

She simply raises her head, and waits for the knife.

Eve tries to mouth the word "Violet". To ask after the girl who would not stop looking for answers, even when her questions brought her within kissing distance of evil.

'Let go,' says Freya, quietly. 'He's waiting for you. They're all waiting for you.'

When it comes, there is something almost compassionate in the way the blade saws across her withered flesh.

40

The Wasdale Valley
February 15, 2020
8.30pm

Violet is adrift in delirium, her thoughts a jumbled mass. She is at once herself, and another. She is now, and she is then: woman and child, united in one body. She feels like a skin-suit, stitched tight over two people.

She tries to make sense of herself. Opens her eyes.

She's back where it began. She's beneath the ground, in the great silvery-black space where she and her friends had tasted death.

Ahead, she sees the woman who Freya has become. Shaved head and round hips, black eyes in a peat-stained face. She glimpses a recent memory. She had found Freya, had she not? Reached out online and reconnected with the girl whose disappearance has gnawed at her for three decades. She had travelled to Scotland to be healed by her old friend. Had undergone a ceremony in a leathery, fetid yurt. And then the demons in her mind had become flesh. She had folded inside herself, wrapped in terrifying hallucinations and memories. And Freya had bound her wrists and ankles and dragged her from the yurt with a strength that seemed unnatural. She had glimpsed her foraging through her possessions – taking her mobile phone and demanding the code to unlock it.

Violet had done as she was bid. Had watched as Freya posted a message to Facebook, saying she would be out of contact for a while. And then Freya had tipped more of the bitter potion down her neck and dragged her to a vehicle that stunk of pig flesh and sweat.

She tries to speak. Calls out to Freya, begging for help.

And suddenly she is turning inside out, falling into the darkness inside herself, watching, terrified as the years fall away like dead skin.

Fourteen again. Fourteen and terrified.

She wears a long white nightdress. The hem is torn and the delicate embroidery is obscured beneath splashes of mud. In places, the material clings to her skin. She's plump and pink. There are patterns on her flesh; serpentine sigils and jagged circles, daubed in sticky fingerprints on the ripe fruit of her skin. Her mind is a basket of slithering shapes, interweaving, gorging on one another. She cannot distinguish her own consciousness from the voices that whisper, sibilant, in the shushing of the trees and the fizzing of her blood.

Her throat is agony. Her mouth is bitter with the taste of burned herbs, a tingling numbness in her tongue and gums. From somewhere, Catherine's voice.

'Violet! Violet, please…!'

A branch snaps in two beneath the sole of her left foot, gunshot-sharp against the silence of the night. Unbidden, her eyes flutter open. She glimpses her surroundings and feels panic claw its way up her aching throat. Mist rises from the mulch of the woodland floor; shapeless wisps that coil around the bases of the rain-blackened trees. The moon is a leering eye, half hooded by a skein of thick cloud. It finds its likeness in the flat, bronze-black surface of the lake.

She sees a shape, moving towards her through the trees. A round, motherly shape. She reaches down and the action makes her stomach heave. She throws up onto the forest floor; the bitter drink and the green liquor spattering onto the ground. She scrabbles in the mulch. Her hands close on something hard and sharp – a twisted tent peg, rusted and bent. She clutches it like a blade.

'Violet... Violet, I'm frightened.'

She hisses Catherine's name. Looks back and sees the small, pathetic figure of her best friend, wriggling out of the hole beneath the twisted tree roots, mud and blood and tears and snot forming a mask upon her flesh as terrifying as the pig skin shaman mask that the man had handed to Freya with the reverence of an acolyte.

Her mind feels as though it has been ripped into strips. She needs to get somewhere safe, somewhere loud, where she can try and put the picture into focus.

She runs. Runs until Catherine's voice fades away.

A twig whips at her face as she pushes through a tangle of spindly branches. She becomes aware of a sound, a keen-edged rhythm: a saw finding purchase in wet wood. She realises that it is the sound of her own breathing; that she is softly hyperventilating. Ghosts of warm breath gather in the black air around her face, drifting away to mingle with the mist and the cold night air.

She pushes through the arch of trees, trying to steady her breathing.

She emerges in a small clearing. On all sides, the trees form a tight mesh, snarled up with blackberries and thorns. She suddenly thinks of fairy tales. Of Sleeping Beauty. The thought emerges as if from nowhere and is met with a screech of pain inside her skull, as if the simplicity of the memory has caused physical pain to the voice that whispers inside her. She shakes her head, angry wasps inside her skin; scratching at herself so hard that she scores red lines into the bare skin of her chest.

The clouds uncouple for a moment and a little yellow light anoints the clearing. There is a hole in the earth; a yawning maw of disturbed ground. A mound of loose stones has been built into a cairn at the far end of the hole. She starts towards it, her feet moving over damp grass. The light reveals the wildflowers that rise from the flattened ground: purple foxgloves, violet knapweed; a constellation of gold and yellow blooms, winking like the lights of a distant town. She reaches the edge of the hole and leans forward. She gasps, sucking in a lungful of cold air. She smells decay. Spoiled meat and sour milk. She catches a taste of her own scent; all sweat and churned roots.

There is a moment's hesitation. The voices in her head fall silent, cowed, as a new voice enters her consciousness. It is a funereal monotone, a throat-sung requiem, but somehow each syllable throbs with a power that makes her flesh prickle. She feels flies landing upon her bare skin, attracted to the stink of her sweat. She hears a low buzzing sound, more of a vibration than a noise, and she realises that there is a part of her that does not want this. A part of her that still fears the dark. That wants to turn and run and rip the darkness with raucous screams.

At the edge of the clearing, a twist of blackness takes shape. Even in the swirl of her delirium, she identifies it as a yew tree, its circumference vast, its branches splayed out like the fingers of an upturned hand. There are great scars in the trunk; the bark ripped away and the wood exposed. She finds her vision blurring as she gazes into the face of the ancient tree. Sees knotholes become eyes, a porcine snout, a hanging mouth of obsidian black.

'She's here! Christ, Derrick, she's here!'

She spins at the sound of the new voice. Slashes upwards with the hard metal skewer she holds in her right fist. It rips through the flesh of Eve Cater's gut as easily as a spoon through ripe melon.

Through the disarray of her thoughts, she becomes aware of the sound of footsteps. She can make out the sound of small, running feet – a haphazard scuttling noise, as if the clearing has suddenly come alive with children. She realises she is on her belly, on the ground, and that the small cop who came looking for her is trying to stuff her guts back in; blinking and pale, telling her it will be okay, that help is coming – that they'll get him for this.

Something seems to vibrate beneath her. She hears chattering, high and childlike, then peals of bright laughter. It seems to come from all sides. She pulls her arms in to her waist. Woodlice scamper across her exposed face; bristly, multi-legged creatures criss-cross her skin, trailing webs; as if lacing her into a corset. She tries to raise her head but some sinewy root has wound itself into her hair and as she pulls herself upright it holds her fast.

She glimpses bone. The yellow-white of a leathery skull, all bristles and tusks, the insinuation of matted hair over bare, brick-red skin. She opens her mouth as the walls of the grave begin to close around her; a toothless maw engulfing her in one slow, slithering swallow. She feels roots tangle about her limbs; tiny, wriggling things climbing into her hair, the weight of cold earth pressing upon her like tombstones. She cannot breathe. Cannot see. Cannot hear the voice.

Darkness takes her, nightmarish visions dancing just out of reach. The last thing she feels is a distant sense of pain, some vague apprehension that her skin is beginning to sizzle and blister; that the leather shroud around her skin is evaporating into the earth, leaving her body to be devoured and digested by the hungry soil beneath the ancient tree.

Here, now, she tries to move but her limbs refuse her commands. Her eyes bulge in their sockets as she tries to see the thing that stands beside and above her, looking down, pig-faced and hideous.

Freya leans down, leather and sweat and rotten meat. Her words are muffled by the mask. They echo, inhuman, inside her skull.

'You're home, Violet. Here, safe. We are going to journey together. I'm going to take you through the veil. Take you to the other place, again and again and again. And every time I come back, there will be a little less of you. I'm bringing him back in pieces, do you understand? Bringing back the one who understood. He's there, waiting for us both. I can feel him. I would never have understood if you hadn't tracked me down. You opened my eyes. You showed me what I had been. All those years, wasted on lies. All I had to do was find you. Find Catherine. You were the ones who left him there. Ended him. Abandoned him to this place. It will take time, but together we will bring him back.'

Violet feels a fresh pain at her wrists. Feels herself dragged upwards as Freya leans her weight on a length of slimy climbing rope and hauls her into a standing position.

'See,' whispers Freya at her ear.

A rough hand at her jaw, angling her head towards the floor.

She sees bones. Scraps of tattered flesh. Sees Freya bend down and stroke the rancid, age-slimed jawbone like a lover.

'He's been waiting for us.'

She stands in front of Violet, close enough for her to see the stitches in the pig-flesh mask. Close enough to see the bristles and dimples in the shaved swine flesh.

'Do you think he will be pleased with me?' asks Freya, her lips moving beneath the covering. 'I've done so much in his name.'

'You're insane,' breathes Violet, desperately.

'Oh yes.' Freya smiles behind the yellow teeth. 'But all the best people are.'

41

Rowan squints out through the window. It's cold and black and the rain comes in handfuls. He should probably have walked Snowdrop home, he realises. Should have put on his coat and acted like a grown-up...

He opens a cupboard and roots around for something drinkable. There's a sloe-and-damson gin that looks as though it might be good for his chest pains. He'd like to roll a joint but isn't sure his fingers can manage it. He groans as the phone begins to trill. He stomps back to the sofa. Looks at the number and curses. It's Serendipity again – no doubt planning on delivering another saccharine homily about his failings as a grown-up and the importance of trying harder. He can't face it. He knows he's done wrong but he can't imagine himself suddenly starting to get things right anytime soon. An apology would be fatuous. How could he apologise for misdeeds that he knows he is destined to repeat? He'd rather wait until Death is knocking at the door then repent for his entire life in one go.

The ringing stops and immediately starts again. It's a withheld number this time. He shakes himself, screwing up his eyes, intent on sounding sober.

'Rowan Blake...'

Nobody speaks. He can hear breathing, the slightest hint of a painful exhalation; a bronchial rattle to the out breath.

'Hello? It's a bad line. This is Rowan Blake – I can't hear you.' He listens again, his patience dissolving. 'You're welcome to call back on a different line. Or email me. I'm available.'

He hangs up, his head thumping. He feels as though he should drink a big glass of water but his body is craving something he can turn into the right kind of fuel. He knows he's nearly there – that the pieces are all laid out in front of him and all he has to do to complete the jigsaw is to chew one or two errant edges into a more pleasing shape. He wonders if he should call Matti. Maybe it would be better to go straight to Aubrey. He can picture her at some book launch, a glass of white wine in one hand and a tote bag full of paperback samplers in the other, toasting the launch of some hot new thing destined to set the publishing world alight. He'd like to remind her that she's already got a bona fide A-plus true crime writer on her books.

He thinks of Sumaira, suddenly. He's no doubt that when it comes to taking his findings to the police, she'll be the friendly face best suited to the task. Just as quickly, his mind fills with the mingled faces of Violet and Catherine. Of two women who spent a weekend being tormented by a sadist and have spent the last thirty years trying to be something other than victims. He shakes his head, angry with himself for considering it. Screws up his hands, painfully, as the thought trails another... Where is Violet now? He suddenly comes to the inescapable conclusion that the right thing to do would be to report his findings to the police and insist they begin treating her as an active missing person. All that is stopping him is the thought of the story leaking out to a competitor before he's able to make it truly his own. And he isn't sure that he really believes that's a good enough reason to stay quiet.

He crosses to the sink. Turns on the taps; pushes his face under the stream, enjoying the sensation of sudden icy cold on skin turned soft and pink by the scorching heat of the fire. It wakes him like a slap. He straightens up, hair dripping onto his bare shoulders and chest, dribbling down to soak the waist of his trousers.

He presses his forehead to the glass. Feels the chill upon his skin. Stares into his own eyes and tries to focus on the view beyond. He can't seem to make anything out. The darkness is oily and absolute, an iridescent shade of gleaming black that makes him think of raven wings. He crosses to the little lamp by the chair and flicks it off. Crosses back to the window in the dark. Resumes his position, leaning against the cold glass, eyes shut.

Counts down in his head.

Three

Two

One

Opens his eyes and feels a frozen, gauntleted hand close around his heart.

An inch away, beyond the mullioned glass, two eyes are staring straight back into him, glaring into his irises like infra-red beams through a magnifying glass. He staggers back, goose pimples rising on his skin.

Sees a face; all snout and teeth and leather; all tusks and meat.

Sees the thing smear breath and spit upon the glass.

He staggers backwards, his hand rising to the inked symbols on his chest. Clatters over the armchair and tumbles to the floor, the last of the red wine spilling onto the carpet: the smear of red expanding like a bloodstain.

He moves towards the door and trips over his own feet. Tumbles to the floor and catches his head upon the edge of the table, pain exploding behind his eyes.

He looks up into the leather and the hair and the round yellow eyes: porcine teeth curving down like swords. He opens his mouth. Feels the sudden thudding impact of a round, flat stone, beating down upon his skull as if pounding in a nail.

Feels the cold and the darkness wash over him like silk.

42

Rowan wakes to pain. He feels as though hot iron is being pressed against his flesh. There is a pain in his shoulder joints; an agony so hot and perfect that for one delirious moment he feels as though wings have been stitched to his back.

He traces the source. Tries to make sense of himself. It's almost as dark with his eyes open as closed. Away from the places where his skin seems to sizzle, he is cold. A sharp breeze lashes at his skin.

Icy cold water drips upon his face from above. He tastes something brackish and mineral. He spits, his tongue too big for his mouth. Something about the action feels wrong. Skin is touching his cheeks. His face feels as if it is being pushed into his sternum.

There had been a creature, he remembers. Pig-like. Leering. Leather and sweat and gone-off pork. He remembers strong hands beneath his armpits, dragging him outside. Remembers the cool of the air on his bleeding skull. Remembers being manhandled and jostled: hauled unceremoniously into a dark space that stunk of diesel and earth. There had been more pain, then. A face, looming in his vision: tanned skin, bald head, piercing eyes. Then something had been poured into his mouth; bitter and brackish and harsh upon his throat. There had been the sudden soft cough of an engine. Darkness, and pain, then the smell of standing water and fallen trees. Metal, upon his ruined skin. Earth and knife-sharp stones, puncturing his flesh as something, someone, dragged him towards a patch of woodland that stunk like dead flesh.

Panic blooms in his chest: fresh blood blotting funeral shroud. He realises he is not touching the ground. His arms are above his head. Something hard and metallic is chewing into the skin of his wrists, deep enough to touch bone. He's dangling over nothingness. He jerks, instinctively. The parts of him that were numb come to life: a shriek of pain emanating through every part of him. He jerks and hears metal upon metal – feels the cold bindings at his wrist take another bite of his skin. He kicks out again, legs moving in ragged circles in the pitch dark, pumping his legs like a cyclist. The constriction in his throat suddenly the centre of his being. He is sinking into himself. The weight of his own body is pulling him down into a cold, dank darkness.

He can't speak. Can't lift his head. Something is crusted to his face. He takes a choking breath and tastes blood. He begins to cough, each gasp seeming to pull the manacles deeper into his flesh. He stretches his neck. Reaches out with his fingertips and touches a link of metal with his middle fingers. They're looped over a cold metal rod.

Handcuffs.

The rung of a ladder.

He tries again to speak. Forces his head out of his neck and stares upwards. Little droplets of water catch a faint, almost phosphorescent light. The darkness seems to shimmer.

A cave, he thinks. *Underground. A shaft. One of the old copper shafts from when they built the house...*

He hears the sound of distant running water.

He can feel his heart beating faster, responding to the desperate fight-or-flight burst of adrenaline that is rushing through his system. He tries to slow it down. To focus. And yet the pain and the fear are absolute. All he wants is for this horror to stop.

A voice drifts up from below. It echoes against the wall. It sounds like more than one voice. Sounds as if a dozen or more people are reading from the same script.

He kicks out again, trying to turn himself as if he is suspended in water. Bites back the hiss of pain that threatens to erupt from his bloodied, dry mouth.

He twists, suspended in the darkness: his arms two snakes joined at the mouth. He glares into the dark. Slowly, the shapes begin to come into focus.

A woman with pale skin is laid out on her back. She wears a light shift dress, filthy and ragged. She is little more than skin and bone. Streaks and swirls have been daubed upon her skin. Even in the darkness and after the desecration of her flesh, Rowan recognises her. It's Violet.

He twists, desperately, and a fresh burst of pain rips down his arms. He bites down upon the fat of his cheek to stop from screaming. Peers through the half-light and tries to make sense of what lies below him.

There are bones scattered on the damp floor. Too many bones. Hundreds of bones. Rowan pictures a bear cave – the lair of something carnivorous and unstoppable.

He spins, helplessly. He feels as if something has broken in his head.

He hears movement, down there, in the shadows by the cave. He sees the thing that haunted Violet's dreams. Sees *Erlik*. The shaman. Cormac Pearl...

Rowan narrows his eyes.

The shaman wears only the mask: eyes like saucers, grey white tusks; stitches jagged where the flesh has been pulled too tight.

The body beneath is female. Rounded shoulders and motherly hips; a triangle of greying fire at her thighs.

Freya.

The girl nobody looked for, because she never really existed.

Despite the pain, despite the fear, Rowan suddenly understands. Thirty-five years ago, Mr Sixpence tried to help a troubled young boy called Cormac Pearl. He taught him how to meditate. To breathe. To channel his energies. He showed him how to journey into the next world and to return stronger than before. But Cormac had no interest in helping people. The darkness inside him swallowed the light. Sixpence cast him out and he returned home to the family that he had already sickened with his violence. They took him in, only for him to betray them.

He fled Blackpool in the company of a young woman – a drifter; an alternative – somebody who had slipped through the cracks. He discarded her soon after, but he found a new world of willing victims. Found broken souls who allowed him to place his healing hands upon them. Who held his hand in the moment of their death so he could ride their dying spirits like a jockey.

Rowan glances down again. Violet is stirring. He can see from the terrible state of her that she has been here, in this place, for a long time. He watches as Freya nudges her with a naked, dirty foot. The nails are painted green.

Beside her, on a little mound of mouldy books, the light of a mobile phone. Freya has been answering his messages. Freya has been keeping the world oblivious to Violet's fate.

'I'm sorry,' he whispers, blood dripping onto his chest. 'So sorry…'

Rowan closes his eyes. He feels as though his arms are going to come out of their sockets. He looks up, into the darkness and the tumbling rain of dirty water. Tastes metal on his tongue. Questions line up in his mind like bullets. What had happened to Sixpence? To Tunstall? To Cormac Pearl?

He swallows, his throat an agony. Then he yells her name. 'Freya!'

Below, the pig face jerks upwards. Rowan spins: a moth twisting in a noose of spider silk. She stares a hole through him – the eyes of the boar and the ones beneath drilling into him like twisted iron. Slowly, as if there is a thread connecting them, she turns her head towards the pile of rags and sticks that lies, scarecrow-like, amid a jagged outcrop of sparkling rocks.

'She did that,' shouts Freya, her voice echoing off the walls. She slides off the mask, glaring up, madness in her eyes but face as still as water. 'Destroyed something beautiful. We would have let her go. Her and Catherine. But they had to fight him. He would have shown them such beautiful things, the way he showed me. His father never understood what he was trying to do. Just saw the darkness in him. I saw so much more. There's a beauty in fire, don't you think? It hurts, but it's beautiful. I didn't understand that until Mr Pearl asked me to help find him. He said he knew his son's habits. That old copper with the dark hair – he'd found the route he liked to take. He was always going to come back to where it began. To where Sixpence showed him the truth of things.

'I still looked young enough to pass for fourteen. That's what people liked about me. That's what the punters had liked. He took me off the streets and paid to pretty me up. Got me in to Silver Birch without anybody asking questions. I was just Freya. The new girl. And I went along with it because it was exciting, and because I didn't really believe it, and because before Mr Pearl found me I was sleeping in doorways and sewers and letting men stick themselves in me for the price of a bag of chips. He told me what to be. How to behave. Who to make friends with. And he told me that all I had to do was keep watch for a drifter called Cormac.'

Rowan tries to make fists. Tries to stop himself screaming as the metal bites into his flesh.

'I never met Cormac, but I found Erlik,' she says, smiling. 'Woke up to find him at the end of my bed. He said he knew who I was. What I was. Said he understood my pain and could help me use it to grow strong. He showed me things I didn't believe were possible. He said his father wanted him dead and that I was nothing but bait. That as soon as I told Mr Pearl or his tame copper that I'd made contact with him, they'd swoop in and take him away and he'd end up with a bullet in his brain. Put down, like a dog. He said to give him a chance to show him he didn't deserve that sort of end. He said he could show me the nature of things. All he needed was the two girls who were sleeping in the next room. Said to put my faith in him.'

Freya shakes her head, twitching as if stung by countless invisible bees. 'So much of it vanished afterwards. After they escaped. After that fat little policewoman got hurt. They broke the circle, do you see? The sacred place. He was jockeying their souls, taking them to the next world, showing them all the wonders that were going to be his to control. Something must have scared them. Woke them. I remember him inside me. Remember seeing with his eyes, with my own; looking out through the consciousness of Violet; of Catherine... and then it was all darkness. They climbed the ladder. Wriggled through the earth. He'd tried to stop them, you see. Tried to pull them back. But his consciousness was still in the place beyond. He fell. Came apart like he was made of straw. They left me down here. Erlik spoke to me long after his heart stopped beating. Spoke to me until I could hear nothing else but his voice.' She presses her hands to her head and lets out a high, tittering laugh. 'By the time I emerged from the ground I think I had gone a little mad. I didn't know what was real and what was not. But I knew I'd done wrong. That I had let people down. That there was a bad man who would want to know why I hadn't kept my side of the bargain...'

A hiss of pain shoots from Rowan's locked teeth. He feels himself slipping. Looks down at the sparkling black floor; the carpet of bones, and feels as though he is dangling over a void of absolute blackness.

Freya looks down at Violet, helpless and broken on the floor. 'She helped me remember. For so many years I hid the

truth from myself. For three decades I tried to be good –
to turn the things Erlik had shown me into a positive force
– a way to help people. The ayahuasca – the drink that
we had shared – it turned those days and weeks beneath the
ground into something unreal. I'd run so fast and so far
that by the time I stopped running I had all but lost sight of
what had caused me to flee. And I didn't want to remember
– not really. I wanted to forget. The money he'd had in
his bag – I spent it on forgetting. On drugs and drink and
anything that closed the windows in my head. By the time
I was locked up – by the time they sectioned me – I didn't
know what was memory and what was hallucination.

'But I found my peace, I need you to know that. I
made sense of it. I knew I would never disentangle it so
I concentrated on being as good as I could be. I took all the
courses, all the classes. I learned to be a healer. I took classes
in reiki, in shamanism, and all the while the voice in my
head kept trying to break through, to force me to remember.
Only when I took control of myself, when I began to believe
myself to be well – only then did it break through. Only
when I felt well enough to face the past did it all come back
like a punch.'

She looks down at Violet. Replaces the mask.

'She found me. She made me remember. She brought Erlik
out of the space behind my heart and put him at the front
of my mind. She did this. And she deserves everything that's
been done to her.' She looks up at him, eyes narrowing. For
a moment it seems as though something else is staring out
through her black lenses; a sensation of snout and tail. 'You
will too.'

She turns away from him. Reaches down and takes Violet

by the hair. Drags her closer to where the cavern becomes nothing but darkness.

Rowan glances up at his ruined hands. The bandages have come loose. His churned, glistening skin oozes blood; the meat of his hands shredded to offal.

Slowly, he becomes aware of a rhythm. It surges up from the cavern floor like a wall of foaming water; a sensory avalanche; an ancient thunder of wood upon skin; the tempo furious, the reverberations striking him in the heart and vibrating down to the bone.

He hears a voice inside himself. Sees in a thousand shades of crimson and vermillion; his every sense crystallising into a vision of colours so vibrant they threaten to overwhelm him. He smells ammonia and burning sage.

Rowan feels himself slipping. It is as if strong, desperate hands are holding his legs and pulling at him. He can't decipher how high above the ground he is. The figures below seem at once close and far, far below. He can make out a colour that seems familiar: a flash of something bright and oddly cheerful – a flower among dead leaves.

He feels himself dying. His head sinks back into his chest, compacting his airways, wrenching harder at the sockets of his shoulders. Over the thunder of the drum he hears tendons and bones creak and strain.

He hears a voice inside himself. A small, quiet sound, like a child still unsure of their voice.

Your hands.

The new flesh.

Rowan yanks down. Feels the cuffs bite into the fat of his hands, gnawing into the pink and blue skin below the ball of his thumb. The pain is like nothing he has ever known before. He does it again. Again.

He squints into the blackness. Sees. Curled up like a foetus, her skin faded alabaster-white, is the outline of a woman who nearly died here, in this place beneath the ground, some thirty years ago. Violet Rayner. He can't see whether she is breathing. But he hears Snowdrop's shouts – a harsh, desperate screech over the heartbeat syncopation of the drum.

He glances at the ladder from which he hangs. There's another set of cuffs, dangling from the rusted run. Somebody died here. Dangled in the dark until their heart gave out and didn't fall to the cave below until their flesh and bones rotted through.

He tugs. Pulls. Grits his teeth.

He feels the metal slide under the tortured epidermis of his ruined hands. Feels skin and pus-soaked bandages peel away from the meat beneath. He cannot contain the scream. It explodes from his mouth: a screech of bats and ravens erupting from the jaws of an ink-dark cave.

He hears a sound like sailcloth being torn in two.

His hands, pared almost to the bone, slip through the teeth of the old handcuffs. He falls into the darkness like a stone.

Freya beats her drum. Raises her voice to the old gods and the new. Feels the spirits rise around her. Feels the void opening around her: the thinning of the veil between worlds. Here, in this place where she was reborn.

There is a sound from above – the screech of a rabbit taken by a crow.

She looks up, glaring out through the pig mask: eyes huge, all tusks and teeth and hair.

And the man with the fleshless hands falls from the sky.

She folds in on herself beneath the impact, her head slamming into the hard ground. The tusks in the porcine mask are pressed upwards by the impact, skewering the soft flesh beneath her jawbone. Both legs snap at the knees. Something splinters inside her; split rib bones pushing out through the flesh of her gut.

Rowan tumbles away, bones breaking, blood pouring from his nose, his mouth, his ears. He cannot see. Cannot make sense of himself. Puts out a hand and slips to the floor. He raises his arms and looks at his palms. Sees bones. Tendons. Sees something flash – a shape in the darkness, a sudden surge of frenzied movement.

Freya should not be able to move. Her bones are broken. Her torso is a mess of blood and paint and splintered bone. And yet she moves with a strength and speed that is the product of pure and perfect hate.

Instinctively, Rowan scrabbles behind him, his ruined flesh sliding off stone and drenched wood. His fleshless palms close upon something firm. He brings it up, blood frothing from his mouth, eyes wide and white and terrified.

The fractured bone punctures Freya's heart like a lance plunged into the flank of a charging boar.

Her dying breath, all spit and blood and foulness, rushes into Rowan's open mouth like a gust from an open door.

He does not try to move her. Does not try to stand.

Just lies on the floor of the cave and watches the distant, twinkling lights.

It feels like a long time before he hears the voice. He feels the pressure on his chest ease a little as the corpse that sits astride him is levered onto the floor. Then Violet's face is above him; all wide eyes and matted hair.

'I saw,' she whispers. 'Saw what was out there...'

Rowan swallows. Tastes blood.

She looks at him, reading something that perhaps only she can see. 'You helped me. You did.' She says it as if making a decision – as if the alternative would be to bring down a rock upon his skull. 'Can you walk? I remember the way...'

Rowan closes his eyes. Finds the strength to raise his arm and to proffer a bloodied, skin-stripped hand.

'Rowan Blake,' he says, trying to smile. He manages to hold her gaze for a moment. 'I want to tell your story.'

Epilogue

Rowan's brought flowers. Half a dozen red roses and half a dozen white. They lie on the table, wrapped in shiny plastic. There are tiny bugs climbing in and out of the velvety folds. He doesn't know what he's trying to say with the gesture, but a gesture seems important, in this place and at this time: at St Olaf's Church in the Wasdale Valley, on the day Derrick Millward's bones are given some company.

Rowan leans against the headstone of a mountaineer who died on Pillar Rock in 1923. He doesn't imagine he will be reprimanded for the sacrilege. He already has the look of a resurrected corpse. He walked here with the aid of a stick, Sumaira's arm always close enough to reach for if needed. Snowdrop stayed within hailing distance, her whole being radiating pride. She'd been told to dress respectfully for the internment of Eve Cater's mortal remains. In her rainbow wellingtons and short tie-dyed dress, she strikes Rowan as impossibly perfect. She's a floral tribute among the cold, dark graves.

Dippy and Jo stand shoulder to shoulder. They both wear black, though Dippy is wearing a floppy-brimmed hat that looks to Rowan as though it would better suit a cartoon donkey.

He turns at the sound of a cough behind him. It's Vicki. She's looking well. She sports a Marbella tan. She didn't cry during the service. Just gave a little nod as she tossed her handful of earth onto the coffin and told her boss she understood. Rowan, watching, had fought the urge to climb into the grave: to start clawing through Millward's rotten coffin and half-eaten bones to look for the papers Rowan still suspects he was buried with. He resisted the urge. He was too tired; too sore.

'You going to write it then?' she asks, looking him full in the face.

Rowan readjusts himself, putting his palm down on the ram's-head walking stick. It was a gift from Violet's mum, hand-carved by a man in the valley. It's been smoothed down so as to keep the friction against the new flesh upon his hands to a minimum. They hurt every day, but it is the damage to his legs that is taking longest to heal. Both legs broke when he smashed down from the cavern roof and crushed Freya into the hard ground. Were it not for Violet he would still be there.

'Write about it, Vicki?' he asks.

'You're the man who solved it, aren't you? Put the pieces together and made sense of it all. Who nearly died and who saved the day…'

'Bollocks.' Rowan smiles. 'I'm an arsehole who blundered about like a carrier bag on the breeze and who only stopped a killer because he fucking landed on her.'

'Aye, but that's not what you'll write.'

'Who says I'll write anything?'

Vicki looks at him. 'You know, don't you? Eve. What she did. The way she played it…'

'Like I say, I might not write a word...'

'You will,' she says, smiling. 'Your sort. You're a slave for the adulation. Either way, I hope you write it here. In the Lakes. I hope you put down roots.'

Rowan glances at his niece. At his sister and her wife. On, across the endless silver of the waters to where the red-grey mass of screes plunges into the depths like a blade. He listens to the rustling of the birds in the branches of the yew trees. Watches the clouds scudding across the indigo sky like the baggage cars of a ghost train.

'I need to get well before I decide anything,' he says. 'I'll recuperate for a while, then see what happens.'

Vicki rolls her eyes. Looks at Sumaira, playing with her phone, and across to where Rev Marlish and his wife stand in silent prayer.

'Best of luck to you,' she says, at last. 'There's a wake at Haskett's. A few coppers. A few friends. You're welcome to join us. There might be some people to talk to for your book...'

Rowan shakes his head. 'It's a bit of a hike on the bad leg. I'll stay here for a bit.'

Later, alone, Rowan finds himself wondering what he truly thinks. There are days in which he yearns for simplicity. Peace. He daydreams of some rural idyll with a beautiful barefoot girl who will cook fruit pies in the morning and walk with him in the woods each afternoon. Other days bring less humble ambitions. He imagines an existence of spectacular debauchery. Of whisky poured onto his tongue by masked courtesans. Sees himself as Caligula amid ghoulish tableaus of fire and gold and flesh.

He does not know if a man who can hold two such

disparate concepts in equal esteem is deserving of either. Doesn't know, in truth, if what comes next will be an improvement or merely an alteration. He simply knows that he wants his tomorrows to contain fewer problems than his todays.

He tries to ride the feeling as if he were a passenger on a wave. Feels his consciousness reaching and the air above the church flares briefly crimson and gold; a shimmering outline around its hard edges. He wonders what he knows and what he fears and what any of it matters to anybody.

His phone pings. It's a suggestive message from Sumaira, overlaid like decoupage atop get-well wishes from Catherine Marlish, and Rosie, the neighbour who is helping Violet put herself back together.

He smiles to himself as he tucks the phone away without replying. Looks at his hands and shakes his head. He's trying to be a better man. He hasn't given the order for the thug who hurt him to be beaten beyond regret. He supposes, in some weird way, the little prick saved his life.

He sniffs. Breathes in the smell of sunlight and fresh air. He glances to his left to check that Vicki has drifted away. He doesn't want to spoil his surprise.

He hears the swish of footsteps on the grass.

'I'm really pleased you're not dead,' says Snowdrop, earnestly. 'I don't know what happened. I can't remember. But I know it was you. You and me. You're my favourite. My best.'

He turns to her, and grins. 'You have a way with words.'

'I'm a writer,' she says, and looks as though she would give the earth for a hug.

'You are,' he says, and means it. 'You really are.'

He pulls a thick proof copy of a book from the pocket of his coat. 'It's with the lawyers,' he says, giving a lopsided smile. 'I don't know if it will see light of day but I've bought some time at least. Time to make it true. And look,' he says, as she clumsily peels back the title page.

Snowdrop smiles like summer as she looks at the dedication.

For Snowdrop, with love

THE END